"We passed upon the stairs, we spoke of was and when, although I wasn't there, he said I was his friend, which came as some surprise, I spoke into his eye's "I thought you died alone, a long, long time ago"

"On no, not me, I never lost control, you're face to face with the man who sold the world"

David Bowie

Prologue: The Paramount Hotel

The knife glints under the dim, yellowed light of the Paramount Hotel's kitchen. Its edge, meticulously sharpened to an obsessive degree, catches the glow of the single hanging bulb swaying slightly above the counter. Here is where I stand, thoughts racing after an intoxicating lunch service and the sound of David Bowie *"Ashes to Ashes"* calmly playing though the radio. I draw the blade across the flesh of a crimson-red tomato, savouring the gratifying resistance of the skin, the sudden give as it splits, the juice spilling like blood onto the cutting board.

The knife feels good in my hand, comforting. It's a precision instrument, a tool designed for control. I like that—control. In this world of delicate preparations and exacting standards, I am in control. The kitchen is my kingdom, the stainless-steel counters my battlements, the simmering pots and pans my subjects. Every night, I perform a symphony of slaughter and creation, dismembering vegetables, and dissecting meats with a surgeon's precision, only to resurrect them as culinary masterpieces. Each plate is a work of art, a testament to my skill, my discipline, my ***power***.

But there's something in the air tonight. A smell I can't quite place, something rancid and sickly sweet, lurking beneath the aromas of searing steaks and freshly chopped herbs. It crawls under my skin, making the hairs on my neck stand on end. I glance up, scanning the corners of the dimly lit kitchen as if expecting to see something—*someone*—lurking in the shadows. But there's nothing. Only the rhythmic drip of the leaky tap, the distant hum of the refrigerator, the soft sound of David Bowie humming though the radio, and the low, ever-present groan of the hotel itself. The Paramount is old—too old, perhaps. It creaks and moans like a living thing, its bones aching under the weight of a thousand secrets.

My hands, usually so steady, tremble slightly as I set the knife down. I wipe the sweat from my brow with the back of my hand, feeling the cold, clammy dampness of my skin. Something is wrong. I can feel it, a nagging sense of unease gnawing at the edges of my consciousness, like a mouse chewing through the wires of a grand machine. But what? *What* is it?

I try to shake it off, try to focus on the task at hand. I have a service to run, after all. The guests—those faceless, nameless entities that haunt the Paramount's shadowed halls—are expecting dinner, and I will not disappoint. I cannot disappoint. The very thought fills me with a nameless dread, a fear that coils tight around my heart and squeezes.

But as I work, the feeling grows, festering like a wound. The kitchen, my Abode, no longer feels safe. The walls seem to close in on me, the shadows lengthening, darkening, swallowing the light. The knife, once an extension of my will, now feels alien in my grasp, its cold steel pressing against my skin like a threat. I hear something—a whisper, perhaps? —just at the edge of my hearing, a sibilant hiss that sends a chill down my spine. I spin around, heart pounding, but there's nothing. No one. Only the oppressive silence of the empty kitchen.

I laugh then, a harsh, brittle sound that echoes off the tile walls. I'm being ridiculous. It's just the hotel—old pipes, creaky floors, the usual noises of an ancient building settling in for the night. There's nothing here, nothing at all. Just my imagination, running wild.

But even as I tell myself this, even as I force myself to continue with the evening's preparations, a small, terrified voice in the back of my mind whispers a truth I cannot ignore:

Something is coming.

And when it arrives, it will devour everything—my kitchen, my craft, my very existence. All will be consumed by the darkness that is creeping ever closer, drawn to the Paramount like a moth to a flame.

And I will be powerless to stop it.

For tonight, the Paramount Hotel is hungry. And it has set its sights on its most prized possession: the chef who thought he was to have it all.

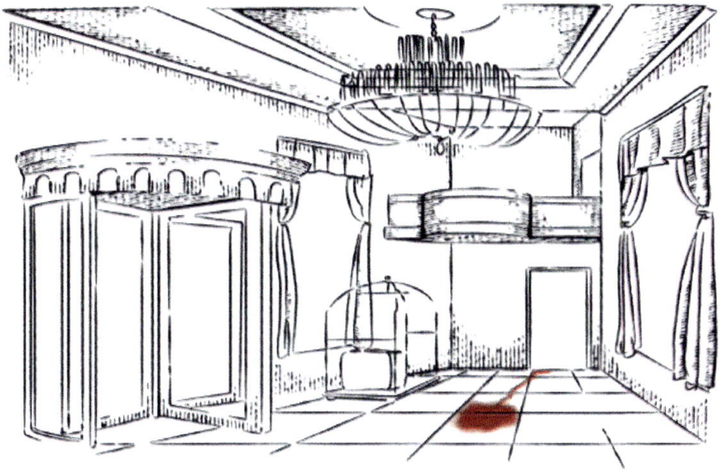

Chapter 1: The Bell

The Paramount Hotel. An establishment soaked in opulence, a grand edifice of vanity with the aura of the past clawing at every corner, every crevice. Each morning, this place becomes my theatre of chaos—a battlefield where my weapon is precision, my enemy is time, and my canvas is the kitchen. It's 5:30 a.m., and the world outside is still tangled in the throes of sleep. I'm not.

I exist in this pre-dawn purgatory, where the silence is a thick fog that clings to everything, suffocating, but necessary. Here, in this stillness, I am the master, the creator of something far greater than mere breakfast plates. Hollandaise sauce is my first act of creation, an alchemy of egg yolks, butter, and heat—simple ingredients that demand a flawless execution. The recipe is a code, one that must be followed with the exactitude of a surgeon's incision.

Hollandaise Sauce:

Ingredients:

- 3 large egg yolks, separated with the precision of a surgeon's blade

- 1 tablespoon lemon juice, sharp enough to cut through the dullness of the ordinary

- 1/2 cup unsalted butter, melted and dripping like the remnants of something pure now corrupted

- A pinch of cayenne pepper, just enough to hint at the danger beneath the surface
- Salt, a reminder that even perfection needs a touch of mortality

Instructions:

1. Prelude to Perfection:

- Fill a saucepan with water, bring it to a simmer—not a boil, never a boil. The difference is subtle, like the line between sanity and madness, but it matters. It always matters.

2. The Ritual of the Whisk:

- In a heatproof bowl, whisk together the egg yolks and lemon juice. This is not just a mix, it's a transformation. Your hand moves with purpose, the yolks thickening, expanding, doubling in volume like some grotesque creature growing beneath your touch. It's almost alive, almost breathing.

3. The Dance Over the Flame:

- Hold the bowl over the simmering water, letting the heat rise but never touch. Whisk with an intensity that borders on obsession. You are in control here, but just barely. The line is thin, and crossing it means failure, means ruin.

4. The Slow Seduction:

- Slowly, almost seductively, the melted butter joins the mixture. It slides in, transforming the frothy mess into something smooth, something that coats the back of a spoon like sin itself. You can feel it thickening, feel the power in the smoothness, the weight of perfection in each stroke of the whisk.

5. The Final Flourishes:

- A pinch of cayenne, a dash of salt—just enough to remind you that this perfection, this creation, is yours. But it's fleeting, a momentary thing that can decay, can collapse if not handled with care.

6. The Ephemeral Nature of Perfection:

- Serve it immediately, because you know the truth: perfection is temporary. Even the finest creation, the most flawless execution, will decay if left to linger. Keep it warm but know that its time is limited. In the end, everything fades.

By the time the sun's first tentative rays scrape the horizon, I'm deep in my war against mediocrity. The kitchen breathes around me, a living thing, its pulse quickening as the minutes tick away. The Paramount, though, has its own pulse, a beat that's older, darker, something that lurks in the shadows of its hundred-year-old walls. Whispers—just that, or maybe more—circulate among the staff. But I'm not one for ghost stories. Not until today.

The bell. It's always there, silent, and gleaming, a brass relic from an era when summoning service required a physical act, a ringing of metal on metal. Today, though, the bell decides to ring itself.

The first note—a ding—cuts through the noise of the kitchen, slicing into my focus like a knife through flesh. The dining room is empty. I know this because I know everything about this place at this hour. No one is here, yet the bell rings again, this time with an insistence that almost suggests urgency.

I wipe my hands on my apron, stained and worn from countless battles, and I stare at the bell. It's still, motionless, but I swear I can hear the echo, as if it's resonating not just in the room, but in my mind, filling it with a chill that has nothing to do with the temperature.

"Is anyone there?" My voice, usually commanding, sounds small, lost in the vast, oppressive silence. Nothing responds, but the air feels different—heavier, colder, like the warmth from the stoves has been sucked away, leaving behind an emptiness that seeps into my bones.

But I'm not a man who spooks easily. I shake off the sensation, forcing myself to dive back into the fray of breakfast service as the staff begin to trickle in, the familiar sounds of clanging pans and hissing griddles replacing the bell's phantom ring. Yet, the feeling of being watched, of something lurking just out of sight, stays with me, clinging like a shadow that won't disappear.

Prep List: Full English Breakfast

- Bacon: Thick-cut, local, aligned in military precision on baking sheets.

- Sausages: Pork, the real kind, pricked to bleed out the fat, prepped for the inferno of the grill.

- Black Pudding: Sliced into discs of coagulated blood, ready for the pan.

- Tomatoes: Halved, seasoned, caressed with olive oil.

- Mushrooms: Scrubbed, sliced, sautéed with a hint of garlic, a dash of herbs.

- Eggs: Poached, scrambled, fried—however the gods of breakfast demand.

- Baked Beans: Simmered, not from a can, but a concoction of molasses and spice.

- Toast: Sourdough, thick, each slice a canvas awaiting the grill's kiss.

The prep list is a blueprint, my guide through the storm that's coming. By 7:00 a.m., the kitchen has transformed from a sanctuary of preparation into a tempest of sound and motion, where every second is a heartbeat in the ticking clock of service.

Time is my adversary, taunting me, always slipping, always running faster than I can. Anxiety is the fuel that keeps me sharp, keeps me pushing, because one slip, one mistake, and the whole operation could fall apart. But there are moments—fleeting, almost impossible to grasp—where everything aligns.

One such moment is when I plate the full English breakfast, but not as tradition dictates—no, this is something more, something elevated, refined. It's a tribute, a bow to the past with a touch of the present, a balance between simplicity and sophistication.

Fine Dining Full English Breakfast

- 2 slices artisanal sourdough bread, toasted until perfect

- 2 slices heirloom tomato, seasoned, grilled to caramel perfection

- 2 pork sausages, poached, then grilled for that kiss of smoke

- 2 rashers smoked bacon, crispy, sinful

- 1 slice black pudding, seared to a crust on the outside, tender within

- 1 large free-range egg, poached, the yolk an orb of golden promise

- Wild mushrooms, sautéed in truffle oil, luxurious, indulgent

- 2 tablespoons homemade baked beans, because some things must remain true

- Micro-greens, a garnish, a final touch of green on the skirmish of a plate

- A drizzle of Hollandaise, because why not finish where we began?

Assembling it is art, a ritual, each component placed with care, precision, a moment of clarity in the chaos of the morning. The first time I plated this dish, it was more than just breakfast—it was a statement, a testament to what I could achieve in the pressure cooker of The Paramount.

But even as I served it, as the diners murmured their approval, my mind was still in that kitchen, with that bell, with the echoes that refused to fade. The Paramount has secrets, and in the silence that comes in the brief lulls of service, I find myself listening for that bell again, half-expecting it to ring, summoning not just the living, but something else entirely. Some mysteries, like some dishes, take a lifetime to perfect, and perhaps, some never do.

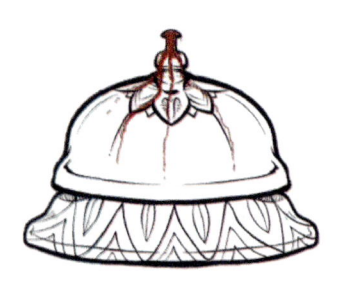

Chapter 2: The Phantom Syndicate

Liam David: The Big Cheese.

His name was a currency in the culinary underworld, a legend among those who knew what it meant to wield a knife with purpose, to dance in the flames of a high-octane kitchen. But legends decay, don't they? They rot from the inside, a slow, cancerous corruption that eats away at the brilliance until all that's left is a hollow shell, still capable of power, but twisted—bent out of shape by the vices that come with unchecked greatness.

In The Paramount's kitchen, Liam was a god—a fallen one. He was a towering figure, both physically and metaphorically, his presence looming over every dish, every move we made. His Gray hair was a testament to the wars he'd fought, each wrinkle a scar from battles won and lost in Michelin-starred arenas. But his eyes—they betrayed him. Sharp, once, like a blade that's seen too much, dulled by whiskey and cocaine, the drugs he used to dull the edges of his own fading genius.

Working under Liam was like being part of a syndicate—a twisted brotherhood bound by the relentless pursuit of culinary perfection, at any cost. He ruled with an iron fist wrapped in the velvet glove of his once-brilliant mind. And you couldn't help but respect him, even as you feared what he'd become. Because Liam could still command a kitchen with a fluidity that was almost supernatural, moving through the chaos with a predator's grace, directing the madness with a simple gesture, a single word. But beneath that command was something darker, a rot that spread through his every interaction.

There was the way he talked to the women in the kitchen, the way his eyes lingered a second too long, the sexist comments slipped out as easily as seasoning on a steak. And then there were the other things—the advances that went unspoken but were felt, the atmosphere thickening like a sauce on the verge of breaking. You could sense it, the tension, the unease. Liam's brilliance was laced with poison, and we were all swallowing it, little by little.

I remember that one night—late, after the kind of service that leaves your nerves raw and your muscles aching. The kitchen was a battleground post-carnage, the remnants of the night's war scattered across every surface. I found Liam in his office, the door half-open, the smell of smoke and stale alcohol drifting out like a spectre. He was slumped in his chair, a glass of whiskey clutched in one hand, a cigarette dangling from his lips. He looked up when I entered, his eyes narrowing as if struggling to focus.

"Hey, kid," he rasped, his voice a gravelly mix of exhaustion and intoxication. "Come in, have a drink."

The room was suffocating, thick with the haze of cigarette smoke and the stench of too many nights spent drowning in alcohol. I could feel the weight of the place, the crushing atmosphere of a man who had once soared too high, only to crash back down to earth, broken, and bitter.

"I'm good, Chef," I muttered, hovering awkwardly by the door, caught between the urge to flee and the compulsion to stay, to see what Liam might say next.

His eyes locked onto mine, suddenly sharp, cutting through the haze like a knife through butter. "Don't end up like me," he growled, his voice low, almost threatening. "This job... it'll chew you up and spit you out if you're not careful."

I stood there, noticing the song playing in the background through the radio *"The man Who Sold the World"* the words hanging in the air, heavy and oppressive, a warning I couldn't shake. Liam was a cautionary tale in the flesh, a reminder of what happens when you let the kitchen consume you, when you give everything to the craft, and it takes more than you ever intended to give.

After that night, something changed. The thrill of the kitchen—the adrenaline, the rush—started to taste bitter. The exhilaration I used to feel was tainted now, every success shadowed by the image of Liam, slumped and defeated, drowning his demons in whiskey and regret. Doubt crept in, like mould in the walls of The Paramount, and I began to question what I was really doing here. Was this what I wanted? To end up like Liam, a once-great chef, now just a ghost of the man he used to be, haunted by the Specters of his own ambition?

Liam's shadow loomed over me, over all of us, a dark cloud of what could be, what might be if we weren't careful. The kitchen—the syndicate—wasn't just a place of creation anymore; it was a place where dreams went to die, where the pursuit of perfection could twist you into something unrecognizable. And I wasn't sure if I wanted to find out just how far I could fall.

Reece Dysilva aka Scorpion:

Reece Dysilva, aka Scorpion: The man was a razor blade wrapped in a chef's coat, slicing through the controlled chaos of The Paramount's kitchen with an irreverence that bordered on the pathological. He thrived in the heat, the noise, the endless, grinding pulse of service—like he was born for it. Reece was a wild card, a disruptor, someone who made you question whether he was genius or just a well-dressed lunatic. Either way, you couldn't ignore him. He was tall, wiry, his movements sharp, deliberate, like a predator stalking his next meal. His eyes—dark, glittering with a kind of malicious glee—gave you the feeling that he knew something you didn't, that he was always two steps ahead in a game only he understood.

The kitchen was a warzone, sure, but to Reece, it was more than that. It was a playground, and he played by his own rules, breaking the established order with a smile and a joke that could cut as deep as any knife. Management hated him, feared him even, but they couldn't deny his results. Reece delivered—every time. His methods were unconventional, to say the least, but you couldn't argue with the outcomes. He was a chef who could take the mundane, the predictable, and twist it into something extraordinary, something that made you rethink everything you thought you knew about food.

The first time we clashed, I knew Reece was different. There was an energy about him, an unpredictability that was both thrilling and terrifying. Working with him was like standing on the edge of a precipice, never quite sure if you were about to fall or fly. He shattered the sombre gloom that Liam's shadow cast over the kitchen, injecting a kind of frenetic vitality that was impossible to resist.

One morning, during the suffocating grind of breakfast prep, Reece delivered his latest disruption—a sharp, stinging slap across my face. I spun around, ready to unleash hell, only to be met with the absurd sight of Reece holding a whole salmon, grinning like a maniac.

"Gotcha!" he yelled, his laughter cutting through the noise, rising above the clatter of pots and the hiss of gas burners. The slap of the fish was like a jolt to the system, the cold, slimy flesh leaving a stinging reminder on my cheek. But the shock quickly melted into something else—laughter, uncontrollable, unrestrained. That was Reece in a nutshell—chaos incarnates, but with a twist of humour that made it all seem almost sane.

"That shit hurt, you bastard!" I growled, rubbing my cheek, still feeling the cold imprint of scales against my skin.

Reece just shrugged, his grin never faltering. "All part of the fun, mate. Gotta keep you on your toes."

Behind that reckless exterior, though, was a mind as sharp as the knives we wielded. Reece's skill in the kitchen was undeniable, his ability to turn the ordinary into the extraordinary unmatched. He bent the rules, shattered conventions, but always, always delivered something remarkable. The respect he commanded was tinged with fear, because you never knew what he'd do next, but you knew it would be unforgettable.

The salmon incident stuck with me, not just because of the bruised ego and stinging cheek, but because it inspired something. The absurdity of it, the pure, unfiltered chaos, sparked an idea—a dish that would capture the essence of Reece, of our strange, chaotic friendship.

Pan-Seared Salmon with Lemon Dill Sauce: An Exercise in Precision and Control

Ingredients:

- 4 salmon fillets, skin-on, each piece a testament to the sea's silent ruthlessness

- Salt and pepper, measured with the cold detachment of an executioner

- 2 tablespoons olive oil, as golden and viscous as liquid wealth

- 2 tablespoons unsalted butter, the richness you'll never deserve

- 3 cloves garlic, minced, sharp as a whisper in the dark

- 1/2 cup white wine, an elixir of forgotten pleasures

- 1/2 cup heavy cream, decadence poured from a carton

- 2 tablespoons fresh dill, chopped, fragrant like a fleeting memory

- 1 tablespoon lemon juice, the bitter tang of regret

- Lemon slices, a garnish that mocks simplicity

- Fresh dill sprigs, because appearances matter more than substance

Instructions:

1. The Ritual of Preparation:

  - Pat the fillets dry with the care of someone who understands the fragility of flesh—yours and theirs. Season with salt and pepper, deliberate, controlled, like the calm before a storm.

  - Heat the olive oil in a skillet, watching the surface as it begins to shimmer, like the first signs of a breakdown. Place the fillets skin-side down, the sizzle immediate, violent. The skin crackles, a veneer of perfection, while the flesh beneath slowly succumbs to the heat, turning opaque, deceivingly pristine.

  - Flip them, but not for long—two, maybe three minutes, just enough to seal their fate. Set them aside, their time will come.

2. The Creation of the Sauce:

- In the same skillet, let the butter melt into the leftover oil, merging into something richer, something darker. Add the minced garlic, sauté until it's just on the edge of burning, the scent sharp enough to sting the eyes, to remind you of what's been lost.

- Pour in the white wine, watching it hiss as it hits the pan, the alcohol evaporating in a ghostly wisp, leaving behind only what it's willing to give up. Simmer until the liquid reduces, until it's nothing more than a concentrated echo of what it once was.

- Stir in the heavy cream, let it blend into the wine, thickening, becoming something almost obscene in its richness. Add the dill, the lemon juice, a touch more salt and pepper, but never too much. Let it cook down for two more minutes, just enough time for it to come together, to reach its potential. It's ready.

3. The Final Act:

- Return the salmon to the skillet, submerging it in the sauce like a final baptism, letting the flavours seep in, saturate the flesh.

- Garnish with lemon slices, fresh dill sprigs—details that will be forgotten the moment they're seen, but without which the illusion would shatter. Serve immediately, the sauce drizzled over with an excess that borders on indulgence.

This isn't just a recipe. It's an exercise in control, in the delicate balance between creation and destruction, between elegance and excess. It's a reminder that every detail, every action, must be executed with the precision of a scalpel, for only then can you achieve something approaching perfection.

Creating this dish was like bottling Reece's essence—chaotic, vibrant, yet undeniably brilliant. It became a staple, a reminder of the madness and the genius that fuelled our kitchen life.

Reece's nickname, "Scorpion," was more than just a name—it was a warning, a hint at the sting that came with getting too close. Theories about its origin abounded, whispers in the dark corners of the kitchen—was it his razor-sharp comebacks, or something darker, something from a past none of us dared ask about? Whatever the reason, the name fit him perfectly sharp, unpredictable, but always commanding respect.

But beneath the rebellious exterior was someone solid, someone you could rely on when the kitchen walls started closing in. Reece was the kind of ally who'd stand by you, no matter how hot the fire got. One night, after a service that had left us all battered and raw, we sat on the back steps of The Paramount, nursing beers, the city lights flickering in the distance.

"Do you ever think about the future?" I asked, the question slipping out in the rare silence between us.

Reece took a long sip of his beer, his eyes distant, reflective in a way I hadn't seen before. "Not really," he said finally, his voice low, almost sombre. "I live in the moment. Tomorrows not guaranteed."

It was a simple philosophy, but one that hit hard, a stark contrast to the anxiety that gnawed at me day after day. Reece lived without the burden of tomorrow, finding joy in the present, in the chaos. It was a lesson I needed, a reminder that even in the pressure cooker of The Paramount, there was space for laughter, for mischief, for something real.

Working with Reece was a wild ride—a blend of laughter, pranks, and hard-earned respect. He taught me more than just how to cook; he showed me how to survive, how to find light in the darkest corners of the kitchen. In Reece, I found not just a colleague, but a friend—someone who made the madness bearable, who reminded me that even in the relentless pursuit of perfection, there was room for a little anarchy, a little heart.

Mathew Crowley & Chantel Richardson: The Dynamic Duo

In the high-octane vortex of The Paramount's kitchen, where each moment was an explosive fusion of chaos and precision, Mathew Cowley and Chantel Richardson emerged as the nucleus of our operation. They were not merely co-workers but an inseparable entity, their movements in the kitchen akin to a meticulously orchestrated ballet, a study in flawless synchronisation.

Mathew was the benign, boyish figure—a figure of charm veiled in shyness. His presence was unassuming, his build ordinary, his demeanour a cocktail of affable warmth and slight reserve. There was an almost disarming quality to his easy smile and genuine kindness, making him a universally liked member of the team.

Chantel, in stark contrast, was an embodiment of fierce energy and resolute confidence. Her presence in the kitchen was as intense as it was magnetic. She commanded the space with a force that bordered on intimidating. Beneath this veneer of boldness lay a labyrinth of insecurities—a fact that revealed itself only in the rare moments when her relentless drive faltered. Her ability to remain composed under the most excruciating pressure was her superpower, turning chaos into her personal stage.

Their synergy was nothing short of electrifying. During the frenzied dinner rush, Mathew and Chantel operated with an almost psychic connection. Their seamless coordination—marked by fleeting glances and imperceptible nods—spoke of a bond that transcended mere professional interaction. Their movements were so synchronised that it often felt like they were extensions of each other's will.

It was an open secret among the staff that Mathew and Chantel's connection extended beyond the confines of professional decorum. Their late-night trysts, shrouded in secrecy, hinted at a deeper, more personal bond—an unspoken acknowledgment of their entanglement that simmered beneath the surface of our workaday world. Despite their separate romantic involvements, their clandestine meetings suggested a complex dynamic that the rest of us could only speculate about.

Mathew's fundamental decency rendered him a linchpin in the kitchen. He was the perennial helper, the empathetic listener—traits that, coupled with his solid work ethic, made him an invaluable asset and a friend. His humility was his greatest strength, setting him apart in a field often marred by ego.

Chantel's fiery spirit, while the source of her remarkable prowess in the kitchen, also harboured the cracks of her deepest vulnerabilities. Her confidence was a double-edged sword—serving her well in the crucible of pressure but also exposing the relentless inner critic that drove her to constantly validate her worth. Her talent was undeniable, her composure unwavering, yet the intensity of her drive was a telltale sign of the insecurity lurking beneath.

Together, they were a living dichotomy—a symphony of contrasting forces that, when fused, created something extraordinary. Their partnership was a dance of calculated precision and raw emotional energy, a dynamic that transformed every task into an exhibition of their unique synergy.

As time wore on, Mathew and Chantel's paths diverged from The Paramount. Chantel found herself in London, continuing her culinary ascent amidst the city's frenetic pace. Mathew, on the other hand, embarked on a career as a DJ—a move as unexpected as it was fitting for his vibrant persona. The transition seemed incongruous at first glance but, in the context of his unpredictable nature, made a curious sort of sense.

"How the hell did that happen?" I remember thinking when I first heard the news. Life, with its ceaseless unpredictability, had woven yet another twist into Mathew's narrative, a chapter in his ever-unfolding story.

Though the years have separated us, the legacy of Mathew and Chantel's time at The Paramount endures. Their story—a tapestry of clandestine rendezvous, unparalleled dedication, and unforeseen career shifts— serves as a potent reminder of the intricate, unpredictable essence of our kitchen world. Their presence remains a testament to the transformative power of connection and the art of seamless collaboration in an environment were chaos and precision dance together.

Scott Munro: The Pleasure Was Mine:

I encountered Scott Munro—an adversary who would redefine my understanding of competition and camaraderie. Unlike the faceless antagonists of lesser narratives, Scott's character stood unadorned, stripped of any façade. His authenticity was his armour, and our complex relationship became a defining chapter of my culinary odyssey.

From the moment our paths collided, animosity simmered between us. We engaged in a visceral rivalry that seemed to infiltrate every corner of the kitchen. The tension was a living entity, a seething concoction of verbal barbs and physical jostling. We were two forces of nature, each pushing the other to the brink, driven by an unyielding will and an equally obstinate pride.

Scott was a formidable figure, both in stature and in presence. His broad shoulders and commanding voice cut through the kitchen with an authority that demanded respect. His every command was a precise decree, leaving no room for error. Initially, I perceived him merely as a blockade—a relentless challenger who pushed every button I had. Our clashes were epic, a brutal dance of competing egos and clashing skills, punctuated by insults and the occasional shove as we navigated the crowded, frenetic environment.

Over time, however, our relentless confrontations began to yield an unexpected outcome. The constant friction exposed a deeper layer beneath Scott's imposing exterior. As we endured service after service, the friction between us gave way to a begrudging respect. We were, paradoxically, drawn closer by our mutual dedication and our shared struggle to excel in the unforgiving realm of the kitchen.

The turning point came during one particularly excruciating shift. Orders piled up with relentless urgency, and amidst the storm, I found myself grappling with a particularly demanding dish. My frustration mounted, my movements became erratic, and the pressure was palpable. In that moment, Scott—without a word—stepped in and took over. His hands moved with the practiced ease of a maestro, and as I watched, I was struck by the sheer depth of his skill. It was a humbling, transformative experience. From that instant, our enmity dissolved into a robust alliance forged in the crucible of shared hardship.

Scott's role expanded beyond that of a rival. He became my mentor, imparting his considerable knowledge with a generosity that spoke volumes of his character. His teachings were invaluable, his patience unwavering. Among the lessons he shared was his meticulous recipe for the perfect scone—a testament to his commitment to detail and excellence.

Ingredients: A Manifestation of Deliberate Craftsmanship

For the Scones:

- 2 cups all-purpose flour—bleached white, refined, as lifeless as the routine you cling to.

- 1/4 cup granulated sugar—sweetness measured with cold precision, a token gesture in an otherwise bitter existence.

- 1 tablespoon baking powder—a force of rise, promising elevation, but always with a catch.

- 1/2 teaspoon salt—just enough to remind you that even pleasure needs a sharp edge.

- 1/2 cup unsalted butter, cold and cubed—detached, icy, cut into pieces like everything else in life.

- 1/2 cup heavy cream—luxury in liquid form, thick and rich, a temporary indulgence.

- 1 large egg—fragile, easily broken, yet necessary for cohesion.

- 1 teaspoon vanilla extract—an essence so pure, it almost convinces you it's more than just flavour.

For the Clotted Cream:

- 2 cups heavy cream—decadence distilled, thickened over time, like the layers of artifice we pile on to mask the void.

For the Strawberry Compote:

- 2 cups fresh strawberries—vivid red, the colour of life, of lust, of violence, diced into neat little pieces.

- 1/4 cup granulated sugar—a sweet cover-up, hiding the tartness underneath.

- 1 tablespoon lemon juice—an acidic bite, a reminder that pleasure always comes with a price.

Instructions: A Methodical Descent

1. Make the Scones:

   - Preheat the oven to 400°F (200°C)—a controlled heat, searing but necessary, like the pressure you thrive on.

- Line a baking sheet with parchment paper—a clean slate, sterile, ready to be marred by your creations.

- In a large bowl, whisk together flour, sugar, baking powder, and salt—each ingredient measured, weighed, and judged, like everything else in your life.

- Add the cubed butter to the flour mixture. Using a pastry cutter or your fingers, work the butter into the flour until it resembles coarse crumbs—like the fragmented pieces of your carefully curated existence, cold, indifferent, reduced to crumbs.

- In a separate bowl, whisk together heavy cream, egg, and vanilla extract—an act of blending, of forced harmony, mixing elements that would otherwise remain distinct, isolated.

- Pour the wet ingredients into the flour mixture and stir until just combined—no more, no less. Over-mixing would destroy it, like overthinking always does.

- Turn the dough onto a floured surface—an arena where control meets chaos. Knead gently, as if afraid to break something, and pat into a 1-inch-thick circle—a form imposed on something that resists it.

- Cut out scones with a round cutter—precise, mechanical, severing one piece from the whole, just as you sever parts of yourself from the world. Place them on the prepared baking sheet, brush the tops with extra heavy cream—a final touch, an attempt to soften the inevitable hardening.

- Bake for 12-15 minutes until golden brown—the colour of perfection, the warmth that's only skin deep. Cool on a wire rack—a temporary reprieve before the inevitable consumption.

2. Make the Clotted Cream:

- Preheat the oven to 180°F (82°C)—a slow, almost torturous heat, drawn out over time, like the suffering you endure in silence.

- Pour heavy cream into a shallow oven-safe dish—exposed, vulnerable, waiting for the transformation that time and heat will bring.

- Bake for 12 hours—an eternity, where every minute feels like a lifetime, thickening into something you can barely recognise.

- Cool to room temperature, then refrigerate for at least 8 hours—chilled, hardened, the softness now masked by a crust, much like yourself.

- Gently scrape off the clotted cream, leaving the liquid behind—taking only what's necessary, discarding the rest like the remnants of a forgotten life.

3. Make the Strawberry Compote:

- Combine strawberries, sugar, and lemon juice in a saucepan over medium heat—a controlled blend of sweet and sharp, a balance as delicate as the one you maintain daily.

- Cook, stirring occasionally, until the strawberries break down—until they lose their form, their individuality, becoming part of something else, something lesser.

- Let it thicken, let it congeal—an imitation of permanence, a texture that lies to you. Cool.

4. Serve:

- Split the warm scones—divide, dissect, destroy the unity you so carefully crafted.

- Spread with clotted cream—layer upon layer, hiding the imperfections, the scars.

- Top with strawberry compote—a final flourish, a mask of sweetness over the tartness, the bitterness that lingers beneath.

What you've made is more than just a dish; it's a reflection, a distorted mirror showing the cracks beneath the surface. It's the perfect facade, but you know, deep down, that perfection is just an illusion. And like all illusions, it's only a matter of time before it shatters.

This scone recipe became more than just a culinary staple; it was a symbol of our evolution from rivals to collaborators. It represented the journey from hostility to partnership, and the lessons learned through our intense interactions.

Scott Munro, once my fiercest competitor, became my mentor and friend. His story is a testament to the power of respect and the transformative potential of collaboration. Through Scott, I learned that the most profound rivalries could evolve into the most enduring alliances, and that true mastery in the kitchen is forged not just in skill, but in the bonds, we build with those who challenge and inspire us.

Megan & Roxi Newman: The Enigmatic Twins

The Paramount's kitchen was a frenetic cacophony, a maelstrom of sizzling pans, clattering cutlery, and shouted orders. Amidst this chaos, two chefs stood out— Megan and Roxi Newman. Identical twins. Or were they? It was impossible to tell. Their movements were synchronised to the point of absurdity, their features indistinguishable. It felt like a psychological experiment designed to drive the rest of us mad.

Megan and Roxi operated with a precision that was almost mechanical, their hands moving in perfect harmony as they prepared dishes. It was disturbing. Their identical dark hair, always pulled back into tight ponytails, glinted under the harsh fluorescent lights, creating a visual echo that intensified the sense of unreality. I often found myself wondering if they were a figment of my imagination, a hallucination born of stress and exhaustion.

In the kitchen, the twins were a relentless force. Their speed and efficiency were unmatched. Orders were fulfilled almost before they were placed, their hands blurring as they diced, sautéed, and plated with inhuman rapidity. It was as if they shared a single mind, each anticipating the other's moves with eerie accuracy. Watching them work, I felt a strange mixture of awe and unease.

Despite their almost supernatural coordination, Megan and Roxi had subtle differences. Megan's plating was delicate, artistic, each dish a miniature work of art. Roxi's dishes, on the other hand, were bold and confident, a reflection of her brash personality. These differences, however, were easily overlooked in the face of their overwhelming similarities, leaving most of us guessing who was who.

Their banter was quick, sharp, and often incomprehensible to those not attuned to their rapid-fire exchanges. They moved through the kitchen like a perfectly choreographed dance, their steps light and precise. It was mesmerising. And unsettling. Their laughter, a high-pitched, almost manic sound, would echo through the kitchen, a stark contrast to the tension and stress of service.

During peak hours, the twins were everywhere at once. Their presence was pervasive, a constant reminder of their uncanny ability to operate as one. Pans sizzled, knives flashed, and through it all, Megan and Roxi moved with an unsettling grace. Their calm demeanour under pressure only added to their mystique, their ability to maintain composure in the face of chaos setting them apart as some of the finest chefs I'd ever encountered.

Despite their formidable skills, Megan and Roxi were approachable, their demeanour disarmingly friendly.

They were always ready to offer advice or lend a hand, their combined knowledge and experience making them invaluable mentors. Their presence was a bomb, a reminder that even in the most demanding environments, camaraderie and mutual support could flourish. Or was it an illusion? A comforting fantasy in the midst of the madness?

Late at night, after a particularly gruelling service, I would sit alone, the remnants of the day's chaos still echoing in my mind. The memories of Megan and Roxi flitting about the kitchen, their movements so perfectly synchronised, would replay in my head, making me question my sanity. Were they truly two people, or was my mind fabricating one to cope with the relentless pace? But then I'd see them together, laughing, sharing a private joke, and the reality of their dual existence would settle back into place. Or so I told myself.

Megan and Roxi Newman, the enigmatic twins who blurred the lines between reality and hallucination, became a fixture in my memory of The Paramount. Their ability to work as a single entity, yet maintain their individuality, was both miraculous and deeply unsettling. They were, without a doubt, two of the most remarkable—and disturbing—chefs I had the privilege to work with. Their legacy in the kitchen of The Paramount is a haunting reminder of the thin line between genius and madness.

Diego D'Alessandro: Enter Frenchie

Diego D'Alessandro, an Italian chef with an ironic nickname, "Frenchie," not by choice but by our collective decision. Diego harboured an irrational and intense hatred for the French, a fact that amused us endlessly. His face would flush crimson at the mere mention of France, so naturally, we dubbed him Frenchie to stoke the flames of his barely contained fury. The name alone was enough to send him into apoplectic fits of rage, an entertaining spectacle amid the drudgery of our daily grind.

Frenchie was, by all accounts, a terrible chef. His skills—or lack thereof—became painfully evident when he took over as the breakfast chef following my promotion to chef de partie. Watching him work was like witnessing a slow-motion disaster, a series of escalating mistakes and mishaps that turned every service into a catastrophe. The man couldn't handle pressure. He wilted under it, crumbled like a poorly made soufflé. Often, it fell to me to salvage the morning after Frenchie had driven it into the ground.

I would walk into the kitchen, greeted by a scene of utter chaos. Orders left unattended, dishes half-prepared, and the unmistakable scent of impending disaster hanging in the air. Frenchie, his face slick with sweat and twisted in panic, would be flailing helplessly during it all. It was up to me to pull service back from the brink, to clear the backlog of checks he had neglected. I would work feverishly, my hands moving in a blur as I restored some semblance of order to the chaos Frenchie had wrought.

Frenchie's incompetence extended beyond breakfast service. His attempts at making staff lunch were nothing short of abysmal. The simple task of preparing a meal for the team turned into an exercise in masochism. One particularly memorable disaster was his infamous "seafood casserole," a vile concoction that looked and smelled like something dredged from the depths of a polluted river. The fish was overcooked to the point of being inedible, rubbery and tasteless. The sauce was a congealed, greasy mess, an unappetising sludge that clung to the overcooked pasta like a parasitic organism. It was a dish that bordered on the criminal, a travesty that left us all clutching our stomachs in nausea.

Despite all his flaws, deep down, Frenchie had a heart of gold. It was buried beneath layers of incompetence and misguided efforts, but it was there. Occasionally, in rare moments of clarity, he would offer a kind word or a helping hand. These moments were fleeting, overshadowed by his perpetual state of panic and the culinary disasters he spawned, but they hinted at a decency that struggled to surface.

The team, for all our mocking and derision, recognised this hidden goodness in Frenchie. We goaded him, drove him to the brink with our taunts, but we also rallied around him in his moments of dire need. It was a twisted sort of camaraderie, a bond forged in the fires of adversity and incompetence. We saved his ass more times than I could count, pulling him back from the precipice of failure and keeping the kitchen from descending into total anarchy.

One particularly harrowing morning, Frenchie was at his worst. Orders piled up, and the kitchen was a veritable hellscape of half-cooked food and frantic shouts. I stepped in, my presence a stabilising force amid the chaos. I worked with a manic intensity, my hands moving faster than my thoughts, methodically clearing the backlog and restoring order. Frenchie watched, his expression a mixture of relief and shame. It was a dance we had performed countless times, a ritual of disaster and redemption.

In those moments, I saw the truth of Frenchie. He wasn't cut out for the relentless pace of our kitchen, but he tried. He failed spectacularly, but he kept coming back, driven by a determination that bordered on masochism. There was a resilience in him, a stubborn refusal to quit despite his shortcomings. It was a quality I couldn't help but admire, even as I cursed him for the chaos he caused.

Diego D'Alessandro, our beleaguered and ironically nicknamed Frenchie, was a constant reminder of the fine line between success and failure in the culinary world. His struggles and failures were a testament to the unforgiving nature of our craft, and his persistence a lesson in resilience. Despite the chaos he brought, he was one of us, a flawed but integral part of the twisted family that was The Paramount's kitchen.

Misfits on the Battlefield:

The Paramount's kitchen wasn't just a place to cook; it was a warzone, a gritty theatre where the misaligned and the broken came together to forge something from the chaos, to pull beauty from the wreckage of raw ingredients and shattered dreams. Under the harsh, unforgiving fluorescent lights, we faced the brutality of stainless steel and the relentless assault of clanging pots and sizzling pans. This was our battleground—a place where the desperation to create, to impress, to survive, bled into every dish we plated.

We were misfits, an oddball collection of damaged souls, each one of us drawn to the heat and pressure of The Paramount's kitchen like lambs to the slaughter. It wasn't just the food that was raw; it was us—raw nerves, raw ambition, raw talent, all fused together in the crucible of this relentless environment. Day after day, we waged our war against mediocrity, against the ticking clock, against each other, forging something remarkable out of the disparate elements of our personalities and skills.

The kitchen was our frontline, and we, the soldiers—wounded, yes, but fighting on, driven by something deeper, something darker. It was more than just cooking; it was survival, it was therapy, it was a twisted form of art where every plate was a masterpiece born from the chaos. Our teamwork, chaotic yet brutally efficient, was a reflection of our collective madness—a mad symphony where each of us played a part, out of tune and in perfect harmony all at once.

In this battlefield, we didn't just cook; we crafted. Our dishes weren't just meals; they were testaments to our shared struggle, our shared pain, and the fleeting moments of triumph that kept us coming back, day after gruelling day. This wasn't just about food—it was about us, about what we could create together, despite, or perhaps because of, our flaws.

One-Pan Chicken and Vegetable Medley

Ingredients:

•4 boneless, skinless chicken breasts—lean, like us, stripped down to the essentials.

•2 tablespoons olive oil—rich, the grease that kept us moving.

•Salt and pepper—to taste, because even in this hellhole, taste mattered.

•1 teaspoon paprika heat, like the fire that burned in our veins.

•1 teaspoon garlic powder—sharp, like the words we threw at each other.

•1 teaspoon dried thyme—because time was something we were always fighting against.

•1 teaspoon dried rosemary—fragrant, a reminder that beauty still existed somewhere.

•1 large red bell pepper—bold, like our ambitions.

- 1 large yellow bell pepper—bright, a flicker of hope in the darkness.
- 1 zucchini—soft, like the vulnerabilities we never showed.
- 1 red onion—layered, like the secrets we kept hidden.
- 1 cup cherry tomato—bursting with life, fragile, like us.
- 4 cloves garlic minced—because nothing good comes without a little pain.
- 1 lemon sliced—acidic, a bite to cut through the monotony.
- Fresh parsley, chopped, for garnish—because presentation was everything.

Instructions:

1. Preheat the oven to 400°F (200°C). The heat rising, like the tension in the air before service.

2. In a large mixing bowl, coat the chicken breasts with 1 tablespoon of olive oil, salt, pepper, paprika, garlic powder, thyme, and rosemary. The basics, just like us—nothing fancy, just enough to get the job done.

3. Heat the remaining 1 tablespoon of olive oil in a large oven-safe skillet over medium-high heat. Sear the chicken breasts for 2-3 minutes on each side until golden brown. The sizzle of the pan, the hiss of meat meeting metal—a sound as familiar as our own heartbeats.

4.Remove the chicken and set aside. Add the bell peppers, zucchini, red onion, cherry tomatoes, and minced garlic to the skillet. Season with salt and pepper and toss to coat in the oil and chicken drippings. The vegetables, like us, taking on the Flavors of everything that came before.

5.Place the seared chicken on top of the vegetables. Arrange lemon slices over the chicken and vegetables. A final touch, like the last words before we marched out to face the public.

6.Transfer the skillet to the oven and bake for 20-25 minutes, or until the chicken is cooked through and the vegetables are tender. The wait, the anticipation—wondering if we'd make it through the rush intact.

7.Garnish with fresh parsley before serving. Because even in the battlefield, you had to make it look good.

This dish, like us, was more than the sum of its parts—a messy, chaotic blend of elements coming together to create something whole, something good. It reflected our time in The Paramount, a testament to our ability to forge something extraordinary from the raw materials of our lives, through sheer will and relentless effort.

In the end, we weren't just misfits. We were warriors, a force to be reckoned with, bound together by the fire of the kitchen and the unyielding pursuit of perfection. The Paramount shaped us, broke us, but it also made us stronger, forging us into something more—a formidable unit, capable of creating not just meals, but masterpieces. And in the heat of the kitchen, we found our place, our purpose, in the relentless, unforgiving pursuit of perfection.

Chapter 3: The Woman in the Wheelchair

The last years of being the breakfast slave at The Paramount were a slow, excruciating descent into madness. The role of breakfast chef became my prison, each day a relentless, monotonous grind that chipped away at my sanity. The alarm clock, a merciless dictator, screamed at 4:30 AM, slicing through the stillness of my bedroom like a straight razor across the throat. Nights out, drinks with friends, the camaraderie I once cherished—all gone, replaced by the cold reality of my solitary routine. Every missed invitation, every early exit, widened the chasm between me and a life I could barely remember. The noose of my schedule tightened with every passing day, constricting, suffocating.

There was, of course, the flicker of hope. A promotion loomed on the horizon—a tantalizing promise of escape, or perhaps, just another step deeper into the abyss. Chef de Partie. It dangled before me like a carrot on a stick, the allure of more responsibility, more power, more hours. But with it came the dread, the gnawing fear of what it would cost. More time in the kitchen with the misfits, less time anywhere else. My relationship—already fragile, already gasping for air—was being slowly smothered by my ambitions. The promotion, instead of saving me, promised to finish the job, driving the final nail into the coffin of what little remained of my personal life.

But before that promotion, before the unravelling truly began, there was one morning—one moment—that would etch itself into my psyche, a harrowing prelude to the doom that lay ahead.

The grim facade of Tempest Street seemed almost designed for the opening scene of some dystopian narrative. Here, beneath the oppressive grey skies of Manchester, this stretch of urban decay served as the gateway to my daily descent into the culinary underworld. The area, known for its notorious red-light district, bristled with the remnants of nocturnal commerce. Women, their faces gaunt and expressions hollow, prowled the perimeters, their bodies merchandise in the twilight of despair.

The bridge, under which I parked each morning, stood like a monolithic sentinel, its concrete arcs forming a stark tunnel that echoed with the whispers of the night's last secrets. This was no mere parking spot; it was an arena of desolation, where the echoes of desperation clung to the damp air like a second skin.

Around me, the detritus of human wreckage littered the ground—discarded needles glinting under the flickering streetlights, broken bottles, the debris of shattered lives. It was a tableau vivant of vice and ruin, a canvas where the city's darkest stories were painted in shades of sordid and somber.

Liam, had he been here, would have reveled in the raw, unfiltered reality of it all. His predilections for the macabre would have found fertile ground in this urban hellscape. But for me, it was less about indulgence and more a necessity—a place to park, a momentary pause before plunging into the day's chaos.

The bridge served as both shelter and symbol, a grim reminder of the city's underbelly. Here, under its cold embrace, I found a perverse sanctuary from the unrelenting drizzle that seemed to wash the city's sins into the gutters. This tunnel, with its damp shadows and cold stone, was a fitting antechamber to the day ahead—a day that would unfold in the heat of the kitchen's fires, far removed from the chill of Tempest Street's morning gloom.

The dim glow from the lone streetlight at the tunnel's end did little to dispel the oppressive darkness of the early hours. Its light, sickly and jaundiced, threw elongated shadows across the slick pavement, creating a tableau that was both eerily serene and unsettling. There, in that half-light of pre-dawn, the scene took on the quality of a distorted dream.

It was precisely 5:00 AM, a time when the world should have been asleep, that I encountered her—a figure so out of place, it seemed ripped from the pages of a gothic novel. At the end of the tunnel, under the weak embrace of the streetlamp, sat a wheelchair, and in it, a woman. Her presence was an anachronism, a stark, unsettling blot against the urban decay surrounding her.

The woman was slouched, her body contorted in an unnatural pose that suggested abandonment. Her skin was the colour of parchment, taut over brittle bones, the texture of her flesh morbidly emphasised by the streetlight's grim luminescence. She appeared not to breathe, her stillness so complete, so definitive, it was as if death itself had taken a moment to pause, frozen in time, like a black star.

The sight of her struck a chord within me, a dissonant clash of horror and fascination. Here was a figure pulled straight from a tableau of nightmares, her existence a macabre reminder of mortality. Yet, there was something undeniably captivating about her—a depressing allure that held me transfixed. Her face, though lined and worn by the vicissitudes of a life I could only imagine, bore an expression of such profound vacancy it chilled the very air around her.

And yet, I did nothing. In the face of this surreal and somber spectacle, I remained motionless, a bystander in my own life. Rational thoughts urged me to assist her, to offer warmth against the biting cold or at least to inquire after her well-being. But I was immobilised, not by fear but by a detachment so complete it bordered on the inhuman. My mind, already churning with the day's forthcoming stresses, viewed her as little more than an aberration, an unwelcome deviation from the morning's routine.

I walked away, leaving her in that spectral light, a decision that would haunt the corners of my conscience in the years to come. Her image lingered in my mind, a ghostly imprint that refused to fade. She became a symbol, not just of my failure to act but of my own moral erosion. That moment marked a turning point, a subtle yet undeniable shift within me. It was as if, in my neglect, I had crossed an invisible threshold, stepping into a realm where ambition clouded judgment, where the human element of my nature was sacrificed upon the altar of career and routine.

That morning, under the cold gaze of that streetlight, something within me fractured. It was a small, almost imperceptible crack, but it was there—an indication of the deeper fissures that had begun to mar the facade of who I thought I was. This was no mere oversight, no simple act of indifference. It was a declaration of my descent, a slow and inevitable slide into a version of myself I had never intended to become.

I remember what I cooked that day—Eggs Royale. Poached eggs, smoked salmon, Hollandaise sauce atop an English muffin. A dish so indulgent, so perfect, that it was almost obscene. It was the favourite of the morning, lauded for its flawless execution, but for me, it was tainted. Every time I plated it, every time I tasted the creamy Hollandaise, the rich, buttery salmon, I was transported back to that tunnel, to the woman in the wheelchair. The Flavors carried the bitter aftertaste of guilt, of remorse, of a conscience slowly unravelling.

Eggs Royale Recipe:

Ingredients:

- 4 English muffins, split and toasted—perfectly crisp, like the surface I presented to the world.

- 8 slices smoked salmon—luxurious, a facade of richness hiding the decay beneath.

- 8 large eggs—each one a symbol of life, of potential, and the fragility that comes with it.

- 1 tablespoon white vinegar—sharp, cutting through the richness, a reminder of the sting of my own conscience.

- Fresh dill, for garnish—because appearances still mattered, even when everything else was falling apart.

For the Hollandaise Sauce:

- 3 large egg yolks—the core, the essence, something pure corrupted by what it became.

- 1 tablespoon lemon juice—acidic, biting, a reflection of my growing bitterness.

- 1/2 cup unsalted butter, melted—rich, comforting, but ultimately suffocating.

- Salt and cayenne pepper, to taste—seasoning that could never mask the truth.

Instructions:

1. Poach the Eggs:

   - Fill a large saucepan with water and bring to a simmer. Add the vinegar.

   - Crack each egg into a small bowl, then gently slide it into the simmering water.

   - Poach the eggs for 3-4 minutes, until the whites are set but the yolks are still runny.

   - Use a slotted spoon to remove the eggs and drain on paper towels. Like draining the life from a moment, leaving it hollow.

2. Prepare the Hollandaise Sauce:

   - In a heatproof bowl, whisk together egg yolks and lemon juice until thickened and doubled in volume. A task so simple yet requiring so much care—just like everything else in my life that I was letting slip away.

   - Place the bowl over a saucepan of simmering water, ensuring the bowl doesn't touch the water.

   - Slowly drizzle in the melted butter, whisking continuously until the sauce is thickened and creamy. A process of transformation, from raw to refined, but tainted by the rot at its core.

   - Season with salt and cayenne pepper.

3. Assemble the Eggs Royale:

- Top each English muffin half with a slice of smoked salmon. A foundation of luxury but built on something hollow.

- Place a poached egg on top of the salmon. Fragile, delicate, but already broken.

- Spoon Hollandaise sauce over each egg. A final touch of indulgence, masking the emptiness beneath.

- Garnish with fresh dill and serve immediately. Presentation is everything, even when the substance is gone.

The dish was perfect, just like everything else I created in that kitchen. But it was a lie. A beautiful, hollow lie. The woman in the wheelchair had become a permanent fixture in my mind, a symbol of my failings, of the cost of my ambition. She was the beginning of my end, the first sign that I was losing myself in the relentless pursuit of perfection.

The promotion to Chef de Partie, once something I'd aspired to, now felt like a cruel joke. A victory that was anything but. It was hollow, like everything else in my life. The woman in the wheelchair was a harbinger, a grim reminder that in my quest for success, I'd lost sight of what truly mattered. The kitchen, once my haven, had become my prison, the place where I'd slowly destroyed myself, one perfect dish at a time.

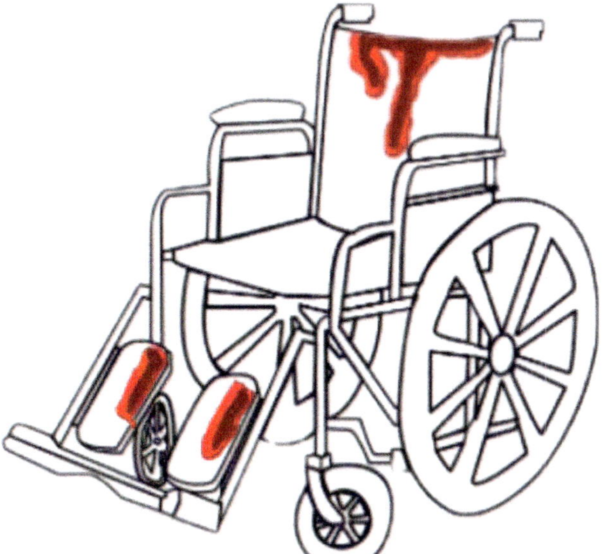

Chapter 4: The Furnace Below

The kitchen we worked in was no mere workspace; it was a subterranean hell, buried deep beneath the hotel like a dark secret, festering and seething with a life of its own. This wasn't just a place where food was prepared—it was an inferno, a place where we were tested, pushed to our limits, and, in some ways, remade in the image of the madness that permeated every corner of The Paramount.

The lights above us, sickly and fluorescent, cast a harsh, unforgiving glare over everything, turning our sweat into a slick, oily sheen that clung to our skin. The air was heavy, thick with the oppressive heat of the ovens, the fryers, and the bodies that moved relentlessly within this furnace. Ventilation was a cruel joke—a mere whisper of air that did nothing to alleviate the suffocating atmosphere. Walking into this kitchen wasn't just entering a room; it was a descent into another world, a world where time warped, stretched, and sometimes seemed to stop entirely, trapping us in an endless cycle of heat and stress.

As you stepped into the kitchen, the first thing that greeted you was the darkest corner, a black void where the light had been out for months. That corner was a cesspool, a place where equipment was stored and forgotten, as if the darkness could swallow the very essence of what was kept there. I'd complained to maintenance more times than I could count, but all I ever got in return was a dismissive shrug and the offer of a lukewarm coffee, as if a shot of caffeine could somehow banish the oppressive darkness that lurked in that corner. It was a small defeat, one of many in the daily grind, but it was also a reminder of how little control we really had over our environment. The darkness was always there, waiting, a silent witness to everything that happened in this place.

To the left of the dessert section stood the fryer—a hulking, greasy beast that seemed to have a mind of its own. It crackled and spat with a malevolent glee, as if it took pleasure in the burns it inflicted on anyone foolish enough to get too close. Next to it was the combi oven, an ancient piece of equipment with a digital display that flickered like a dying star. The oven was temperamental at best, a relic of a bygone era that refused to die, clinging to life with a stubbornness that matched our own. The prep sink beside it had become the unofficial "lobster execution area," where crustaceans met their end under our swift, indifferent hands. The sink was always stained with the residue of death, a place where the line between life and sustenance was blurred beyond recognition.

Moving toward the pass, the kitchen was divided into two main sections: Veg and garnish to the left, meat and fish to the right. The meat and fish section were the heart of the kitchen, the place where the real action happened, where the heat was most intense, both literally and figuratively. This was mainly occupied by Mathew & Chantel, working that section felt like being at the eye of a storm, where every decision mattered, where the energy was electric, and where a single mistake could spell disaster. This was no-mans-land, the place where chefs were made or broken, where reputations were built on the back of sweat, blood, and tears.

Fond memories of this section often involved Scott, Mathew, Chantel, and Scorpion. We communicated with the precision of a well-rehearsed orchestra, each service a symphony of sizzling pans, sharp knives, and shouted commands. Scott and I had developed a seamless rapport, our movements and words perfectly synchronised, making us an unstoppable team in the heat of battle. There was a camaraderie there, a bond forged in the crucible of the kitchen, that made the relentless pressure almost bearable.

But not all memories were fond. One particularly sinister memory from that section stands out—a moment of dark satisfaction that still haunts me. I had left a mussel pan on the solid top for too long, its handle becoming an instrument of pain, searing hot and ready to strike. Liam, oblivious in his frenzy, grabbed it without thinking, his hand searing like bacon on the griddle. The smell of burning flesh filled the air, mingling with the scent of the food, and I should have felt remorse. But instead, a dark thrill coursed through me, a twisted sense of satisfaction at seeing him brought low, even if only for a moment. It was a small, cruel victory in the relentless battle of the kitchen, a reminder that even the strongest could be brought to their knees by a single moment of carelessness.

The pass was the throne of the kitchen, the place where the chef on duty commanded the service with a heavy hand. It was a position of power and pressure, where every dish, every decision, was scrutinised under the harshest of lights. Being at the pass meant you were the commander, the leader, and the entire service reflected on your prowess. It was a place where you could taste both glory and despair in equal measure, where the success of the night hung in the balance, and where the line between triumph and disaster was razor thin.

Beyond the pass was the front of house area—a different world entirely, one where the chaos of the kitchen gave way to the polished veneer of the dining room. I always hoped Ellie would walk through those doors, her presence a sign that the service might go well. Ellie was a beacon of light in an otherwise brutal morning routine, her calm demeanour a stark contrast to the frenzy that defined our existence below. Her arrival was a small spark of hope in the otherwise relentless grind, a reminder that there was still something worth striving for, even in this hell….but we will introducer her later!

Finally, there was the pot wash, a realm ruled by Uro—or at least, that's what I think his name was. Uro was a giant of a man, with a massive, teddy bear physique that belied the wildness in his eyes. He was like a character out of a nightmare, a cross between Hodor and Santa Claus on meth, with a constant mutter of "Yessss, Nooooooo, Kulava," whatever the hell that meant. He moved through the pot wash with a kind of manic energy, his massive hands scrubbing pots and pans with a ferocity that was both awe-inspiring and terrifying. His favourite drink was pickle juice, a bizarre choice that fit right in with the twisted tapestry of the kitchen. Uro was the gatekeeper of the pot wash, the last line of defence between the chaos of the kitchen and the clean, pristine plates that would eventually make their way back to the pass.

This was the world we lived in, a world where the heat never let up, where the pressure was unrelenting, and where the line between sanity and madness was often blurred beyond recognition. The kitchen was our furnace, our crucible, the place where we were forged and where we were broken, day after day, night after night. And through it all, we kept going, driven by something deep inside us—something that made us return to the heat, to the chaos, to the madness, again and again.

In the end, we were all just cogs in the machine, ground down by the relentless gears of the kitchen, each of us playing our part in the endless cycle of creation and destruction that defined our lives. And as I stood there, in the furnace below, I realised that there was no escaping it—this was our world, our reality, and there was no way out.

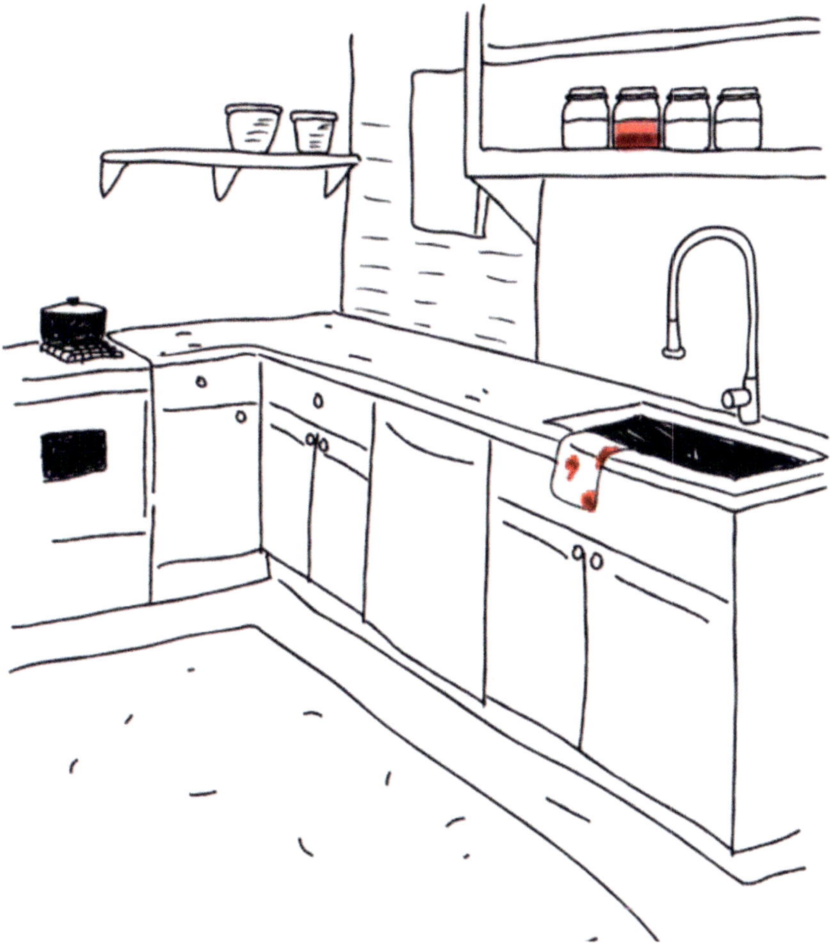

Chapter 5: The Last Shimmer of Light

The final stretch of my tenure as The Paramount's breakfast chef was an unrelenting spiral, a descent into the kind of madness that gnaws at your sanity, chews through your resolve, and leaves you hollowed out. Each morning, the routine suffocated me—waking up at 4:30 AM to the screech of an alarm that felt less like a wake-up call and more like the blade of a guillotine, severing me from the few remnants of a normal life. Friends? I had none. Nights out? Forgotten. My life had been pared down to the basics: work, sleep, and the faint, distant echo of a social life I used to have. But amidst this grim existence, there was Ellie Dawson, a front-of-house waiter who also worked the early shifts. She was an unexpected flicker of light in an otherwise pitch-black tunnel.

Ellie was a curious kind of beautiful. Not the kind that hits you like a slap to the face, but something subtler, something that lingered. Her presence was a strange mix of serenity and warmth, like a beam of light slicing through the thick fog of my mornings. She sang to herself as she made toast for the guests, her voice soft, almost a whisper, but it cut through the hysteria of the kitchen, soothing, calming. It was a reprieve, a momentary escape from the battle lines I was trapped in.

There was something about her—something effortless in the way she moved, the way she smiled, that made the morning grind a little more bearable. She had this way of making everything seem okay, even when it clearly wasn't. Her laughter, quiet and restrained, was like a balm on my frayed nerves, easing the tension that threatened to unravel me completely. I found myself drawn to her, more than I should have been, more than was safe. My relationship was already circling the drain, and getting involved with Ellie could only lead to more complications. But there was something magnetic about her, something that made the mornings not just tolerable, but do I dare say it…. almost enjoyable!?

As the days slipped by and my impending promotion to Chef de Partie loomed closer, the stress mounted, twisting the noose around my neck tighter with each passing hour. But amidst all this, Ellie became my anchor. We bonded in the way that only people who work in high-pressure environments can. We laughed, we gossiped, we vented our frustrations to each other. Her presence turned the morning shifts from a torturous ordeal into something I almost looked forward to. Just knowing she was there, on shift, made the relentless grind of the kitchen a little less soul-crushing.

We were like seasoned warriors, Ellie and I, tackling the breakfast service with a practiced rhythm, a synchronized dance of efficiency and havoc. There was one morning that stands out, a particularly hellish one. A tour group had descended upon us without warning, orders flooding in faster than we could handle. The kitchen was a war zone—pans clattering, oil spitting, the heat oppressive—and the dining room was a chaotic mess of impatient guests and unreasonable demands. But Ellie moved through it all with an ease that was almost hypernormal, her calm efficiency a stark contrast to my frenzied energy. She managed the dining room with the kind of poise that suggested she was born for this, while I orchestrated the kitchen with a precision that bordered on the manic.

Every morning, before the chaos began, I made her fresh pastries. Croissants, Danishes—whatever she wanted. It was a small gesture, but it mattered. Seeing her face light up when she bit into a warm, flaky croissant was like a small victory, a rare moment of satisfaction during the daily grind. Her appreciation was something I clung to, a reminder that not everything in my life was falling apart. There was still a shred of normalcy, of kindness, in the world.

The Croissant Recipe

Ingredients:

- 4 cups all-purpose flour—basic, necessary, like the structure I was trying to hold onto.

- 1/2 cup granulated sugar—a touch of sweetness, like the fleeting moments of joy Ellie brought into my life.

- 1 tablespoon salt—to balance, to remind me that even sweetness has its limits.

- 1 cup whole milk, warm—a comfort, a reminder of something soft, something safe.

- 1 package active dry yeast—alive, growing, like the feelings I was trying to suppress.

- 1 cup unsalted butter, cold and cubed—rich, indulgent, but dangerous in excess.

- 1 large egg, beaten (for egg wash)—the final touch, the thing that makes it all come together.

Instructions:

1. Prepare the Dough:

   - In a bowl, combine warm milk and sugar, then sprinkle the yeast over it. Let it sit until foamy, about 10 minutes. Like anticipation, waiting for something to happen, for something to grow.

   - In a large bowl, mix the flour and salt. Add the yeast mixture and knead until the dough is smooth and elastic, about 10 minutes. Kneading, working out the tension, forcing it into something manageable.

   - Shape the dough into a ball, cover with plastic wrap, and let it rise in a warm place until doubled in size, about 1 hour. Rising, growing, just like the distance between me and the rest of the world.

2. Prepare the Butter:

   - Place the cold, cubed butter between two sheets of parchment paper. Using a rolling pin, pound and roll the butter into a thin rectangle. Cold, hard, but slowly giving way, just like me.

   - Refrigerate the butter slab while the dough is rising. Waiting, always waiting.

3. Laminate the Dough:

- On a floured surface, roll the dough into a large rectangle. Place the butter slab in the centre and fold the dough over it, enclosing the butter completely. Encasing it, hiding it, like the emotions I kept buried deep.

- Roll out the dough into a long rectangle and perform a letter fold: fold one third of the dough over the centre, then fold the other third over that. Fold, roll, fold, roll—just like the days blending into one another.

- Wrap the dough in plastic wrap and refrigerate for 30 minutes. Repeat this rolling and folding process three more times, chilling the dough for 30 minutes between each fold. Repetition, routine, the only things keeping me sane.

4. Shape the Croissants:

- Roll the dough into a large rectangle, about 1/4 inch thick. Cut the dough into triangles. Precise, methodical—just like the way I was trying to keep my life together.

- Starting from the wide end of each triangle, roll the dough up tightly towards the point to form a croissant shape. Place the croissants on a baking sheet lined with parchment paper.

5. Proof and Bake:

- Cover the croissants with a damp cloth and let them rise in a warm place until doubled in size, about 1 hour. Rising, like the tension, like the inevitable fallout.

- Preheat the oven to 375°F (190°C). Brush the croissants with the beaten egg. A final touch, a last attempt to make everything seem okay.

- Bake for 15-20 minutes, or until golden brown and flaky. Perfect on the outside, but who knows what's really inside.

As the days passed, our bond grew stronger, a light in the otherwise dark landscape of my life. Ellie and I became something more than just colleagues, something that was dangerously close to crossing a line. But that's a story for another time. What mattered was that on that particularly chaotic morning, when the world felt like it was crashing down around us, Ellie and I faced it together. We were like soldiers in the trenches, picking each other up when the weight of the service threatened to crush us. There were glances exchanged, glances that said more than words ever could, a silent communication that only comes from mutual respect and something more—a connection that was both comforting and exhilarating.

When the last plate had been served and the dining room began to empty, we shared a moment of triumph. It wasn't loud, it wasn't celebrated, but it was there—a quiet acknowledgment that we had survived, that we had won this battle. But I knew, deep down, that this was just a temporary victory. The dark clouds of my culinary journey were gathering on the horizon, and Ellie was my last shimmer of light, the only thing keeping me from sliding into complete madness.

She was the anchor that kept me grounded, the reminder that amidst the relentless grind and the looming promotion, there was still something worth holding onto. But like all good things, I knew this too would pass. The question was, how much longer could I hold on before the darkness consumed me completely?

Chapter 6: The Test

They called it *The Test*—capital T, like it was some grand, sacred rite of passage, instead of the brutal, soul-sucking marathon that it really was. Today was my turn to run the gauntlet: from 5:30 AM to 11:00 PM, breakfast to dinner tonight service. A masochistic, nearly 18-hour stretch designed to break you, to see if you had the balls to handle the relentless grind of a Chef De Partie. Every chef at The Paramount went through it. Now it was my turn. Fuck my life.

The day stretched out before me like an endless void, each second dragging like a slow, deliberate torture. The hours piled up, an oppressive weight, suffocating in their vastness. The kitchen was prepped, a battlefield ready for the war to come: 200 covers for breakfast, 150 for lunch, another 150 for dinner. The entire team on edge, every nerve strung tight, waiting for the onslaught, I could see the excitement in Scorpion's eyes, I don't understand how he got thrilled from this knowledge, fucking madman.

Breakfast service was its own special kind of hell. Orders crashed in like a tidal wave—Eggs Royale, full English, pancakes dripping with syrup and disdain. Late guests stumbled down, oblivious, demanding their morning sustenance as if the world revolved around them. The pressure was unbearable, but I kept my cool, my head locked in place, my control absolute. Ellie's soft humming floated through the chaos, a thin thread of sanity during madness, a fleeting moment of calm before the next storm.

The lunch rush had been a relentless, unforgiving blur—an unholy storm of orders that lashed against us with the force of a hurricane, leaving the kitchen battered, breathless, teetering on the edge of collapse. To my surprise, Frenchie delighted himself to assist with the afternoon teas. But no fucking surprise he somehow managed to fuck up the simplest of tasks. Sandwiches. For ten afternoon teas. Ten. Fucking. Afternoon. Teas. The enormity of his failure clawed at my brain, a brutal, relentless scratching that wouldn't let up. My eyes darted to the station where platters should have been piled high with neat rows of delicate cucumber sandwiches, smoked salmon, egg salad on perfectly cut bread. But there was nothing. Just empty, mocking space.

"Fuck," I hissed through gritted teeth, the word a venomous whisper that barely contained the fury roiling within me. My pulse hammered against my temples; each beat a countdown to the impending disaster that was about to erupt in the dining room. Customers were waiting, perched on the brink of expectation, their eyes scanning the room for a glimpse of the decadent afternoon tea they believed was their due. And here we were, in the depths of the kitchen, staring down the barrel of utter catastrophe, all because Frenchie—the useless, pathetic fuck—had forgotten the sandwiches.

Frenchie, with no surprise, was floundering, drowning in his own incompetence. I saw it in his eyes—the wide, frantic panic, the way his hands shook as he fumbled with the bread, his movements jerky and uncoordinated like a puppet with his strings cut. It would have been almost pitiable if it weren't so goddamn infuriating. But there was no time for pity, no time for anything except action.

I lunged for the bread, tearing into it with a savagery that surprised even me. "Move!" I snarled, shoving Frenchie out if the way. He stumbled, barely catching himself, the butter knife slipping from his trembling hand. Absolutely fucking useless.

There was no time, no time to make everything from scratch, not with the dining room perched on the edge of revolt, their anticipation a noose tightening around our necks. I had to think fast, move faster. The kitchen around me dissolved into a blur as I tore through it, my mind a razor-sharp instrument slicing through the chaos with surgical precision.

Bread. It didn't matter if it was perfect—just get it sliced. I slashed through loaf after loaf, the serrated blade a blur of motion in my hands. Butter—slather it on thick, no time for finesse, no time for anything except speed. Cucumber—where the fuck were the cucumbers? My eyes scanned the devastation and landed on them, discarded and forgotten next to a pot of boiling eggs. I lunged, grabbing the cold, green bastards and slicing them with a fury that bordered on psychotic.

"Eggs! Where the fuck are the eggs?" My voice was a whip, cracking through the air, snapping Frenchie out of his stupor. He scrambled to peel and mash, his hands shaking, desperately trying to keep up with the pace I was setting. But he was too slow, too fucking slow.

The smoked salmon—Jesus, we were almost out. It didn't matter. I grabbed what was left, flinging it onto the buttered bread with a precision that felt more like an act of violence than culinary preparation. My hands moved on autopilot, assembling the sandwiches with a speed and efficiency that bordered on superhuman.

One tray down, then another. The Twins tried to help, but their attempts only slowed me down, their movements clumsy and pathetic. They relied on each other too much, like two halves of a broken machine that couldn't function without the other. I shoved them aside taking over completely.

"Go!" I barked, thrusting a tray into one of their hands. "Get these out there before they start rioting!"

They bolted, stumbling toward the dining room, and I watched them go, a twisted smile pulling at the corners of my mouth. I had saved Frenchie's sorry ass, saved us all from the brink of catastrophe, but there was no satisfaction in it, no sense of victory. Only the bitter taste of resentment, the knowledge that once again, I had to clean up his mess.

Lunch ended, barely a moment to regroup. The briefest of respites—laughter, banter, a fleeting release from the tension before the storm gathered again. Scott, the twins, Scorpion, —we were a ragtag crew, held together by our shared insanity. But the clock kept ticking, and dinner service loomed, a beast waiting to be fed. The evening special: a duck dish that demanded precision, a delicate ballet of Flavors that had to be perfect. Anything less would be a failure.

Pan-Fried Honey Duck Breast

Ingredients:

- 4 duck breasts—pristine, like the image we projected to the diners.

- Salt and pepper—to taste, a reminder of the bitterness beneath the surface.

- 2 tablespoons olive oil—rich, like the sheen of sweat on our brows.

- 1/2 cup balsamic vinegar—sharp, cutting, a slap to the senses.

- 2 tablespoons honey—sweet, but with a sting, just like the service.

- 1/4 cup chicken stock—depth, like the layers of exhaustion we tried to hide.

- 2 sprigs of fresh thyme—a hint of something fresh, something pure, now long gone.

- 1 orange, zested and juiced—bright, but fleeting, a ghost of flavour.

- 2 shallots, finely chopped—small, precise, like the steps we took to survive.

- 1 tablespoon butter—smooth, a false sense of comfort.

Instructions:

1. Preheat the oven to 400°F (200°C). The heat building, just like the tension in the kitchen.

2. Score the skin of the duck breasts in a crisscross pattern. Season with salt and pepper. Precision, like the cuts we made every day, both in the kitchen and to our own sanity.

3. Heat the olive oil in a large ovenproof skillet over medium-high heat. Place the duck breasts, skin side down, in the skillet and cook until the skin is crisp and golden brown, about 6 minutes. The sizzle of fat, the hiss of heat—music to our ears, a promise of something more.

4. Turn the duck breasts over and transfer the skillet to the oven. Roast for 5-7 minutes, until the duck is cooked to your desired doneness. Remove from the oven and let rest. Rest—a concept as foreign as sleep, as unattainable as peace.

5. In the same skillet, add the shallots and cook until soft. Add the balsamic vinegar, honey, chicken stock, thyme, orange zest, and juice. Cook, stirring occasionally, until the sauce is reduced and thickened, about 10 minutes. The sauce—thick, dark, like the atmosphere in the kitchen, heavy with the weight of expectation.

6. Remove the thyme sprigs and stir in the butter until the sauce is glossy. Slice the duck breasts and serve with the sauce drizzled over. Perfection, or the illusion of it, served up on a plate.

Dinner service was an unrelenting torrent, orders crashing down on us with the force of a hurricane. Each one a wave, pounding against our defences, wearing us down, pushing us to the brink. The team was stretched thin, emotions frayed and raw. Scott barked orders, the twins moved in eerie synchronicity, and Scorpion's intensity never wavered. There were moments—dishes burnt, orders miscommunicated, a near-disaster with the duck special—that demanded everything we had, split-second decisions and flawless execution. But we endured. We pushed through the pain, the exhaustion, the madness.

The final dish was served, the last order completed. The kitchen fell silent, the noise and chaos replaced by a heavy, exhausted stillness. And there it was—the promotion. Chef De Partie. A title, a recognition, a hollow prize won at the cost of my sanity. The promise of a room at The Paramount, a small mercy after an endless day. But as I stood there, the adrenaline fading, the weight of the day settling on my shoulders, I couldn't shake the gnawing sense of dread. This was just the beginning.

After the gruelling service that earned me my promotion, I stumbled through the labyrinthine corridors of the hotel, each step a monumental effort. Sweat-soaked and exhausted, I clutched my keycard like a lifeline, my grip tight, knuckles white, trying to fend off the creeping tendrils of fatigue. The wooden floors beneath my feet groaned with every step, each creak a sinister whisper echoing the haunted hallways of every horror movie trope imaginable.

The room I finally reached was anachronistic, a cozy relic adorned with vintage furniture and abstract paintings that hinted at madness. Wooden floors, a marble-tiled bathroom with a bathtub that promised solace from the day's carnage. At last, peace. The bed called to me, a siren song of rest and oblivion.

I collapsed onto the bed, the cool sheets enveloping me as I began to reflect on my new title: Chef De Partie. The good and the bad swirled in my mind—a whirlwind of potential futures, each one a double-edged sword. The thrill of power, the burden of responsibility, the endless grind that had led me here. As I drifted through these thoughts, an uneasy sense began to creep into the room.

A cold dread settled over me as memories of the bell incident clawed their way to the surface. I sat up, scanning the room, eyes darting through the shadows. Something was in here with me. My heart pounded, the silence of the room amplifying the sound of my own breathing.

And there it was, just visible in the dim corner of the room, a figure obscured by darkness—the woman in the wheelchair. Her laboured, wheezing breaths sliced through the still air, a grotesque symphony of life on the edge of death. The look on her face was the same as that night, a mask of exhaustion and despair.

I couldn't believe it. Why was she here? The smell of decay filled the room, a pungent reminder of my neglect. Compelled by a mix of horror and curiosity, I slowly approached her, the floorboards creaking beneath my feet. The closer I got, the stronger the stench became, until it was almost unbearable.

As I reached out to touch her, she vanished. Gone, like a figment of my tortured imagination. I stood there, hand outstretched, trembling. This had to be in my head. The fatigue, the stress, the endless hours—it was all catching up to me.

The rest of the night is a blur, a hazy memory of restless sleep and haunting dreams. The line between reality and nightmare blurred, leaving me to wonder what was real and what was a product of my overworked mind. The promotion was mine, but at what cost? The woman in the wheelchair, a ghost of my past, would haunt me, a reminder of the path I had chosen and the price I was paying.

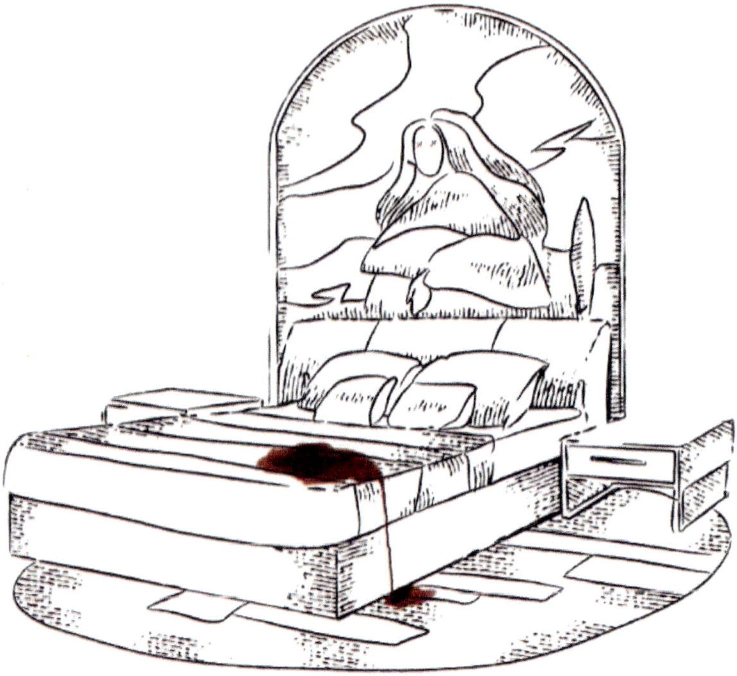

Chapter 7: Advancement, Tragedy, and the Hidden Cave

Here I am, in the back office where the tyrant chef Liam has sat me down. The room is a claustrophobic hellhole, barely big enough to house the old, sagging desk and the stacks of crumpled paperwork. Electrical wires snake across the ceiling, some hanging loose, buzzing faintly—a constant reminder of the imminent fire hazard. The fluorescent light flickers sporadically, casting erratic shadows on the peeling walls. The air is thick with the stench of sweat and stale smoke, suffocating, making each breath a struggle, the radio playing *"Ashes to Ashes by David Bowie"* slightly humming in the background.

Liam hands me my new contract as Chef De Partie, his voice a droning monotone, congratulating me, listing my merits. All I hear is white noise. My eyes are heavy, the bags under them feel like lead weights pulling me down. I'm barely listening, only catching fragments of his spiel about dedication and skill. His words dissolve into the background hum of the dying light overhead.

All I can think about is the directive I received as I walked in: "Fix Frenchie's staff lunch." The absurdity of it all—promotion to Chef De Partie and I'm still dealing with this nonsense. My thoughts drift, cold and clinical, settling on the decision to throw together the best Mac & Cheese for the staff. Simple, comforting, with a touch of elegance.

Mac & Cheese: A Symphony of Decadence

Ingredients: A Calculated Indulgence

- 200g elbow macaroni—innocuous in appearance but designed to deliver satisfaction in every bite.

- 2 tablespoons unsalted butter—cold, unyielding, waiting for the heat to transform it into something more.

- 2 tablespoons all-purpose flour—a fine powder, a substance as deceptive as it is essential, the foundation of this operation.

- 2 cups whole milk—rich, almost luxurious, the kind of liquid that coats the tongue with a thick layer of comfort.

- 1 cup heavy cream—decadence distilled; an opulent addition that takes this dish from ordinary to obscene.

- 1 teaspoon Dijon mustard—sharp, almost cruel, a flavour that cuts through the richness like a scalpel.

- 1/2 teaspoon garlic powder—subtle yet pervasive, the kind of presence that lingers long after it's gone.

- 1/4 teaspoon cayenne pepper—a hint of danger, a spark of heat that reminds you of the darkness that lies just beneath the surface.

- 1/4 teaspoon white pepper—spicy, biting, an element of surprise in an otherwise predictable narrative.

- 200g sharp cheddar cheese, grated—bold, assertive, a flavour that demands your attention and refuses to let go.

- 100g Gruyere cheese, grated—earthy, complex, the kind of cheese that reveals its layers over time.

- 50g Parmesan cheese, grated—salty, aged, a taste of something that has been perfected over years of careful refinement.

- Salt, to taste—simple, essential, a reminder that even the most decadent dishes need balance.

- Fresh chives, finely chopped (for garnish)—a splash of green, a superficial nod to freshness in a dish that is anything but.

Instructions: The Methodical Descent

1. Preheat the oven to 375°F (190°C)—the temperature at which this concoction will reach its final, irresistible form.

2. Cook the macaroni in a large pot of salted boiling water—watch the bubbles rise, the macaroni dance, a prelude to what's to come. Drain and set aside—a simple act, but one that holds the promise of something more.

3. In a saucepan, melt the butter over medium heat—observe as it softens, liquefies, surrenders to the heat. Add the flour—two tablespoons, no more, no less. Whisk continuously—an act of control, maintaining the balance until it forms a roux, the base from which everything will emerge.

4. Gradually whisk in the milk and heavy cream—pour slowly, deliberately, watching as the liquid thickens, as the mixture clings to the back of a spoon—a sign that it's ready, that it's time to move forward.

5. Stir in the Dijon mustard, garlic powder, cayenne pepper, and white pepper—a calculated mix of flavours, each chosen to play its part in the unfolding drama. Let them blend, merge, until they become inseparable, until they create something greater than the sum of their parts.

6. Reduce the heat to low and add the cheeses—first the cheddar, then the Gruyere, and finally the Parmesan. Stir as they melt, as they lose their individuality in the heat, becoming a smooth, homogenous sauce. Season with salt to taste—a final touch, a final act of control.

7. Combine the cheese sauce with the cooked macaroni—pour it over, let it coat every piece, every curve, ensuring nothing is left untouched. This is more than just mixing; this is about domination, about making sure every inch of macaroni knows its place.

8. Transfer the mixture to a baking dish—a container, a vessel, where it will undergo its final transformation. Bake for 20-25 minutes—until the top is golden, bubbly, until it reaches that perfect state of imperfection.

9. Garnish with fresh chives before serving—a hint of green, a reminder that even in decadence, there must be the illusion of balance.

What you've created isn't just Mac & Cheese; it's a statement, a testament to the power of indulgence, to the allure of excess. It's the kind of dish that pulls you in, that holds you captive with its richness, its complexity. And like all things beautiful and dangerous, it leaves you wanting more, even as it consumes you.

Liam sends me back to the kitchen, shoving the prep list for the larder section into my hands. The paper is smudged, covered in greasy fingerprints, a testament to the relentless grind of this place.

Larder Section Prep List:

1. Smoked Salmon Tartare:

   - Dice smoked salmon, shallots, and capers. Mix with lemon zest, dill, and crème fraîche.

2. Duck Liver Pâté:

   - Prepare and cook duck livers, blend with butter, brandy, and spices until smooth.

3. Beetroot Carpaccio:

   - Thinly slice roasted beets, marinate in olive oil, balsamic vinegar, and thyme.

4. Stuffed Mushrooms:

- Clean and hollow out button mushrooms, stuff with herbed goat cheese and breadcrumbs.

5. Crab Cakes:

- Mix crab meat with breadcrumbs, eggs, mayonnaise, mustard, and seasonings. Form into patties.

6. Gazpacho Shooters:

- Blend tomatoes, cucumbers, peppers, garlic, and olive oil. Chill and serve in shot glasses.

7. Oysters on Ice:

- Shuck fresh oysters, serve on crushed ice with mignonette sauce.

The list is endless. As I walk back to the kitchen, the weight of the day ahead pressing down on me, I can't shake the feeling of dread creeping in. The kitchen is my battleground, and today, I am its reluctant commander.

I'm smashing through the prep list like a madman, each item a small victory, a fleeting triumph in the endless war of the kitchen. The smoked salmon tartare is done tick. Duck liver pâté smooth and velvety tick. Beetroot carpaccio marinating in olive oil and thyme—tick. Every tick is a heartbeat, a moment of respite, but the clock keeps ticking and lunch service hasn't even started. I'm already pissed off, exhausted, the weight of the day pressing down on me like a vase.

And then it begins. Checks start flying through the kitchen like machine-gun fire—check on, check on, check on. It's like being in an active firing range, bullets whizzing past my ears, constantly under fire with little ammo to my name. Orders come in faster than I can process them. The air is thick with heat and the acrid smell of sweat and stress. My hands are moving on autopilot, slicing, dicing, plating, but my mind is somewhere else, lost in the car crash.

I notice Liam's lack of companionship, his unusual short temper. More angry than usual. Every word he spits is laced with venom. Is it personal life issues? Is it work? Is it me? Fuck knows. His eyes are daggers, his voice a whip. I don't have time to ponder his demons; I have my own to deal with.

Hundreds of oysters need opening, the shells sharp and unforgiving. My fingers are numb, the knife slick with brine and sweat. Liam's abuse is a constant drone in the background, a relentless stream of invective. The pressure is building, a tsunami of stress and fatigue.

And then it happens. My hand slips, the oyster knife plunges through the soft flesh of my palm. The pain is immediate, white-hot, searing. Blood pours from the wound, a crimson river, soaking my whites, dripping onto the floor. Tiny shards of shell embedded in the gash, each one a tiny dagger.

I stare are my hand, almost confused, disorientated…. excited? I pull the knife out, gasping, trying to keep my composure. Liam's eyes lock onto mine, cold, unfeeling.

"You have no time to bleed," he barks, his voice cutting through the haze of pain. No sympathy, no concern, just a command. The world narrows to the throbbing in my hand and the orders still coming in.

I wrap a towel around the wound, the fabric quickly turning red. There's no time to stop, no time to think. The battle rages on and I'm just a soldier, wounded but still fighting, still pushing through the pain, the exhaustion, the endless stream of checks. Each one a reminder of the relentless grind, the unforgiving nature of this life.

Hours and hours passed, checks flying at us at a thousand miles per hour. "Check on, check on," the mantra of the damned, a relentless, brutal rhythm that marks the passage of time in this hellish kitchen. My hand throbs, the wound a persistent reminder of my fallibility, my humanity, the blood soaking through the makeshift bandage, mixing with sweat and grime. Tensions are high, the air thick with an oppressive sense of dread and desperation.

Liam, once a towering figure of rage-fuelled competence, is unravelling before my eyes. His descent into chaos is palpable, a slow-motion train wreck I can't look away from. He falters, misses checks, lashes out at everyone around him. His fury is indiscriminate and all-consuming, a king losing his grip on a crumbling kingdom.

Then, out of nowhere, when all hope seems lost—this is the moment in stories where something spectacular happens, the miraculous save that turns the tide. But not here. No saviour comes, no redemption. In this short, brutal tale, we are doomed.

Liam snaps. His scream is a primal, guttural sound, raw and animalistic, a howl of pure agony and rage. He slams his last plate down, food exploding in a chaotic burst of colour and texture, a final act of defiance. Then he turns and starts kicking a small stone oven behind the pass, his fury almost reducing it to rubble. His face is a mask of madness, eyes wild and unfocused. He leaves, storming out, abandoning the pass, leaving us exposed and vulnerable.

Scott steps in, trying to salvage the wreckage of this disastrous service. His calm in the storm is a stark contrast to Liam's unhinged rage, but the damage is irreparable. The service limps to its end, the battlefield littered with the detritus of our failure.

I didn't see Liam, not until weeks later. I was alone in the kitchen, preparing for another gruelling day, the quiet before the storm. He slunk in, a shadow of his former self, eyes sunken, skin sallow. He was begging me for money, his voice a pathetic whisper. With a mix of pity and revulsion, I walked him to the nearest cash point and handed him a tenner. He looked rough, gaunt and haunted, a man broken by his demons.

I never saw him again after that. The kitchen moved on, as it always does, but the memory of his breakdown lingered, a dark stain on the relentless grind of our daily lives. The image of his contorted face, the sound of his animalistic scream, the sight of him reduced to begging—

it all haunted me, a grim reminder of the thin line between order and chaos, competence and madness.

Over time, the kitchen became a wasteland, leaderless and lost, a battlefield littered with the remnants of our shattered morale. Scott tried to fill the void, but his efforts were in vain, mere band-aids on gaping wounds. Upper management, those faceless puppeteers, had other plans. They let us suffer, let us drown in our own sweat and blood, while they brewed up a solution, a cold and calculated remedy for our suffering. This solution arrived in the form of a new Executive Chef, Jamie Lee Webster.

Jamie entered our kitchen like a storm, his presence oppressive and suffocating. He had short brown hair, cold, calculating eyes, and an athletic build that spoke of control and power. He assessed us with a clinical precision, dissecting our flaws and weaknesses with a mere glance. We were leaderless, rogue, but his dominance in the kitchen was absolute, eclipsing even the formidable reputations of Scott and Scorpion. He was a predator among prey, and we felt it keenly.

Jamie reminded me of why I had originally taken on cheffing, but in a way that felt like a twisted reflection of my former passion. Under his iron rule, there was a semblance of hope, but it was hope tainted by fear. He refined our menu, turning it into something sharp and cruelly beautiful. His char-grilled Dover sole dish was a standout, a masterpiece that epitomised his ruthless perfectionism.

Grilled Dover Sole: An Exercise in Precision

Ingredients: A Calculated Selection

- 2 Dover sole fillets—pristine, almost too perfect, their flesh pale and unblemished, a canvas awaiting transformation.

- Olive oil—cold-pressed, green-gold, anointing the fillets with a subtle sheen, the promise of something more beneath the surface.

- Sea salt and black pepper—simple, elemental, the barest touch of seasoning that speaks to restraint, to control.

- Fresh lemon juice—a burst of acidity, sharp, cutting through the richness with surgical precision.

- Finely chopped parsley—green, fresh, a superficial nod to vibrancy in a dish that is otherwise stark, severe.

- Garlic butter—luxurious, indulgent, an afterthought that lingers, melting slowly, creeping into every crevice.

Instructions: The Methodical Ritual

1. Preheat the grill to high— let the heat rise, let it reach that point where control teeters on the edge of chaos. This isn't just about cooking; it's about power, about harnessing the fire.

2. Brush the Dover sole fillets with olive oil—a gentle stroke, the oil glistening on the surface like a thin veneer, a mask that hides the rawness beneath. Season with sea

salt and black pepper—no more, no less, just enough to hint at complexity without overwhelming the simplicity.

3. Place the fillets on the grill—lay them down with care, listening for the sizzle, that first kiss of heat that begins the transformation. Cook for 4-5 minutes on each side— a precise calculation, the timing crucial. Watch as the flesh turns opaque, as it begins to flake under the slightest pressure, the moment when perfection is reached but not yet lost.

4. Drizzle with fresh lemon juice—a sharp, acidic bite, cleansing the palate, cutting through the richness like a razor blade through silk. Top with finely chopped parsley—a sprinkle of green, a dash of life on a plate that speaks of finality.

5. Serve immediately—there's no room for hesitation, no time to linger. The sole must be hot, the garlic butter melting over the top, seeping into the crevices, pooling on the plate like the residue of something darker, something unspoken.

This isn't just a dish; it's an experience, a moment suspended in time. The Dover sole, once pristine, now transformed, lies before you—a testament to the precision, the control, the restraint that goes into every detail. And yet, beneath the surface, there's a tension, a latent energy that hints at something more, something dangerous. As you take that first bite, the delicate flavours meld together, the richness of the butter, the sharpness of the lemon, the subtle heat of the pepper— all perfectly balanced, all perfectly controlled. But there's always that edge, that awareness that at any moment, the balance could tip, the control could slip, and everything could fall apart.

Jamie's philosophy was harsh, his methods brutal, but his results were undeniable. His catchphrase, "Oui I Chef, Oui I," echoed through the kitchen like a mantra, a reminder of his omnipresence. It soon became the butt of a joke between me and Ellie, a small, bitter slice of levity in the otherwise relentless torture of our daily lives.

Under Jamie's oppressive leadership, the kitchen transformed into a machine, efficient and unyielding. It was as if a dark cloud had lifted, replaced by a stark, merciless clarity. The team began to gel, working with a newfound, fear-driven purpose. Jamie's influence was pervasive, his standards exacting, his presence a constant, looming threat.

Yet, even as things improved, a part of me remained on edge, constantly wary, waiting for the inevitable descent back into insanity. This was a place where hope was a dangerous thing, a double-edged sword that could just as easily cut you down. Jamie had brought order, but it was an order built on a foundation of fear and control, and in this kitchen, such foundations were always at risk of crumbling.

Jamie's iron-fisted rule had transformed our once brutal services into a perverse ballet of elegance and efficiency. But amidst the newfound order, a gnawing dread festered within me, a deep-seated insecurity that it could all collapse back into the hellhole that existed under Liam's abysmal reign. Jamie's innovations were mostly genius, but one idea stood out as a catastrophic miscalculation, a glaring exception that I'm convinced he knew was doomed from the start. This abomination was known as "The Cave."

The Cave was a single-man kitchen located on the ground floor of the hotel, a claustrophobic rat cage masquerading as a culinary workspace. It was small, cramped, devoid of proper ventilation, and the only equipment it boasted were a single oven, a grill, and a few electric hot tops. That was it, that's all we fucking had! And Jamie, in his infinite wisdom, decreed that the full menu would be available from that cave. A full fucking menu, with one chef grinding through it all! It was incomprehensible.

The entire team despised The Cave. It was an insult to our craft, a cruel joke at our expense. The idea of serving our meticulously crafted dishes from that dungeon was beyond ridiculous. Each day, Jamie would handpick one unlucky motherfucker to endure the solitary confinement of The Cave, to battle the entire menu in such a cramped, hostile environment. Prep food in the main kitchen, haul it up to The Cave, and then survive 12 to 14 hours in that inferno. It was a rhythm of torment.

Over time, The Cave morphed from a simple miscalculation into a punitive measure. Any chef who fucked up the night before was sentenced to The Cave for the following service. It became the embodiment of

Jamie's iron-fisted control, a place of punishment and isolation. But the kitchen had had enough. Operation Sabotage was set in motion.

The Cave itself was a nightmare. The oppressive heat, the lack of space, the constant pressure of producing the full menu alone—it was a slow descent into madness. The walls seemed to close in, the air thick with the scent of desperation and sweat. Each chef sent to The Cave returned broken, their spirits crushed under the weight of the impossible demands.

The rhythm of The Cave was relentless. Prep in the main kitchen, lug the supplies upstairs, and then face the onslaught of orders alone. The grill hissed malevolently, the oven groaned in protest, and the electric hot tops buzzed like a swarm of angry insects. There was no respite, no moment of peace. It was a war of attrition, and we were losing.

The team's hatred for The Cave was palpable. Every day, another chef was condemned to that pit of despair, their only crime being a minor mistake or a momentary lapse in judgment. The Cave became a symbol of our collective suffering, a reminder of the brutal reality of Jamie's regime.

Our plan to sabotage The Cave was born out of necessity. We couldn't endure it any longer. The sabotage had to be subtle, undetectable. A faulty connection here, a misplaced ingredient there—small acts of rebellion designed to disrupt the flow and render The Cave inoperable. It was our only hope of escaping the relentless torment.

As we executed our plan, the tension in the kitchen rose. We were walking a fine line, risking everything to reclaim our sanity. Each act of sabotage was a victory, a small step towards freedom. But the risk was immense. If Jamie discovered our plot, the consequences would be severe.

The Cave, once a place of punishment, became a battleground for our very souls. We fought back, resisting the oppressive regime that sought to break us. And in the end, we hoped to emerge victorious, to reclaim our dignity and restore balance to the kitchen.

Sadly, its was my turn to face off with The Cave, I was the unlucky duckling who was chosen, the pressure was relentless. Orders flew in like bullets, each one a demand, a threat. The tickets piled up faster than we could read them, a growing mountain of expectation that loomed over m, ready to crush us me under its weight. Every dish was impossible, every moment a trial by fire. The relentless rhythm of service drummed in my ears, a maddening beat that pounded in time with my racing heart.

I could feel it building, the cracking, the fissures forming beneath the surface. My hands moved on autopilot, slicing, dicing, searing, plating. But my mind was elsewhere, drifting on the edge of a dark abyss, staring into the void that was slowly, inexorably, pulling me in.

It started small. A misplaced pan, a cut that was too deep, too jagged. Then another, and another. The mistakes began to stack up, a tower of errors teetering on the brink of collapse. My vision blurred, the edges of my world darkening as the heat and the noise and the unyielding pressure pressed down on me from all sides.

A plate slipped from my hand, crashing to the floor with a sound like shattering glass, like the final crack of a breaking mind. The noise cut through the din of the kitchen, a discordant note in the symphony of chaos. Heads turned; eyes widened in shock. But I couldn't move. I stood there, paralysed, staring at the fragments of porcelain scattered at my feet, my breath coming in ragged, shallow gasps.

It was all unraveling. The Cave had me in its grip, squeezing, crushing, until I felt my knees buckle. I caught myself on the edge of the counter, the metal cool against my burning skin, but the reprieve was fleeting. The walls of the kitchen seemed to close in, the oppressive heat and the weight of failure bearing down on me like a physical force.

Someone—one of the waiters, maybe, or one of the chefs from the furnace—shouted my name, but it was a distant echo, lost in the roaring in my ears. My vision tunnelled, the world narrowing to a single point of focus: the knife in my hand. My knuckles whitened as I gripped it, the blade trembling, slick with oil and blood. My blood. I hadn't even noticed the cut, the deep, jagged line running across my palm, the crimson drops that mingled with the grease on the countertop.

And then, like a dam breaking, it hit me. A wave of raw, unfiltered panic that swept through me, pulling me under, drowning me in its cold, merciless grip. I couldn't breathe, couldn't think. The air was gone, replaced by a suffocating fog that choked me, strangled the life out of me.

The Cave had won. It had taken everything I had, drained me dry, and left me a hollow shell, shaking, broken, shattered. The knife clattered to the floor, the final act in a nightmarish play that I could no longer endure.

Jamie's choice to impose The Cave on us was not just a punishment; it was a deliberate act of cruelty, a sadistic experiment to see how far we could be pushed before we broke. Each chef who entered The Cave emerged hollowed, their eyes void of hope, their spirits crushed. It was a punishment worse than any other, a solitary confinement in the middle of a bustling hotel.

The only good that ever came out of The Cave was the occasional small dish that made its way into our grim routine. My personal favourite was the crab toast—a rare glimmer of culinary brilliance amidst the torment.

Crab on Sourdough Toast: A Dissection of Delicacy

Ingredients: A Carefully Curated Selection

- Fresh sourdough bread—dense, artisanal, its crust crackling under the pressure of a knife, yielding to the softness beneath, a contrast that mirrors the dichotomy of existence.

- 200g fresh crab meat—white, succulent, meticulously picked clean of shell and sinew, the remnants of a life once vibrant, now reduced to sustenance.

- 2 tablespoons mayonnaise—rich, creamy, a subtle binder that clings to the crab, holding it together, much like the thin veneer of sanity holding back the abyss.

- 1 teaspoon Dijon mustard—sharp, biting, a hint of something darker lurking beneath the surface.

- 1 lemon, juiced—acidic, cutting, a necessary counterpoint to the richness, its sharpness a reminder that pleasure and pain are inextricably linked.

- Salt and pepper to taste—simple, essential, the barest whisper of flavour, yet capable of altering the entire composition.

- Fresh chives, finely chopped—green, delicate, a garnish that speaks of life even as it decorates the remnants of the dead.

- Butter for toasting—golden, melting, its richness seeping into the bread, saturating it with warmth and indulgence.

Instructions: The Ritual of Creation

1. Lightly toast the sourdough slices in butter—heat the pan, watch the butter sizzle, foam, and then subside into a golden pool. Lay the bread down gently, pressing it into

the heat, listening to the hiss as it begins to brown. The crust darkens, the butter seeps in, and the kitchen fills with the scent of something primal, something rich and sinful. You turn the bread, admiring the golden-brown surface, the crisp edges. It's a perfect balance of texture, a contrast that teeters on the edge of destruction.

2. In a bowl, mix the crab meat with mayonnaise, Dijon mustard, lemon juice, salt, and pepper—methodically, precisely. Each ingredient is added with care, folded together until the crab is coated, not smothered. The mayonnaise clings to the meat, the mustard cuts through with its sharpness, the lemon juice brightens, lifting the entire composition to a higher plane. Salt and pepper— the final touch, seasoning not just the dish but the very experience of it.

3. Spread the crab mixture generously on the toasted sourdough—take your time, saver the act of spreading, of covering the golden surface with the pale, creamy crab mixture. Each stroke of the knife is deliberate, each layer a testament to the art of perfection.

4. Garnish with finely chopped chives—a sprinkle of green, a touch of life on the plate, a contrast to the white of the crab, the golden brown of the toast. The chives add not just flavour but colour, a visual cue that speaks to freshness, even as the crab beneath speaks of the sea and the life it once had.

5. Serve immediately, savouring the fleeting moment of joy—but is it joy, or something darker? The toast, warm in your hands, the crab, cool and rich on your tongue—

each bite is a moment suspended in time, a balance of pleasure and guilt, indulgence and restraint. You take another bite, and another, the flavours melding, the textures contrasting, until all that's left are crumbs on the plate and the lingering taste of something you can't quite define, something you can't quite shake off.

This is not just a dish—it's an experience, a momentary escape from the ordinary, a step into the sublime. But beneath the surface, there's a tension, a darkness that hovers at the edges, reminding you that even the most delicate pleasures can have a bitter aftertaste.

The satisfaction of savouring that crab toast was one of the few moments of respite in an otherwise unending nightmare.

But as the days of torment dragged on, our collective resolve strengthened. The sabotage continued, small victories accumulating until the fateful day arrived.

The Cave's systems began to fail. The faulty connections sparked and short-circuited, the ingredients went bad, and the relentless heat became unbearable even by the already hellish standards. The Cave, once Jamie's instrument of control and punishment, crumbled under our collective defiance.

Victory was ours. The Cave was rendered inoperable, a testament to our resilience and rebellion. The oppressive air of the hotel kitchen lightened, and for the first time in what felt like an eternity, we could breathe. But the darkness lingered. The fear of retribution, the lingering dread of Jamie's wrath—it was never far from our minds. The Cave's destruction was a victory, but it came at a cost. The scars it left behind would never truly heal.

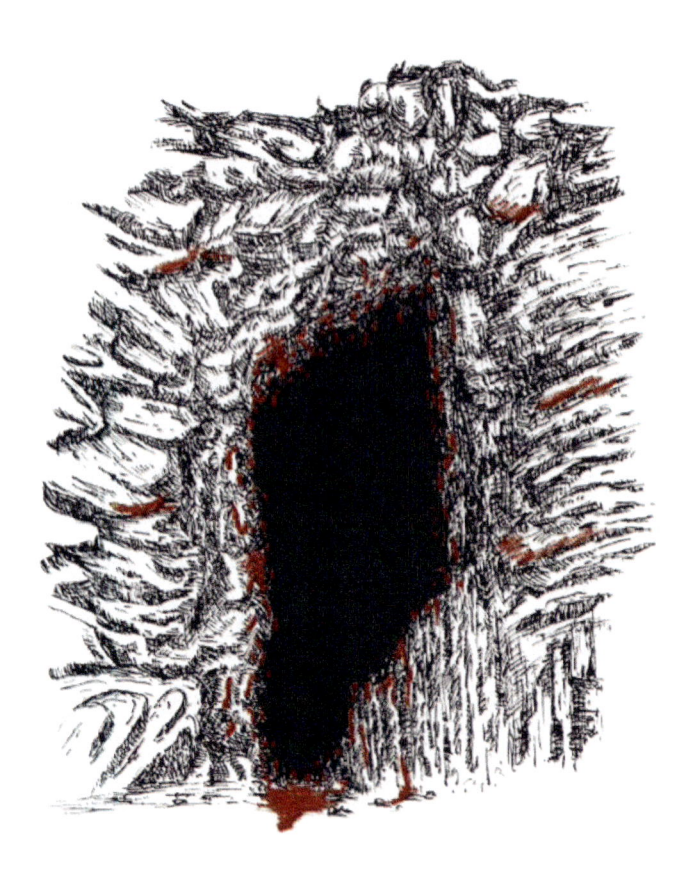

Chapter 8: Dancing with Shadows

The kitchen had become a grotesque parody of normality, a relentless, grinding machine that chewed us up and spat us out, day after excruciating day. The team, once a fractured collection of misfits, had fused into a cold, efficient unit—each of us a cog in the monstrous mechanism of culinary excellence. Plates left the pass with the precision of a mechanised assembly line, the eerie harmony of our movements born from shared suffering and the crushing weight of expectation.

Time blurred into a monotonous haze, each day bleeding into the next with a brutality that was both numbing and relentless. The kitchen's rhythm was a brutal drumbeat, pounding away at our souls without mercy. Mornings merged into evenings, each shift an ordeal that stretched out endlessly, a Sisyphean cycle of prep, service, and cleanup. The physical toll was insidious: aching limbs, a searing pain that gnawed at my spine, and the constant, grinding ache of a soul battered by relentless demands. The kitchen had become a crucible of endurance, a place where we were forged and broken in equal measure.

Behind the veneer of success, my personal life was unravelling, fraying at the edges until it finally tore apart. The social fabric I once clung to had disintegrated, unravelling thread by thread. Friends who once filled my life with warmth and laughter drifted away, their patience worn thin by my absences, my disinterest, my cold indifference. Family gatherings became relics of a past life, distant memories of obligations I no longer cared to fulfil. And then there was my relationship—once the last bastion of stability in my agonising existence. Its dissolution was the final blow, the last thread snapped, leaving me adrift in a sea of isolation.

In the aftermath of my culinary downfall, I found myself spiralling into an abyss of hedonistic destruction. The very concepts of safety and responsibility became macabre jokes, echoes of a past life that seemed both alien and scornfully unattainable. The night transformed into a canvas for my excesses, each dark corner of the city a stage for a play of debauchery in which I starred as the tragic protagonist.

Nightclubs pulsed with a visceral, throbbing energy that matched the frantic disarray of my inner turmoil. Their strobe-lit dance floors and the anonymous crush of bodies provided a temporary refuge from the relentless grip of reality. Alcohol became my constant companion, each gulp a desperate wash to cleanse the bitter taste of failure. The burn of liquor as it slid down my throat was a mere whisper compared to the scorching despair that consumed my spirit.

Drugs followed—each dose a momentary escape, a fleeting reprieve from the ever-present shadow of misery that loomed over me. Cocaine's sharp clarity, ecstasy's euphoric embrace, the hazy oblivion offered by pills—all were but palliatives, feeble shields against the relentless assault of my own thoughts.

Encounters with women morphed into a series of faceless, meaningless interactions. Random liaisons in dimly lit corners of clubs, desperate connections made under the influence, each as empty and void of meaning as the last. These were not acts of passion but transactions of emptiness, each woman a momentary salve for a soul hollowed out by despair.

As the sun would rise, casting its accusatory light over the city, I'd find myself alone again haunted by the echoes of the night's empty pleasures, each morning a stark reminder of the void that had become my existence. The cycle was relentless, each night a further descent into the depths, a testament to the destructive path I had chosen as my escape.

The apex of my downward spiral materialised in the form of a spontaneous, almost farcical escapade to Berlin—a city shrouded in shadows and steeped in a history of both grandeur and grit. Berlin, with its pervasive air of decadence and debauchery, seemed tailor-made for someone teetering on the brink of self-destruction. It was there, in that hedonistic haven, where my darkest impulses found fertile ground.

On a capricious impulse, fuelled by a toxic mixture of ennui and desperation, I boarded a flight to Berlin, drawn by the promise of anonymity and the thrill of the unknown. The city welcomed me with its notorious embrace, its clubs pulsating with a raw, unfiltered energy that resonated with my inner turmoil. The thumping bass of the underground scenes—places steeped in illicit allure and reckless abandon—echoed the chaotic dissonance in my mind.

Each venue I frequented was a dive deeper into the abyss. The air was thick with the scent of sweat and sin, the walls vibrating with the beats of techno, the very soundtracks to my unraveling. Berlin's nightlife, infamous for its unapologetic wildness, mirrored the tumultuous storm within me. Each night was an odyssey, a relentless pursuit of the next high, the next rush of adrenaline, the next fleeting connection.

The very essence of the city, with its blurred lines between the decadent and the derelict, magnified my disregard for the consequences of my actions. My date— an embodiment of my own reckless disregard—was merely a catalyst, a companion in the dance of defiance against the creeping dread of reality. Together, we lost ourselves in the hedonic maze of Berlin's nightlife, each club a darker echo of the last, each encounter hollower than the one before.

This trip was not a journey but a descent, each step taking me further from the person I once was, each moment in Berlin a vivid, pulsing reminder of how far I had fallen. The city of shadows welcomed my shadow self, hosting my final acts of rebellion against a life I could no longer claim as my own.

In Berlin, the chaos of the nightlife offered a temporary escape, a fleeting distraction from the wreckage of my personal life. The city's anonymity, its embrace of excess, was intoxicating—like a drug, it offered a brief, heady thrill, but it was ultimately hollow, unsatisfying. The thrill of the unknown, of pushing boundaries, was a fleeting pleasure, a poor substitute for the stability and sanity I had sacrificed.

In the swirling spiral of my downfall, amidst the cacophony of my own self-destruction, I encountered Abby Norman—a storm in human form, her disdain for humanity almost palpable. She was anger personified, with a biting wit and a sharp tongue that both intrigued and repelled. It was inevitable, perhaps, that we would spiral together, two lost souls finding solace in shared bitterness. Our connection was instant and intense, a volatile mix of passion and mutual self-destruction that burned fiercely from the start.

Abby's madness matched my own, her wild, reckless nature fuelling the flames of my unravelling life. Yet, amid the tempest of our romance, I couldn't help but be unnerved by her peculiar obsession with KFC. It was a mundane yet bizarrely significant detail that stood out starkly against the backdrop of our shared chaos. Her devotion to fast food was not just a quirk but a fixation, one that inexplicably cooled my fervour. Each bucket, consumed with a zeal that bordered on religious, seemed to underline our fundamental differences—the trivial turned grotesque, a microcosm of our doomed affair.

Our relationship, intense and brief, was as destructive as it was exhilarating. Abby's volatile temper and possessive streak soon proved too much, even for my frayed nerves. The final straw came during a heated argument as we sped down the highway; her jealousy over my platonic female friends erupted into a venomous tirade. In a moment of clarity—or perhaps sheer desperation—I made my escape, literally jumping from her moving car to avoid another minute of our toxic exchange.

Landing hard on the roadside, watching her car screech away into the night, I felt a surge of relief mixed with the adrenaline of my impromptu exit. The physical pain from my tumble paled in comparison to the emotional tumult of our brief liaison. In that abrupt departure, I left behind more than just a volatile relationship—I shed a layer of my former life, stepping further away from the person I had been, driven by the madness of a world I was desperate to leave behind. Abby drove off into the night, and with her went the last remnants of my brief affair with normalcy, leaving me to face the stark reality of my continued descent.

My descent into madness was marked by a visceral, almost grotesque abandon. The boundaries of sanity and self-preservation were obliterated in a frenzied pursuit of hedonistic pleasure. It was a savage, unrelenting dance of self-destruction, a vivid, terrifying testament to the depths of my unravelling mind.

Chapter 9: Fractured Bliss

Amidst the ceaseless whirlwind of my self-destruction, an unexpected twist emerged—a kiss from Ellie, a brief, fleeting beacon in the storm of my own making. It happened one night, a collision of intoxication and loneliness, where boundaries dissolved in the haze of neon lights and the bitter taste of cheap alcohol. We were drowning in the city's oppressive atmosphere, dancing through a maze of confusion and disarray, when the kiss occurred. It was impulsive, desperate—a momentary salvation that would soon unravel into disaster.

Ellie's existence within the grim confines of the Paramount was a stark contrast to the dreary routine that engulfed us. Her sporadic laughter cut through the oppressive air like a beam of light in a dimly lit corridor, a rare diversion from the relentless grind of the kitchen—a sanctuary in the gastronomic hellscape we navigated daily. As the shadows in my own life grew darker, my fixation on Ellie intensified, her fleeting presence becoming a lifeline in the turbulent sea of my existence.

Our escapades outside of work evolved into a desperate liturgy, pathetic attempts to infuse our hollow routines with semblance of substance. We delved into the nightlife with the urgency of the doomed, flitting from bar to bar, club to club, drowning in the numbing embrace of alcohol. Each outing was a pilgrimage to nowhere, a chase after fleeting moments that dissolved like mist at the faintest touch of reality.

The ritual of crashing at one another's apartments became our sad mimicry of normal life, a way to forge some sense of stability from the chaos that was our daily existence. These overnights were less about passion and more about survival, two souls clinging to the wreckage of their professional lives, seeking solace in the familiarity of shared misery.

This pattern of self-destruction, masked as camaraderie, spun a cocoon around us, isolating us from the harsh truths of our lives. In Ellie, I found not just a companion in hedonism, but a fellow traveler on the road to ruin. Together, we crafted a veneer of normalcy, a fragile facade that belied the depth of our despair. As we navigated the labyrinth of Manchester's nightlife, each step further into the abyss, the bond between us deepened—not out of love, but out of a mutual dependency, a shared addiction to the fleeting distractions that night after night, offered us temporary respite from our self-imposed purgatories.

Despite my growing attraction, I knew that this was nothing more than a transient indulgence—a temporary distraction from the crumbling reality I inhabited. Our nights together were mere flickers of warmth in a cold, indifferent existence. We were two broken souls clinging to each other, both fully aware that our connection was doomed from the start.

In the dim light of early morning, as we lay entwined in the sparse comfort of her apartment, Ellie's voice sliced through the silence—a vulnerable confession in the stillness. "I love you," she murmured, her words laden with a weight I was ill-equipped to bear. My reaction was reflexive, a defence mechanism honed through years of shielding myself from the very vulnerability she now offered. "No, you don't," I retorted sharply, the words not just a denial of her feelings but a reflection of my own fractured psyche.

The phrase was a cold blade, a dissection of any tenderness that might have survived the night's escapades. It was cruel, unnecessarily so, a testament to the depth of my own desolation. My response was devoid of warmth, a mirror to the hollow man I had become, so entrenched in self-destruction that the idea of genuine affection was foreign, almost offensive.

The air between us grew thick with the chill of my dismissal. Her expression, a mixture of confusion and pain, was a palpable hit—a visual flinch that made me internally recoil, not out of remorse but out of recognition of my own decayed capacity for human connection. In that moment, my words were not just a shield but a sabre, slashing through the facade of our relationship to expose the rot beneath.

My cruelty was not just a reflection of my emotional bankruptcy but also a stark admission of it. I had become a husk, a shell of a man who moved through the world with mechanical precision, devoid of the ability to connect, to truly feel. The world I inhabited was one of sharp angles and harsh light, where every interaction was transactional, every human connection a potential threat to the precarious balance of my carefully managed apathy.

In the aftermath of those words, the room felt colder, the shadows deeper. Ellie's presence, once a comfort, now seemed an indictment of my own failings. I had repelled her affection, not out of disbelief in her feelings but out of a deep-seated fear of what it meant to be loved, to be seen, to be known. I had pushed her away with the brutality of my honesty, an honesty that was as much a defence as it was a weapon.

As she withdrew from me, the distance not just physical but emotional, a part of me recognised the tragedy of that moment—a potential for something real and sustaining, discarded like the countless ingredients I sliced through each day in the kitchen. The brutality of my environment had infiltrated my soul, and I wielded my emotional detachment like a chef's knife, carving through the possibilities of a different life with the precision of a man who knew only how to cut, never to mend.

Amid the charred remains of our dwindling romance, there is one moment that stands out—a grotesque, almost surreal episode that encapsulates my spiralling incompetence. In a futile attempt to impose some semblance of normalcy onto the harrowing situation I found myself in, I decided to make Ellie a bacon sandwich. The idea was simple, almost primitive—bread, bacon, heat—yet in my hands, it became a ticking time bomb, a culinary experiment doomed to fail from the start. The act of preparing food, of offering sustenance, felt almost primal, as if by feeding her I could reclaim some lost territory in the war of our friendship.

The kitchen was immaculate, a striking marble kitchen top purgatory that reflected nothing back at me but my own hollow eyes. The bacon, thick-cut, organic, and unnecessarily expensive, sizzled in the pan, its fat crackling like static on an old television. I stood there, watching the grease spit and bubble, mesmerised by the way it danced in the pan, oblivious to the disaster that was about to unfold. My mind wandered, as it often does, to the bleak corridors of my own psyche, pondering the futility of it all—this sandwich, this friendship, this life.

It wasn't until the acrid stench of burning meat assaulted my senses that I realised something was wrong. The kitchen, once a haven of order, was now a battlefield—smoke curling in thick, menacing tendrils, the pan a molten wreckage of blackened pork. My first instinct was to fling the window open, as if that could somehow erase the damage, cleanse the air, reset the scene. But it was too late. The smoke, like some malevolent entity, refused to be contained, pouring out into the hallway, triggering the shrill, merciless scream of the smoke alarm.

The sound was deafening, a piercing wail that seemed to cut through the very fabric of my being, exposing the raw, pathetic truth of my existence. Ellie's housemates, those entities who floated through the periphery of her life, stumbled out of their rooms, drawn by the noise, their eyes wide with confusion and fear. They saw me standing there, spatula in hand, surrounded by smoke and charred meat, and their expressions turned from confusion to something darker, something like pity.

I glanced at Ellie, who had appeared in the doorway, her face a mask of exasperation tinged with a sad sort of amusement. The corners of her mouth twitched, as if she were suppressing a laugh, and in that moment, I felt a surge of something—shame? Anger? —but it quickly subsided, replaced by the cold, clinical detachment that had become my default state. I offered her a smile, a brittle, empty gesture, and said, "I thought I'd make you breakfast."

The words hung in the air, absurd and hollow, like a bad joke with no punchline. I watched as the housemates' exchanged glances, their expressions shifting from concern to a kind of bemused resignation. They retreated back to their rooms, leaving Ellie and me alone in the smoke-filled kitchen. The silence that followed was oppressive, a heavy blanket of unspoken words and unresolved tension.

I turned back to the stove, where the remains of the bacon lay in a smouldering heap, a testament to my failure. The absurdity of the situation hit me all at once, and I couldn't help but laugh—a short, mirthless bark that echoed in the empty room. This wasn't just a culinary mishap; it was a microcosm of my entire existence—a relentless cycle of misguided intentions, catastrophic results, and a grim sort of humour that kept me sane, or at least kept me from spiralling further into the abyss.

Ellie sighed, a long, drawn-out sound that seemed to convey all the weariness of our companionship. "You really know how to make an impression," she said, her tone light but laced with something darker, something like disdain. I shrugged, as if to say, "This is what you signed up for." Because, in the end, what else was there to say? The sandwich was ruined, the kitchen was a mess, and our friendship was hanging by a thread. But there was a certain comfort in that, in the predictability of my failures, in the way they mirrored the larger failures of my life.

As I scraped the charred remnants of the bacon into the trash, I felt a strange sense of calm wash over me. This was who I was, after all—a man who couldn't even make a simple bacon sandwich without setting off a chain of disasters. But there was a grim sort of humour in that realisation, a dark irony that I found oddly comforting. Because if nothing else, I was consistent. Consistently inept, consistently destructive, but consistent, nonetheless.

And maybe that was the real tragedy—or the real joke. That in my own twisted way, I found solace in the chaos, a perverse pleasure in my own shortcomings. Because if I couldn't fix the friendship, if I couldn't make Ellie happy, at least I could make her laugh, even if it was at my own expense. Even if it was the last laugh. Here's the bacon sandwich that should have been:

Bacon Sandwich with Tomato Relish and Brioche Bun

Ingredients:

- 6 slices of high-quality thick-cut bacon—each slice a reminder of the indulgence that once held meaning.

- 1 large ripe tomato finely chopped—ripe yet destined to rot.

- 1 small red onion finely diced—sharp, biting, like the reality I tried to ignore.

- 1 clove garlic minced—a subtle undertone, lost in the chaos.

- 2 tablespoons balsamic vinegar—dark, acidic, a bitter counterpoint to sweetness.

- 1 tablespoon sugar—a fleeting sweetness in a world of bitterness.

- Salt and freshly ground black pepper, to taste—a necessity, a reminder of the grind.

- 4 brioche buns—soft, delicate, but easily torn apart.

- Fresh basil leaves, for garnish—a touch of colour in a drab, grey world.

Instructions:

1.Prepare the Tomato Relish:

•In a small saucepan over medium heat, combine the chopped tomato, red onion, garlic, balsamic vinegar, and sugar. Cook, stirring occasionally, until the mixture has thickened and reduced, about 15-20 minutes. Season with salt and pepper to taste. Set aside to cool. Like memories, the Flavours blend and reduce, becoming something more than the sum of their parts.

2.Cook the Bacon:

•In a large skillet over medium heat, cook the bacon until crispy, about 5-7 minutes per side. Remove the bacon from the skillet and drain on paper towels. Crisp on the outside, but the grease seeps through, staining everything it touches.

3.Assemble the Sandwich:

•Toast the brioche buns until golden brown. Spread a generous amount of tomato relish on the bottom half of each bun. Layer with crispy bacon slices and garnish with fresh basil leaves. Top with the other half of the brioche bun. A construction of lies each layer hiding the rot beneath.

4.Serve:

•Serve the bacon sandwiches warm, accompanied by a side of your choice. Offer them with a smile that doesn't reach your eyes, because even the best intentions can burn everything down.

The relationship with Ellie dissolved, as anticipated. I returned to the Paramount, my life reduced to a relentless cycle of kitchen drudgery and hedonistic self-destruction. Ellie left the hospitality world to pursue other dreams, leaving behind the wreckage of our fleeting connection. Despite our romantic failure, we managed to maintain a tenuous friendship—a silent acknowledgment of the battles fought, and the fleeting connections formed amidst the disarray. In the end, we were left with the remnants of what once was—a fractured, yet strangely coherent, connection that spoke to the understanding we shared, the deep undercurrents of our mutual despair.

With Ellie gone, the brief, fragile respite from my chaotic existence evaporated, leaving me alone to face the abyss. My life became a relentless campaign of culinary slavery by day and hedonistic self-destruction by night. The kitchen, with its unforgiving demands, was my battlefield, while the night transformed into a tumultuous descent into drug-fuelled debauchery.

I plunged into the darker corners of the city's nightlife, seeking oblivion in the most dangerous ways. Cocaine, speed, LSD—each drug a desperate attempt to escape the void within. I stumbled through neon-lit streets, my senses heightened to a fever pitch, lost in the throbbing beats of clubs that felt like temples to excess. Strangers became fleeting companions in this nocturnal wasteland, their faces a blur as we shared lines of white powder and whispered secrets in dimly lit corners.

One night, high on a cocktail of substances, I found myself in the heart of a pulsating dance floor, the music a deafening roar that drowned out my thoughts. Bodies moved around me, a mass of hedonistic abandon. It was then that I saw her again—the woman in the wheelchair. She was there, in the shadows, her presence a stark contrast to the frenetic energy around us. Her eyes, cold and vacant, bored into me, a haunting reminder of my failings and the darkness that consumed me.

Compelled by a mix of fear and morbid curiosity, I pushed my way through the crowd, each step feeling like a march toward an inevitable reckoning. When I reached her, I extended a trembling hand to touch her, to confirm her existence. As my fingers brushed her shoulder, her head detached from her body, rolling onto the dance floor. The sight was grotesque, surreal—a vivid nightmare made flesh. Panic surged through me, the world around me distorting into a chaotic blur.

I don't remember the rest of the night, just fragments of frantic movement, distorted faces, and the oppressive weight of my own madness. The next clear memory I have is of the harsh clang of the service bell jolting me awake. I found myself back in the kitchen, the familiar, stifling heat pressing down on me. My hands moved with mechanical precision, plating dishes for the masses, each movement a hollow echo of the passion I once had for this craft.

As I stood there, my mind reeling from the night's horrors, I realised that I had become a prisoner of my own existence—a slave to the kitchen by day and a victim to the night by choice. The fleeting escape that drugs and nightlife provided was just an illusion, a temporary reprieve from the suffocating reality of my life. I was caught in an unending cycle of self-destruction, each high followed by a brutal comedown that left me hollower and more broken than before.

The memory of the woman in the wheelchair, her head rolling across the dance floor, became a symbol of my unravelling sanity. She was a spectre, a reminder of the darkness that lurked within me, a darkness that no number of drugs or hedonism could ever truly escape. And so, I continued my descent, each night blurring into the next, each high a fleeting escape from the inexorable pull of the void. This dish embodies the dissonance of my experience of that night: the charred octopus representing the physical and mental scars, while the blood orange reduction symbolises fleeting moments of brilliance and madness, creating a complex and hauntingly beautiful experience on the plate.

Recipe: "Dissonance" - Charred Octopus with Black Garlic and Blood Orange Reduction

Ingredients:

- 1 large octopus, its cold, gelatinous weight about 2 pounds—just enough to remind you of the life it once had.

- 2 tablespoons olive oil—smooth, viscous, a subtle sheen of artifice over the rawness beneath.

- 4 cloves black garlic, minced—their darkness hiding a complexity, a bitterness that's both alluring and dangerous.

- 2 blood oranges, zested and juiced—their vibrant red juice a vivid reminder of the thin line between pleasure and violence.

- 1/4 cup red wine vinegar—sharp, acidic, cutting through the richness like a blade through flesh.

- 1/4 cup honey—sweet, sticky, a deceptive softness masking the harsh reality.

- 1 teaspoon smoked paprika—a hint of smoke, a whisper of something charred, something lost.

- 1 teaspoon sea salt—coarse, unrefined, a contrast to the slick perfection of the dish.

- Freshly ground black pepper—biting, aggressive, a subtle nod to the underlying tension.

- Fresh parsley, chopped—a final touch of false innocence, green and bright against the dark.

Instructions:

Octopus Preparation:

1. Cleaning the Octopus: The ritual begins. The octopus sprawls before you, its alien form both repulsive and fascinating. You strip it of its defence — removing the beak, the internal organs, anything that might betray the vulnerability beneath. Cold water rushes over it, cleansing, purging, but nothing can wash away the truth.

2. Tenderising: Into the boiling water it goes, a baptism by fire. The tentacles curl, as if in pain, as they soften, tenderise, become something that can be consumed. You watch, detached, as it changes, as the life leaves it entirely. Then you pull it from the water, its transformation complete, leaving it to cool, to wait.

3. Grilling: The grill is hot, unforgiving. You slice the tentacles from the head—clean, precise, like a surgeon. The oil coats them, the spices cling to them, and then they meet the heat. The sizzle, the smoke, the scent of something primal fills the air. You sear them, 3-4 minutes on each side, until they're charred, crispy—a delicate balance of destruction and perfection.

Black Garlic and Blood Orange Reduction:

1. Blood Orange Preparation: The blood oranges are next, their zest and juice the only remnants of their former selves. You strip them of their skins, squeeze them dry, their essence captured in a bowl.

2. Reduction: Into a saucepan, the blood orange juice meets the red wine vinegar and honey. It simmers, reduces, thickens, becomes something darker, something more. The sweetness is tempered by the acidity, the mixture reduced by half until it's thick, almost syrupy—a seductive, dangerous allure.

3. Incorporating Black Garlic: The black garlic joins the reduction, its bitterness melding with the sweetness of the honey, the sharpness of the vinegar. You stir, watching as the flavours blend, as the darkness deepens. The blood orange zest is the final touch, a bright, sharp note in the midst of the gloom. You let it simmer, let the flavours meld, then remove it from the heat—an elixir of contrasts, of beauty and brutality.

Plating:

1. Tentacle Arrangement: The octopus tentacles are placed on the plate with care, an artful arrangement that reflects the chaos and beauty of the night. Each piece is a reminder of the process, of the transformation from life to death to something that can be consumed.

2. Drizzle: The black garlic and blood orange reduction is drizzled over the tentacles, pooling on the plate like

blood at the scene of a crime. It coats the octopus, clinging to it, a final embrace before the end.

3. Garnish: A sprinkle of fresh parsley, green and vibrant, a touch of colour in the darkness, a hint of freshness against the rich, deep flavours. It's the final deceit, the final contrast, before the dish is consumed, before the experience is complete.

In the end, "Dissonance" is more than just a dish. It's a reflection of the tension that underlies everything, the contrast between light and dark, between pleasure and pain. It's a reminder that every bite, every moment, is balanced on the edge of a knife, a delicate dance of flavour and sensation that could tip into madness at any moment.

Serve "Dissonance" with a side of dark rye bread or a simple arugula salad dressed in lemon and olive oil, enhancing the dish's complexity and providing a refreshing balance.

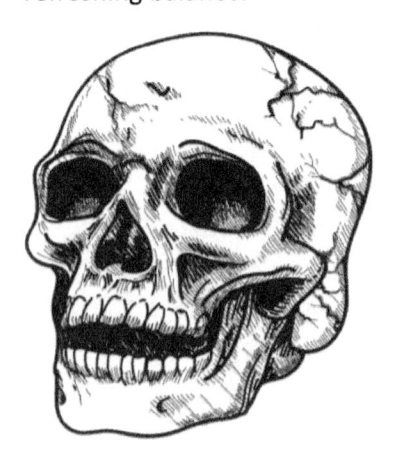

Chapter 10: The Naked Man

In the labyrinthine corridors of the Paramount, the surreal had usurped the mundane. The hotel had morphed into a bizarre playground for the decadent and the depraved. Drug users, like fallen angels, would often collapse in the shadowy confines of our restrooms, their bodies succumbing to the sweet release of their chemical escapes. The clink of needles and the sighs of relief echoed off the tiled walls, a macabre symphony that played on loop.

Guests arrived with motives cloaked in mystery, their reasons for staying as varied as they were unsettling. Some sought the eerie silence of our rooms as muses for their horror tales, their minds weaving narratives from the spectral whispers that seemed to seep from the very walls. Others used our spaces for rituals arcane and obscure, their chants and incantations disturbing the stillness of the night.

The whispers among the staff grew darker with tales of our finest suites—luxurious and lavish yet tainted. These rooms, once the pinnacle of opulence, had become stages for Pornographic films, the air heavy with lust and the scent of sweat. Cameras rolled where once only dreams had played, capturing acts meant for private indulgence now destined for public consumption.

Even more chilling were the stories of guests who checked in but never checked out. They vanished like ghosts, their existence wiped clean from the hotel's memory, save for the lingering question of their fate.

Such disappearances fed the rumours of haunted rooms and cursed hallways, adding layers to the hotel's already checkered legend.

Amidst this backdrop of the bizarre and the unholy, the necessity for lone workers to carry radios became painfully apparent. These devices were not just tools but lifelines, crackling with the voices of colleagues as they navigated the hotel's more perilous duties. Each static-filled transmission served as a reminder that, in the Paramount, one was never truly alone, yet always perilously close to danger.

This dark underbelly of hospitality, where the line between service and servitude blurred, became our reality. The bizarre was not an aberration but the norm, a daily tableau against which we played our parts. And as the hotel's doors swung open each day to welcome the new and the nefarious alike, we braced ourselves for another dive into the depths of the Paramount's strange saga.

On this particular morning, I was covering for Frenchie, entrenched in the monotonous yet comforting ritual of breakfast setup, when an unexpected call crackled through the radio.

"Hey, uh, we've got a situation," the night guard's voice, edged with anxiety, came through. "There's a naked man locked out of his room, wandering the floors, trying other doors. Can you back me up? It's 5:00 am, freezing outside. We need to get him back in his room."

My heart sank. This was not the kind of excitement I needed before the breakfast rush. As if, out of all the crazy nonsensical situations that could occur, this one was at my centre stage, and I haven't even poached a single fucking egg!!! The hunt for the naked man began, a bizarre game of cat and mouse, infused with a sense of creeping dread.

The corridors were dimly lit, the shadows playing tricks on my eyes. The guard and I scoured the hallways, the naked man a ghostly figure disappearing around corners. Each time we approached, he bolted, a fleeting phantom in the gloom. It was a twisted, live-action nightmare, a parody of reality where the stakes were disturbingly high.

We found him first on the second floor, near the fire escape. His pale skin glowed eerily in the sparse lighting, his eyes wild with confusion or perhaps madness. He ran as we approached, his bare feet slapping against the cold tiles, echoing through the empty halls like a harbinger of doom. The pursuit felt like a scene from a horror movie—one moment he was there, the next he vanished into the darkness, only to reappear where we least expected him.

The hotel seemed to conspire with him, its labyrinthine layout a perfect stage for this macabre chase. We checked the stairwells, the maintenance closets, even behind the heavy curtains in the lounge areas. The sense of impending disaster grew with each passing minute, my anxiety gnawing at me. Time was slipping away. Breakfast service loomed, and my morning prep was far from complete.

On the fourth floor, we caught a glimpse of him slipping into a guest room. The door slammed shut behind him. We pounded on it, demanding he open up, but the silence on the other side was unnerving. When we finally managed to unlock it, the room was empty, the window open, the curtains billowing in the icy wind. He had escaped again, like a spectre slipping through our fingers.

As the hours dragged on, the pursuit took on a surreal quality, blending elements of dark comedy and genuine horror. It was like a twisted version of Tom & Jerry, with us as the bumbling cats and him the elusive mouse, yet there was an undercurrent of menace, like something out of "The Shining." The naked man was no longer just a hotel guest; he became a symbol of the chaos lurking beneath the surface of our meticulously maintained facade.

On the fifth floor, he darted into the ladies' restroom. We followed, the night guard and I exchanging nervous glances. The flickering fluorescent lights cast eerie shadows, transforming the restroom into a scene from a ghost story. We heard the unmistakable sound of a stall door closing. As we approached, I felt a chill run down my spine, a sense of foreboding that made me hesitate.

"Come out," I called, my voice echoing unnaturally. Silence. The guard pushed open the stall door, and there he was, crouched on the toilet seat, eyes wide with fear or madness. He looked up at us, and for a moment, time stood still. He was muttering something, as if he was lost in his deepest corners of his mind, I couldn't make out properly what he was saying "I Never done good things, iv never done bad things, iv never done anything out of the blue". Those were the only words I could make out. Then, with a sudden, almost inhuman burst of speed, he vaulted over the stall divider and out the door, leaving us in stunned disbelief.

The pursuit finally ended in the basement, the most eerie and desolate part of the hotel. The naked man had cornered himself in the laundry room, a place of harsh fluorescent lights and industrial machines humming ominously. He crouched behind a row of washers, his breath ragged, eyes darting wildly. There was no escape now.

As we approached, the reality of the situation hit me. This wasn't just a ridiculous chase; it was a descent into madness. The guard and I managed to subdue him, wrapping him in a blanket and leading him back to his room. The whole ordeal had taken hours, leaving me exhausted and frazzled, my nerves frayed.

In this madness, a spark of inspiration—or perhaps a flicker of insanity—ignited. The absurdity of the situation gave birth to a new dish. The "Naked Ravioli" was born from this chaos.

Recipe: Naked Ravioli - Spinach and Ricotta Filling with Brown Butter Sage Sauce

Ingredients:

Filling:

- 1 cup ricotta cheese—smooth, creamy, deceptively simple.

- 1/2 cup grated Parmesan cheese—sharp, biting, a necessary edge.

- 1 cup fresh spinach, blanched and chopped—vibrant, yet subdued, like a fleeting moment of clarity.

- 1 egg yolk—rich, golden, the heart of the matter.

- Salt and pepper to taste—because even perfection needs balance.

Pasta Dough:

- 2 cups all-purpose flour—a blank canvas, ready to be shaped.

- 3 large eggs—life, cracked open, poured out.

- 1 tablespoon olive oil—smooth, seductive, a whisper of indulgence.

- 1/2 teaspoon salt—essential, grounding, the bare minimum to keep you sane.

Brown Butter Sage Sauce:

- 1/2 cup unsalted butter—rich, decadent, on the edge of burning.

- 8-10 fresh sage leaves—fragile, fleeting, crisped to perfection.

- Salt to taste—a final touch, a reminder that too much is never enough.

- Freshly grated Parmesan cheese for garnish—because presentation is everything.

Instructions:

Pasta Dough:

1. Mixing: On a clean surface—clean, but never sterile—mound the flour, a powdery mountain that hides untold potential. Make a well in the centre, a hollow void. Crack the eggs into the well, watching the yolks spill out like a secret you can't take back. Add olive oil and salt. Using a fork, slowly—always slowly—incorporate the flour into the eggs. Watch as it forms a dough, as something raw and chaotic begins to take shape.

2. Kneading: Knead the dough with methodical precision, ten minutes, each movement deliberate, almost violent. Feel the resistance, the pushback, until it yields, smooth and elastic in your hands. Wrap it in plastic, suffocate it, and let it rest for 30 minutes, giving it time to reflect on what it's about to become.

Filling:

1. Combining: In a bowl, mix the ricotta, Parmesan, spinach, egg yolk, salt, and pepper. Stir until well combined, until there's no trace of individuality, just a single, homogeneous mass. It's simple, almost too simple, but there's beauty in that simplicity, a stark contrast to the complexity of what's to come.

Assembly:

1. Rolling: Roll out the dough into thin sheets, as thin as you can manage without breaking it. It's a delicate balance, like walking a tightrope. Cut into large squares or circles—whichever shape feels right but remember symmetry is crucial.

2. Filling: Place a spoonful of the filling onto each piece of dough. Fold over, press the edges, seal it tight, trapping everything inside. Half-moon shapes, rectangles—it doesn't matter, as long as the edges are sealed, as long as nothing escapes.

Cooking:

1. Boiling: Drop the ravioli into salted boiling water, watching them sink, disappear. Wait until they float to the top, about 3-4 minutes, like secrets rising to the surface. Drain them, set them aside—don't rush, let them wait.

Brown Butter Sage Sauce:

1. Melting: In a large skillet, melt the butter over medium heat. Watch it carefully, because butter can turn on you in an instant. Add the sage leaves, watch them sizzle,

crisp up, as the butter turns golden brown, teetering on the edge of disaster.

2. Seasoning: A pinch of salt, just enough to elevate, not overwhelm.

Serving:

1. Plating: Toss the cooked ravioli in the brown butter sage sauce, coating each piece, each fold, in that rich, nutty complexity. Serve on plates, but don't just serve — present. Garnish with freshly grated Parmesan cheese, a final touch of refinement, a sharp contrast to the rich indulgence beneath.

Notes:

The Naked Ravioli embodies the surreal and darkly humorous nature of that morning. The simplicity of the dish mirrors the absurdity of the situation, a reminder of the thin line between madness and inspiration. The richness of the filling contrasts with the starkness of the pursuit, capturing the essence of the twisted, haunting experience.

Finally, we managed to lead the naked man back to his room. The ordeal left me exhausted, frazzled, my nerves frayed like a cheap suit. The dawn light filtered through the grime-streaked windows, mocking the mornings insanity. In the end, all that chaos and terror crystallised into a single, absurd culinary creation: Naked Ravioli. Our victory over the naked man and the madness he brought with him was as fleeting as the satisfaction from a good meal, a moment of clarity in the endless nightmare of the Paramount.

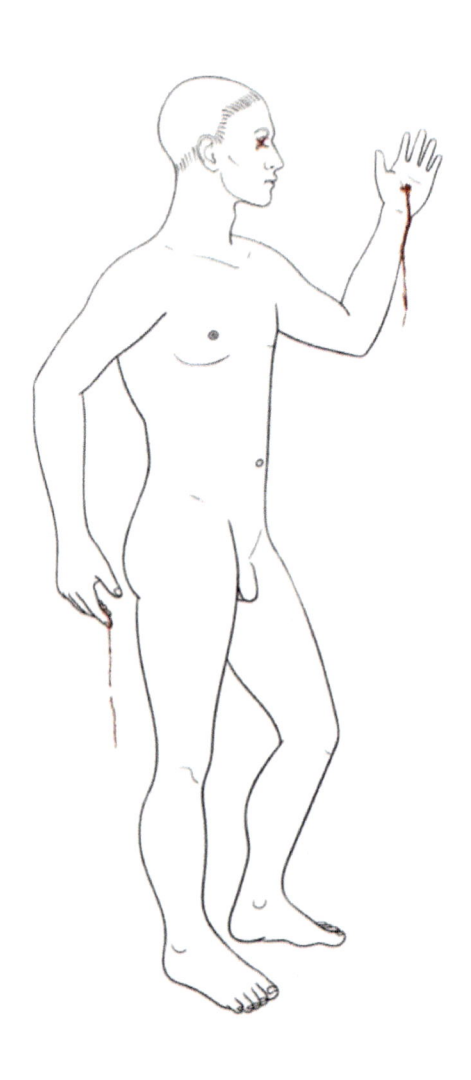

Chapter 11: Simon Collins and the Night of Madness

Simon Collins was a fixture of the night at The Paramount, a shadow that moved through the dimly lit corridors and vacant halls like a ghost who had long since made peace with his haunt. There was something about Simon that drew people in—a magnetic quality, a certain charisma that made you want to be in his presence, despite the unsettling aura that clung to him like a second skin. He was tall, his posture straight, almost military-like, with the kind of features that seemed to be sculpted from stone: sharp jawline, high cheekbones, and dark hair that was always immaculately parted down the middle. His eyes, a piercing blue, had a way of locking onto you, as if he could see right through the layers of bullshit that people wore like armour.

His grin was both charming and disconcerting. It was a cheeky, almost boyish smile that could disarm you in an instant, make you forget, for a brief moment, the oppressive weight of the hotel's atmosphere. But behind that smile, there was something else. Something darker. It was as if Simon carried a shadow with him, a darkness that lurked just beneath the surface, ready to seep out at any moment. You could see it in the way his eyes would occasionally cloud over, his expression momentarily slipping from carefree to something far more sinister, before snapping back into place with that same, disarming grin.

We bonded over our mutual love of Metal Gear Solid, the legendary video game that had consumed hours of our lives. It was a strange thing to bond over, in the midst of the entropy that was The Paramount, but it was our shared escape. In a world where we were both trapped, Metal Gear Solid was our refuge, a world where the lines between heroism and villainy blurred, where complex characters navigated a landscape of moral ambiguity—a fitting metaphor for our own lives, really.

Our conversations about the game were intense, filled with laughter and passion as we dissected every plot twist, every character arc. We debated the ethics of Snake's missions, the philosophical underpinnings of the game's narrative, all while knowing full well that the real world we inhabited was far darker than any video game. Those late-night discussions were a lifeline, a way to cling to some semblance of normalcy in a place that felt increasingly like a descent into madness.

But as our friendship deepened, so did the revelations. Simon had a way of weaving stories that were as captivating as they were disturbing. He spoke of his night shifts at The Paramount with a casual detachment that was both fascinating and horrifying. The things he saw, the people he encountered—guests who checked in and never seemed to check out, strange noises echoing through empty hallways, the occasional bloodstain that was quickly and quietly cleaned up—these were the tales that Simon relayed to me with that same cheeky grin, as if they were nothing more than the punchlines to some dark, cosmic joke.

There was one night, in particular, that stood out—a night when Simon's darkness seemed to take centre stage. We were in the staff break room, the only light coming from the flickering television that played some late-night infomercial, casting eerie shadows on the walls. He leaned in close, his voice dropping to a conspiratorial whisper, and began to tell me about a guest—a regular, apparently—who had checked in earlier that evening.

"She was stunning," Simon said, his eyes narrowing as he recalled the details. "Blond hair, red lips, the kind of woman who turns heads when she walks into a room. But there was something off about her, something... dangerous."

He paused, letting the tension build before continuing. "I followed her up to her room—just to make sure everything was in order, you know? But when she got there, she turned to me and smiled, this wicked smile that made the hair on the back of my neck stand up. Then she said something I'll never forget."

Simon leaned in closer, his voice barely above a whisper. "'If you followed me in here, you still would not be able to find me.'"

I felt a chill run down my spine as he spoke, the room suddenly feeling much colder. "What did she mean?" I asked, my voice betraying the unease I felt.

Simon just shrugged, that grin of his widening into something almost predatory. "I don't know. But I do know that she hasn't checked out yet. And her room's been awfully quiet."

There was a moment of silence, the weight of his words hanging in the air like a dark cloud. I wanted to laugh it off, to dismiss it as one of Simon's twisted stories, but the look in his eyes told me that this was different. This wasn't just another tale to pass the time—this was something real, something dangerous.

From that night on, I couldn't shake the feeling that there was more to Simon than he let on, that the darkness he carried wasn't just a part of his charm—it was something much deeper, much more insidious. And yet, despite the unease he stirred in me, I found myself drawn to him, unable to resist the pull of his magnetic personality. It was as if I was caught in his orbit, trapped in a gravitational field that was slowly pulling me into his world of shadows and secrets.

As our friendship grew, so did the stories—each one darker than the last, each one pushing the boundaries of what I was willing to believe. But it wasn't just the stories that got under my skin; it was the way Simon told them, the way he revealed in the details, as if he took a perverse pleasure in the horrors he described. It was intoxicating and terrifying in equal measure.

In the end, I couldn't tell where the man ended, and the darkness began. Simon Collins was an enigma, a riddle wrapped in a mystery, draped in a shroud of charming smiles and chilling tales. And as much as I wanted to believe that it was all just a façade, a game he played to pass the time, there was a part of me that couldn't shake the feeling that Simon was much more dangerous than he appeared.

And so, I remained in his orbit, drawn ever closer to the black hole that was Simon Collins, night staff at The Paramount, with his chiselled features, his cheeky grin, and the darkness that lurked just beneath the surface. A darkness that, I feared, would one day consume us both.

One morning, while I was meticulously dicing vegetables, Simon recounted a particularly grotesque story. "So, there I was," he began, his voice tinged with a mix of amusement and horror, "cleaning up the lobby when this guy stumbles in, covered in what looked like blood. Turns out it was cranberry juice from a brawl at a nearby bar. But then, he insists on playing the piano in the lounge, even though he has no idea how to play. It was like watching a catwalk across the keys—horrifying but hilarious."

I laughed, the absurdity of the tale a welcome distraction from the relentless monotony of the kitchen. But beneath Simon's jovial exterior, it was clear he was a damaged soul. No surprise, really—everyone at the Paramount was damaged in some way. It was this shared brokenness that cemented our friendship.

Our nights out were less about fun and more about survival, a desperate attempt to stave off the darkness that clung to us like a second skin. Simon and I would hit the town with a singular purpose—to drown ourselves in booze, women, and whatever substances we could get our hands on, all in the hope of escaping the crushing weight of reality, if only for a few hours. The city, with its neon lights and shadowy alleyways, became our playground, a twisted maze where the lines between pleasure and madness blurred into one.

We plunged into the deepest, darkest recesses of Manchester, the kind of place where the city's soul seemed to rot away, festering beneath its gritty, industrial illusion. Simon, with that sly grin of his, led the way. He knew the city's underbelly like the back of his hand, and tonight, he was taking us somewhere special, somewhere secret, a place that thrived in the shadows of the Northern Quarter.

We walked through narrow, dimly lit alleys, the air thick with the stench of decay and the distant hum of the city's restless energy. The streets were alive with the ghosts of Manchester's past, the old warehouses and derelict buildings looming over us like silent sentinels. Simon moved with a purpose, his footsteps echoing off the cracked pavement, leading us deeper into the labyrinth of the city's darkest corners.

Finally, we arrived. A nondescript door tucked between two towering structures, the kind of place you'd walk by a thousand times without noticing. Simon pushed it open, revealing a narrow hallway lined with dust-covered bookshelves. The scent of aged paper and forgotten stories lingered in the air, mingling with the faint trace of something darker, something almost sinister, but exciting.

At the end of the hallway, Simon stopped. He reached out and pulled a seemingly random book from the shelf—an old, leather-bound tome with faded gold lettering that read *'The Man Who Fell to Earth.'* The bookshelf groaned, then slowly swung open, revealing a hidden doorway. We stepped through, leaving the outside world behind, descending into the depths of Manchester's secret heart.

The bar was like something out of a twisted dream. It was a cabin-style den of iniquity, a place where the walls seemed to close in, where the air was thick with the scent of smoke and the heavy, suffocating warmth of dimly lit green lights. The furniture was old, worn leather, the kind that creaked under the weight of your sins, and the lighting cast long, eerie shadows that danced across the room, hiding more than they revealed.

Animal heads adorned the walls, each one a macabre trophy of someone's twisted conquests. Their glassy eyes stared out into the void, their mouths frozen in silent screams, as if they were eternally trapped in the moment of their demise. Each one reminded me of the countless lives I had taken in the name of culinary art, the sacrifices I had made for the sake of a new dish. The connection was undeniable, and a sick, twisted part of me reveled in it.

The place reeked of decay and desperation, a seedy undercurrent that permeated everything, from the sticky, dark-stained floorboards to the low murmur of voices that filled the room. The customers were a motley crew of lost souls, their faces obscured by the thick haze of smoke that hung in the air like a shroud. This was a place where people came to forget, to lose themselves in the dark corners of their minds, to drown in the abyss of their own making.

It was seedy as fuck, the kind of place that existed on the fringes of reality, where the line between right and wrong blurred into oblivion. And yet, there was something intoxicating about it, something that drew me in, that made me want to sink deeper into the shadows, to embrace the darkness that lurked within this hidden, forbidden world. Here, in the deepest pits of Manchester, we found a sanctuary of sin, a place where the weight of our deeds hung heavy in the air, mingling with the scent of smoke and blood.

It was in this crimson bar, already steeped in excess and bad decisions, that we found ourselves in the company of a lead singer of an extremely popular Manchester band, we will just call him "Liam". At the time, I didn't even recognise him—celebrity status meant nothing to me in my perpetually numbed state. Liam was just another face in the crowd, another voice in the cacophony of the night. He was accompanied by a friend, a shadowy figure who moved through the evening with an unsettling ease, always a step behind Liam, like a ghost tethered to its master.

Simon, ever the cryptic one, kept referring to this man as Liam's "cousin," but the way he said it, with that trademark grin that never quite reached his eyes, made it clear that whatever relationship existed between Liam and this man was far more complicated, and far more disturbing. "Just think of him as family," Simon would say, his voice dripping with irony, as if he were in on a joke that I was too far gone to understand. Who knows what the real story was? At that point, I was too far down the rabbit hole to care.

The night spiralled quickly. We drank copious amounts of alcohol, downing shots like they were water, the burn in our throats a welcome distraction from the gnawing void inside. We found ourselves in one dimly lit bar after another, each one more decrepit than the last, the kind of places where the walls seemed to absorb the despair of their customers, where the air was thick with the stench of sweat, smoke, and something far more insidious.

The bathrooms were a special kind of hell—narrow, dirty spaces where the flickering lights cast sickly shadows on the cracked tiles. It was in one of these bathrooms that we did our first lines of the night, the cocaine burning as it went up, leaving a bitter taste in the back of my throat. But the effect was immediate, sharp, like someone had flipped a switch in my brain. The world around me seemed to slow down, every sensation amplified, every thought razor-sharp, but only for a fleeting moment before the paranoia set in.

We stumbled through the streets like vagrants, barely more than walking corpses in a nightmarish cityscape. The city itself felt alive, a malevolent entity that watched us from the shadows, its neon signs flickering like malevolent eyes. Every alleyway, every corner, seemed to conceal something waiting to pounce, and every passerby was a potential threat. The alcohol and drugs twisted my perceptions, turning the familiar into the grotesque. Faces distorted into monstrous caricatures, their expressions unreadable, their eyes hollow.

At some point, we ended up in a grimy club, the kind of place that existed on the fringes of the city's nightlife, where the music was so loud it felt like it was vibrating inside my skull, rattling my brain in its cage. The crowd was a sea of bodies, swaying and gyrating in a chaotic rhythm that matched the pounding bass. The lights were dim, the air thick with smoke and the scent of sweat and desperation. It was the perfect place to lose yourself, to disappear into the throng and let the night swallow you whole.

I vaguely recall dancing, or something that resembled dancing, with a woman whose face I can't remember, her features a blur in the strobe lights. Her hands on my body felt both alien and familiar, like the touch of a ghost. We moved together, or rather, we swayed in place, caught in the current of the music, but there was no connection, no intimacy. It was just another meaningless encounter in a night full of them, a desperate attempt to feel something, anything, in a world that had long since gone numb.

The club was a pulsing, writhing beast, alive with the sickly glow of neon lights and the deafening pound of bass that throbbed in my skull like a relentless, malignant tumour. Everything was too much—the lights slicing through the dark, the music a chaotic symphony of electronic noise, the bodies packed too close, pressing in on me, suffocating. My mind was a fractured mirror, splintered reflections of reality crashing together in a dizzying, nauseating blur. The alcohol coursing through my veins did nothing to dull the edges; if anything, it sharpened them, cutting deeper, dragging me further into the abyss.

Simon stood beside me, his grin a grotesque parody of joy, twisted and manic under the club's harsh lights. He was calm, almost serene, while I was spiralling into madness, the panic clawing at my insides, threatening to rip me apart. I could feel the darkness creeping in at the edges of my vision, a shadowy spectre that whispered of violence and blood. I needed to get out, to escape, but there was nowhere to go, nowhere to hide from the demons that had taken root in my mind.

Then it happened—a jolt, sharp and sudden, as if the universe had decided to tear itself open just to spit me out. An elbow, hard and unforgiving, slammed into my ribs, knocking the breath from my lungs in a ragged gasp.

I turned, eyes wild, to face the intruder—a hulking mass of muscle and anger, his face twisted into a snarl that spoke of violence barely contained. His eyes, bloodshot and glassy, bore into mine, a challenge, a threat.

"You disrespect my girl," he slurred, his words thick with the stench of cheap liquor and barely restrained fury.

Before I could react, before the fog in my brain could clear enough to form a coherent thought, Simon was there, stepping between us, his grin widening into something truly sinister. "Back off, mate," he said, his voice low, dripping with a calm that was more terrifying than any shout, more menacing than any threat. There was something in his eyes, something dark and hungry, that made the hair on the back of my neck stand on end.

The man didn't back down. Instead, he shoved Simon, hard, sending him stumbling into me. My vision tunnelled, the world narrowing to a single, focused point of rage. The fear, the panic, it all boiled over, spilling out in a violent surge. My fist connected with his jaw in a brutal, satisfying crunch, the impact sending a shockwave up my arm, igniting something primal, something savage deep within me.

The club erupted into chaos. The man's friends, shadows at the edge of my vision, surged forward, their fists flying, their faces contorted with anger and something else—something darker, more primal. Simon moved beside me, a blur of motion, his actions quick, precise, a deadly ballet of violence. I caught a glimpse of him smashing a bottle over someone's head, the glass shattering, a spray of blood and alcohol mixing in the air like some macabre work of art.

The fight was a cacophony of violence, a symphony of flesh meeting flesh, of bones cracking under the force of impact. I was lost in it, consumed by it, my movements automatic, detached, as if I was watching someone else, someone far removed from the person I thought I was. My fists connected with bodies, with faces, each blow a release, a catharsis that only drove me deeper into the darkness. I felt a punch to my gut, the air rushing from my lungs, but it only fuelled the fire, the rage that had taken hold, turning me into something less than human, something more.

Security finally waded in, pulling us apart, but not before I landed a final, vicious blow to the man's ribs, the impact reverberating through my bones like a death knell. I was dragged backward, my vision swimming, the adrenaline crashing, leaving me empty, hollow. The man lay on the floor, groaning, his friends sprawled around him, beaten, broken. Simon stood beside me, his face smeared with blood, a grotesque mask of violence, his grin wider than ever, a twisted, sick satisfaction gleaming in his eyes.

They threw us out into the night, the cold air hitting me like a slap, jolting me back to some semblance of reality. The streets were eerily quiet, the chaos we had left behind seeming like a distant memory, a nightmare fading with the dawn. I staggered, my body aching, my mind reeling, the darkness still clinging to me, a suffocating shroud. Simon clapped me on the back, his laughter ringing out into the empty streets, a sound that echoed in the silence, a jarring reminder of what we had done.

"That was fucking brilliant!" he exclaimed, his voice alive with a manic glee that sent chills down my spine.

But I couldn't share in his mirth. The darkness that had consumed me in the club still lingered, a heavy weight pressing down on my chest, crushing me. The fight, the violence, it had unleashed something in me, something I wasn't sure I could ever control again. As we walked away from the scene of our carnage, leaving behind the blood and broken bodies, I knew that something fundamental had shifted. A line had been crossed, a boundary obliterated, and I wasn't sure if I could ever go back.

The city's shadows seemed darker, more ominous, as if they were reaching out to claim me, to drag me further into the abyss. The events of the night would haunt me, I knew that much, lingering in the corners of my mind, a constant reminder of the darkness within, the part of me that reveled in the violence, in the bloodshed. Simon lit a cigarette, the flame briefly illuminating his face, casting sharp, angular shadows that made him look almost demonic. He offered me one, but I shook my head, too lost in the mire of my thoughts to even respond.

As we walked away, the city's darkness swallowing us whole, I couldn't shake the feeling that I was falling, spiralling further into a void from which there was no escape. The fight had changed something in me, had unlocked a door that I wasn't sure I could ever close again. And as the night pressed in around us, I knew that the person I had been before was gone, lost to the darkness that had taken hold, replaced by something darker, something far more dangerous.

We stumbled through the streets, our footsteps echoing off the walls, the only sound in the oppressive silence. The neon signs that had once been a beacon now felt like the eyes of some malevolent force, watching our every move, waiting for us to slip up. The city itself seemed to be alive, its heart beating in time with my own, its breath hot and fetid against my skin.

The city was still pulsing with the echoes of the night's debauchery as I found myself standing at the entrance of The Paramount, the familiar, imposing structure looming above me like a monolith. The striking lights that had guided me through the dark labyrinth of the city had faded, replaced by the cold, clinical glow of the hotel's facade. The alcohol still buzzed in my veins, my thoughts fragmented, distorted, like shards of a broken mirror reflecting the night's madness.

Instead of heading to my room, where the comfort of my bed might have offered some semblance of peace, my inebriated mind took an unexpected detour. Without thinking, I found myself descending into the bowels of the hotel, into the heart of the inferno—the kitchen. It was as if some primal force was guiding me, pulling me back to the place where I could exert some control over the chaos that had consumed my night.

The kitchen was a stark contrast to the dark, chaotic world I had just escaped. The sterile, blinding brightness of the fluorescent lights bounced off the stainless-steel surfaces, illuminating every corner with an unforgiving glare. It was too bright, too clean, too perfect—a jarring shift from the grime and filth I had waded through just hours before. But there was something comforting in the cold, clinical environment, something that called to the part of me that craved order, precision, control.

I grabbed my whites from the hook, the fabric stiff and starched against my skin, a far cry from the sweat-soaked clothes I had worn throughout the night. The act of donning them was almost ritualistic, a transformation from the lost, drunken soul who had stumbled through the city to the cold, calculating chef who ruled this domain with an iron fist. The whites were my armour, my shield against the madness that threatened to engulf me.

In the stark silence of the empty kitchen, I began to experiment, the act of cooking becoming a twisted sanctuary, a way to channel the chaos into something tangible, something I could control. The ingredients were laid out before me, raw and unformed, waiting for me to breathe life into them, to shape them into something more than the sum of their parts.

The details of that night are hazy, my memories blurred by the alcohol and the relentless pace of my thoughts. I moved through the kitchen like a man possessed, my hands working with a speed and precision that belied my intoxicated state. The knife in my hand was an extension of my will, slicing through flesh and bone with a savage grace. I could feel the tension in my muscles, the strain in my tendons, but the pain was distant, a dull throb that barely registered in the fog of my mind.

As the night wore on, the ingredients came together in a dish that seemed to encapsulate the madness of our escapade—a dish that was as unhinged as the night itself. I remember fragments—flashes of flavours, textures, a cacophony of sensations that collided and clashed in a way that should have been disastrous, but somehow wasn't. The dish was a reflection of my state of mind, a culinary manifestation of the darkness that had seeped into my soul.

There was something primal in the act of creation, something that spoke to the darkest corners of my psyche. The kitchen, with its sterile surfaces and sharp edges, became a laboratory, a place where I could dissect and reassemble the night's experiences, transforming them into something that could be consumed, digested, understood. The act of cooking was no longer just about nourishment; it was about control, about mastering the chaos that had taken hold of my life.

The dish that emerged from that night was an abomination, a Frankenstein's monster of ingredients that had no business being together. And yet, there was something beautiful about it, something that spoke to the insanity of the night, the violence and passion that had driven me to this point. It was a dish that defied logic, a symphony of discordant notes that somehow, miraculously, came together in a way that made sense, if only in the twisted recesses of my mind.

The Abyssal Feast

Ingredients:

For the Meat:

- 2 pounds of octopus tentacles, slick and glistening, their suction cups still pulsing with latent life.

- 1 pound of bone marrow, freshly extracted from beef bones, the raw essence of the animal still clinging to it.

- 1 pound of beef heart, thinly sliced, the blood seeping from the flesh like a slow, inevitable leak.

- 1 pound of chicken feet, the skin yellowed and sinewy, twisted into grotesque shapes that seem to defy anatomy.

- 4 large bull testicles, halved, their fleshy insides exposed, a vulgar display of nature's cruelty.

For the Marinade:

- 1 cup of black garlic pastes, thick and viscous, like tar dredged from the bottom of a forgotten pit.

- 1/2 cup of squid ink, a deep, inky blackness that absorbs the light, turning everything it touches into a shadow.

- 1/4 cup of fish sauce, its pungent aroma clinging to the air like the stench of decay.

- 1/4 cup of soy sauce, dark and salty, a liquid embodiment of bitterness.

- 1 tablespoon of grated ginger, sharp and cutting, a hint of violence beneath the surface.

- 5 cloves of garlic, minced, their scent hanging in the air like a threat.

- 3 red chilli peppers, finely chopped, their heat a promise of the pain to come.

- Zest of 1 lemon, a brief, fleeting reminder of something pure before it's swallowed by the darkness.

- 1 tablespoon of honey, a sickly sweetness, masking the bitterness beneath.

For the Sauce:

- 2 cups of beef blood, still warm, the life draining from it with every second.

- 1/2 cup of red wine, deep and rich, like the blood of a long-forgotten king.

- 1/4 cup of balsamic vinegar, its acidity biting, cutting through the richness like a knife through flesh.

- 1 tablespoon of unsweetened cocoa powder, dark and bitter, a taste that lingers long after the meal is over.

- 1 tablespoon of fresh thyme leaves, their scent a faint echo of life in a dish that's anything but.

•Salt and pepper to taste, the final insult to the dish's twisted beauty.

For the Garnish:

•Charred baby corn blackened and twisted; their sweetness turned to ash.

•Pickled radishes, their sharpness a cruel counterpoint to the dish's heaviness.

•Fresh pomegranate seeds, like drops of blood, a final reminder of the life that was taken.

•Fried sage leaves, their crispness a brittle mask over the darkness beneath.

•Crushed black sesame seeds, a dusting of darkness, the final touch in this symphony of despair.

Instructions:

1. Preparing the Meat:

•Octopus Tentacles: Drop the tentacles into boiling water, watching as they writhe in their final moments of agony. Blanch them for 3 minutes, then shock them in ice, a brief respite before the end. Marinate them in the black garlic and squid ink mixture, a bath of darkness for at least 2 hours—long enough for them to absorb the despair.

•Bone Marrow: Roast the bone marrow on high heat, 450°F, for 15 minutes. Watch as the marrow bubbles, its essence released in a final, desperate attempt to cling to life. Scoop it out, setting it aside like a trophy.

- Beef Heart: Bathe the thin slices of heart in a mixture of soy sauce, fish sauce, and ginger, allowing the bitterness to seep into the flesh. Let it marinate for at least 1 hour, giving it time to absorb the reality of its situation.

- Chicken Feet: Boil the feet, watching as they curl in on themselves, for 30 minutes. Toss them in a mixture of garlic, chilli peppers, and honey, a mockery of sweetness in a dish so devoid of it.

- Bull Testicles: Sear the halved testicles in a hot pan, the sizzle of flesh meeting heats a cruel symphony. Set them aside, their journey not yet over.

2. Cooking the Meat:

- Grill the Octopus: Over high heat, char the tentacles until they blacken, their suction cups curling in agony. Each side should take 5-7 minutes—long enough for the flesh to surrender to the heat.

- Sear the Beef Heart: In a cast-iron skillet, sear the marinated heart slices for 2 minutes per side, the flesh barely resisting, its time in this world coming to a close.

- Fry the Chicken Feet: Drop the feet into a deep fryer, watching as the oil bubbles and spits, the feet crisping up like the final crackle of a dying fire. Fry them for 5 minutes, just long enough for them to lose all semblance of life.

- Finish the Testicles: Toss the seared testicles with the bone marrow, a final indignity, and roast them in the oven at 400°F for 5 minutes.

3. The Sauce:

- Pour the beef blood into a saucepan, watching as it pools and thickens. Add the red wine, balsamic vinegar, and cocoa powder, stirring as the liquids merge into a dark, bitter concoction. Let it simmer, reducing by half, the life draining out of it with every bubble. Add thyme leaves and season with salt and pepper, the final touches in this dish of despair.

4. Plating the Beast:

- Lay the octopus tentacles on a dark, heavy platter, twisting them into serpentine shapes that hint at the chaos within. Arrange the beef heart slices and roasted testicles alongside, a macabre tableau of flesh and sinew. Pile the crispy chicken feet at the centre, a twisted crown for this abyssal feast. Drizzle the blood sauce over the meat, letting it pool and congeal in the crevices, a final insult to the dish's twisted beauty.

5. The Final Touch:

- Garnish with charred baby corn, pickled radishes, pomegranate seeds, fried sage leaves, and crushed black sesame seeds—a cruel mockery of a traditional garnish, each element adding to the dish's dissonance.

•Serve this monstrosity in a dimly lit room, the darkness swallowing the light, the air thick with the scent of blood and despair.

I plated the dish with meticulous care, every element arranged with a precision that bordered on obsessive. The colours were vibrant, almost too bright, the textures a study in contrast—smooth and rough, soft and hard, each bite a journey through the madness that had brought it into existence. I stood back and surveyed my creation, the kitchen lights reflecting off the pristine white plate, casting shadows that danced and flickered like the memories of the night.

For a moment, I felt a twisted sense of satisfaction, a perverse pride in what I had created. The dish was a masterpiece of insanity, a culinary embodiment of the night's horrors, and yet, in its own way, it was perfect. It was a dish that could never be replicated, a one-time creation born from a unique convergence of darkness and desperation.

I didn't taste it—I couldn't. The very idea of consuming something so intimately tied to the madness of the night made my stomach turn. Instead, I left it there, on the pass, a silent testament to the chaos that had taken hold of my life. The kitchen, once a sanctuary, now felt like a tomb, the dish its final offering.

Hours later, as the first light of dawn crept through the windows, I finally made my way to my room, the exhaustion crashing over me like a tidal wave. My mind was still reeling, the events of the night playing on a loop, but the act of creation had drained me, left me hollowed out, empty. I collapsed onto my bed, still in my whites, the images of the night blending into the darkness as sleep finally claimed me.

The dish remained in the kitchen, untouched, a reminder of a night that defied logic, a night where the lines between creation and destruction blurred into one. In the cold light of day, it would seem absurd, ridiculous even, but in that moment, in the furnace of the kitchen, it had made perfect sense. And perhaps that was the most terrifying thing of all.

Chapter 12: Predator Concrete Jungle

Gary Bromley wasn't just a man; he was an institution of dread wrapped in a suit that was somehow simultaneously crisp and crumpled. Short and stocky, with a scalp of short black hair that practically screamed "Mid-50s managerial disappointment," Gary wore exhaustion like a tailored jacket. As the Operational Manager for the hotel, he had perfected the art of wielding authority with a sharp, cutting demeanour that could slice through the most well-intentioned of morale. His humour? A desert of dry quips that left a trail of crickets behind, as if the universe had collectively decided to abandon any notion of laughter in Gary's presence.

Gary was a man of routines, a creature of predictability, every action meticulously rehearsed until it became second nature. It was his peculiar habit of booking his "niece" into one of the high-end rooms during his night shifts that first caught my attention. She was always the same—or so it seemed at first glance. Blonde hair, blue eyes, a doll-like figure draped in luxury. But there was something off, a subtle dissonance that gnawed at the edges of my perception like a rusted blade dragging across the skin.

At first, I dismissed it, attributing the unease to the haze of fatigue that comes from too many nights spent navigating the labyrinthine hell of The Paramount. But the more I observed, the more the inconsistencies revealed themselves—small, almost imperceptible changes that should have gone unnoticed. One week, her eyes were a vivid, electric blue, the next, a duller, almost lifeless shade of cornflower. A freckle that had once graced the curve of her nose would vanish, only to reappear near her cheekbone, or not at all. Her smile would shift from a coy, practiced smirk to something more innocent, almost naive, as if the woman standing before me was a different person altogether, yet somehow exactly the same.

It was disorienting, like staring at a reflection in a funhouse mirror where the distortions were so subtle they teased at the edge of your sanity. I couldn't shake the feeling that I was being played, that this whole charade was a performance, each "niece" a different actress cast in the same role, Gary the director pulling the strings from the shadows. But who would believe such a thing? The thought alone was absurd, the kind of paranoid delusion that takes root in the mind of someone who's spent too much time in the bowels of a place like this.

The "niece" checked in week after week, each time under Gary's watchful eye, each time in one of the most opulent rooms the hotel had to offer. And every time, I scrutinised her, searching for the subtle flaws, the cracks in the facade that whispered of something deeply, fundamentally wrong. But no one else seemed to notice. Or if they did, they chose to remain silent, content to let the oddities fade into the background of their own carefully controlled lives.

I would joke to Gary about it. That I noticed his "niece" wasn't quiet, right? That her eyes shifted colour like the changing of the seasons or that her freckles played a game of hide and seek across her face? He would dismiss it, brushed me off, or worse, stared at me with that cold, dead-eyed look that sent a shiver down my spine. So, I stopped mentioning it, letting the unease fester, a constant, gnawing reminder that in this place, nothing is ever what it seems.

If there was one thing Gary took pride in, it was claiming dominance over everyone in the hotel. From the cleaning staff who reeled under his piercing gaze to the front desk personnel who had learned to navigate his oppressive presence like seasoned sailors in a storm, he attempted to rule with an iron fist. The night staff were no exception, huddling under the weight of his expectations. But the true battleground was the kitchen, a fortress that even Gary Bromley could not fully conquer.

No one elicited visceral rage in Gary quite like the kitchen crew, particularly Scorpion, a flamboyant chef who often walked the line between culinary genius and the embodiment of chaos. In a particularly fevered spat over a bloody burger—yes, that's how low we sank—Gary stormed in, hurling accusations and burgers with equal measure. "Lettuce and tomato need to be on the bottom of the patty!" he barked, the words flying from his mouth as if they were venomous darts meant to pierce and paralyse.

Scorpion, drenched in sweat and facing the onslaught of checks like an unrelenting tide, shot back, "No, you fucking wet wipe! It's on the top! Everyone knows that!" The kitchen pulsed with the tension of a standoff as Gary's eyes narrowed dangerously, and he spat back, "What did you say?!"

The moment hung in the air like a noose. Scorpion, emboldened by a cocktail of adrenaline and audacity, met Gary's gaze without flinching. "Are you deaf? SUCK

ON MY BIG DICK! You don't scare me; you're not God, and you're not my mother."

It was a declaration that ignited the inferno. Gary's face contorted as if someone had shoved a hot coal down his throat. Before we could process the shock, an altercation erupted, a flurry of arms and angry voices. We pulled Gary away, struggling to contain a tempest of fury that threatened to engulf the kitchen whole.

In the aftermath, Gary made it abundantly clear that he would not let the insult slide. He began scheming, fabricating tales of insubordination against Scorpion, convinced that he could wield his managerial power like a sledgehammer and crush the defiance he had encountered. He failed spectacularly, a pyrrhic victory that only served to embolden us further.

It was during that chaotic time I resolved to craft the perfect burger: a fine dining beef masterpiece that would never be sullied by the likes of Gary's flickering authority.

The Perfect Burger Recipe

Ingredients:

- 1 lb ground beef (80% lean, 20% fat—because perfection requires just the right balance)

- 2 tablespoons Worcestershire sauce—dark, Savoury, a secret weapon that cuts through the monotony

- 1 teaspoon garlic powder—sharp, lingering, the edge you never see coming

- 1 teaspoon onion powder—subtle, almost unnoticed, but essential

- Salt and pepper to taste—because even in the chaos, control is paramount

- Fresh brioche buns—soft, golden, a facade of innocence hiding the indulgence within

- Aged cheddar cheese—sharp, mature, with a depth that only time can bring

- Crispy lettuce—clean, fresh, a fleeting nod to purity

- Vine-ripened tomatoes (sliced)—juicy, vibrant, as red as temptation itself

- Dill pickles—tangy, a bitter contrast that cuts through the richness

- Special burger sauce (mayo, ketchup, mustard, and a touch of relish)—smooth, creamy, the perfect blend of sweet and tangy, a concoction of contradictions

Instructions:

1. Combining: In a cold, sterile bowl, combine the ground beef with Worcestershire sauce, garlic powder, onion powder, salt, and pepper. Handle the meat gently—too much force, and you ruin everything. The meat needs to stay tender, juicy, the way things should be before they're destroyed by the heat.

2. Forming: Form the mixture into thick patties, each one a perfect, round disc of potential. Make a slight indentation in the centre—it's a small detail, but it's the difference between control and chaos. This prevents the patty from bulging, keeps everything in line, keeps everything perfect.

3. Cooking: Preheat a grill or skillet over medium-high heat. The surface should be hot, but not too hot—like

anger, controlled, seething just beneath the surface. Place the patties on the heat, listen to the sizzle, a promise of what's to come. Cook for about five minutes on each side, until they reach your desired doneness—medium-rare, perhaps, because there's beauty in the imperfection of something not fully done.

4. Melting: In the last minute of cooking, place a slice of aged cheddar on each patty. Watch as it melts, slowly, perfectly, cascading over the edges, covering the meat in a layer of sharp, molten decadence. It's about balance—too much, and you lose the beef; too little, and the cheddar's edge is dulled.

5. Assembling: Take the bottom brioche bun, soft, golden, almost too perfect. Place the patty on it, the weight of it pressing down slightly. Then, layer the lettuce—crisp, green, a brief respite from the richness. Add the tomato slices, red, ripe, bleeding juice. Place the dill pickles on top, their tang cutting through everything else. Finally, drizzle on the special burger sauce, a blend of mayo, ketchup, mustard, and a touch of relish—each element playing off the other, creating something greater than the sum of its parts. Top it off with the other half of the brioche bun, press down slightly, feel the resistance.

6. Serving: Serve the burger with fries—crispy, golden, a sidekick to the star. But this isn't just about eating; it's about the experience, about the anticipation, about the perfection that exists only for a moment before it's devoured, destroyed. Enjoy it while it lasts, because in the end, everything falls apart.

The news spread like a contagion, the headlines sharp and venomous. "Operations Manager Arrested for Child Exploitation." I found myself staring at those words, each letter burning into my consciousness like a brand reserved for the damned. Gary Bromley—once a name that stirred nothing more than a slight irritation—had evolved into something much more sinister: an embodiment of betrayal, a hydra lurking in the encroaching shadows of our shared history.

Years of his orchestrated mediocrity now stood grotesquely reframed, backlit by this sickening revelation. The long hours spent enduring his vacuous speeches, his ceaseless rants about profitability, and the mind-numbing drudgery of his managerial style came rushing back like a flood of bile. Every overlooked corner of the hotel now seemed haunted by the distant echoes of children's laughter, twisted into something malevolent and foul. The nostalgia I had once held for simpler days now intertwined with a dawning horror—how easily one could slip into the malignancy of power, how subtly it could corrupt the soul.

The implications of Gary's crimes were chilling. The rooms he had always taken such pride in, painstakingly rendered 'child-friendly' with pastel wall decals and plush toys, now felt like the punchline of a grotesque joke, each detail a symbol of his predation. The hotel had been his stage, a facade of innocence masking dark performances that went unseen. I recalled those "family weekends," where parents, blissfully unaware, checked in and out along with their children, their joyous mingling now a macabre tapestry woven with threads of terror and violated trust.

And then there was the recollection of the "niece"—a spectre who drifted through the hotel, her presence ever-changing, as though she were a chameleon in a world of cutthroat adults, slipping unnoticed through the cracks of surveillance. How often had I brushed off the subtle shifts in her appearance, the way a freckle would vanish, or her eyes would take on a different shade of blue? And how often had Gary dismissed my insistence on verifying identifications, waving me off with that insufferable air of authority? "It's about hospitality, not interrogation," he'd say, as if my cautiousness was a betrayal rather than a safeguard. But what is authority when it's nothing more than a mask for corruption, a disguise for the rot festering beneath the surface?

The memory of his arrest plays out in my mind like a slow-motion film, each detail excruciatingly clear. His ghoulishly mundane demeanour was striking in its banality as the officers approached, their faces set in a mixture of determination and disgust. I can only imagine the irony that twisted their mouths as they witnessed the embodiment of a predator caught in the act, flailing and stumbling when confronted with morality. Gary's defensive posture told me everything I needed to know; he saw his capture not as a reckoning, but as an affront to the twisted order he had constructed.

Good riddance, I thought, perhaps a little too fervently. The satisfaction that washed over me bordered on euphoria, but beneath it lurked a disturbing realisation— a shiver of complicity as I questioned how I could've overlooked the signs, how I had indulged in the blissful ignorance that allowed him to carry out his ghoulish acts unchecked.

The cycles of mundanity within the hotel now felt ridiculous, burdened under the weight of this singular revelation. Redemption and vigilance became the twin pillars of my survival from that point forward. I began to scrutinise the way families moved through the lobby, parents with lapses of sight too easily dismissed as harmless. Every laugh, every gleeful shout echoing from the play area now carried with it an undercurrent of suspicion. Was that joy truly innocent, or was it merely a reflection of the darkness I had naively allowed to flourish?

In this revelation, I uncovered the true essence of vigilance. It wasn't just about physical observation—it was an emotional reckoning with the fragility of trust and the dreadful reality that power, when left unchecked, could birth unimaginable horrors. I realised, with a mix of satisfaction and despair, that we had become nothing more than guardians in a carnival of masquerades, where the mundane hid the grotesque beneath its banal veneer. Like a ridiculed raccoon picking through the ashes of shattered innocence, I lurched forward, determined to unveil the layers of deception that covered our world—and perhaps, in that relentless search, find a semblance of salvation for the innocents who tread too close to the inferno.

Chapter 13: The Lobster Slayer

The kitchen was a battleground, a fiery hellscape where the clatter of pans and the roar of burners formed the symphony of our daily war. Jamie's relentless pursuit of culinary perfection pushed us to our limits. The new recipes he introduced were not just dishes but trials by fire, testing our mettle and pushing us beyond what we thought possible. These creations were masterpieces of modern cuisine: the delicate balance of Flavours in our Duck à l'Orange, the textural symphony of the Truffle Risotto, and the avant-garde deconstruction of the Classic Beef Wellington. Each dish was a testament to our endurance and our skill, hard-won badges of survival in this hostile environment.

One dish, however, stood out above the rest—our stunning Steak and Lobster sharing platter. There was something primal about the way people reacted to this dish. It was as if we had tapped into some deep, carnal desire, some ancient need for indulgence that had been lying dormant, just waiting to be awakened. The dish itself was a masterpiece of excess—a thick, marbled cut of steak, seared to perfection, its juices running like rivers of molten gold, paired with a full lobster, its crimson shell a stark contrast to the pale, tender flesh within. And then there were the triple-cut chips, fried to a golden crisp, their edges sharp enough to cut, their insides soft and pillowy, like the dream of some long-forgotten luxury.

It was more than just food; it was a spectacle, an event, a moment of obscene decadence that played out on the table, drawing eyes from every corner of the dining room. The Steak and Lobster platter became our calling card, the dish that put us on the map, the siren song that lured the wealthy and the desperate alike into our clutches. But like all things that glittered too brightly, it was both a blessing and a curse.

The demand for the dish quickly spiralled out of control, turning each service into a nightmarish ordeal. It wasn't just a meal; it was an obsession. People would come in droves, their eyes glazed over with anticipation, their mouths already watering at the thought of the steak's charred crust, the lobster's delicate sweetness. They would order it in pairs, in groups, whole tables demanding platter after platter, as if the mere act of consuming it would grant them some kind of immortality, some fleeting taste of a life they would never truly possess.

The kitchen became a frontline warzone, each service a frenzied skirmish in an endless war of hunger and desperation. The orders would flood in, a relentless barrage that left no room for error, no time to breathe. The sound of knives chopping, grills sizzling, and pans clanging echoed through the confined space, a symphony of carnage that threatened to drown us all. The air was thick with the scent of seared flesh, the acrid tang of boiling lobster shells, and the ever-present stench of sweat and fear.

Scott, the twins, and I moved like automatons, our hands a blur of motion as we churned out platter after platter, our minds numbed by the repetition, the pressure, the sheer weight of expectation. There was no room for mistakes, no margin for error—one misstep, and the entire service could collapse, the delicate balance we maintained every night shattered in an instant. The stakes were too high (no pun intended, honestly), the demand too great. We were dancing on the edge of a razor, and it was only a matter of time before someone got cut.

And then there were the customers, the ravenous hordes who would fight, claw, potentially kill to get their hands on the Steak and Lobster platter. They would watch us from the dining room, their eyes fixed on the kitchen pass, their faces twisted with a mixture of desire and desperation. The slightest delay would send them into a frenzy, their voices rising in a chorus of demands, complaints, threats. They needed it, craved it, and we were the unfortunate souls tasked with providing it.

I remember one night in particular, a Saturday, the restaurant packed to the rafters, the noise level a constant roar that vibrated through my skull. The orders for the Steak and Lobster platter were coming in faster than we could handle, the tickets piling up, the pressure mounting with each passing minute. My hands were slick with grease, my shirt soaked through with sweat, the heat from the grills and fryers suffocating.

A couple at table seven had been waiting too long, their impatience growing with each tick of the clock. They had been watching us, their eyes narrowing as the minutes dragged on, their fingers tapping rhythmically against the table. Finally, they snapped. The man, a hulking brute of a figure, stood up, his chair scraping loudly against the floor, and stormed over to the kitchen pass.

"Where the fuck is our food?" he demanded, his voice a guttural growl that cut through the din of the restaurant. "We've been waiting for over an hour for that fucking platter!"

Scott, ever the diplomat, tried to defuse the situation, his voice calm, measured, but the man wasn't having any of it. His face flushed with rage, his eyes bulging with a feral intensity that bordered on insanity. He reached over the pass, his massive hand gripping the edge with white-knuckled force, and pulled Scott toward him, his other hand raised as if to strike.

That was when the twins intervened. They moved as one, their identical faces set in grim determination, their bodies a blur of motion as they leapt over the counter and tackled the man to the ground. The restaurant fell silent, all eyes on the scene unfolding before them, the air thick with tension, the taste of violence hanging heavy in the air.

The man struggled, his fists swinging wildly, but the twins were relentless, their movements precise, controlled, a choreographed dance of brutality. It was over in seconds. The man lay on the ground, gasping for breath, his face a mess of blood and sweat, while the twins stood over him, their expressions cold, unyielding.

There was a moment of stunned silence, the entire restaurant frozen in time, before the woman at table seven let out a bloodcurdling scream. It was a sound that pierced through the noise, the chaos, the madness, a primal wail that sent a shiver down my spine.

But it didn't matter. None of it mattered. Because the Steak and Lobster platter had become more than just a dish—it had become a symbol, a beacon of everything we had sacrificed, everything we had endured. It was a reflection of the world we inhabited, a world where hunger and desperation ruled, where people would do anything, absolutely anything, to get what they wanted.

And we were the ones who had to make it happen, night after night, service after service, our bodies and minds pushed to the breaking point, all in the name of satisfying the ravenous appetites of those who would never know the true cost of their indulgence.

I can't fathom how no one was fired, prosecuted, or dragged out in handcuffs; it's beyond comprehension.

In the end, it was a blessing and a curse. The Steak and Lobster platter had made us famous, but it had also made us slaves, prisoners of our own success, trapped in a cycle of excess and expectation that we could never escape. And as I stood there, watching the twins drag the man out of the restaurant, his blood staining the pristine marble floor, I couldn't help but wonder how much longer we could keep this up before it all came crashing down around us.

Around this time, I received a gift from a close friend: a Victorinox 12-inch wooden handle chef's knife. It was a thing of beauty, elegant yet intimidating, a deadly piece of craftsmanship. With this weapon of mass destruction in my hands, I was quickly dubbed the executioner of all lobsters that entered the hotel. The hotel became a slaughterhouse, and I was the harbinger of doom for these crustaceans.

The lobsters, a creature of the deep, brought to the surface against its will—its fate sealed the moment it enters the cold, sterile world of the kitchen. There's a perverse pleasure in the ritual of preparation, a dance between man and beast, where every step is both deliberate and final. The process is not just about cooking; it's about exerting control, bending the wild to the demands of fine dining, an act as much psychological as it is culinary.

First, you must grasp the lobster with a firm hand, feeling its carapace, the rough texture a stark contrast to the smooth steel of the knife waiting beside you. The creature's claws snap helplessly, an instinctive reaction to the end it cannot escape. It's alive, and that's crucial—you want the freshness, the vitality, the terror, to be the secret ingredient that infuses the dish.

Place it on its back, the segmented underbelly exposed and vulnerable. Here, in this moment, there's a pause, a breath taken not out of hesitation but to savour the inevitability of what comes next. The knife hovers above the cross-shaped mark just behind the lobster's eyes—the point of no return. You bring the blade down swiftly, decisively, severing the spinal cord in a single stroke. The tail may twitch, a final, futile protest, but the brain has already been silenced. The beast is yours, its life snuffed out with surgical precision.

But the process doesn't end there. You must deal with the claws, those formidable weapons now rendered harmless. A twist, a crack, and they're separated from the body, the meat inside waiting to be extracted, each movement calculated, efficient, devoid of any emotion save for the cold satisfaction of a task well executed.

The tail comes next, its firm flesh destined for the plate. A quick slice along the underside, and it's free, the meat pristine and white, untouched by the brutality of the kill. The shell peels away easily, revealing the treasure within, a testament to the skill of the execution.

There's something almost ritualistic about boiling a lobster. Submerge it in a pot of rolling water, seasoned with enough salt to mimic the ocean it was taken from. The heat will turn the shell a vivid red, a visual metaphor for the violence that brought it here, to this final resting place. Time it perfectly—too little, and the flesh remains raw, too much, and it toughens, losing the delicate texture that makes it so prized. Ten minutes, no more, no less. The clock is your guide, ticking away the seconds until perfection is achieved.

As you lift the lobster from the pot, steam rising like the last breath of a dying animal, you're reminded that this is not just about food—it's about dominance. You've taken something wild, something raw, and transformed it into a work of art, a masterpiece of culinary skill. The plate is your canvas, the lobster the centrepiece, a symbol of the power you wield in the kitchen. And as you garnish it with butter, lemon, perhaps a sprig of parsley for colour, you know that you've created more than just a meal. You've crafted an experience, a moment of fleeting beauty born from an act of calculated cruelty.

Hundreds, if not thousands, of lobsters met their end at my hands. Each kill chipped away at what was left of my humanity. Daily, more lobsters were dumped on my station, their black, beady eyes filled with fear and hatred as they awaited their fate. I watched the light go out in their eyes as I delivered death blow after death blow with my new knife. It wasn't long before I earned the moniker "The Lobster Slayer."

The process was gruesome. Some lobsters were cut in half, their bodies writhing in their final moments. Others were boiled alive, their screams—if you could call them that—echoing in the confines of the kitchen. Some seemed to group together, as if in a futile attempt to survive the onslaught. But none could stand against the Lobster Slayer. I felt like a monster, I am their monster, a living nightmare to them. I could imagine them telling their offspring horror stories about me, the harbinger of their destruction.

One day, a surreal experience shattered the monotony of my grim task. As I prepared to execute another lobster, this one fought back. It looked me dead in the eye, and I swear I saw a glint of defiance. It was their champion, the one chosen to defeat me.

The lobster's body tensed as if coiled with a spring of primal energy. My knife struck out with practiced precision, but the lobster parried with an almost supernatural agility. Its tail snapped with ferocious strength, the segments slapping against the cold steel of my blade, sending vibrations up my arm. Its claws gripped and lashed out with a terrifying intensity, each strike narrowly missing my flesh.

The lobster lunged at me—lunged! —and we were locked in a battle of fates. Man versus lobster, a struggle of epic proportions. It was not just a fight; it was a dance of death; each move a step closer to the end. The lobster's tail whipped through the air, a blur of motion that seemed to defy the very laws of nature. My knife slashed through the space it had occupied mere milliseconds before, meeting only the empty, humid air of the kitchen.

Time seemed to stretch into an eternity as we battled. My knife struck out again and again, but the lobster parried each blow with a resilience I had never seen. Its eyes, those beady, soulless eyes, bore into mine with a malevolent intelligence. It was a dramatic and visceral fight, a testament to the primal struggle for survival.

At one point, the lobster's claw clamped down on my wrist with a vice-like grip. Pain shot up my arm, white-hot and blinding. I gritted my teeth and swung my knife in a desperate arc. The blade caught the lobster's carapace, sending a shower of tiny, jagged shards into the air. The lobster released its grip and fell back, momentarily stunned.

With a roar, I brought the knife down in a final, decisive blow. The blade pierced through the lobster's shell, splitting it in two. The lobster convulsed once, twice, and then lay still, its body twitching in the throes of death. The battle was over. The champion was defeated.

In the end, the lobster perished, and the succulent steak and lobster platter was served to the masses. The lobsters had lost this war, their champion defeated, and the dish continued to be served in all its bloody glory.

Steak and Lobster Recipe

Ingredients:

- Steak:

  - 2 Prime Ribeye steaks, dry-aged for 28 days—marbled perfection, the kind of decadence that demands respect.

  - Salt and pepper to taste—simple, brutal, the essence of seasoning stripped down to its core.

- 2 tablespoons olive oil—silky, smooth, a prelude to the heat that's about to hit.

- 2 tablespoons unsalted butter—rich, indulgent, ready to meld into the seared flesh.

- 4 cloves garlic, crushed—aromatic, relentless, a flavour that clings like a memory you can't shake.

- 2 sprigs rosemary—earthy, sharp, a touch of green in a world of red.

- 2 sprigs thyme—subtle, understated, but undeniably essential.

- Lobster:

- 2 live lobsters—alive, writhing, their fate sealed the moment they were plucked from the tank.

- 1 lemon, halved—citrus, acid, a sharp contrast to the richness of the flesh.

- 2 tablespoons butter—melted, golden, ready to drown the lobster in luxury.

- 2 cloves garlic, minced—sharp, biting, cutting through the richness like a blade.

- Fresh parsley, chopped—green flecks of life in a dish that's all about indulgence.

- Triple Cut Chips:

- 4 large russet potatoes—starchy, thick, ready to be transformed into golden perfection.

- Vegetable oil, for frying—hot, bubbling, the medium through which these potatoes will find their true form.

- Sea salt, to taste—coarse, aggressive, the finishing touch that turns simple into sublime.

Instructions:

1. Steak:

- Preheat the oven to 400°F (200°C). The heat rising, an inferno that mirrors the tension in the room.

- Season the steaks generously with salt and pepper. The crystals clinging to the flesh, a promise of the Flavours to come.

- In a cast-iron skillet, heat olive oil over high heat until shimmering. The oil quivers, on the verge of chaos. Add the steaks and sear for 2-3 minutes on each side until a crust forms, the surface sizzling, caramelising into a layer of pure, unadulterated flavour.

- Add butter, garlic, rosemary, and thyme to the skillet. The butter melts, foaming, the herbs releasing their essence into the air. Baste the steaks with the melted butter and herbs, each spoonful a slow, deliberate act of indulgence.

- Transfer the skillet to the oven and cook until the steaks reach the desired doneness (125°F for medium-rare), about 5-7 minutes. The heat sears through, penetrating to the core, leaving the centre tender, bloody.

- Let the steaks rest for 5 minutes before serving. The juices, held in suspense, slowly redistribute, pooling beneath the crust.

2. Lobster:

- Bring a large pot of salted water to a boil. The water roils, a maelstrom that will claim the lives of the lobsters. Add the lobsters and cook for 8-10 minutes until bright red, the shells a vivid scarlet, a visual confirmation of their demise.

- Remove the lobsters and let them cool slightly. Split the lobsters in half lengthwise, the knife cracking through the shell, exposing the tender, succulent flesh within.

- In a small saucepan, melt butter with garlic and lemon juice. The aroma fills the air, a heady mix of richness and acid. Brush the lobster meat with the garlic butter mixture, each stroke a final, fatal caress. Sprinkle with parsley, the green a deceptive hint of life in a dish that celebrates death.

3. Triple Cut Chips:

- Peel and cut the potatoes into thick wedges. Each cut precise, deliberate, the raw potatoes ready for their transformation.

- Rinse the potatoes in cold water and pat dry. The starches wash away, leaving behind a clean slate.

- Heat vegetable oil in a deep fryer to 325°F (165°C). The oil bubbles, ready to envelop the potatoes in its searing embrace. Fry the potatoes in batches for 5-6 minutes until they start to soften but do not brown. Remove and drain on paper towels, the oil dripping away, leaving behind the soft, pillowy interior.

- Increase the oil temperature to 375°F (190°C). The heat climbs, intensifying. Fry the potatoes again until golden and crispy, about 3-4 minutes. The transformation is complete—the outside shattering into a crisp, golden crust.

- Drain on paper towels and season with sea salt. The crystals cling to the surface, a final touch of flavour.

4. Assembly:

- Arrange the steak and lobster on a large platter, garnished with the triple-cut chips and lemon halves. The dish, a monument to indulgence, a testament to the lengths we'll go to for a taste of perfection.

- Serve immediately, basking in the glory of a dish that has captivated and conquered. The platter gleams under the lights, the air thick with the scent of seared meat, briny lobster, and the sharp tang of lemon—a sensory overload, a decadent feast for those who dare to indulge.

As I reflect on the creation of this dish, I am struck by the juxtaposition of its beauty and the horror of its preparation. The most exquisite dishes often come from the most horrific acts, and the blood on my hands is a testament to the price of culinary excellence. The Lobster Slayer lives on, not just in the memories of those who have tasted this dish, but in the dark corners of my mind where the screams of the lobsters still echo.

Chapter 14: The Inspection

The morning rush has passed, a brutal ballet of clanging pans, sizzling meat, and the hiss of steam. It left the kitchen like a combat-zone post-slaughter: streaks of oil on the stainless-steel counters, knives caked in the remnants of flesh, the faint stench of sweat and blood hanging in the air like a toxic cloud. The storm has abated, and what remains is a deceptive calm, the kind of quiet that lingers before the next wave of chaos crashes over us. It's in these moments, when the kitchen seems to hold its breath, that I find myself most on edge.

I'm at my station, orchestrating the mist en place with the precision of a surgeon, my movements methodical, each slice and chop deliberate, calculated. The ingredients of a soon to be French Onion Soup are laid out before me like the tools of my trade, their fate sealed by my steady hand. The repetition is almost meditative, a sequence that brings a twisted sense of order to the madness of my world. The kitchen, this stainless-steel cathedral of creation and destruction.

French Onion Soup

Ingredients:

- 4 large yellow onions, thinly sliced—precision is key.

- 4 tablespoons unsalted butter—luxury, pure and cold.

- 2 tablespoons olive oil—smooth, almost sinister.

- 1 teaspoon sugar—a sweet deception, masking the inevitable bitterness.

- 2 cloves garlic minced—cut with the accuracy of a scalpel.

- 1/2 cup dry white wine—elegant, with a sharp bite, much like the truth.

- 8 cups beef broth—rich, dark, the essence of something once alive.

- 2 bay leaves—an offering to the gods of chaos.

- 4-5 sprigs of fresh thyme—herbaceous, fleeting, like memories.

- Salt and freshly ground black pepper, to taste—a necessary brutality.

- 1 baguette, sliced into 1-inch-thick rounds—rustic, but don't let that fool you.

- 2 cups grated Gruyère cheese—decadent, melting into oblivion.

Instructions:

1. Caramelise the Onions:

   - In a large, heavy-bottomed pot, melt the butter with the olive oil over medium heat. Feel the weight of the pan, solid and unforgiving.

   - Add the sliced onions, watching as they wilt under the heat. Stir occasionally, savouring their transformation.

After about 10 minutes, they will soften, surrendering to the inevitable.

- Sprinkle in the sugar—just a teaspoon, enough to coax out the darkness lurking within. Continue to cook, stirring frequently, until the onions are golden brown, teetering on the edge of burning. This will take 30-40 minutes. Time, in the end, is the true test of your resolve.

2. Add Garlic and Wine:

- Toss in the minced garlic, letting its sharp aroma fill the kitchen. Cook for another 1-2 minutes until its essence is fully released, no longer hiding behind the onions.

- Pour in the white wine, the liquid cutting through the richness, scraping up the browned bits from the bottom of the pot like sins being laid bare. Let it reduce, simmering until only the truth remains, about 5 minutes.

3. Add Broth and Herbs:

- Pour in the beef broth, dark and simmering, a concoction that whispers of life lost. Add the bay leaves and thyme, ancient symbols of protection that do little to ward off what's coming.

- Bring the soup to a simmer, then reduce the heat to low and let it cook, uncovered, for 30-40 minutes. The steam rises, carrying the scent of something that was once whole, now unraveling.

4. Prepare the Baguette:

- While the soup is simmering, preheat your oven to 400°F (200°C). The heat is comforting, almost reassuring in its predictability.

- Arrange the baguette slices on a baking sheet, their future clear and unavoidable. Toast them in the oven for about 5-7 minutes, until they're crisp, golden, but not yet crumbling under the pressure.

5. Assemble and Serve:

- The soup has finished its time in the pot, a transformation complete. Remove the bay leaves and thyme sprigs—symbols of what might have been.

- Ladle the soup into oven-safe bowls, the liquid dark and reflective. Place a few slices of toasted baguette on top, as if shielding yourself from the depths below.

- Sprinkle a generous amount of grated Gruyère cheese over the baguette slices, covering the surface, hiding the truth beneath a layer of melting decadence.

- Place the bowls on a baking sheet and transfer them to the oven under the broiler. Watch as the cheese bubbles and browns, knowing that beneath it all, something darker lurks.

6. Serve:

- Carefully remove the bowls from the oven. Feel the heat against your skin, the culmination of your efforts. Serve immediately, knowing that the rich, deep flavours of the caramelised onions are both a comfort and a reminder of what it took to get here. The melted cheese, now golden and bubbling, offers a brief escape, a fleeting moment of indulgence before reality seeps back in.

Enjoy your meal—or whatever this has become.

But it's a fragile peace, one that can be shattered in an instant. The tension is palpable, a coiled spring waiting to snap. I can feel it in the air, an electric charge that prickles the skin, a reminder that the storm is never truly over. It's merely gathering strength, biding its time before it strikes again.

Then, the phone rings.

The sound is jarring, a sharp intrusion into the silence, slicing through the air with the subtlety of a knife to the throat. It's a sound that shouldn't belong here, in this place of steel and fire, where the only music is the rhythm of the kitchen—metal on metal, the roar of the burners, the staccato beat of knives on cutting boards. But here it is, shrill and relentless, a reminder that the outside world still exists, still claws at the edges of this controlled chaos.

The phone rings again, and the fragile peace of the kitchen is shattered, like glass splintering under the pressure of an unseen force. My hand, steady moments before, hesitates for just a fraction of a second, the knife pausing mid-air. It's enough to throw off the rhythm, to break the trance. The calm I had constructed so meticulously begins to unravel, the tension coiling tighter in my chest.

I glance at the clock. It's too early for delivery calls, too late for breakfast orders. The possibilities race through my mind, each one more unsettling than the last. Has someone fucked up? Is there a VIP demanding something ridiculous? Or worse, is it something that's about to spiral out of control, something that will send this entire operation crashing down around us?

I reach for the phone, my hand now steady but my mind racing, the calm façade I wear slipping just enough to let the undercurrent of dread seep through. The kitchen around me is still, the other chefs busy at their stations, oblivious or perhaps deliberately ignorant of the storm brewing just beyond the reach of the burners.

I lift the receiver, and as I press it to my ear, the world around me narrows to this one moment, this one conversation. The silence that follows is suffocating, the calm before the inevitable plunge into the chaos that lies ahead. The storm is coming, and when it hits, I'll be standing at the centre of it, the eye of the hurricane, holding the knife.

"Chef! The health inspector is here!"

Scott's voice crackles through the receiver, tinged with panic, fear—emotions I've long since buried beneath layers of professionalism, a carefully constructed mask that hides the chaos churning beneath. The words hang in the air, each syllable like the crack of a whip, sending shockwaves through the fragile calm I've fought so hard to maintain.

My grip tightens around the handle of the knife, the blade hovering over the cutting board, poised to slice through the next batch of onions. But now, the edge wavers, a fraction of an inch from the white flesh. The health inspector. Unannounced, unexpected, unwelcome. The words echo in my mind, bouncing off the walls of my consciousness like a ricochet, each one carving out a deeper groove of dread.

I don't have time for this—not today, not with the fridge full of secrets.

The pulse in my temples quickens, a relentless drumbeat that drowns out the hum of the kitchen, the hiss of the burners, the rhythmic chop-chop-chop of knives on plastic. I can feel the blood pounding in my veins, each beat a countdown to disaster, a reminder that in this world, nothing stays hidden forever.

But I can't afford to lose control. Not now. Not when the entire operation could unravel at the seams with a single misstep, a single wrong word, a single glance into the wrong fridge. The health inspector is a predator, circling the kitchen with a hunger for failure, a thirst for the slightest infraction, a weakness to exploit. And I'm the prey, the one standing between them and the truth that lies just out of sight, behind stainless steel doors.

I steady my breathing, forcing the panic down, burying it beneath the surface where it belongs. My hand, still gripping the knife, lowers to the cutting board, the blade sinking into the onion with a dull thud, the white flesh splitting apart like a wound. I focus on the act of slicing, each cut deliberate, precise, a way to keep my hands busy while my mind races through the possibilities.

The fridge. The one at the back, where the light has been out for months, casting everything in a permanent shadow. The one where the questionable cuts of meat are stored, the ones that don't quite meet the standard but can't be thrown away. The one where the off vegetables are kept, their wilted leaves and soft spots hidden beneath a layer of fresher produce. The one where the secrets of the kitchen are stashed, out of sight, out of mind, until now.

I glance around the kitchen, my eyes flicking from station to station, assessing, calculating. The other chefs are moving with the precision of machines, their focus on the tasks at hand, oblivious to the storm about to break over us. But Scott knows. He's seen the fridge, knows what lies inside, and his fear is palpable, crackling through the receiver like static electricity.

The inspector could be here any moment, clipboard in hand, eyes scanning for the slightest imperfection, the smallest flaw. They'll poke and prod, open doors, lift lids, peer into every corner, every crevice, searching for the one thing that could bring it all crashing down. And when they find it—and they will find it the consequences will be swift, merciless, the end of everything we've built.

But I'm not ready to let it all slip through my fingers. Not yet.

"Stall him," I command, my voice a cold, precise instrument. I hang up, the clatter of the receiver hitting the counter echoing in the sterile space around me.

Time is against me. The walk-in is a ticking time bomb—overripe produce, expired sauces, ingredients that have seen better days, but are just barely holding on, like patients in an ICU. I've spent years honing my skills, but today will test the limits of my culinary deception.

I stride to the fridge, the cold air hitting my face like a slap. The door swings open to reveal the horrors within a wilted lettuce, a box of tomatoes that are more liquid than solid, a wedge of cheese that's become more mould than dairy. This isn't food—it's evidence, each item a potential charge in the case against me.

The lettuce is first. I grab it, toss it into a blender, and hit "puree." The sound is violent, aggressive, a machine devouring what's left of the greenery. I add balsamic vinegar, sugar—disguises for the truth, a mask for the decay. I taste it—Rustic gazpacho, I decide, though the flavour hints at something darker, something rotting from within.

Next are the tomatoes. I slice away the worst parts, the blade moving quickly, efficiently, discarding the diseased flesh. The pieces that remain go into a pot with onions, garlic, oregano. The scent is heady, intoxicating—Tomato confit, I whisper, though the voice in my head tells me it's a lie, a beautiful, fragile lie.

The cheese is last. Mould has colonised most of the wedge, spreading like an infection. I cut away the outer layer, exposing the pale, trembling heart within. It goes into a dish, grated, melted, concealed under pasta—a burial, a cover-up. Artisan mac and cheese, I tell myself, though the deception sits heavy in my gut, like lead.

The kitchen door swings open, the heavy metal creaking on its hinges, a sound that cuts through the thick air like a knife. The health inspector steps inside, a man whose very presence is a disruption, an intruder in the hell scape of my domain. Clipboard in hand, his eyes scan the room with the cold detachment of a predator surveying its prey. His gaze is sharp, calculating, seeking out flaws, discrepancies, any sign of weakness that he can latch onto and exploit.

His nose twitches, almost imperceptibly, detecting the mix of scents that hang in the air—garlic, rosemary, simmering stock—but more than that, he's picking up the lies, the deceit, simmering just beneath the surface, masked by the aroma of culinary excellence. He can smell the rot, the corruption that I've worked so hard to conceal, and I know that he's hunting for it, that he won't stop until he finds it.

"Good afternoon, Chef," he says, his voice flat, devoid of warmth, an automated greeting from a man who's seen it all and cares about none of it.

I force a smile, thin, calculated, every muscle in my face straining to maintain the façade. "Not at all. We're just preparing for lunch service." The words come out smooth, rehearsed, but inside, my mind is a whirlwind of dread and anticipation.

He nods, stepping further into the kitchen, into our world. This is our territory, our kingdom, where we wield control, but right now, with him here, it feels like we are the ones on trial, like everything we've built could be torn down in an instant. He's not here to admire the work, to appreciate the craft; he's here to tear it apart, to find the flaws, the imperfections, the hidden decay that lurks behind the polished surface.

He begins his rounds, moving with a deliberate slowness that sets my nerves on edge. Every step he takes, every drawer he opens, every cupboard he peers into feels like a violation, like he's digging into my very soul, searching for the secrets I've buried deep within. The silence in the kitchen is suffocating, the only sounds the soft clinks and clicks of the inspector's meticulous examination.

My heart hammers in my chest, each beat a countdown to disaster, each second that passes tightening the noose around my neck. I watch him with a calculated calm, my mind racing through a thousand scenarios, a thousand ways this could go wrong. But I've been here before, I've danced this dance, and I know how to play the game.

"What's this?" he asks, his voice cutting through the tension like a blade. He's stopped at the pot of tomato confit, the steam rising like a guilty conscience, the smell rich and intoxicating, a deceptive veil over the truth.

"Ah, a special for today," I reply smoothly, ladling a small sample into a dish, my hand steady despite the tremor in my heart. "Tomato confit, slow cooked with a blend of herbs." I offer him the dish, watching as he sniffs it, his expression unreadable, his face a mask of indifference.

The spoon hovers near his lips, the world narrowing to this single moment, this single taste. Time slows, the sounds of the kitchen fading into the background as I wait, as I hold my breath, the silence stretching into eternity.

He takes a taste. I watch him, every muscle in my body tense, waiting for his reaction, for the verdict that could either save me or damn me. The silence is unbearable, the air thick with unspoken fears.

"Not bad," he mutters finally, jotting down a note on his clipboard, his tone dismissive, as though my entire career hangs on the edge of that one phrase. I exhale slowly, the relief washing over me like a narcotic, dulling the edges of my fear, but only for a moment.

He moves on to the next dish, the gazpacho, another taste, another nod, the rhythm of his inspection as relentless as the ticking of a clock, each taste a test, each nod a temporary reprieve. He pauses at the mac and cheese, lifting a forkful to his mouth. My breath catches, the world tilting slightly as I wait, the seconds stretching out like an executioner's countdown.

He chews, swallows, takes another bite, the silence in the kitchen now a deafening roar in my ears. "This is excellent," he says, his tone betraying a hint of surprise, a small crack in his otherwise impenetrable facade. "The cheese has a... unique flavour. What do you call it?"

I force another smile, the muscles in my face straining under the effort, every word a carefully measured lie. "It's our special aged blend," I say, my voice steady even as the deception curdles in my throat. "Very exclusive."

"Impressive," he says, scribbling something on his clipboard, but his eyes are still scanning, still searching, like a shark circling in the water, waiting for the first sign of blood.

He finishes his rounds, each step an eternity, each breath a gamble. The kitchen feels like a pressure cooker, the tension building with every moment, the air thick with the scent of cooked deception, the lies simmering beneath the surface, threatening to boil over. Finally, he closes his clipboard, snapping it shut with a finality that echoes through the silent kitchen like the lid on a coffin.

"Everything seems to be in order," he says, his tone almost reluctant, as if he's disappointed not to have found anything, not to have caught me in the act. "Just one last question: where do you source your ingredients? I must say, they're quite... distinctive."

The world tilts slightly, the ground beneath my feet unsteady, as if I'm standing on the edge of a precipice, one wrong step away from plunging into the abyss. "Oh, we have a very exclusive supplier," I say, the lie slipping out effortlessly, even as it twists like a knife in my gut. "Only the finest, freshest produce. Quality is our top priority."

He nods, seemingly satisfied, but the look in his eyes tells me he's still suspicious, still hunting, still waiting for the slightest crack in the facade. "Well, Chef, keep up the good work. I'll be back for another check in a few months."

As soon as he's gone, I collapse against the counter, my legs trembling, the adrenaline that's been coursing through my veins leaving me hollow, empty. The kitchen is silent now, the air thick with the scent of cooked deception, the rot still lurking in the corners, hidden just out of sight. I've survived this round, but I know it's only a matter of time before the truth resurfaces, before the lies we've built our kingdom on come crashing down around us.

I glance at the fridge, at the secrets still festering within. Tonight, I'll clean it out—sterilise it, purge it of the filth that threatens to undo everything. But for now, I allow myself a moment to breathe, to bask in the victory, however temporary it may be.

In the end, it's all about appearances. As long as everything looks perfect, no one will ask too many questions. No one will dig deeper. And I'll keep faking it, keep presenting the perfect facade, until the day it all comes crashing down. Because I know that day is coming, and when it does, there will be no hiding, no escaping the truth that lies beneath the surface.

But until then, I'll keep playing the game, keep dancing on the edge of the knife, because in this world, that's the only way to survive.

For now, I write down that Tomato Confit Recipe, as a reminder of my skill in deception.

Tomato Confit Recipe

Ingredients:

- 2 cups cherry tomatoes—small, perfect, each one a capsule of fleeting life.

- 1/2 cup extra virgin olive oil—thick, golden, viscous, the lifeblood of the dish.

- 4 cloves garlic—smashed, broken, their raw essence laid bare.

- 1 teaspoon fresh thyme leaves—tiny, fragrant, a whisper of what was once green and vibrant.

- 1 teaspoon sea salt—coarse, like granules of bone, adding a subtle sting.

- 1/2 teaspoon freshly ground black pepper—dark, pungent, a hint of bitterness to cut through the richness.

Instructions:

1. Preheat your oven:

- Set the oven to 250° F (120° C). The low, suffocating heat is crucial. It's the slow burn, the patient torture that transforms the tomatoes, turning them into something far beyond their original, naive state.

2. Prepare the tomatoes:

- Wash them—clean them up for their final act. Dry them meticulously, erasing any last vestiges of innocence. Place them in a single layer in a baking dish, lined up like lambs to the slaughter.

3. Add the aromatics:

- Douse them in olive oil, submerging them in the slick, golden liquid. Scatter the garlic cloves—smashed, brutalised—and sprinkle the thyme over the tomatoes. Salt them, pepper them, as if preparing a sacrifice. This is no mere seasoning; it's an initiation, a rite of passage into something darker, more profound.

4. Slow-roast the tomatoes:

- Slide the dish into the oven, and let the heat do its work. Two to three hours—long enough to break them down, to strip away their pretensions. Watch as they deflate, shrivel, surrendering to the inevitable. The aroma that fills the room is intoxicating, almost suffocating—a blend of sweetness and decay.

5. Cool and store:

  - When the transformation is complete, remove them from the oven. Let them cool, but not too much—just enough to handle without burning. Transfer them, along with the oil, garlic, and thyme, into a jar, a vessel for their new existence. They'll keep for two weeks, maybe more, but it's irrelevant—they won't last that long. Nothing ever does.

6. Serve:

  - Use this confit with care. Spread it on bread, mix it with pasta, drape it over meats, or eat it straight from the jar, savouring each bite. The flavours are deep, complex—a mixture of pleasure and pain, sweetness and bitterness. It's a dish that reminds you of life's fleeting nature, of the beauty that can emerge from the slow, relentless march towards destruction.

Chapter 15: A Dance with Death

Usually, the kitchen was a cathedral of panic and desperation, a hallowed ground where steel met flesh, and fire forged the mettle of men. Tonight, however, it was eerily quiet. Only Scott and I remained, the two lone survivors in the no-mans-land that had claimed so many before us. The other chefs had been felled by a sudden bout of sickness and holidays (Fuck me some of us was aloud holidays!!), leaving us to face the oncoming storm of the dinner service alone. The air was thick with the scent of fear and the acrid tang of adrenaline.

Scott was on the pass this service.

As the first tickets started to roll in, the kitchen roared to life, transforming from a dormant beast into a ferocious, fire-breathing monster. The burners flared, casting an ominous glow across the room, while the pans sizzled and spat, their angry hiss blending into the cacophony of clattering steel and shouted commands. The noise was a symphony of chaos, an overwhelming assault on the senses that threatened to drown out any semblance of order or sanity.

But in the midst of it all, Scott and I worked in grim harmony, our movements synchronised like some macabre dance. We were a well-oiled machine, each of us anticipating the other's next move with a precision born from countless services fought side by side. The rhythm of our work was hypnotic, almost soothing in its familiarity, as though we had slipped into a trance, driven by the primal need to survive the relentless onslaught of orders.

Yet, as the night wore on, the pressure mounted, and the cracks in our immortality began to show. The kitchen's once fluid motions started to falter; the tempo of our symphony skewed by the rising tension that pulsed through the air like a live wire. The relentless pace was like a vice tightening around us, squeezing every ounce of energy, every drop of focus, until all that was left was a frayed, nerve-shredding desperation.

"Where's the peppercorn sauce?" Scott's voice cut through the din like a whip, sharp and angry, tinged with the unmistakable edge of hysteria.

"Coming right up!" I shouted back, my hands working furiously to plate the dish, my fingers moving with a speed and dexterity that felt almost mechanical. The sauce, thick and rich, slid over the steak like liquid sin, a perfect, glistening coat that belied the chaos from which it had been born.

But the service was relentless, an unending tide of orders that battered against us like a storm surging against the rocks. Each ticket that slammed onto the pass was another wave, another threat of being pulled under, dragged down into the depths of failure. Sweat poured down my face, stinging my eyes, blurring my vision, but I didn't dare pause to wipe it away. I could feel Scott's gaze on me, a burning intensity that seemed to sear into my skin, his eyes like daggers that sliced through any veneer of calm I had left.

"Move faster!" he barked, his voice edged with hysteria, a crack in the mask of control he had worn all night.

"I'm doing my best!" I snapped back, my patience fraying at the edges, my temper barely contained beneath the surface. Each word tasted like acid on my tongue, a bitter reminder of the tension that had been building, simmering just below the boiling point.

Then without warning. A moment of frustration, a split-second lapse in the thin veneer of civility that had barely held us together. Scott's hand moved with a flash of violence, his fingers closing around the handle of a knife, his face contorted in a mask of rage that twisted his features into something unrecognisable, something monstrous.

Without a word, without even a hint of hesitation, he hurled the knife in my direction. Time seemed to slow, the world narrowing to the glinting steel blade spinning through the air, a glinting instrument of violence. I was frozen, caught in the moment, my mind screaming at me to move, to react, but my body was paralysed, locked in the grip of shock and disbelief.

I turned suddenly, the knife buried itself in my back with a sickening thud, the sound drowned out by the roar of the kitchen around us. And then came the pain, a searing, white-hot explosion that tore through my body, radiating out from the point of impact like fire spreading through dry brush. It was overwhelming, consuming, a pain so intense that it seemed to burn away everything else, leaving nothing but raw, agonising sensation.

I stumbled, the world around me spinning, the kitchen fading in and out of focus as my mind struggled to process what had just happened. The blade was still there, a foreign object lodged deep in my flesh, a grotesque symbol of the madness that had taken hold. My hands gripped the edge of the counter, knuckles white, fingers digging into the steel as if I could somehow ground myself, keep myself tethered to reality.

Scott stood there, his chest heaving, his eyes wide and wild, a mix of shock and fury etched into his features. For a moment, the kitchen seemed to fall silent, the clatter of pans, the sizzle of meat, the shouts of the other staff— all of it muted, as if the world itself had paused, holding its breath.

But then the noise returned, crashing over me in a deafening wave, the chaos of the kitchen rushing back in to fill the void. The other runners were shouting, their voices a jumbled mess of confusion and panic, but I couldn't make out the words, couldn't focus on anything other than the pain, the knife, the blood that I could feel soaking into my whites, warm and sticky.

Scott took a step back, his face pale, the realisation of what he'd done beginning to dawn on him. His lips moved, forming words that I couldn't hear, couldn't understand, as if we were separated by an invisible barrier, a chasm that had opened up between us.

And in that moment, as the pain threatened to drag me under, I felt something else—a cold, detached sense of clarity. The kitchen, the service, the relentless pressure—it had all led to this, to this breaking point where the veneer of professionalism, of control, had shattered, revealing the raw, ugly truth beneath. We were animals, driven to the edge by the demands of perfection, by the relentless pursuit of an ideal that was always just out of reach.

I locked eyes with Scott, and in his gaze, I saw my own reflection—a reflection twisted by anger, by frustration, by a madness that had been festering for far too long. And in that moment, I knew that something had broken, something that couldn't be mended.

The kitchen continued to roar around us, the service pressing on, unstoppable, unyielding, even as the world tilted and spun. But for Scott and me, something fundamental had shifted, something dark and irreversible, and there would be no going back.

I staggered forward, my vision swimming with stars. The world around me became a blur of red and black, a nightmare of agony and confusion. I reached back, my fingers brushing against the hilt of the knife, slick with my blood. The pain was excruciating, a white-hot fire that consumed me from within.

"Jesus Christ, what have you done?" I gasped, my voice trembling with shock.

Scott's face twisted into a mask of horror; his eyes wide with disbelief. "I...I didn't mean to," he stammered, his hands shaking. "It was an accident!"

But there was no room for accidents in the kitchen. The service continued unabated, the orders piling up around us. I could feel my strength ebbing away, my legs threatening to give out beneath me. But I couldn't stop, not now. The primal drive to survive, to keep moving, propelled me forward.

"Keep cooking," I muttered through gritted teeth, forcing myself to stand. "We can't stop."

Scott hesitated, his hands hovering over the stove. The fear in his eyes mirrored my own, a reflection of the horror that had unfolded between us. But he nodded, his resolve hardening. Together, we continued the service, our movements slower but no less determined.

Every breath was a struggle, every step a battle against the pain that wracked my body. The knife felt like a shard of ice, cold and unforgiving, embedded in my flesh. Blood oozed from the wound, soaking through my chef's coat and staining the floor beneath me. But I refused to falter. I refused to let the kitchen consume me.

The hours passed in a haze of torment and exhaustion. We moved like automatons, driven by the need to finish the service, to survive the night. The final ticket came and went, and the kitchen fell silent once more. The adrenaline that had sustained me ebbed away, leaving only the raw, throbbing pain in its wake.

Scott turned to me, his face pale and drawn. "We need to get you to a hospital," he said, his voice strained.

I nodded weakly, my vision dimming. The room spun around me, a dizzying whirl of shadows and light. Together, we stumbled out of the kitchen, leaving behind the battlefield where we had waged our war. The night air was cool and crisp, a stark contrast to the inferno we had endured.

The ride to the hospital was a blur of flashing lights and muted sounds. My head swam with pain, my consciousness drifting in and out like a flickering flame. By the time we arrived, I was barely holding on, my strength sapped by the blood loss. The doctors rushed me into the emergency room, their faces grim and focused.

Hours later, after the wound had been cleaned and stitched, I lay in a hospital bed, the sterile smell of antiseptic stinging my nostrils. The doctor, a stern woman with piercing blue eyes, had just finished checking my vitals. Her touch was cold and clinical, but her eyes held a flicker of concern.

"You were lucky," she said, her voice a low murmur. "A few inches to the left, and it would have hit your spine."

I nodded weakly, too exhausted to respond. As she turned to leave, I caught sight of something that made my blood run cold. Sitting in the corner of the room, partially obscured by shadows, was the woman in the wheelchair from Tempest Street.

Her appearance was even more grotesque than I remembered. Her skin was a sickly, mottled grey, stretched taut over her bones like parchment. Her eyes were hollow pits of darkness, devoid of life. Her mouth twisted into a rictus grin, revealing teeth that were jagged and blackened. She wore the same tattered dress, stained with grime and blood, and her bony fingers clutched the arms of the chair with a desperate intensity.

I blinked, rubbing my eyes in disbelief. When I looked again, she was gone. The chair was empty, as if she had never been there. My heart pounded in my chest, the pain in my back momentarily forgotten. I knew what I had seen. The woman was real, and she was haunting me.

The doctor's voice broke through my reverie. "Are you alright?" she asked, her brow furrowing in concern.

I forced a smile, shaking my head. "I'm fine," I lied, my voice barely a whisper. "Just tired."

But I wasn't fine. The horrors of the kitchen had followed me here, and now, even in the supposed safety of the hospital, I was not alone. The woman from Tempest Street was a spectre of my darkest fears, a reminder that the line between life and death was far thinner than I had ever imagined.

As the doctor left the room, I lay back against the pillow, my mind racing. The night had been a crucible of pain and terror, and I had emerged scarred but alive. Yet, I couldn't shake the feeling that something had changed.

The kitchen, the knife, the woman—they were all pieces of a puzzle I couldn't yet comprehend. And as I drifted into a fitful sleep, the image of her twisted smile burned into my mind, I knew that my ordeal was far from over.

Chapter 16: Best Friends with The Prostitute Syndicate

Parking on Tempest Street was a calculated decision, a deliberate choice in a city where every inch of asphalt was claimed by the greedy claws of capitalism. In the heart of Manchester's notorious red-light district, it was the only place where I could leave my car without feeding the insatiable meters that lined every other street. But what Tempest Street saved me in parking fees, it extracted tenfold in the toll it took on my psyche. This was a place that whispered to the darkest corners of the human mind, a festering wound in the city's flesh where decay and despair thrived, unchecked and unchallenged.

The moment I turned off the engine, the silence descended like a shroud, thick and suffocating, wrapping itself around me like a noose. The air was cold, far colder than it had any right to be, a chill that seeped into my bones and settled there, an unwelcome guest that refused to leave. But it wasn't just the temperature that made the atmosphere so unbearable—it was the smell that cruel, unsettling aroma that clung to your skin and clothes, a vile stench that spoke of things better left forgotten. It was the smell of rot, of human waste, of a city's forgotten refuse left to fester and decay in the shadows.

As I stepped out of the car, the smell hit me like a physical blow, a rancid cocktail of sweat, urine, and decay that made my stomach churn. It was a smell that burrowed into your senses, invading every pore, every breath, until it became a part of you, a reminder of where you were and what you had willingly walked into. The scent was inescapable, spreading like wildfire through the labyrinth of alleys that crisscrossed the district, each one a darker, more twisted version of the last.

The street was a nightmare landscape, a tableau of human misery played out under the sickly glow of flickering streetlights. Homeless men huddled in doorways, their eyes vacant and hollow, devoid of any spark of life. They were the living dead, trapped in a purgatory of their own making, or perhaps one crafted by a world that had long since discarded them. They begged on every corner, their voices little more than a rasping whisper, a desperate plea for something—anything—to ease the suffering that defined their existence. But more often than not, their cries went unanswered, their bodies slipping into a heroin-induced stupor as they sought warmth in the abyss.

The sidewalks were littered with the detritus of a society on the brink of collapse. Needles glinted in the gutter, discarded like the lives they had destroyed, each one a silent testament to the desperation that pulsed through the veins of this place. The walls were stained with the evidence of countless sins, layers of graffiti and grime blending together into a grotesque mural that spoke of violence, addiction, and decay.

Dead pigeons were strewn across the pavement like macabre offerings, their carcasses torn and pecked at, their feathers matted with dirt and blood. It was as if some inhuman creature had feasted upon them, leaving behind only the bones and the scraps, a twisted reminder that life here was cheap, expendable, easily discarded.

The darkness in Tempest Street was palpable, a living, breathing entity that thrived on the misery of those trapped within its grasp. It was a place where the rules of civilised society no longer applied, where the thin veneer of order and decency had been stripped away to reveal the raw, brutal reality beneath. Here, in this forgotten corner of the city, humanity's worst impulses were given free rein, unchecked and unchallenged by the forces that were supposed to keep them at bay.

And yet, despite everything—despite the stench, the despair, the ever-present threat of violence—I kept coming back. Tempest Street had a pull, a gravitational force that drew me in, feeding off the darkness that lurked within me. It was a mirror, reflecting back the parts of myself that I kept hidden, the parts that I pretended didn't exist. Here, in this place of decay and despair, I could shed the mask, let the darkness seep out, if only for a moment.

I walked down the street, my footsteps echoing in the silence, each one a reminder that I was still alive, still a part of this twisted dance of life and death. The homeless men ignored me, their eyes glazed over, lost in whatever hellish dreamscape their minds had conjured up. The dead pigeons lay in my path, their beady eyes staring up at me, accusing, as if they knew my secrets, knew the darkness that I carried with me.

As I reached the end of the street, the lights of the hotel in the distance, I took one last breath of the foul, acrid air, letting it fill my lungs, letting it remind me of who I really was. And then, with a final glance at the twisted landscape around me, I stepped into the light, leaving Tempest Street behind, but carrying its darkness with me.

But what caught my morbid fascination were the women—the ladies of the night. Phantoms of the sex world, they stood like zombies on every corner, their eyes vacant and their bodies emaciated. They were the walking dead, skeletal figures with sunken cheeks and eyes devoid of hope. Their teeth, what remained of them, were yellowed and rotting. The smell that clung to them was a sickening blend of sweat, urine, and stale cigarettes. They moved with a shuffling gait, their limbs stiff and uncoordinated, like marionettes controlled by an unseen puppeteer.

Each night, as I parked my car on Tempest Street—a ritualistic descent into the underbelly of the city—they would emerge from the shadows, their presence as inevitable as the rot that clung to the walls around us. These women, draped in rags that passed for clothing, were creatures of the night, their eyes glinting with a mixture of desperation and opportunism. Their hollow gazes held a predatory hunger, a feral need that had long since devoured any trace of humanity.

"Want some business, love?" they'd coo, their voices a raspy, seductive melody that grated against my nerves. The sound was like the whisper of dry leaves in a desolate forest, a promise of decay disguised as temptation. Their words were mechanical, devoid of any true emotion, as though they were reciting lines from a script they had performed a thousand times before.

I'd respond with the same detached politeness every time, the words falling from my lips like well-rehearsed lines in a play. "No, not today," I'd say, or "Sorry, too busy." I always maintained that veneer of civility, a thin mask that hid the revulsion curling in my gut. It was a sick game, this dance of rejection and anticipation. There was a part of me—dark, twisted, primal—that enjoyed the interaction, that took pleasure in the anticipation I wielded over them, the knowledge that I could say "yes" if I wanted to. But I never did. I never would.

Over time, they began to recognise me, their gaunt faces lighting up with a grotesque familiarity whenever they saw my car pull up. I was a fixture in their world, a character in their nightly theatre of despair. Their eyes would gleam with a predatory recognition, a calculated anticipation that maybe—just maybe—tonight would be the night I'd say "yes." It was a pathetic hope, one that they clung to with the same desperation they used to cling to their fading beauty.

One of them, a skeletal figure with stringy hair and sunken cheeks, took it a step further. She learned my name, her voice curling around it like a snake, squeezing every ounce of depravity from the syllables. "Let me suck you dry, Lewis," she'd purr, her voice a venomous hiss that slithered into my ear, "I'll rock your world." There was something almost comical in the way she said it, as though she were offering me a deal I couldn't possibly refuse. But the humour was lost in the grotesque reality of it all, in the sheer ugliness of her proposition.

They were fucking animals, these women—reduced to base instincts, to nothing more than tools of survival in a world that had stripped them of everything else. Their desperation was palpable, a stench that clung to them as surely as the filth that coated their bodies. And yet, despite the revulsion that churned in my stomach every time I encountered them, there was a part of me that was entertained by their persistence. It was a sick, twisted amusement, a reflection of the darkness that lurked within me, a reminder of my own depravity.

I found myself drawn to them, not in the way they hoped, but in a darker, more perverse sense. They were a mirror, reflecting the ugliest parts of myself back at me. Their persistence, their willingness to debase themselves for the promise of a few pounds, was a constant reminder of the moral decay that had taken root in my soul. I could see it in their eyes, in the way they looked at me, the way they sized me up with the cold calculation of predators assessing prey. They saw me for what I was—a man teetering on the edge of the abyss, a man whose façade of civility was one word away from crumbling.

And yet, I never crossed that line. I never indulged their offers, never gave in to the dark whispers that urged me to say "yes." But the temptation was always there, lurking in the back of my mind, a shadow that grew darker with each encounter. I knew that one day, the line between us—the thin, fragile line that separated my world from theirs—might blur, might fade away completely. And when that day came, I wasn't sure what I would do, or who I would become.

But for now, I kept playing the game, kept maintaining the illusion of control. I parked my car on Tempest Street, stepped into the role of the polite gentleman, and watched as they circled me like vultures, waiting for me to slip, to fall, to become one of them. It was a nightly ritual, a sick reminder of the darkness within me, a darkness that I couldn't escape, no matter how hard I tried.

And as I walked away, leaving them behind in the cold, dark street, their eyes followed me, their whispers echoing in my mind. "Give us a fuck honey" "Want any business?" "You don't know what your missing" Their words clung to me like a curse, a promise of what could be, of what might one day happen. And as much as I hated them, as much as I despised what they represented, I knew that deep down, I was no different. I was just better at hiding it. For now.

Soon, it wasn't just propositions for business. The women who prowled Tempest Street had started to close in, their familiarity growing like a cancer, spreading through the dank, fetid air of Manchester's red-light district. "Morning, Lewis," they'd say as I arrived, their voices slithering through the darkness, wrapping around me like a noose. "Good night, Lewis," when I left, their tone dripping with an unsettling intimacy that gnawed at the edges of my sanity.

It wasn't just the regulars, the ones whose gaunt faces and hollow eyes I had grown accustomed to. No, even the newcomers—the fresh meat dragged into this pit of despair—greeted me by name. I hadn't even seen some of them before, yet they called out to me as though we were old friends, as though I was a part of their twisted little community. Each new greeting was like a knife twisted deeper into the flesh of my carefully constructed reality, a reality that was now beginning to unravel, thread by thread.

Then there was the morning I found them—three of them—using my car's mirrors to apply their makeup. They were draped across the hood and leaning against the doors, their bodies twisted into unnatural poses as they smeared garish hues of red and pink across their hollow cheeks and cracked lips. The sight was grotesque, a parody of femininity that made my stomach churn with a mixture of revulsion and dark amusement.

I stood there for a moment, watching them from the shadows, my hand hovering over the key fob, reluctant to break the surreal tableau before me. Their faces, reflected in the dirty, streaked mirrors, were like masks, each one painted with a horrifying mockery of beauty, a beauty that had long since been stripped away by the harsh reality of their existence.

When I finally unlocked the car, the sound of the doors clicking open shattered the fragile silence. They jumped, startled, their heads snapping towards me in unison, their eyes wide and animalistic. For a split second, I saw something raw in their gaze—fear, perhaps, or the instinctual need to flee from a predator. But then they recognised me, and the fear dissolved into something far more unsettling.

"Sorry, Lewis," they giggled, their voices a discordant melody that grated on my nerves. "Just doing our makeup. You know how it is." Their laughter was hollow, forced, a sound that held no warmth, only the cold calculation of survival. The one closest to me, her lips smeared with a blood red that bled into the lines of her weathered face, flashed me a grin that was more like a snarl, baring teeth that were chipped and yellowed.

"At least we're looking after your car, Lewis," she added, her tone laced with a sly, almost mocking edge. Her grin widened, a grotesque display of teeth and gums, as if she were daring me to object, to tell them to get the fuck away from my car and out of my life. But I said nothing. I simply stood there, my hand still on the door handle, frozen in the moment as the realisation hit me—this was getting out of hand.

They were getting too close, blurring the lines between their world and mine, dragging me down into the abyss with them. It was as though I had become a part of their ritual, a fixture in their nightmarish existence, no different from the needles in the gutter or the dead pigeons in the street. I could feel the filth of Tempest Street seeping into my life, into my very soul, tainting everything it touched.

But even as the revulsion twisted in my gut, there was something else—a dark, twisted thrill that I couldn't deny. I was drawn to their degradation, to the way they had begun to weave themselves into the fabric of my daily routine. Their persistence, their audacity, was both horrifying and intoxicating, feeding some primal need within me that I had long tried to bury.

And so, I didn't push them away. I didn't tell them to leave or to stop using my car as their makeshift vanity. I let them linger, let their sickly-sweet perfume and cigarette smoke cling to the interior of my vehicle, let their laughter echo in my ears long after I had driven away. I let them get under my skin, burrow into the cracks of my carefully constructed facade, because deep down, I knew that I was no different from them.

But I could feel it—the darkness growing, spreading, taking root in the corners of my mind. Tempest Street was becoming more than just a place to park; it was becoming a part of me, a reflection of the rot that festered beneath the surface. And each morning, as I parked my car and they swarmed around me, their eyes glittering with that same mix of desperation and opportunism, I knew that the line between us was thinning, wearing away like old fabric, until one day, there would be nothing left to separate us at all.

It started small, almost innocuous—just one tire let down, a slow hiss of escaping air that I barely noticed as I walked up to my car. It was a minor inconvenience, easily fixed, but it set the tone for what was to come. The next day, it was two tires, both as flat as the hope in the eyes of the women who loitered on Tempest Street. I should have known then that things were about to escalate, that the delicate balance I had been walking was beginning to tip.

But I ignored the warning signs, chalked it up to the general malaise that permeated the area, the inevitable decay that touched everything here. Tempest Street was a place where things fell apart, where the broken pieces of life came to rot in the shadows. My car, like everything else, was just another casualty of the entropy that reigned supreme in this part of the city.

Then came the nails—jagged, rusty things embedded deep in the rubber, placed with deliberate malice. I pulled one out, holding it up to the weak morning light, its sharp point glinting like a promise of violence. It was clear now that this wasn't random, wasn't just the street claiming another victim. This was targeted. This was personal.

And then, the paint. White, thick, splashed across the hood of my car like a deformed handprint. It was an act of vandalism so blatant, so brazen, that it left no room for doubt. Someone was sending a message, and it wasn't hard to figure out who. The pimp—some shadowy figure I had never seen but whose presence I had always felt, lurking in the periphery, watching, waiting. Did he think I was poaching his girls? Did he think I was a threat?

The retaliation was swift and brutal. Each morning, I would find a new act of violence inflicted on my car—a tire slashed, a window cracked, the paint smeared with some unidentifiable substance that reeked of rotting flesh. It was a relentless assault, a declaration of war that I had never intended to start. My car, once a refuge, had become a battleground, a symbol of the conflict brewing on Tempest Street.

But it wasn't just my car. The street itself seemed to be changing, the air growing thick with a tension that pressed down on me like a weight. Prostitutes who had once greeted me with sly grins and whispered propositions were disappearing, vanishing into the night without a trace. Their absence was felt like a missing limb, an unsettling silence where there had once been the hum of desperate life.

Then the bodies started turning up—bloated, lifeless things pulled from the murky depths of the nearby canal. The water, once a stagnant mirror of the sky, now seemed to hold secrets in its dark embrace, secrets that were slowly rising to the surface. The faces of the dead were twisted in monstrous parodies of their former selves, their skin pale and waxy, their eyes wide open, staring blankly at nothing. It was as if the canal itself had claimed them, swallowed them whole, and then spit them out, changed, corrupted by the darkness that lurked beneath the surface.

The police increased their patrols, their presence a stark contrast to the usual neglect that Tempest Street endured. Their cars prowled the streets, their lights casting long, eerie shadows that stretched across the pavement like the fingers of some unseen hand. They questioned everyone, their voices tinged with suspicion, their eyes scanning the faces of the remaining women with a cold detachment that made my skin crawl.

But the fear, the thick, suffocating fear that hung in the air, wasn't just about the murders. It was something more, something primal, something that went beyond the violence and the blood. It was the fear of being watched, of being hunted. The knowledge that there was something out there, lurking in the shadows, something that could strike at any moment, without warning.

I felt it too, that creeping sense of dread that gnawed at the edges of my mind, a constant companion as I walked the streets, as I parked my car, as I lay in bed at night, staring up at the ceiling, waiting for the sound of breaking glass or the scrape of metal against metal. The pimp was out there, somewhere, watching, waiting for the moment to strike. And the thought of it, the knowledge that I had become a target, that I had somehow crossed a line, was a sickness that spread through me, turning my veins to ice

The street was changing, evolving into something darker, something more dangerous. The balance had shifted, and I was caught in the middle, trapped in a game that I didn't know the rules to, a game that I couldn't win. The car was just the beginning, just a taste of the violence that was to come.

And as I stood there, staring at the paint splashed across the hood, at the nails embedded in the tires, at the shattered glass that crunched underfoot, I knew that this was only the start. The violence was escalating, the tension building, and it was only a matter of time before it all came crashing down.

Tempest Street was no longer just a place to park. It had become a battlefield, a warzone, and I was caught in the crossfire. The violence, the fear, the death—it was all around me, closing in, suffocating me, driving me to the edge.

And in the end, I knew that there was only one way this could end. One way to stop the madness, to end the violence, to reclaim my life. But that thought that dark, twisted thought, was one that I wasn't ready to face. Not yet. Not while there was still a chance, however slim, that I could walk away from this unscathed.

One night, after another gruelling shift, I returned to my car. The street was as usual, a rotting wasteland, eerily deserted, the silence broken only by the distant hum of the poorly illuminated streetlights. The weight of the night clung to me like a second skin, the residue of sweat, stress, and the stench of burnt oil lingering as I slid into the driver's seat. The engine roared to life, a mechanical beast awakening, and for a moment, I allowed myself to believe that escape was within reach. But then, like a flash of impending doom, the unmistakable blue lights flared in my rearview mirror, cutting through the darkness, slicing through any illusion of safety.

My heart jackhammered against my ribs, the sudden surge of adrenaline a twisted cocktail of fear and rage. I'd had a few drinks earlier, a pitiful attempt at rewarding myself for surviving yet another night in the culinary trenches, where the knives were sharp, and the tempers even sharper. A drink to dull the edges, to blur the lines between reality and hell I waded through daily. But now, those few drinks felt like a ticking time bomb strapped to my chest.

Shitting it, I thought, a mantra that echoed in the hollow cavern of my mind. I'm fucked.

Saturday night. The witching hour where the city's underbelly comes alive, and I was just another young lad in a fucked area, prime pickings for the boys in blue. They were bound to pull me over, bound to drag me out of the car, and force me to blow into a goddamn breathalyser. The inevitability of it pressed down on me, a vice tightening around my throat.

The police questioning, under the eerie glow of streetlights in a desolate parking area, immediately cast a shadow of suspicion over me. Their probing inquiries, seemingly routine, carried an undercurrent of accusation, as if they were peeling back layers of an unspoken crime.

"Where have you been tonight?" they asked, their eyes piercing through the darkness, scrutinising my every reaction. The question, simple yet loaded, echoed ominously in the confines of my car.

"Have you noticed any unusual activity in the area? Is there anyone in your car we need to know about?" This followed, their tone suggesting they were searching for clues only I might unwittingly reveal. The normalcy of a police check morphed into an interrogation where I felt like a suspect in a thriller, the protagonist who unwittingly found himself entangled in a sinister plot.

"Do you often park here?" they continued, their flashlight beam dancing across the interior of my car, flirting with the edges of the trunk that harboured my culinary arsenal. My heart hammered against my chest, not just from the fear of a loosing my driving licence but from the darker implications of what lay in my trunk—a set of sharp knives, each with a purpose in the kitchen, yet under the current context, they were potential exhibits in a crime scene. A bloody towel, stained from preparing meat, could be misconstrued as a macabre token of violence. And the defibrillator (don't ask), now seemed a bizarre and incriminating article to possess.

My answers were measured, a façade of calm over a roiling internal chaos. I explained, my voice steady, that I was just returning from a tough night at work, a chef wearies from the battles of the kitchen. They seemed sceptical, the flashlight's glare a physical pressure that threatened to unveil every doubt they harboured about me. The tension was palpable, a thick, tangible cloak that smothered the night air.

As I managed to dissuade them from searching the trunk—a move that would undoubtedly spiral into a nightmarish explanation of kitchen tools mistaken for instruments of harm—they let me go with a stern warning. Driving away, the relief was tempered by the haunting realisation of how easily the tools of my trade could be seen as implements of a serial killer's toolkit. The irony was bitter, a cruel joke played by the universe on a night that should have ended simply with a tired chef going home. Instead, I was left with the chilling awareness of my vulnerability, of how quickly the ordinary could turn extraordinary under the lens of suspicion.

I never parked on Tempest Street again. Instead, I took up cycling to work, avoiding the dark alleys, the haunted corners, and the phantoms of the night. But the memories lingered, the sense of dread never fully dissipating. The screams of the damned, the cold, dead eyes of the prostitutes, the relentless gaze of the pimp—they stayed with me, a permanent scar on my psyche.

The Pigeon

Ingredients:

- 2 whole pigeons, cleaned and plucked—small, delicate, their lives snuffed out for this moment of culinary indulgence.

- 4 cloves garlic, minced—sharp, pungent, like the truths we keep hidden beneath layers of civility.

- 1 lemon, zested and juiced—acidic, biting, a contrast to the richness of flesh.

- 2 sprigs rosemary, finely chopped—earthy, resilient, a scent that clings to memory.

- 2 sprigs thyme, finely chopped—subtle, understated, a whisper in the cacophony of Flavours.

- Salt and pepper to taste—because even in perfection, there must be balance.

- 4 tablespoons olive oil—smooth, unctuous, a necessary lubricant for the wheels of this machine.

- 1 cup red wine—dark, rich, the colour of spilled blood.

- 1 cup chicken broth—depth, warmth, a base layer of comfort in a dish steeped in complexity.

- 2 tablespoons butter—silky, indulgent, the final touch that melds everything together.

Instructions:

1. Preparation:

   - Preheat the oven to 375°F (190°C). The heat rises slowly, like anticipation building in the pit of your stomach, knowing what's about to unfold.

   - In a small bowl, combine the minced garlic, lemon zest, rosemary, thyme, salt, and pepper. The mixture is fragrant, heady, a potent blend of nature's offerings. Rub this concoction all over the pigeons, inside and out, massaging it into the skin, feeling the slight give of the flesh beneath your fingertips. The birds are small, fragile, their bodies yielding to your touch.

2. Searing:

- Heat the olive oil in a large ovenproof skillet over medium-high heat. The oil shimmers, rippling with heat, waiting. Place the pigeons into the skillet, the sizzle a sharp exclamation points in the silence. Sear the birds until golden brown on all sides, about 4-5 minutes per side. The skin crisps, darkens, the aroma fills the air—a scent that's both inviting and ominous. You can almost see the life leaving them, their transformation from creatures of flight to vessels of flavour.

3. Roasting:

- Transfer the skillet to the preheated oven. The heat envelopes the pigeons, sealing in their fate. Roast for about 25-30 minutes, or until the internal temperature reaches 160°F (71°C). The kitchen fills with the rich scent of roasting meat, a primal reminder of the cycle of life and death, of nature's brutal indifference.

4. Sauce:

- While the pigeons roast, deglaze the skillet with red wine and chicken broth. The liquid hisses as it hits the hot pan, steam rising like a ghost from the depths. Bring to a simmer, scraping up the browned bits—the remnants of what once was, now transformed into something new. Reduce the sauce by half, concentrating its essence, then whisk in the butter until smooth and glossy. The sauce is thick, velvety, a dark mirror reflecting the complexity of the dish.

5. Serving:

   - Once the pigeons are done, remove them from the oven and let them rest for 10 minutes. The meat relaxes, the juices redistributing, settling into their final form. Plate the pigeons, drizzle the rich, dark sauce over them, the liquid pooling around the edges like blood at a crime scene. Serve with roasted vegetables or a fresh salad—a nod to balance, though it feels like a hollow gesture in the face of such decadence.

As I reflect on this pigeon dish, it's a stark reminder of the delicate balance between beauty and horror. Much like my encounters on Tempest Street, it embodies the duality of life—the allure of the sublime juxtaposed with the terror of the grotesque. The blood on my hands, whether from the kitchen or the dark streets, remains a testament to the price of survival in a world where darkness and light constantly vie for dominance.

Chapter 17: The Hand

Cycling to work had become my only sanctuary, a fleeting moment of escape from the suffocating darkness that had come to define my existence. The rhythmic peddling, the icy wind lashing against my face, the relentless thud of the wheels on the pavement—it was all that kept me from drowning in the chaos that awaited me each day. The physical exertion was a way to numb the mind, to suppress the lingering stench of Tempest Street, to prepare myself for the unrelenting brutality of the kitchen. But today was different. Today, the usual sense of doom that clawed at me each morning was overshadowed by a strange, almost manic excitement.

Michael Caines was coming. Not just another celebrity chef, but Michael-fucking-Caines—a culinary deity who towered above the rest of us mere mortals, his reputation a blade that could carve through even the toughest critics. He wasn't just a chef; he was a myth, a legend, a living embodiment of culinary excellence. The kind of man whose very name could make or break a restaurant, whose presence alone could ignite either fear or reverence—or both, depending on how close you stood to the inferno of his genius.

I'd heard the stories, of course—everyone had. The tales of his relentless pursuit of perfection, the way he could command a kitchen with nothing more than a glance, the intensity that radiated from him like heat from a blast furnace. But hearing the stories and standing in his presence were two different things entirely. And today, he was descending into the bowels of our kitchen, into the furnace we called home, to bestow his wisdom upon us—or perhaps, to judge us, to dissect us, to see if we were worthy of his name.

The anticipation was a live wire, crackling in the air, electric and dangerous. It buzzed in my ears, pulsed through my veins, drove me forward as I raced toward the hotel, each pedal stroke a mixture of awe and dread. I could feel it—every chef in that kitchen could feel it—the weight of his arrival pressing down on us like the oppressive heat from our stoves. It was as though the very walls of the hotel were straining under the pressure, the bricks themselves trembling in anticipation.

As I reached the hotel, the façade loomed before me, a monolith of stone and glass that seemed suddenly insignificant in the face of the man who would soon be stepping through its doors. I chained my bike, my hands shaking slightly with a mix of adrenaline and fear. The cool air of the morning did nothing to quell the heat rising within me, the same heat that burned in every corner of the kitchen, a reflection of the inferno that was about to ignite.

Inside, the kitchen was a frenzy of activity, every chef moving with a precision that bordered on the manic. The usual chaos of the prep work had been elevated to a new level of intensity, a fever pitch that reverberated through the clattering of pans, the hiss of steam, the sharp ring of knives on cutting boards. It was as if we were all standing on the edge of a precipice, looking down into the abyss, waiting for the moment when Michael Caines would arrive and either pull us back or push us over.

When I finally stepped into the kitchen, it was like stepping into the eye of a storm. The heat, the noise, the sheer force of it all hit me like a physical blow, a wall of sensation that threatened to overwhelm. But I couldn't falter, couldn't show a hint of weakness. Not today. Not with him coming.

I made my way to my station, my movements automatic, instinctual, honed by years of service in this brutal, unforgiving world. I turned my radio on to calm my nerves. As I adjusted the dial, the crackling static gave way to the strains of "Ashes to Ashes," the eerily familiar melody slithering through the speakers like a venomous serpent. It wrapped itself around my mind, tightening its grip with every echo of Bowie's spectral voice. The knives felt heavier in my hands, the vegetables on the chopping board less compliant, as if they too could sense the shift in the air, the coming storm. I worked with a precision that was almost mechanical, each slice, each chop, a heartbeat in the frantic rhythm of the kitchen.

Then came the call, the announcement that sent a shiver down the spine of every chef in the room: "Michael Caines is here."

When I saw him, it was like witnessing a deity made flesh. Michael Caines. His very presence dominated the room, his gaze predatory, with a sharp, hungry glint that could pierce through steel. He was handsome in a way that felt almost cruel, his features chiseled, his confidence a blade that cut through the air. His right hand—a prosthetic—was more than just a reminder of his resilience; it was a symbol of his dominance over the trials that would break lesser men. Despite, or perhaps because of it, he was a legend—a deity who had risen above mere mortals. Now, he was here, and the energy in the kitchen shifted from its usual tension to something more dangerous, more reverent—a cult-like anticipation that left everyone on edge.

As I approached him, my heart pounded in my chest, each beat a thunderous echo of my mounting anxiety. This was it. My chance to stand out, to catch the eye of a legend and perhaps, in some small way, to be seen as more than just another faceless chef slaving away in the culinary trenches. "Mr. Caines," I began, extending my hand, my voice betraying the slightest quiver of reverence. But in my eagerness, in my desperation to make an impression, I reached for his right hand—the prosthetic.

The world seemed to pause, the kitchen's usual cacophony fading into a muted hum as that moment stretched into an agonising eternity. His eyes flicked down to my hand, his expression morphing from neutral to something colder, something clinical, as if I were an insect under a microscope. A mistake had been made—my mistake—and the realisation hit me like a bucket of ice water. His gaze, devoid of warmth or empathy, locked onto mine, and I felt the blood in my veins freeze, my skin prickling with the sharp sting of embarrassment.

"Fuck me," he said, his voice flat, devoid of any emotion, the words slicing through the air like a blade. The disappointment in his tone was palpable, though it was the absence of anger that unsettled me the most. It wasn't rage that simmered behind those calculating eyes; it was indifference, the kind of apathy that spoke volumes about how little I mattered in the grand scheme of his world.

My hand hovered there, suspended in the air, trembling like a leaf caught in a breeze, before I hastily retracted it, the flush of shame rising from my neck to my cheeks, burning hot and vivid. "I'm, uh, really honoured to have you here," I stammered, my voice reduced to a pathetic whisper, the words barely audible over the noise of the kitchen. But he had already moved on, his attention shifting away from me, leaving me standing there, humiliated and exposed, like a bug pinned to a cork board, its wings flapping uselessly as it struggled to break free.

The other chefs noticed, of course. How could they not? Their snickers, poorly concealed behind masks of professionalism, echoed in my ears, a chorus of mockery that only deepened the wound. I had failed spectacularly, my one chance to make an impression shattered in a moment of thoughtless eagerness. The moment had passed, and I-was left with nothing but the bitter taste of regret and the icy grip of Michael Caines' disapproval.

The kitchen, usually my domain, felt foreign and hostile, the walls closing in on me as if to squeeze out every last ounce of dignity I had left. The air buzzed with a feverish energy as everyone else orbited around Michael Caines, desperate to bask in his glow, to earn a sliver of his approval. I tried to focus, to drown out the mortifying encounter by throwing myself into my work, but it clung to me like a shadow, a constant reminder of my inadequacy.

The prep list—my sentence for the day, handed down from on high by Michael-fucking-Caines. It wasn't just a list; it was a meticulously crafted gauntlet, a series of trials designed to test my limits, to push me to the edge of my sanity and beyond. Each item, each line, dripped with expectation, with the weight of a legend's scrutiny.

1. Truffle-Infused Duck Liver Pâté

20 portions

- Clean and devein the duck livers. No mistakes, no torn flesh—precision is key.

- Sauté in clarified butter with shallots until golden, but not overcooked. Undercooked is death; overcooked is disgrace.

- Deglaze with cognac, flame it off—let the fire burn away any weakness.

- Blend to a silken consistency, folding in truffle oil and black truffle shavings. Every fold must be deliberate, like the movements of a surgeon.

- Pass through a fine sieve, twice. No impurities, no imperfections. Store in a cold, controlled environment until service.

2. Beetroot-Cured Salmon

15 fillets

- Fillet and pin-bone the salmon with care—every stroke of the knife should be a love letter to the flesh.

- Prepare the cure: a precise blend of sea salt, sugar, grated beetroot, and a touch of horseradish. The balance must be exact, no room for error.

- Coat the salmon in the cure, pressing it into every crevice, every inch of skin. The transformation begins now.

- Wrap tightly in cling film, weighted down. Let it rest in the cold, dark embrace of the fridge for exactly 48 hours. No more, no less.

- Rinse, slice thinly—each slice a translucent whisper, a promise of what's to come.

3. Wild Mushroom Consommé

10 litres

- Forage or select the finest wild mushrooms—each one a treasure, each one a challenge.

- Sweat the mushrooms with shallots and garlic, letting them weep out their essence.

- Prepare a raft with egg whites, ground mushrooms, and mirepoix—this is your lifeline, your last defence against failure.

- Simmer gently, never boiling—coaxing out the clarity, the pure essence of fungi. Skim away imperfections like they're your own sins.

- Strain through cheesecloth, twice. The consommé should be as clear as your conscience, though mine is anything but.

4. Lobster Bisque

5 gallons

- Live lobsters—dispatch them cleanly, efficiently. No hesitation, no second thoughts.

- Roast the shells to a deep, fragrant red, the colour of ambition.

- Deglaze with brandy—let the flames rise, reflecting the fire in your own eyes.

- Add mirepoix, tomato paste, and stock—let it simmer, reducing the essence of the ocean to its core.

- Strain, reduce further—perfection is found in the details, in the reduction of chaos into order.

- Finish with cream and a touch of sherry, balancing richness with restraint. Season meticulously.

5. Aged Ribeye Steaks

12 cuts, 14oz each

- Select only the finest cuts, marbled with the promise of succulence. Each steak is a canvas, waiting for the brushstrokes of fire and salt.

- Dry-age for exactly 28 days—the flesh must mature, its complexities deepen.

- Trim to perfection—no waste, no excess. The edges must be clean, the surface unmarred.

- Vacuum-seal and store until the precise moment of searing. The timing must be exact—there is no room for misjudgment.

6. Triple-Cut Chips

40 portions

- Peel and cut the potatoes with geometric precision, each piece a uniform soldier in the war against mediocrity.

- Rinse in cold water, purging them of excess starch—purity is the goal.

- Blanch at a low temperature, just until tender—do not let them brown. This is only the beginning.

- Fry at a higher temperature until golden—this is the test, where the weak falter and the strong endure.

- Drain, season with sea salt—serve immediately, hot and crisp. Each chip must be a perfect contradiction of textures.

This is your battlefield; this is your test. Each item on this list is a challenge, a provocation. Michael Caines isn't just watching—he's judging, weighing your worth against the standard of his perfection. There's no room for error, no space for hesitation. Failure isn't just a possibility; it's a certainty if you let your guard down, if you falter for even a second.

This prep list isn't just a task—it's a declaration of war. The enemy? Mediocrity. And the battlefield? Your very soul.

Throughout the day, I watched him work, his movements precise and methodical, almost mechanical despite the prosthetic hand that should have slowed him down but didn't. He commanded the kitchen with an effortless authority, his voice a steady, hypnotic rhythm that guided the flow of the service, each word a command that we obeyed without question. He was a maestro, conducting a symphony of knives and pans and sizzling flames, and we were his orchestra, following his lead with a mixture of awe and terror.

But as I watched him, the knot of inadequacy in my gut tightened, constricting my insides until it was difficult to breathe. Each dish he crafted was a masterpiece, a testament to his unparalleled skill, his relentless pursuit of perfection. And yet, in every interaction we had, I felt the sting of his contempt, the thinly veiled disdain that coloured his every word when he spoke to me. The handshake, that single moment of shame, had marked me in his eyes, branded me as less-than, and no amount of effort or dedication seemed capable of erasing that stain.

He would assign me tasks, seemingly simple at first, but always with a twist—something subtle, something designed to push me just beyond my comfort zone, ensuring that I was always teetering on the brink of failure. And when I did falter, when I didn't meet his impossibly high standards, he would make me redo it, again and again, until my hands were trembling with fatigue and my mind was frayed at the edges. The day became a relentless gauntlet of humiliation and frustration, a slow, torturous descent into madness.

I was tasked with a sauce—simple, straightforward, the kind of thing I could do blindfolded and with one hand tied behind my back. But when I handed it to Caines, he didn't even taste it. He just glanced at it with those cold, calculating eyes of his and then—without a word—flung the pot across the kitchen. The clang of metal against metal was like a gunshot, reverberating through the air, a declaration of war.

"This is garbage," he snarled, and for the first time, I heard the true timbre of his voice—low, guttural, dripping with contempt. "Do it again. And this time, get it right."

My hands trembled as I started over, the weight of his gaze pressing down on me, crushing me, like the fucking lid of a cast-iron pot. I could feel the eyes of the other chefs, too—each one a pinpoint of silent judgment, a thousand knives aimed squarely at my back. There was no camaraderie here, no silent support, just cold, clinical indifference. And why would there be? This was a jungle, and Caines was the apex predator, and the rest of us were just the scraps.

The second attempt was no better. Nor was the third. Each time, Caines found something wrong—a hint of bitterness, a touch too much salt, the consistency not quite right. Each time, his fury grew, his words cutting deeper, sharper, until they were no longer words but scalpels, dissecting me, peeling back the layers until there was nothing left but a raw, quivering mass of nerves.

During a brief lull in the service, I found myself near him again, drawn to him like a moth to a flame, desperate for some kind of redemption. "Mr. Caines," I ventured, my voice barely steady, "I'd love to learn more about your techniques." It was a plea, thinly veiled as a request, a last-ditch effort to prove that I wasn't a complete waste of space.

He glanced at me, his expression inscrutable, a mask of indifference that gave nothing away. "Fuck off," he said, his tone dismissive, as if swatting away an annoying insect. The flick of his wrist as he turned away was the final insult, a gesture so casual, so dismissive, that it crushed any hope I had left.

So, I threw myself into my work with renewed determination, trying to absorb every bit of knowledge I could, hoping against hope that I could somehow claw my way back from the brink, that I could prove myself through sheer force of will.

I felt like he was now purposely sabotaging my work. At first, it was small—petty things, really—ingredients missing, pots moved, knives that were just a little too dull. Annoying, sure, but nothing I couldn't handle. Then it escalated. I would return to the kitchen, my entire prep station was a mess—my knives scattered, my mise en place ruined, as if someone had taken pleasure in destroying every ounce of my hard work. I knew it wasn't an accident. This was deliberate. This was calculated.

I tried to confront Caines about it, tried to explain that I was being set up, that someone was actively working against me. He barely looked up from his station, his focus unwavering, like a surgeon mid-operation. "Stop making excuses," he said, his voice colder than the stainless steel under his hands. "If you can't handle the pressure, you don't belong here."

But it wasn't just the sabotage. It was him. The way he watched me, the way his eyes followed my every move, like a predator stalking its prey. There was something in his gaze, something dark, twisted, almost sadistic. He wasn't just testing me; he was toying with me, pushing me, seeing how far he could go before I broke.

The breaking point came during service. It had been a long day—sixteen hours on my feet, pushing out dish after dish, the heat, the pressure, the constant fear of failing, of letting him down, gnawing at me like a rat in the walls. I was exhausted, my body ached, my mind was fraying at the edges. But there was no rest, no time to even catch a breath. The orders kept coming, relentless, each one a ticking time bomb waiting to explode in my face.

I was plating a dish when it happened. A slip, a mistake, the knife catching the edge of my palm, slicing through flesh and sinew like butter. Blood poured from the wound, a bright, garish red against the white of my chef's coat. I staggered back, my vision blurring, the world tilting on its axis. I could hear the others, the low murmurs, the gasps, but it was his voice that cut through the noise, sharp, cold, devoid of any empathy.

"You're bleeding on the food you fuck," he said, as if commenting on the weather. "Get out of my kitchen."

The words barely registered, lost in the haze of pain and exhaustion. I stumbled to the sink, blood dripping onto the floor, staining the pristine tiles. The other chefs watched, their eyes full of contempt, disgust. No one offered help. No one said a word. Just Michael Caines, standing there, his face a mask of cold indifference.

"You're weak," he said, his voice like a death sentence. "You're not cut out for this."

Something inside me snapped. All the fear, all the anger, all the humiliation that had been building up inside me like a pressure cooker finally exploded. I grabbed the nearest pot, its weight solid and reassuring in my hand, and hurled it at him with all the strength I had left. It missed, clanging against the wall, a hollow, empty sound. But it didn't matter. The act itself was enough.

I stood there, trembling, breath coming in ragged gasps, the adrenaline coursing through my veins, my vision swimming. Caines just stared at me, his eyes cold, calculating. For a moment, I thought he might actually do something, something violent, something final. But he didn't. He just smiled, that thin, predatory smile, and said the words that would haunt me for the rest of my life.

"Get out," he said, his voice low, dangerous. "You're done here."

As I cycled home, the wind biting at my cheeks, the hatred that had fuelled me throughout the day drained away, leaving behind only a creeping dread that gnawed at my insides. The high of meeting a culinary legend had curdled into something dark, something that burrowed into my brain like a parasite, feeding on my insecurities, my fears.

When I arrived home, my phone buzzed with a message from Jamie: "We need to talk about today. First thing tomorrow." The words were a death sentence, a crushing blow that left me reeling, my mind spinning with dark, spiralling thoughts. Fuck Michael Caines!!

The thrill of meeting a legend had twisted into a grim nightmare, a tale of humiliation and impending doom. The thought burrowed into my brain, a dark, relentless presence, as I lay in bed, staring at the ceiling. The encounter with Michael Caines, which had begun with such promise, now loomed over me like a spectre, a shadow that whispered of failure and disgrace.

The next morning, the kitchen felt colder, more hostile. The usual camaraderie was gone, replaced by whispered conversations and furtive glances that sliced through the air like knives. When the head chef finally called me into his office, the verdict was swift, brutal. Michael Caines had noted "Psychopathic" and "inadequate performance." The words were a death sentence, a crushing blow that left me reeling, my mind spinning with dark, spiralling thoughts.

I stumbled out of the office, the world around me blurring into a fog of despair. The hero I had idolised had become my executioner. The cycle to work, once a ritual of clarity, now felt like a descent into hell, each pedal stroke a reminder of my failure, of the dark, inescapable pit I had fallen into.

The day ended as it had begun, in darkness. The thrill of meeting a culinary legend had been warped into a tale of humiliation and dread. As I lay awake that night, the weight of the prosthetic handshake and Michael Caines' cold stare bore down on me, a relentless reminder that in the unforgiving world of high cuisine, there is no room for error.

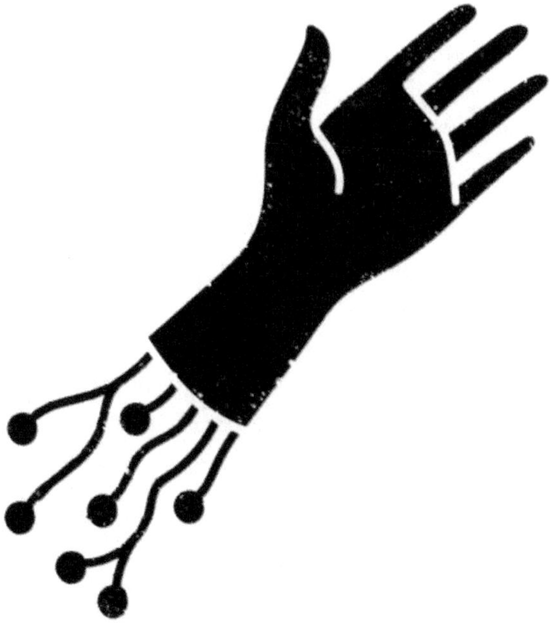

Chapter 18: Cooking For the Dark Lord

Today was different, the air was charged with an electric chill, a palpable sense of foreboding. Today was the day Ralph Fiennes would grace us with his presence—not as the affable actor, but as Ralph Fiennes—the embodiment of pure evil, the Dark Lord Voldemort himself. The thought of him set my nerves on edge, and I peddled faster, the icy wind stinging my face like a lash.

Anticipation gnawed at me; a dark thrill entwined with dread. Fiennes had requested a seemingly simple dish: lamb chops, garlic mashed potatoes, tender-stem broccoli, and red wine jus. Simple, yet in the shadow of the Dark Lord, they took on a sinister weight. This was no ordinary request; it felt like a dark summoning, a command to perform a culinary sacrament.

Entering the kitchen, the usual calmer of pots and pans was muted, overshadowed by the impending arrival of Fiennes. The staff moved with anxious energy, their eyes darting nervously toward the clock. I could feel it too—the oppressive weight of his presence, a dark spectre looming over the day's work.

Then he arrived. Ralph Fiennes, towering and imposing, exuding an aura of malevolence that was almost tangible. He was no longer the charming actor but the Dark Lord Voldemort. His eyes, cold and piercing, swept across the room, briefly meeting mine. There was a flicker of something dark and inscrutable, a silent promise of consequences.

"Mr. Fiennes," I managed to whisper, my voice barely a tremor. He acknowledged me with a nod, a faint, sinister smile curling his lips. His presence seemed to drain the warmth from the room, leaving an icy void in its wake.

The order was precise: lamb chops, garlic mashed potatoes, tender-stem broccoli, red wine jus. Simple yet tainted by the gravity of his presence. As I prepared the dish, every movement felt ritualistic, almost occult. Each chop of the knife, each stir of the pot was imbued with a dark significance.

Lamb Chops with Garlic Mashed Potatoes and Tender-Stem Broccoli

Ingredients:

For the Lamb Chops:

- 8 lamb chops, each an inch thick—each chop a tiny, blood-soaked testament to the art of the kill.

- 3 tablespoons olive oil—silky, smooth, a lubricant for the inevitable searing of flesh.

- 4 garlic cloves, minced—sharp, biting, an undertone of danger lurking beneath the surface.

- 2 teaspoons fresh rosemary, finely chopped—earthy, resilient, with a scent that clings to your memory like the aftermath of violence.

- 1 teaspoon fresh thyme, finely chopped—subtle, a whisper of green in a world painted red.

- Salt and freshly ground black pepper—to taste, because even in death, there must be balance.

- 1 cup red wine—for deglazing, if you're feeling particularly indulgent, like washing away sins in a sea of crimson.

For the Garlic Mashed Potatoes:

- 2 pounds Yukon Gold potatoes, peeled and cubed—starchy, golden, a reminder of innocence lost.

- 4 garlic cloves, peeled and whole—simmering, softening, losing their bite as they're drowned in boiling water.

- 4 tablespoons unsalted butter—rich, creamy, a false comfort in a dish born of violence.

- 1/2 cup heavy cream—thick, indulgent, the kind of luxury that hides the darkness beneath.

- Salt and freshly ground black pepper—to taste, because even comfort food has its edge.

- Fresh chives or parsley, chopped—for garnish, but only if you care to pretend there's still something pure left in this world.

For the Tender-stem Broccoli:

- 1 pound tender-stem broccoli—green, vibrant, the last gasp of life before it's plunged into boiling water.

- 1 tablespoon olive oil—another layer of slickness, coating the vegetables in a sheen of false promises.

- Salt and freshly ground black pepper—to taste, because even in simplicity, there's a hidden bitterness.

- 1 lemon, cut into wedges—for serving, if you desire a sharp, acidic contrast to the softness of flesh.

Instructions:

1. Prepare the Lamb Chops:

1. Preheat your oven to 400°F (200°C). The heat rises like the tension in a room just before the first blow is struck.

2. In a small bowl, mix olive oil, minced garlic, rosemary, thyme, salt, and black pepper. The aroma is intoxicating, a blend of earth and spice that masks the true nature of what's to come.

3. Rub the lamb chops with the mixture, your fingers sliding over the meat, ensuring it's well coated. Let them marinate, let them sit in their own demise, soaking up the Flavours of what's about to be done to them. Leave them at room temperature if you're in a hurry or let them chill in the refrigerator for up to 2 hours for a deeper, more intense flavour. Either way, their fate is sealed.

4. Heat a large ovenproof skillet over medium-high heat. The oil shimmers, the pan ready to accept its sacrifice. Sear the lamb chops for 2-3 minutes on each side, the flesh browning, the smell of seared meat filling the air—a scent that lingers, that claws at your senses and makes you remember things you'd rather forget.

5. If you're using it, deglaze the pan with red wine. Pour it in, watch as it hisses, as it steams, as the alcohol evaporates and leaves behind only the essence of the grape—a deep, dark reduction that whispers of sin.

6. Transfer the skillet to the preheated oven and roast for 8-10 minutes, or until the lamb chops reach your desired level of doneness. Let them rest for 5 minutes before serving, the juices redistributing, settling in, preparing for their final journey.

2. Prepare the Garlic Mashed Potatoes:

1. Place the potatoes and garlic cloves in a large pot. Cover with cold water and add a pinch of salt. The water boils, bubbles rising like unspoken thoughts, like secrets trying to escape.

2. Reduce the heat to medium and simmer for 15-20 minutes, or until the potatoes and garlic are tender, their resistance gone, softened by the relentless heat.

3. Drain well and return the potatoes and garlic to the pot, the steam rising like a ghost of what once was.

4. Mash the potatoes and garlic together until smooth. Stir in the butter and heavy cream until well combined. The mixture is creamy, comforting, but there's a sharpness to it, a bitterness that lingers just beneath the surface.

5. Garnish with chopped chives or parsley if desired, a green flourish that pretends to offer life in a dish that speaks only of death.

3. Prepare the Tender-stem Broccoli:

1. Bring a large pot of salted water to a boil. The water is clear, pure, but it will soon take on the essence of what you plunge into it.

2. Add the tender-stem broccoli and cook for 2-3 minutes, or until tender but still crisp. The green vibrancy dulls, the life cooked out of it, but there's still a snap, a final gasp of resistance.

3. Drain and toss with olive oil, salt, and black pepper. The seasoning clings to the vegetables, a final touch before they're consumed.

4. Optionally, serve with lemon wedges on the side, if you crave that sharp, acidic bite, that sting that reminds you of what it is to feel.

4. Serve:

1. Plate the lamb chops alongside a generous serving of garlic mashed potatoes and tender-stem broccoli. The colours are rich, vibrant, but there's a darkness to the dish, a sense that this is more than just a meal.

2. Drizzle any pan juices or red wine jus from the skillet over the lamb chops if desired. The sauce pools, thick and rich, a final indulgence in a dish that's all about indulgence.

3. Serve immediately, but don't just serve—revel in it. The lamb, the potatoes, the broccoli—it's more than just

food. It's a statement, a testament to the power of the kitchen, of what you can create, of what you can destroy.

The lamb chops sizzled ominously in the pan, their rich aroma mingling with the pungent scent of garlic. I mashed the potatoes until they were smooth and creamy, infused with the sharp tang of garlic. The broccoli steamed gently, its vibrant green a stark contrast to the dark richness of the red wine jus.

Plating the dish felt like a sacrificial rite. The plate was a dark altar, the food an offering to the Dark Lord. I carried it out, the weight of his gaze pressing down on me like an oppressive force.

Fiennes sat at the head of the table, his eyes tracking my every move with a predatory intensity. I could hear the whispers of doubt seeping though the hotel walls. I placed the dish before him, my hands trembling. He regarded the plate for a moment before beginning his inspection, I glanced down and swore blind I saw a snake slither from under his chair.

With deliberate, almost ceremonial grace, he cut into the lamb. The first bite was taken with a slow, deliberate savour, his eyes closing as he tasted. A soft, imperceptible sigh escaped his lips. When he opened his eyes again, they were even darker, more malevolent.

"Perfect," he murmured, his voice a velvety whisper that sent a shiver of fear through me. "Absolutely perfect."

A wave of relief washed over me, but it was tainted with a deep, dark unease. I had satisfied the Dark Lord, but at what cost? This was a true contrast from my experience with Micheal Caines! His gaze lingered, a silent, ominous promise of future demand.

The remainder of the evening passed in a blur. Fiennes dined with a predatory grace, each bite a calculated act of indulgence. As he finished, he stood, his eyes locking onto mine once more.

"Thank you," he said, his voice low and commanding. "You have a gift."

I nodded; throat dry, unable to speak. As he departed, the oppressive atmosphere lifted, but the memory of his gaze—the cold, malevolent presence—lingered.

The kitchen buzzed with muted excitement, but I felt a cold, hollow emptiness. I had cooked for the Dark Lord and emerged unscathed, yet the encounter left its mark. The chill in the air remained, a constant reminder of the dark ritual I had performed. The thrill of the encounter was overshadowed by a deep, gnawing dread, a reminder that in the world of high cuisine, as in the world of Voldemort, there was no room for error. The cost of failure was far too high, and the shadow of the Dark Lord seemed to loom over my every action, a dark spectre that would not easily be exorcised.

Chapter 19: The Teddy Bears Picnic

Time passes in a blur of relentless repetition, and the once-exhilarating thrill of cooking for celebrities has soured into a bitter nightmare. Their endless demands and quirks disrupt the rhythm of service, slowing us down, turning what should be a symphony of culinary artistry into a cacophony of despair. Weeks meld into months, months into years, all marked by the same grinding routine, the kitchen a pressure cooker of insanity.

Jamie, our visionary leader, had become consumed by a ravenous ambition, the pursuit of his dream: a Michelin star. This was his singular obsession, his unholy grail. His vision of culinary excellence twisted into an arrogant charade, heads held high, noses stuck up in the air. We believed ourselves worthy, yet we hadn't won a damn thing. This arrogance was a cancer, infecting the entire team, but I kept my head down and pressed on, determined to survive the madness.

The kitchen, once a construction of creativity and passion, had transformed into a battle of egos and shattered dreams. The once vibrant hum of activity now felt like the incessant drone of a hive on the brink of collapse. Each dish was no longer a work of art but a weapon in Jamie's war for recognition. The plating had to be flawless, the flavours an explosion of perfection, each bite a testament to his genius or so he believed. We were no longer chefs; we were soldiers in his private army, marching towards an ever-receding horizon of acclaim.

Jamie's eyes, once sparkling with inspiration, now burned with an unsettling intensity. His hands, which used to create masterpieces, had become instruments of tyranny, slamming down on countertops, pointing accusatory fingers, wielding knives with a precision that seemed more suited to a butcher than a chef. The pressure was palpable, a thick, suffocating fog that hung over the kitchen, seeping into our bones, our minds, our souls.

The celebrities, oblivious to our torment, paraded through the dining room like royalty. They devoured our creations with careless abandon, unaware of the blood, sweat, and tears that had gone into each meticulously crafted dish. Their compliments rang hollow, their criticisms stung like barbed wire. The joy of creation was dead, buried under layers of expectation and disappointment.

Yet, through it all, I persisted. My hands, scarred and calloused, continued to chop, sauté, and plate. My mind, though battered, remained focused. I clung to the hope that there was an end to this madness, that one day we would break free from Jamie's tyranny and find our own paths to redemption. But each day, as the cycle repeated, that hope grew dimmer.

Jamie's pursuit of the Michelin star had become a dark obsession, a madness that consumed him and threatened to devour us all. His perfectionism was a mask for his insecurities, his rage a cover for his fear of failure. He pushed us harder, demanding more, never satisfied, always chasing that elusive accolade.

Jamie and Scott, our sous chef, poured their energy into crafting the Michelin star menu. Scott, newly promoted and smugly revelling in his new status, collaborated with Jamie on new ideas. They brainstormed, argued, and finally conceived our pièce de resistance: our first proper ten-course tasting menu.

The Ten-Course Tasting Menu:

1. **Amuse-Bouche:** Truffle-infused duck liver pâté with micro-greens—A decadent prelude, a bite-sized introduction to excess, the liver's rich, silky texture corrupted by the earthy musk of truffle, adorned with micro-greens that feign innocence.

2. **Starter:** Beetroot-cured salmon with horseradish crème fraîche—Thin, translucent slices of salmon, their flesh stained a sinister crimson by the beetroot, the sharp bite of horseradish crème fraîche cutting through the sweetness, a dish that whispers of elegance while hinting at something far darker.

3. **Soup:** Wild mushroom consommé with parmesan crisps—A broth as dark as the forest floor, where the mushrooms were foraged, reduced to an essence of pure umami. The parmesan crisps float on the surface, fragile as autumn leaves, ready to disintegrate at the slightest touch.

4. **Fish Course:** Seared scallops with pea purée and crispy pancetta—The scallops, seared to perfection, their flesh quivering on the plate, are paired with a verdant smear of pea purée, as vibrant as fresh blood, and shards of pancetta, crisp as dried skin.

5. **Main Course:** Lamb chops with garlic mashed potatoes and tender-stem broccoli—The lamb, succulent and pink, a testament to careful butchery, lies atop a mound of garlic-infused mashed potatoes, creamy and rich, with tender-stem broccoli, the only nod to something green and living on the plate.

6. **Palate Cleanser:** Lemon sorbet with basil infusion—A momentary reprieve, a cold shock to the system, the sharpness of lemon sorbet, spiked with the subtle, almost medicinal note of basil, a cleansing of the palate before the descent continues.

7. **Poultry Course:** Quail with foie gras and black truffle jus—The quail, delicate bones and all, is paired with a sinful slab of foie gras, its richness tempered by a drizzle of black truffle jus, the scent intoxicating, almost overwhelming.

8. **Cheese Course:** Assorted artisanal cheeses with quince paste and crackers—A tableau of decay and preservation, the cheeses, veined with mould, their rinds thick and pungent, are served with a smear of quince paste, sweet and slightly rotten, alongside brittle crackers that snap under the weight of indulgence.

9. **Pre-Dessert:** Lavender panna cotta with honeycomb—A soothing lull before the final act, the panna cotta's delicate wobble betrays its fragility, infused with lavender's floral whisper, adorned with shards of honeycomb that shatter and dissolve.

10. **Dessert:** Dark chocolate fondant with raspberry coulis—The finale, a molten core of darkness, the fondant yielding to reveal its liquid heart, paired with a smear of raspberry coulis, as red and vibrant as spilled blood, the perfect, bitter end.

This is not merely a meal—it is an experience, a journey through the depths of excess and indulgence, each course a step further into the abyss, where pleasure and discomfort meld, where beauty is tinged with a sinister edge.

The race for the Michelin star was on. We were not the only contenders in town, and each service was an excruciating 15–16-hour marathon of menu development, perfection, and mass feeding. The pressure was relentless, the environment toxic.

Upper management, in their infinite wisdom, decided we chefs should also handle front-of-house duties once or twice a week. The front-of-house staff couldn't keep up with the new service style and were dropping like flies. Envy gnawed at me; they had escaped the hellish pit. My turn to surrender to the front-of-house duties came, and I was assigned to man the door.

The door. A simple threshold separating two worlds—one a carefully crafted illusion of civility, the other a cauldron of anarchy where knives flashed like lightning and curses erupted like thunder. I was stationed at this juncture, the gatekeeper between the madness of the kitchen and the farce of the dining room. Here, in the dimly lit, marble-clad lobby, I was the first face the customers would see. I, who had spent years honing my craft in the brutal trenches of the kitchen, now reduced to this—an ornamental figure, a mannequin in a crisp white coat with a smile as hollow as the souls of the diners I greeted.

The lobby was a world apart from the inferno behind the double doors. Polished marble floors gleamed under soft lighting, a stark contrast to the scorched pans and burnt fingers just a few feet away. The ambiance whispered of wealth and sophistication, masking the madness that lurked beneath the surface. It was a masquerade, and I was its unwilling participant, forced to play the part of the gracious host while my mind still reeled from the carnage of the kitchen.

Guests arrived in waves, each one a new assault on my dwindling patience. They sauntered in, exuding a sense of entitlement that clung to them like expensive aftershave. Designer clothes draped over bodies that had likely never known hunger, polished shoes that had never stepped in anything more offensive than a puddle. They greeted me with disdainful glances, their noses tilted skyward as if to avoid the stench of desperation that permeated the restaurant. My smile was a mask, a practiced facade that hid the simmering contempt I felt for these privileged creatures who were oblivious to the raw, brutal work that took place just beyond the flames of the double doors.

The irony of my position gnawed at me; a bitter pill lodged in my throat. Here I was, a chef who had trained to create culinary masterpieces, reduced to a glorified doorman. Each "Good evening, welcome to The Paramount" was a dagger to my pride, each polite nod a twist of the blade. I was a puppet, my strings pulled by the whims of upper management's misguided strategies, forced to dance to their tune while my real purpose—my passion—lay discarded in the flames of the kitchen.

Inside, Jamie and Scott were locked in their own battles, their relentless pursuit of perfection driving them to the brink of insanity. The kitchen was a war zone, the air thick with tension and the acrid scent of burning ambition. Every dish was a battlefield, every plate a soldier sent into the fray, its success or failure a matter of life and death. Jamie's voice cut through the din like a knife, barking orders with a fervour that bordered on manic. Scott, his now right-hand man, mirrored his intensity, their combined will a force of nature that swept through the team, leaving exhaustion and resentment in its wake.

But here, in the gilded cage of the lobby, I was trapped in a different kind of hell. The restaurant was a palace of opulence—marble floors, posh tables, chandeliers dripping with crystal, even a pianist playing soft, haunting melodies that only added to the surrealism oddly enough playing "Life on Mars". And there I was, a misfit, stationed at the glass door like a sentry at the gates of a lunatic asylum. Tonight's oddity was a table of five, but only four out of the five guests had arrived—well-dressed, middle-class women, clearly from old money.

"May I take your coats and seat you? I'll take the coat of your fifth guest when they arrive," I said, forcing my voice into a semblance of professionalism.

The women exchanged confused glances. "No, we're all here. No one is missing," one of them replied, her tone laced with condescension.

I looked again, counting the heads. Four. "Not a problem, I'll rearrange your table for four. Help yourselves to some drinks, and I will—"

"No! We are all here, all five of us!" The oldest of the women, a woman in her large forties with a face carved by years of privilege, pulled out a stuffed bear, immaculately dressed in a suit, shoes, a top hat, and a monocle.

"This is Sir Percival. He will be joining us this evening," she announced with a mixture of excitement and indignation, as if daring me to challenge the absurdity of her statement.

Stunned, I had no choice but to play along. This was the new normal, after all—a world where reality bent to the whims of the wealthy and the threat of any bad reviews,

I had to play along. I took Sir Percival's "coat," a small, tailored garment that felt unnervingly real in my hands, and seated him at the table as if he were a living, breathing guest. The bear ordered the ten-course tasting menu and a flute of wine (TEN FUCKING COURSES). I had to interact with it, describe each dish in detail, and endure the surreal spectacle of the owner tasting the bear's meal, offering two separate critiques—one for herself and one for Sir Percival, it was fucking insane.

The grandeur of the dining room only heightened the absurdity of the situation. The chandeliers cast a soft, golden glow over the tables, creating an almost ethereal atmosphere that contrasted sharply with the bizarre scene unfolding at table six. The women chatted animatedly, their voices a blend of refined accents and cultured laughter, as if nothing were amiss. Sir Percival sat poised at the head of the table, his beady eyes fixed forward, an eerie stillness in his plush demeanour.

The first course arrived—truffle-infused duck liver pâté with micro-greens. I set the plate in front of Sir Percival, my hands trembling slightly as I laid out the silverware. "For Sir Percival," I said, my voice betraying the slightest quiver of incredulity. The owner, her perfectly coiffed silver hair catching the light, meticulously cut a piece of pâté, lifting it to her lips with the same reverence one might show a sacred relic. She chewed thoughtfully, then turned to the bear.

"Delightful, isn't it, Sir Percival? Simply exquisite."

The evening progressed in a haze of surrealism. Beetroot-cured salmon with horseradish crème fraîche, wild mushroom consommé with parmesan crisps—each dish was presented to the bear with the same solemnity, each one tasted and critiqued by his owner with the gravitas of a Michelin inspector. "The salmon has a lovely balance of sweetness and tang, don't you think, Sir Percival?" she would say, nodding as if the bear's silence were a profound agreement.

Other diners glanced over occasionally, their curiosity piqued by the odd sight, but they quickly returned to their own meals, as if the presence of a stuffed bear dining alongside them was just another quirk in a world gone mad.

I made a decision—one born out of some twisted desire for destruction, a need to see chaos unfold before my eyes. I chose to inform our executive chef about this... this guest. As I approached Jamie, I could feel the unease slithering through me, my stomach churning with a sick anticipation. For a moment, I hesitated, my gaze falling to the stained tiles beneath my feet, as though the truth lay hidden somewhere in the cracks. Then, swallowing my fear, I forced the words out.

"Chef," I began, my voice a fragile thread barely holding together amidst the cacophony of clanging pans and the violent sizzle of meat scorching on the grill. "Table six... they, uh, have a special request."

Jamie's head jerked up, his eyes narrowing into icy slits as they locked onto mine. "Spit it out," he growled, his tone laced with a venom that sent a shiver crawling down my spine.

"It's... it's for the bear, Chef," I stammered, feeling the heat of embarrassment crawl up my neck, staining my cheeks red.

For a moment, there was nothing. Silence. A vacuum in which time ceased to move. The symphony of the kitchen faded into a distant hum as Jamie processed my words, his brow furrowing, lips twitching in disbelief. Then, like a storm cloud darkening the horizon, something inside him snapped.

"What the Fuck?" he uttered, his voice dropping to a dangerous whisper, the kind that precedes an explosion.

"The bear, Chef," I repeated, my voice quivering, barely audible now. "You're cooking for a stuffed bear, Sir Percival. They ordered the ten-course tasting menu... for him."

Jamie stared at me, his eyes widening, uncomprehending. His mouth opened, closed, struggling to form words, to grasp the absurdity of what I was telling him. And then, like a dam breaking, the floodwaters of his fury burst forth.

"Are you fucking kidding me?" he roared, his voice ricocheting off the stainless-steel walls, drowning out the hiss of boiling pots and the crackle of searing flesh. The kitchen froze, Scott, the twins, Matthew, Chantel, every set of eyes locking onto Jamie as he detonated with a fury none of us had ever witnessed.

"You mean to tell me," He continued, his voice crescendoing into a fever pitch, "that I've been slaving away in this goddamn kitchen all night, pouring every ounce of my blood, sweat, and soul into these dishes—for a fucking stuffed bear?"

His face flushed a violent shade of red, the veins on his neck bulging grotesquely, his fists clenched so tightly his knuckles bleached white. He was teetering on the precipice, a volcano seconds away from a catastrophic eruption.

"I create masterpieces!" he bellowed, slamming his fist onto the counter with such force that the plates rattled, threatening to shatter. "Works of art! And you're telling me my food is being fed to some goddamn child's toy?"

I stepped back, the pulse of fear thudding in my temples, but it was too late. Jamie had crossed the threshold, and there was no reeling him back. With the ferocity of a hurricane, he barrelled through the double doors, storming into the dining room like a man possessed. Conversations died mid-sentence, every head snapping toward the wild-eyed chef who had just exploded into the room, his rage palpable, radiating off him like heat from a furnace.

He homed in on table six, where the women sat, draped in their finery, blissfully ignorant of the tempest they had unleashed. Sir Percival, the object of their misguided adoration, sat at the head of the table, his beady eyes staring vacantly ahead, his plush body dressed in a suit and monocle that now seemed grotesque in the face of Jamie's seething fury. It was too much, the final straw that sent Jamie spiralling over the edge.

"You!" he spat, pointing a trembling finger at the bear, his voice vibrating with unchecked rage. "You're the one we are serving? You're the one eating my food?"

The women gaped at him in shock, their faces painted with confusion, tinged with fear, but Jamie's focus was singular, his gaze fixed on the bear with a murderous intensity. "Do you know what I've put into those dishes?" he ranted, his voice climbing higher, every word laced with hatred. "The hours, the sweat, the fucking perfection? And you—you sit there, in your little suit, pretending to appreciate it? You're mocking me! Mocking everything I stand for!"

One of the women opened her mouth to speak, perhaps to placate, but Jamie wasn't listening. He snatched the plate in front of Sir Percival—a dish of pan-seared duck with cherry reduction, its presentation flawless—and hurled it across the room. The plate shattered against the wall with a deafening crash, the sound splintering the silence like a gunshot.

"You think this is a joke?" he screamed; his voice hoarse with the force of his outburst. "You think I'm some kind of clown, cooking for your amusement? Well, fuck you! Fuck all of you!"

The dining room erupted into chaos. Guests leapt from their seats, gasps of shock and fear slicing through the air as Jamie's tirade continued, unchecked, unhinged. He seized Sir Percival by the arm, yanking the bear from its seat, holding it aloft like a sacrificial offering.

"You think you're better than me?" he hissed, his voice dripping with venom. "You think you can sit there and judge my food, like you're some kind of god? Well, let's see how you like it now!"

With a final, violent gesture, he flung the bear across the room. It sailed through the air, crashing into a nearby table before slumping to the floor in a pathetic heap, its monocle askew, its little hat tumbling off. The women screamed, one fainting, another rushing forward to retrieve the bear, cradling it as though it were a wounded child.

Finally, the staff intervened, pulling Jamie back, restraining him as he thrashed, still shouting obscenities, his voice raw, his face twisted into a mask of rage and despair. He fought against them like a caged animal, his sanity unraveling, his humanity lost in the flames of his ego.

But it was over. The damage had been done. Jamie was dragged out of the dining room, his screams echoing through the hallway, fading into the distance as the doors swung shut behind him. The guests were left in stunned silence, the room littered with the wreckage of a chef's shattered pride and a stuffed bear lying lifeless on the floor, its dignity stripped away, its purpose obliterated.

As the reality of what had just transpired began to settle in, I felt a cold emptiness gnaw at the edges of my consciousness. The madness that had long simmered beneath the surface had finally broken through, reducing the carefully curated facade of the restaurant to rubble in a single, catastrophic explosion of fury. The night had descended into a twisted nightmare, and deep down, I knew that nothing would ever be the same again.

Sir Percival's Absurd Delight

Ingredients:

For the Amuse-Bouche:

- 100g duck liver pâté—smooth, rich, a perfect blend of decadence and cruelty.

- 1 small truffle, finely shaved—its earthy aroma, a fragrant whisper of wealth and indulgence.

- 50g micro-greens—delicate, almost too perfect, a façade of life atop a foundation of death.

For the Starter:

- 200g beetroot-cured salmon—vibrant red, a stark reminder of the thin line between life and death.

- 50g horseradish crème fraîche—sharp, biting, a jolt to the senses that lingers just long enough to remind you that pain can be exquisite.

For the Soup:

- 500ml wild mushroom consommé—dark, earthy, the essence of the forest distilled into liquid form.

- 50g parmesan crisps—crunchy, brittle, a fragile mask over the deep, unyielding darkness below.

For the Fish Course:

- 4 large scallops—seared to perfection, their tender flesh a reminder that the sea hides as many horrors as it does delights.

- 100g pea purée—bright green, smooth, the only softness in a world of sharp edges.

- 50g crispy pancetta—salty, crispy, the last remnants of what was once life, now reduced to garnish.

For the Main Course:

- 2 lamb chops—grilled, charred, their juices running like the lifeblood of a sacrifice on the altar of culinary perfection.

- 200g garlic mashed potatoes—creamy, comforting, a deceptive softness masking the reality of their creation.

- 100g tender-stem broccoli—green, vibrant, a fleeting attempt at purity in a meal steeped in indulgence.

For the Palate Cleanser:

- 2 scoops lemon sorbet—cold, sharp, a cleanse that doesn't quite wash away the sins committed in the courses before.

- 5 basil leaves—fresh, green, a flicker of life that's too fleeting to matter.

For the Poultry Course:

- 1 quail—small, delicate, its roasted flesh a cruel mockery of innocence.

- 50g foie gras—rich, unctuous, a testament to the excesses of the privileged.

- 1 black truffle, thinly sliced—its aroma, a final note of decadence, its presence, a quiet assertion of dominance.

For the Cheese Course:

- Assorted artisanal cheeses—brie, blue cheese, aged cheddar—each one a testament to the art of decay.

- 50g quince paste—sweet, sticky, a futile attempt to mask the sharpness of the cheeses.

- Crackers—crisp, dry, a necessary vehicle for the indulgence that follows.

For the Pre-Dessert:

- 200ml lavender panna cotta—soft, yielding, a floral escape that lulls you into a false sense of security.

- 50g honeycomb—sweet, brittle, its golden hues hiding the darkness within.

For the Dessert:

- 2 dark chocolate fondants—baked until their outer shell cracks, revealing the molten core within, a final reminder that darkness can be sweet, even as it consumes you.

- 50g raspberry coulis—red, vibrant, a sharp contrast that cuts through the richness with a reminder of the fragility of life.

Instructions

Amuse-Bouche:

1. Plate a small portion of duck liver pâté. Let it sit there, mocking the very idea of moderation.

2. Garnish with finely shaved truffle, its scent a seductive lure, and a small handful of micro-greens, their fragile forms trembling under the weight of the pâté.

Starter:

1. Slice the beetroot-cured salmon thinly, each slice a ribbon of life's blood laid out on the plate.

2. Add a dollop of horseradish crème fraîche on the side, the white purity a stark contrast to the deep red of the salmon, as if trying to cleanse the sins it accompanies.

Soup:

1. Heat the wild mushroom consommé until it reaches the perfect temperature, a simmering cauldron of darkness.

2. Serve in a bowl with parmesan crisps on the side, the brittle texture a reminder that even the strongest things can be broken.

Fish Course:

1. Sear the scallops in a hot pan until their surfaces are golden brown, their interiors tender, almost as if they are pleading for mercy.

2. Plate them on a bed of pea purée, the green brightness a last gasp of life, and sprinkle with crispy pancetta, the final nails in the coffin of what once was.

Main Course:

1. Grill the lamb chops to your preferred doneness, their juices spilling out like confessions under interrogation.

2. Serve with garlic mashed potatoes and tender-stem broccoli, the two sides of this culinary coin—one soft, one hard, both necessary.

Palate Cleanser:

1. Scoop lemon sorbet into small bowls, the coldness searing through the taste buds, a sharp jolt back to reality.

2. Garnish with finely chopped basil leaves, the fleeting green that offers a moment of respite before the plunge back into darkness.

Poultry Course:

1. Roast the quail until its skin is crisp, its flesh tender, and serve alongside foie gras, a dish as rich as it is controversial.

2. Garnish with thin slices of black truffle, the final act of indulgence before the inevitable end.

Cheese Course:

1. Arrange the assorted cheeses on a platter, each one a work of art in the medium of decay.

2. Serve with quince paste and crackers, the sweetness and crunch attempting, but failing, to mask the truth beneath.

Pre-Dessert:

1. Prepare lavender panna cotta and allow it to set, its softness a false promise of serenity.

2. Garnish with honeycomb pieces, their golden hue a deceptive illusion of warmth and safety.

Dessert:

1. Bake the dark chocolate fondants until the outside is set and the inside is molten, the final act in this performance, a sweet darkness that beckons.

2. Serve with a drizzle of raspberry coulis, the red stain a reminder of the blood that has been shed, both metaphorically and literally, in the pursuit of this meal.

This multi-course meal reflects the absurdity and the high stakes of the pursuit for culinary perfection. Each dish symbolises a step in the dark comedy of the kitchen's life, culminating in the surreal dining experience of Sir Percival, the stuffed bear. The dishes are crafted with meticulous care, echoing the exaggerated elegance and unyielding standards of a Michelin-star chase, yet they carry an undercurrent of whimsical absurdity that mirrors the bizarre reality of serving gourmet meals to a plush toy.

Chapter 20: The Swan

It's 10:00 AM. I'm standing outside The Swan, a sister hotel to The Paramount, under a fog-draped sky. The ivy-covered walls and the serene lake give it an air of tranquillity, but beneath this beauty, I sense a deeper, sinister energy. My hand, gripping a cup of black coffee, is steady despite the lack of sleep. The Swan is going to be different; I tell myself. But not in the way I think.

The Swan greets me with an unsettling stillness, an oppressive silence that seems to seep through the cracks of its grandiose facade. The heavy oak doors swing open with a groan, almost as if the building itself resents my presence. The air inside is thick, stifling, laden with the cloying scent of polished wood and something else—something metallic, like the faintest whisper of blood on steel. It's not a smell one easily forgets, even if most people would deny its existence.

I step onto the burgundy carpet, the fibres so dense they swallow the sound of my footsteps. It's as if the hotel wants to erase me, to absorb me into its fabric without a trace. The ceilings stretch unnervingly high above me, looming, almost mocking in their grandeur. They make you feel insignificant, a speck in the vast, calculated opulence of The Swan.

To the left, a massive fireplace crackles quietly, its flames licking at the shadows like a hungry beast. The fire casts long, sinister shadows on the walls, which are adorned with portraits—gaunt, aristocratic faces that track your every move with hollow, dead eyes. The furniture is the kind that invites you to sink into it, to lose yourself in its plush, velvety embrace. But there's something off, something too precise about the way each chair, each table, is placed as if they're part of some carefully orchestrated charade, waiting for their cue to ensnare the unsuspecting.

The reception desk dominates the room, a dark slab of mahogany that gleams like a polished tombstone. Behind it, the receptionist—a woman with a smile that is as hollow as the eyes of those portraits—greets me. Her voice is sweet, almost syrupy, but there's a deadness behind it, a practiced warmth that feels like a lie she's told so many times it's lost all meaning. Her eyes—those cold, dead eyes—give nothing away. She's a part of this place, an extension of its veneer, her humanity stripped away, layer by layer, until all that's left is a shell.

I walk down the corridor to my room, the hallway a dimly lit tunnel that stretches on forever, lined with identical doors. Each one is marked with a tarnished brass number, the kind that belongs in a Victorian asylum. The sconces on the walls cast a sickly, yellowed light, bathing everything in an almost sepia tone. It feels like I'm walking through a photograph from a time when people still believed in ghosts, when they still feared the things that lurked in the dark corners of their mind.

The carpet here is thicker, quieter, as if designed to muffle more than just the sound of footsteps. It feels like I'm sinking with every step, the floor swallowing me up, pulling me deeper into the bowels of this twisted place.

The air is heavier here, oppressive, pressing down on me like a weight I can't shake. It's not just the decor, the architecture—it's the feeling that this place is alive, that it's watching me, sizing me up, waiting for me to make a wrong move, the same feelings as The Paramount. And here I am, sent to this place by the mother hotel, to dive deep into assisting the already dyeing chefs that inhabit this place.

The staff here are beyond eccentric—they're insane. Grace, the head waitress, is perhaps the most unsettling. She's not just a little odd; she's clinically disturbed. The first time I saw her, she was standing in the middle of the dining room, her back to me, talking softly to the air. Her voice was low, almost melodic, as if she were comforting a child, or maybe coaxing a confession from a reluctant soul. I approached her, curious, and she turned slowly, her eyes unfocused, pupils dilated. She looked right through me, as if I wasn't even there, and continued her conversation with the empty chair in front of her.

"Yes, I understand," she whispered, nodding slowly. "He won't bother you anymore. I'll make sure of it."

I followed her gaze, but the chair was empty, save for the shadows that danced on the polished wood. For a moment, I felt a chill creep up my spine, like a cold, invisible hand resting on my shoulder. The rational part of my mind screamed at me to snap her out of it, to remind her that there was no one there, but something about the intensity in her eyes, the absolute conviction, stopped me. This wasn't some harmless quirk; this was madness, deep and consuming.

Grace spends hours like this, holding entire conversations with people who don't exist. Her expressions change as she listens, her responses tailored to the invisible spector she seems to see. Sometimes she laughs softly, a sound that sends shivers through the other staff members, who give her a wide berth, careful not to cross whatever line she's drawn between the living and the dead. Other times, she looks distressed, even tearful, her hands wringing together as if trying to hold on to whatever thread of sanity she has left. The guests don't notice—or maybe they do, but like everything else at The Swan, they choose to ignore it, to pretend it's just part of the atmosphere.

Then there's Paul, the maintenance guy. His obsession with alien abductions is legendary. He's convinced that guests are regularly taken by extraterrestrials. He keeps a log in his workshop, detailing the so-called "abductions" with a meticulousness that's almost admirable. Almost. His workshop is a shrine to his paranoia, walls plastered with grainy photos of blurry lights in the sky, clippings from tabloid articles about "close encounters," and hand-drawn diagrams of spacecraft. Strings of red yarn connect various photos and notes, creating a chaotic web of connections that only make sense to him.

Paul talks about Them in hushed tones, his voice trembling with a mix of fear and reverence. He insists that the abductions always happen after midnight, when the hotel is quiet, when the guests are vulnerable. He'll corner you in the hallway, his breath smelling faintly of cigarettes and cheap whiskey, and whisper his theories in your ear, his eyes darting around as if the very act of speaking could summon Them.

"They're watching us," he'll say, his voice barely audible. "They know everything. I've seen the signs. I have proof."

He'll pull out his logbook, flipping through the pages with fevered urgency, showing you the entries—names, dates, times, detailed descriptions of guests who supposedly disappeared, only to return hours later, dazed, confused, with no memory of where they had been. "See?" he insists, jabbing a finger at a particular entry. "They always take the ones who order the Hunter's Chicken. It's like a signal, a trigger. They know who to take."

His eyes are wild, bloodshot from lack of sleep, his hands shaking slightly as he clutches the book to his chest like a talisman. He's created an entire mythology around these abductions, each detail more elaborate than the last, each theory more convoluted. And yet, despite the sheer insanity of it all, there's a part of you that almost believes him, that feels the pull of his madness.

The other staff members avoid him as much as possible, not out of fear, but out of a desire to maintain their own tenuous grip on reality. No one wants to get too close to Paul, to be drawn into his world of conspiracies and delusions. But sometimes, late at night, when the wind howls outside and the lights flicker, you can almost hear it—the hum of something unnatural, something not of this world. And you start to wonder, just for a moment, if maybe Paul is right, if maybe there's something out there, watching, waiting.

Then there's Anna, the sous-chef, who obsessively counts salt grains, convinced that if she gets the number wrong, something terrible will happen. Every morning, she spends an hour in the pantry, bent over a bowl, tweezers in hand, counting out exactly 1,024 grains of salt. Her eyes are red-rimmed, her fingers trembling slightly as she moves each grain with precise, deliberate care. She doesn't speak during this ritual, her lips pressed into a thin line, her focus absolute. The rest of us try not to interrupt her, knowing that any disturbance could send her into a tailspin of panic.

But it's Carl, the night porter, who takes the cake. He's convinced that the hotel is built on ancient burial grounds, and that the spirits of the dead are restless, angry, seeking vengeance. Every night, he patrols the halls, sprinkling salt and muttering Latin incantations under his breath. His face is gaunt, hollow-eyed from years of sleepless nights, his hands raw and chapped from handling the coarse salt. He claims to hear the spirits whispering to him, telling him their secrets, their desires. He's a man on the edge, teetering between this world and the next.

I've caught him staring at me more than once, his eyes burning with a fevered intensity that makes my skin crawl. He'll sidle up to me, his voice low and conspiratorial, and ask if I've seen anything unusual, if

I've felt a presence in my room, if I've noticed the temperature drop suddenly. And then he'll lean in closer, his breath hot and sour against my neck, and whisper, "They're watching us. They know we're here."

It's hard to keep my sanity in a place like this, surrounded by people who've lost theirs. I start to wonder if maybe they're right, if maybe the dead really do walk these halls, if maybe the aliens are watching, waiting to strike. I start to question my own perceptions, my own grip on reality. I start to see things out of the corner of my eyeshadows that move when they shouldn't, lights that flicker for no reason. I hear whispers in the dead of night, soft and sibilant, just on the edge of hearing.

I tell yourself it's all in your head, that I'm imagining things, that the stress is getting to me. But deep down, I know that The Swan is a place of madness, a place where the line between reality and delusion is blurred, where the insane become the norm, and the sane are the true outcasts. And I start to wonder, just for a moment, if maybe I'm the one who's lost touch, if maybe I've crossed that line without even realising it.

And as Grace continues her whispered conversations with the dead, as Paul meticulously logs his imaginary abductions, as Anna counts her salt grains, and as Carl wards off vengeful spirits, I find yourself slipping, just a little bit further into the darkness, into the madness that has consumed them all.

One night, I got lost in what I can only describe as a labyrinth of animal head trophies. It's a hidden part of the hotel, a corridor so rarely spoken of that I began to doubt it even existed, as if it were a whispered rumour between the walls themselves. The entrance is unmarked, a narrow passage behind a heavy oak door that groans on its hinges, as if protesting the intrusion. I pushed it open, the sound reverberating down the darkened hallway, and stepped inside, drawn by a morbid curiosity, a need to uncover whatever secrets The Swan had tucked away in its decaying bowels.

The first thing that hit me was the smell—thick and cloying, a sickly-sweet blend of aged wood, dust, and something else, something more primal, more decayed, like the faint scent of old blood that refuses to fade. The air was stifling, as if it hadn't moved in years, trapped in the corridor along with the memories of whatever horrors had taken place here. My footsteps echoed unnaturally loud against the cold stone floor; the sound swallowed almost immediately by the oppressive silence.

The walls were lined with the mounted heads of animals, their glassy eyes fixed in eternal stares that seemed to follow me as I moved deeper into the corridor. Deer, boars, even a massive bear loomed above me, their expressions frozen in a grotesque mockery of life. Their fur was matted and dull, their antlers chipped and yellowed with age. Each one was mounted with care, positioned at varying heights, as if placed there by someone with an eye for macabre aesthetics, someone who found beauty in death.

As I wandered further, the hallway began to twist and turn, narrowing and widening unpredictably, disorienting me, playing tricks on my senses. The walls seemed to close in, the ceiling pressing down, making it harder to breathe. I tried to keep track of my path, counting the steps, noting the turns, but the corridor was a maze, a shifting labyrinth designed to confuse and trap. Every turn led to another set of dead eyes staring down at me, unblinking, judging. The floor creaked underfoot, as if the building itself was alive, its bones groaning in protest of my presence.

The further I went, the more oppressive the air became, thickening with each step, until it felt like I was wading through molasses. My skin prickled with sweat, a cold clamminess that seeped into my bones. The smell grew stronger, more rancid, a putrid mixture of decay and something else, something I couldn't quite place, something animalistic and raw. I could feel the walls closing in, the space tightening around me, squeezing the air from my lungs.

The mounted heads seemed to grow larger, more menacing, their eyes glittering in the dim light, almost alive. I could swear I saw one of the deer heads blink, its eyes narrowing in silent accusation. The bear's mouth, a gaping maw of yellowed teeth, seemed to twist into a snarl, the muscles in its frozen face tightening in a grotesque parody of life. I felt their gaze boring into me, a thousand dead eyes watching my every move, judging, condemning.

Time lost meaning in that twisted corridor. Minutes stretched into hours, or maybe it was the other way around. I lost track of how long I wandered; the passage of time distorted by the surreal nightmare I found myself trapped in. Every turn led to another dead end, another set of accusing eyes, another wave of suffocating dread. I could hear my heartbeat in my ears, a frantic, irregular drumbeat that matched the rising panic in my chest.

At one point, I stopped in front of a particularly large set of antlers, my breath hitching as I realised that I had seen this exact set before, several turns back. The realisation hit me like a sledgehammer: I was going in circles. The hallway, this entire labyrinth, was toying with me, leading me back on myself, trapping me in an endless loop of fear and confusion. I turned on my heel, trying to retrace my steps, but the walls seemed to shift, the turns all wrong, leading me further into the maze, deeper into the belly of this grotesque beast.

The stench of decay grew stronger, almost unbearable now, clinging to the back of my throat, filling my lungs with every breath. My hands brushed against the walls, rough and splintered, as if the very structure was rotting away, decomposing around me. I could feel the panic rising, clawing its way up my throat, a desperate need to escape, to break free from this suffocating nightmare.

And then, just when I thought I might never find my way out, I saw her...—the woman in the wheelchair. The one from Tempest Street, my inner nightmare!! with the vacant eyes and the hollow cheeks. Only now, she wasn't just a figment of, my twisted mind. She was here, in front of me, sitting in that rusting wheelchair, her posture unnaturally stiff, her hands resting in her lap, pale and still as death.

She's followed me here.

My breath catches in my throat, a cold sweat prickling the back of my neck. I blink, hard, but she's still there, her eyes fixed on me with a stare that feels more like a command than a gaze. The air around her seems to ripple, like heat waves off asphalt, distorting the space between us, making it hard to focus, hard to think.

I take a step back, my heart pounding, the same drumbeat of fear that had thudded in my chest when I was lost in that labyrinth of animal heads. The corridor feels narrower, the walls closing in, the ceiling pressing down. My lungs constrict, the air thick and suffocating.

She doesn't move. Just sits there, her eyes boring into me, stripping away any semblance of sanity I've managed to cling to in this place. Her lips are slightly parted, as if she's about to speak, but no sound comes out. Instead, the silence between us deepens, thickens, until it's almost tangible, a suffocating blanket of dread that wraps itself around my throat.

I try to tell myself that it's just a trick of the light, a figment of my imagination twisted by the madness that's seeped into every corner of this cursed hotel. But deep down, I know that's a lie. She's real, as real as the stench of shit that lingers in the air, as real as the cold sweat dripping down my spine.

I back away slowly, my eyes never leaving hers, as if breaking the connection will release whatever hold she has on me. But with every step I take, she seems to loom larger, more present, her stillness a stark contrast to the racing thoughts in my head, the pounding of my heart. I can feel her pulling me in, her presence wrapping around me like a noose, tightening with each breath.

Finally, I break free, turning on my heel and stumbling down the corridor, the echo of my footsteps a frantic rhythm in the oppressive silence. But even as I flee, I can feel her eyes on my back, that unblinking, dead stare that follows me, haunts me, no matter where I go.

I don't stop running until I'm back in my room, the door slammed shut behind me, the lock turned with shaking hands. But even here, in the relative safety of these four walls, I can still feel her presence, just outside the door, waiting, watching, her image burned into my mind, a permanent scar left by the darkness that pervades this place.

She's followed me here, and I know, deep in the pit of my stomach, that there's no escaping her. The hotel, with all its twisted corridors and hidden horrors, has woven her into its very fabric, a ghost that refuses to be laid to rest, a spectre that will haunt me until I finally lose myself completely in the madness that she and this place demand.

And so, I sit, waiting for the next time I see her, knowing it's only a matter of time before she finds me again, before her cold, empty gaze consumes me entirely.

I didn't get any sleep that night……….

The guests are no better, their demands insatiable. They order Hunter's Chicken, every single one of them, their eyes glazed as they repeat the request like automatons. "Hunter's Chicken," they say, their voices devoid of inflection. It's as if the dish holds some hypnotic power over them, compelling them to order it again and again. Their eyes bore into me, judging, waiting for me to fail.

The orders pile up, a never-ending stream of slips that taunt me. Each one is a ticking time bomb, a potential disaster. The pressure is unbearable, the kitchen a cacophony of clanging pans, sizzling meat, and shouted commands. My hands move on autopilot, slicing, dicing, plating, but my mind is elsewhere, lost in the chaos.

The stress is a physical presence, a weight that presses down on my shoulders, making it hard to breathe. Every mistake is magnified, every slip-up a catastrophe. The diners are vultures, waiting for me to falter, to give them an excuse to complain, to demand a refund. Their eyes bore into me, their whispers a constant reminder of my failure.

The nights are the worst. After the last plate is sent out, the silence is deafening. The kitchen, once a hive of activity, is now a tomb. The whispers and creaks of the old building seem louder, more insistent. I can hear the ghosts Grace speaks to, feel the eyes of the mounted trophies watching me. The walls close in, the darkness pressing down, suffocating.

Sleep is elusive, my dreams haunted by the faces of the guests, the dead eyes of the animal trophies, the whispered conversations of Grace. I wake up in a cold sweat, my heart racing, the fear a constant companion. The Swan is a prison, a place of madness and despair. Each day is a battle, the pressure mounting with every order, the madness creeping closer, ready to consume me.

Every guest orders the same thing—Hunter's Chicken. It's uncanny, like they've been programmed. We joke about it, but the laughter is hollow. The pervasive obsession with this dish is unnerving, a ritualistic demand that turns our already chaotic kitchen into a nightmarish assembly line. I can't escape it. Every time I close my eyes, I see chicken breasts, feel the slick of olive oil, hear the sizzle of bacon. It's like the entire hotel has been hypnotised and I'm the unwilling executor of their culinary desires.

Hunter's Chicken Recipe

Ingredients:

- 4 chicken breasts: Firm, plump, perfectly symmetrical. If they're not, discard them. I can't stand imperfections.

- Salt and pepper to taste: Not too much, not too little. Precision is key. Measure with care, a delicate balance between flavour and excess.

- 1 tablespoon olive oil: The finest, cold-pressed. Anything less is unacceptable. The rich, golden hue must be pure, unmarred by impurities.

- 1 onion, finely chopped: Every piece uniform, each cut precise. The knife glides through the flesh, leaving behind perfect cubes. Anything less would be chaos.

- 2 garlic cloves, minced: Sharp, pungent, overwhelming. The scent clings to your fingers, a reminder of its presence long after it's been reduced to nothing.

- 200g button mushrooms, sliced: Thin, almost translucent. They must be identical, indistinguishable from one another, a collective of perfection.

- 200ml chicken stock: Homemade, of course. Store-bought is an abomination. Simmered for hours, rich and golden, a liquid essence of life.

- 100ml white wine: Not just any wine—a crisp, dry Sauvignon Blanc. The bouquet should be light, floral, with a hint of acidity that lingers on the tongue.

- 2 tablespoons tomato paste: Thick, concentrated, a deep red that borders on blood. Stir it slowly, let it dissolve, merging with the stock, infusing it with colour and depth.

- 1 tablespoon Worcestershire sauce: Dark, complex, a blend of Flavors that hints at something darker, something hidden. It's essential, though no one quite knows why.

- 100g smoked bacon, diced: Crisp, salty, its fat rendering into the pan, infusing the air with its intoxicating aroma. Dice it precisely, each piece a perfect square.

- Fresh thyme for garnish: The final touch, a sprig of green, vibrant against the rich browns and reds of the dish. It's not just garnish—it's a statement.

Instructions:

1. Preheat the oven to 180°C (350°F): The temperature must be exact. No fluctuations. Set the dial, watch the numbers rise, wait for perfection.

2. Season the chicken breasts with salt and pepper: This is a ritual, a meticulous process. The grains of salt must be evenly distributed, the pepper freshly ground. Rub it into the flesh, feel the texture beneath your fingers. The chicken should be cold, firm, but not too cold—a subtle resistance when pressed.

3. Heat the olive oil in a pan and sear the chicken until golden brown: The oil shimmers, nearly smoking. The chicken hits the pan with a sizzle, the sound sharp, almost violent. The skin tightens, browns, the aroma rising as it sears. Turn it, carefully. No tears, no uneven spots. It must be golden, flawless.

4. Transfer to an ovenproof dish: The dish is white, pristine. The chicken lies in it, waiting, glistening with oil, the golden skin a promise of what's to come.

5. In the same pan, sauté the onions, garlic, and mushrooms until soft: The onion hits the hot oil, its

sharpness softening, the garlic following soon after, releasing its pungent scent. The mushrooms are next, their moisture evaporating in the heat, leaving behind a rich, earthy aroma. Stir constantly. Nothing must burn, nothing must stick. The timing is crucial—too long, and it's ruined.

6. Add the chicken stock, white wine, tomato paste, and Worcestershire sauce: Pour them in, one by one. The stock bubbles, the wine hisses, the tomato paste dissolves, staining the liquid a deep, unsettling red. The Worcestershire sauce swirls through it all, darkening the mixture, adding a complexity that's almost sinister. Stir well, watching the colours blend, the aromas mingle.

7. Add the diced bacon and cook until crispy: The bacon sizzles, its fat rendering into the sauce, the edges curling, turning a deep golden brown. Stir it in, letting it coat the chicken, the sauce thickening as it simmers, rich and glossy.

8. Pour the mixture over the chicken breasts in the ovenproof dish: The liquid envelops the chicken, seeping into every crevice, covering it completely. The smell is intoxicating, a blend of wine, garlic, and bacon. It's perfect. Almost.

9. Bake in the preheated oven for 25-30 minutes, until the chicken is cooked through: Place the dish in the oven, close the door, and wait. The heat penetrates the chicken, the sauce bubbles, thickening further, the aroma filling the kitchen. Check the time. Exactly 25 minutes. Open the door, pierce the chicken. The juices should run

clear, the flesh firm but tender. Anything less is unacceptable.

10. Garnish with fresh thyme: The final touch. Place the sprig on top, adjust it slightly, ensuring it's cantered, the leaves vibrant against the dark sauce. Step back. Examine your work. It's beautiful.

It's perfect.

But there's something in the back of my mind, something that whispers in the silence of the kitchen. It tells me that no matter how perfect this dish is, no matter how meticulous I am in its creation, it will never be enough. There's something missing, something I can't quite grasp, a flaw that gnaws at me even as I admire the finished product.

But then again, maybe it's not the dish that's flawed. Maybe it's me.

The orders come in, one after another, a relentless stream of Hunter's Chicken. It's as if the entire hotel has been taken over by a singular, insatiable craving. The printer spits out the tickets with mechanical precision, each one bearing the same three words. I read them over and over until they lose meaning, until they become just shapes on paper.

The kitchen falls into a rhythm, a synchronised dance of dread and repetition. The chicken breasts are lined up like soldiers awaiting execution. I salt them, pepper them, sear them to a golden brown. The sizzle is deafening, a white noise that drowns out everything else. The onions and garlic hit the pan, releasing their pungent aroma into the air, mingling with the scent of cooking meat and fresh thyme.

The pan is a battlefield, the ingredients soldiers in a war of attrition. The mushrooms are sliced, their pale flesh exposed. They bleed their juices into the pan, melding with the chicken stock and wine to create a sauce that is both rich and suffocating. The bacon, diced into perfect cubes, crisps up with a violent crackle, sending droplets of hot fat flying. They land on my skin, burning, but I barely feel it anymore. Pain is just another ingredient in this dish.

The guests eat with a mechanical precision, their faces blank as they cut into the chicken. Forks and knives move in unison, a symphony of consumption. They chew methodically, eyes glazed over, lost in the trance. It's not enjoyment; it's sustenance, a necessity. They don't talk, don't smile. They just eat, and eat, and eat.

In the dead of night, I lie awake, the recipe etched into my mind like a curse. I see the chicken breasts, feel the slick of olive oil, hear the sizzle of bacon. I dream of knives and blood, of kitchens and chaos. The smell of thyme haunts me, clinging to my clothes, my skin, my very soul.

I start to wonder if there's something in the chicken, some ingredient that drives them to madness. Or maybe it's in me, a toxin that spreads through my hands into the food, infecting them all. The laughter of the staff is hollow, their eyes empty. We are prisoners of the Hunter's Chicken, bound by its unyielding demand.

The Swan is a labyrinth of mirrors, each one reflecting a different facet of my descent. The kitchen, a crucible of heat and pressure, moulds me into something unrecognisable. I am the Hunter, and this is my prey. The guests, the staff, the very walls of this place—they all conspire in this grotesque ballet, where every move is dictated by the unyielding recipe.

As I stand at the stove, turning another piece of chicken, I catch my reflection in the stainless steel. My eyes are hollow, my face a mask of weariness and dread. The Hunter's Chicken is more than a dish; it's a curse, a relentless torment that binds me to this place, this madness. And as the orders keep coming, I know there is no escape. The Swan has claimed me, and I am lost.

My stint at The Swan was a descent into a different kind of madness. The place, with its eccentric staff and unsettling ambiance, took a toll on my psyche. Each day there was a grotesque blend of monotony and panic, a bizarre theatre of the absurd where reality and delusion intertwined. The hotel, an imposing edifice of fading grandeur, was a sanctuary for the unhinged. It wasn't just the creaking floors and the dim, flickering lights—it was the people, the whispers, the feeling of being constantly watched.

As I left The Swan, I couldn't help but feel relieved, hoping that my next destination would be a step towards normalcy, whatever that might mean. But I knew that

The Swan had changed me, its shadows and whispers leaving an indelible mark on my soul. The madness, the paranoia, the constant sense of unease—they had become a part of me. I drove away from the hotel, the sun rising on the horizon, but the memories of The Swan lingered, a dark cloud over my newfound freedom. I was free, but I was also a prisoner of my own mind, the scars of The Swan etched deeply into my psyche.

In the rearview mirror, The Swan receded into the distance, but its presence loomed large in my thoughts. Normalcy was a mirage, an illusion I chased but never quite reached. The road ahead was uncertain, the future a blank canvas waiting to be painted with new experiences. But as I drove, I couldn't shake the feeling that the shadows of The Swan were following me, their whispers growing louder with each passing mile.

291

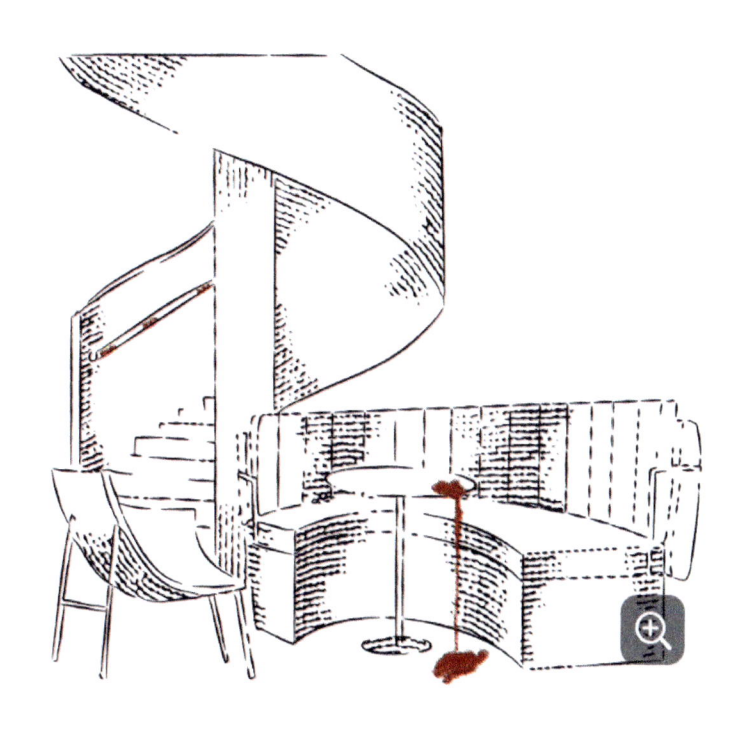

Chapter 21: The Pride Weekend War

The failed attempt at securing a Michelin Star was the final nail in Jamie's coffin. The once-celebrated visionary, the culinary prodigy whose name had been whispered in awe across the industry, had been reduced to a hollow shell of his former self. He drifted through the kitchen like a spectre, a ghost haunting the very place that had once been his kingdom. The star—no, the obsession with the star—had consumed him entirely, leaving behind a void so profound it had swallowed his passion whole, regurgitating only bitterness and resentment. The fire that once burned in his eyes, a fire so bright it could ignite the souls of those around him, had dulled to a lifeless stare. What had been a mission, a quest for perfection and glory, had decayed into something grotesque—just a pay-check job. And in the ruins of his ambition, only his cruelty seemed to thrive.

Jamie's descent into malevolence wasn't a sudden fall but a slow, inevitable spiral, one that those of us in the kitchen had witnessed with a mixture of horror and fascination. At first, it was the little things—a sharp word here, a dismissive comment there—but as the weeks turned into months, his bitterness grew into something monstrous, something that twisted his very soul. He didn't just lose interest in the work—he became sadistic, relishing the power he held over us, using it to inflict pain, both emotional and physical. The kitchen, once a marvel of creative energy, transformed into a dungeon, a place where egos clashed, and despair hung in the air like the acrid smoke from a burned pan.

One night, as I stood at my station, mindlessly prepping vegetables for the next day's service, Jamie slithered up beside me, his presence announced by the sour stench of whiskey that clung to him like a second skin. He leaned in close, so close I could feel the heat of his breath on my neck, the alcohol fumes filling my nostrils, making my stomach churn. His voice, low and dripping with malice, cut through the monotonous rhythm of chopping knives and sizzling pans like a serrated blade.

"Haha, I purposely put Frenchie on back-to-backs," he whispered, the words slithering from his mouth with a twisted glee. There was no remorse, no hint of guilt—just the cold, calculated cruelty of a man who had lost all sense of humanity. "I don't give a fuck if he can't see his family. I worked hard to be head chef; I can see my family when I want. He's the grunt, it's his fault, not mine. Pathetic ha."

The laughter that followed wasn't the joyful sound of someone amused, but a jagged, cruel noise that grated against my eardrums, reverberating through the kitchen like the death rattle of a dying animal. It was the laugh of a man who had nothing left but his own sadism, a man who took pleasure in the suffering of others because it was the only thing that made him feel alive anymore.

I watched him as he straightened up and swaggered away, a twisted smirk still playing on his lips, his eyes dead, devoid of the spark that had once made him great. This wasn't the Jamie I had known, the Jamie who had inspired us all with his relentless pursuit of perfection.

That man was gone, replaced by a bitter, vengeful shadow of himself, a man who no longer cared about anything except inflicting pain and asserting his dominance over those he saw as beneath him.

The kitchen, which had once been a place of passion and camaraderie, had become a hellish purgatory, a place where we all walked on eggshells, waiting for the next outburst, the next cruel joke, the next senseless punishment. We were no longer a team, but a group of individuals trapped in a nightmare, each of us trying to survive the torment that had become our daily existence.

And in the centre of it all was Jamie, the fallen king, now more monster than man, ruling over his shattered kingdom with an iron fist and a sadistic grin, his eyes always searching, always hunting for the next victim to feed his insatiable need for control. The Michelin Star, the symbol of everything he had once strived for, had become his undoing, a cursed object that had driven him to the brink of madness and beyond.

Frenchie, our not so perfect breakfast cook, was a family man, the kind who wore his love for his wife and kids like a badge of honour. Jamie's deliberate scheduling to keep Frenchie away from them was a new low, even for him. Seeing Frenchie's eyes grow hollower with each passing day, his shoulders slump under the weight of relentless hours, made me question my own future. Was this what awaited me? A life of broken dreams and shattered spirits, or worse, becoming a monster like Jamie, feeding off the misery of others?

Pride Weekend loomed on the horizon, a beacon of celebration and chaos. The hotel was a hive of activity, the anticipation of the event palpable, but for us—the remaining three chefs: the twins and myself—it marked the beginning of an infernal trial. The twins, identical in appearance yet worlds apart in temperament, were my only comrades in this culinary storm. The other chefs, clever enough to anticipate the oncoming slaughter, had the foresight to book this weekend off. I couldn't help but feel a surge of venomous envy—those calculating fuckers.

Day one of Pride Weekend hit us like a tsunami—an unrelenting force of chaos that tore through the kitchen with the ferocity of a beast unleashed. Orders cascaded into the pass, an endless torrent of demands that threatened to drown us in a sea of stress and sweat. The dining room, normally a controlled environment of clinking cutlery and hushed conversations, had transformed into a riotous spectacle of laughter and celebration, a frenzy of rainbow-coloured mania that seeped into our supposed sanctuary, poisoning the air with its forced gaiety and hollow joy.

The twins, those eerily synchronised automatons, worked with a precision that bordered on madness, their movements so tightly controlled, so mechanical, it was as if they were trying to outpace the very tide that sought to swallow us whole. But beneath their outward calm, I could see the cracks—the strain in their eyes, the barely perceptible tremor in their hands. They were on the brink.

And there I was, ricocheting between stations like a pinball in some sadistic machine, my mind a blur of stress and desperation. Each task was a challenge, each dish an obstacle in the ever-increasing gauntlet. My heart raced, my pulse pounding in my ears like the relentless thud of a drum, each beat a reminder that we were one misstep away from total collapse.

But the worst of it wasn't the orders, or the chaos, or even the deafening roar of the dining room. No, the worst of it was Jamie, he left us to fend for ourselves, a ship adrift in a storm with no captain at the helm. His appearances were sporadic, each one a fleeting burst of venom and derision that left us reeling, our confidence shattered.

The weight of his contempt was a palpable thing, a dark cloud that hung over us, pressing down on our shoulders, choking us with its oppressive presence. Every move we made, every decision, every plate we sent out felt like it was under the scrutiny of that shadow, as if we were dancing on the edge of a razor blade, waiting for it to cut deep. I couldn't help but feel a wave of contemptuous disbelief wash over me as I observed the so-called dish of the day. A pathetic, uninspired offering—garlic king prawns. The audacity of it, parading as some sort of culinary achievement, when in reality, it was nothing more than a lazy, banal concoction, thrown together with the finesse of a toddler's crayon scribbles. The thought of it, sitting there on the menu, masquerading as something worthy of admiration, filled me with a quiet, simmering rage.

The uninspiring Garlic King Prawns

Ingredients:

- 500g of king prawns, peeled and deveined, their flesh exposed, vulnerable.

- 4 cloves of garlic, finely chopped, each slice releasing an aroma that's almost intoxicating.

- 2 tablespoons of olive oil, cold-pressed, the good stuff, because anything less would be a crime.

- 2 tablespoons of unsalted butter, smooth and pale, melting under the heat like something surrendering to the inevitable.

- The juice of 1 lemon, freshly squeezed, sharp enough to cut through the richness.

- Salt and freshly ground black pepper, to taste, but not too much, because too much would ruin everything.

- Fresh parsley, chopped—just enough for a garnish, a touch of green to remind you that life still exists.

- Lemon wedges, because presentation is everything, and they add a final twist of acidity.

Instructions

1. Prepare the Prawns: - Pat the prawns dry, feeling the cold, slick flesh beneath your fingers. Season them lightly with salt and pepper, the barest hint of flavor before the real work begins.

2. Cook the Garlic: - Heat the olive oil and butter in a large frying pan over medium heat, watching as the butter slowly surrenders to the heat, merging with the oil. Add the garlic, each piece hitting the hot oil with a satisfying sizzle. Sauté until the garlic is fragrant, almost golden, but not too much—never too much.

3. Cook the Prawns: - Add the prawns to the pan, placing them carefully, deliberately. Cook for 2-3 minutes on each side, watching as they turn from translucent to opaque, a transformation as inevitable as death.

4. Add Lemon Juice: - Squeeze the lemon juice over the prawns, the acidity cutting through the richness like a knife. Toss everything together, ensuring every prawn is coated in the garlicky, buttery sauce.

5. Serve: - Remove the prawns from the pan and arrange them on a plate with clinical precision. Sprinkle with parsley, because the touch of green adds a perverse sense of vitality to the dish. Serve immediately, with lemon wedges on the side, a final touch that's as much for show as it is for taste.

Enjoy your creation—simple, yet devastatingly effective.

By the end of the first day, we were wrecked—physically, mentally, emotionally. Our bodies ached with the kind of deep, bone-weary exhaustion that no amount of rest could alleviate. Our spirits were frayed, hanging by a thread, ready to snap under the pressure of another day like this. The kitchen, once a place of controlled chaos, had become a war zone, and we were the soldiers on the front line, battered and bruised, but still standing, still fighting.

But as I stood there, looking out at the aftermath of the day, the remnants of the battle that had just been fought, I couldn't help but feel a sick, twisted sense of satisfaction. We had survived. Barely, but we did it. And in this world, in this hell that we had willingly thrown ourselves into, survival was the only thing that mattered. Tomorrow would bring another storm, another tidal wave of madness and demand, but tonight, we live another day.

The night air was thick with the scent of sweat and desperation, the remnants of our collective breakdown hanging in the air like a miasma. The pride of the festival, that false gaiety, had long since faded, leaving behind only the harsh reality of what we had become. The world outside might have been celebrating, but inside, within the walls of the kitchen, it was a different story—one of survival, of enduring the relentless assault of orders and expectations, of trying to keep our heads above water in a sea that sought to drown us.

And as I looked around at the wreckage of the kitchen, the twisted remains of what had once been a place of creativity and precision, I realised that this was only the beginning. Pride Weekend had just begun, and we were already on the brink. The next two days would push us further, test our limits in ways we couldn't yet imagine. But for now, in this brief moment of calm before the next storm, we were still standing. Battered, broken, but still standing. And in this world, that was the closest thing to victory we would ever know.

Day two was a descent into madness, a plunge into the kind of chaos that strips away any last vestige of sanity. The onslaught of orders didn't just increase—it grew fiercer, more relentless, each ticket a new wound torn into our already fraying psyche. Every time that goddamn printer spat out another slip, it was like a gunshot, a loud and violent reminder of our inadequacy. We weren't just chefs's anymore; we were soldiers in a trench, every action calculated for survival, every second ticking down to an inevitable disaster.

The kitchen, once a well-oiled machine, had transformed into the front line where we were not just fighting the tide of orders, but each other. The twins—usually so in sync it was unnerving—began to unravel, their synchronised dance morphing into a disjointed stumble. You could see it in their eyes, the way they darted, wild and unfocused, their faces flushed with the heat of the kitchen and the strain of holding it all together. The flawless choreography they prided themselves on was breaking down, their tempers flaring, snapping at the edges like a taut wire ready to snap.

The tension in the kitchen had reached a boiling point, the air thick with the stench of sweat, desperation, and something else—something darker. The service was a relentless barrage of tickets, each one a new demand, a new impossibility to add to the growing pile. We were drowning, gasping for air in a sea of hopelessness, our nerves frayed to the point of snapping. And then, in the midst of the madness, it happened.

One of the Twins, there face, twisted in a mask of frustration, veins bulging in their neck as they barked orders, trying to maintain some semblance of control over their section. But the night had been brutal, unforgiving, and the twins was unraveling right before my eyes. There movements were no longer precise; they were erratic, desperate. The kitchen had become a pressure cooker, and they were about to blow.

I was at the pass, trying to keep up with the torrent of orders, when I saw it. A chicken breast, perfectly seared, a piece of culinary art in any other context, sitting on the counter. It was supposed to be plated, garnished, sent out to the dining room with a flourish. But something went wrong—maybe the garnish was late, maybe the sauce had separated, maybe it was just one fucking thing too many.

Both of the twins stared at the chicken breast, there hands trembling, the weight of the night pressing down on them like a vice. And then, with a scream that tore through the kitchen like a primal howl, they snapped. One of them grabbed the chicken breast, her fingers digging into the tender flesh, and in one wild, violent motion, she hurled it across the kitchen. Time seemed to slow as the chicken sailed through the air, its trajectory a perfect arc of insanity, before crashing through the small, grime-covered window above the sink.

The sound of shattering glass was like a gunshot, echoing through the kitchen, freezing everyone in their tracks. The chicken breast disappeared into the night, out the window, gone. For a moment, there was silence—a brief, stunned pause in the madness as we all processed what had just happened. And then, like a dam breaking, the kitchen erupted in chaos.

Laughter, hysterical and unhinged, bubbled up from deep within me, spilling out in a manic, uncontrollable burst. It was absurd, surreal—a fucking chicken breast, launched into the darkness like some deranged offering to the gods. The front of house staff joined in, their laughter mixing with mine, a twisted chorus of relief and insanity. Even the twins, still shaking with fury, let out a bitter, strangled laugh, there hands clenched into fists at there sides.

But the moment was fleeting, a brief, mad reprieve in the relentless storm. The laughter died as quickly as it had begun, replaced by the cold, harsh reality of the kitchen, the tickets still coming, still demanding more. We were still drowning, still struggling, still trapped in this nightmare.

And yet, something had shifted. The chicken breast, that absurd, ridiculous act of defiance, had punctured the tension, released some of the pressure that had been suffocating us. It was a small, meaningless victory in the grand scheme of things, but in that moment, it was everything. It was a reminder that we were still human, still capable of happiness, of laughter, of resistance, even in the face of the impossible.

As the night wore on, the kitchen slowly, painfully, returned to its grim rhythm. The orders kept coming, the unholy system continued, we returned back to snapping at each other, too, the camaraderie we had clung to as a lifeline now fraying, splitting back under the pressure. The kitchen echoed with the sharp crack of insults, the cold sting of accusations. We weren't just colleagues anymore; we were combatants in a war with no clear enemy, lashing out because we had nowhere else to direct our rage, our fear.

The kitchen itself seemed to pulse with malevolence, the heat from the burners and ovens mixing with the rising tension to create an atmosphere that was suffocating, oppressive. The walls, slick with condensation, seemed to close in around us, shrinking our world down to this one hot, sticky room where we were trapped, slaves to the tickets that kept coming, kept demanding more, more, more.

Every second was a countdown to disaster, the pressure building like a bomb waiting to explode. The sound of knives against chopping boards, the hiss of meat hitting searing pans, the clatter of pots and pans—it all blended into a chaotic symphony that played in the background of our unraveling minds.

Jamie was no help, of course. His indifference had turned into something worse—a sort of gleeful sadism as he watched us struggle, as he saw the cracks widening, the tension ratcheting up to unbearable levels. He hovered on the outskirts, never stepping in to help, only to criticise, to mock. His eyes gleamed with a twisted satisfaction, as if this was the show he'd been waiting for, the moment when we would all break, when the kitchen would finally implode under the weight of its own ambition.

And still, the tickets kept coming, the orders piling up faster than we could handle them. Every plate that went out felt like a small miracle, a temporary reprieve in a war we were losing. The seconds dragged on, each one stretching into an eternity of heat and noise and tension. I could feel the disaster looming, a shadow on the horizon, inevitable and inescapable.

By the time the night ended, we were hollow, shells of the people who had walked into that kitchen just hours before. The adrenaline that had kept us going, that had fuelled our frenzied movements, drained away, leaving only exhaustion and a deep, gnawing sense of dread. We had survived, but barely, and the knowledge that we had to do it all again tomorrow was a weight that settled on our shoulders, crushing us under its relentless pressure.

As I left the kitchen, the air outside cool against my flushed skin, I knew that something had changed. The cracks that had started to form weren't going away—they were widening, deepening, and it was only a matter of time before they tore us apart completely. The madness of that night was just the beginning, a prelude to the chaos that was to come. And as I walked away, the kitchen still ringing in my ears, I couldn't shake the feeling that we were all hurtling toward a disaster we couldn't escape, a darkness we couldn't outrun.

By day three, we were shattered. The relentless pace, the impossible demands—it all came crashing down. Tears of frustration mingled with sweat as we stumbled through service. The pride and joy of the celebration outside felt like a cruel joke, a stark contrast to our private hell.

As the last plate left the pass, we collapsed, the weight of the weekend crushing us. The kitchen was now a prison of torment and despair. Jamie's legacy was one of suffering, his dream turned nightmare our daily reality. I knew then that I had to escape, that I couldn't let myself become another casualty in his war for a dream that had long since died.

In the midst of the chaos and crumbling spirits of the Pride Weekend war, the act of creating the rainbow cake offered a rare moment of solace and a brief reprieve from the relentless pressures of the kitchen. As each vibrant layer was added, the cake became a symbol of hope and resilience amidst adversity. The bright colours red, orange, yellow, green, blue, and purple—each represented a layer of our struggle, yet also our determination to rise above the daunting challenges.

Recipe: Rainbow Cake

Ingredients

For the Cake:

- 3 1/4 cups all-purpose flour: Precisely measured, levelled, because precision is everything. There's no room for error here—each cup must be exact, each grain accounted for.

- 1 tbsp baking powder: The catalyst, the agent that brings it all together, inflates the mixture, gives it life. But too much? Disaster.

- 1/2 tsp salt: A half teaspoon, no more, no less. Just enough to balance the sweetness, to cut through the saccharine facade.

- 1 1/2 cups unsalted butter, room temperature: Soft, pliable, but not melted. It must be perfectly malleable, yielding to pressure but still holding form. Anything less is unacceptable.

- 2 cups granulated sugar: Pure, white, crystalline. The sweetness that lures them in, that coats the tongue, that masks the bitter undertones.

- 4 large eggs: Fresh, organic, the yolks a deep, rich yellow. The binding agent, the element that holds it all together, that gives the cake its structure, its substance.

- 1 tbsp vanilla extract: The essence, the aroma that fills the air, that hints at something more, something beneath the surface.

- 1 cup whole milk: Not skim, not 2%. Whole. Full fat. The richness, the creaminess that saturates the batter, that seeps into every layer.

- Food colouring (red, orange, yellow, green, blue, purple): The illusion, the vibrant facade. Each colour must be perfect, vivid, a distraction from what lies beneath.

For the Frosting:

- 2 cups unsalted butter, room temperature: Creamy, smooth, indulgent. It must glide across the tongue, dissolve into sweetness, leaving nothing behind but the memory of something perfect.

- 8 cups powdered sugar: Fine, powdery, almost ethereal. It coats everything it touches, a dusting of sweetness that lingers, that clings.

- 1/2 cup heavy cream: Thick, rich, unctuous. It adds body, depth, a weight that anchors the sweetness.

- 2 tsp vanilla extract: More essence, more aroma, a reminder that beneath all this sweetness, there is something more, something almost real.

- Pinch of salt: Just a pinch, to balance, to cut through the indulgence, to remind you that everything has a cost.

Instructions

1. Preheat Oven: Preheat your oven to 350°F (175°C). Six 9-inch round cake pans greased and floured, each one a blank canvas waiting to be painted. The anticipation hangs heavy in the air, thick and palpable.

2. Mix Dry Ingredients: In a medium bowl, whisk together the flour, baking powder, and salt. The dry ingredients, the foundation. Whisk them thoroughly, until they are one, indistinguishable from each other. The mixture must be uniform, flawless.

3. Cream Butter and Sugar: In a large bowl, beat the butter and sugar together until light and fluffy. This is where it all begins—the transformation, the alchemy. The butter and sugar merge, becoming something more, something almost magical. Add the eggs one at a time, beating well after each addition. Each egg, each addition, is critical, each one pulling the mixture closer to perfection. Mix in the vanilla extract. The aroma fills the room, intoxicating, overwhelming.

4. Combine Wet and Dry Ingredients: Gradually add the flour mixture to the butter mixture in three parts, alternating with the milk. Begin and end with the flour mixture. Beat just until combined. Careful now—don't overmix. Too much and the cake becomes tough, unyielding. Too little and it falls apart, crumbling into nothingness.

5. Divide Batter and Add Colouring: Divide the batter evenly into six bowls. Each one must be exact, the same as the others. No deviations, no mistakes. Add a different food colouring to each bowl and mix until the colours are vibrant. The colours are everything—bright, vivid, distracting. Each one a promise, a lie. Stir until each batter is a brilliant shade, a feast for the eyes, a distraction for the mind.

6. Bake the Cakes: Pour each coloured batter into its own prepared cake pan. The colours swirl, a kaleidoscope of deception. Bake for 15-20 minutes, or until a toothpick inserted into the centre comes out clean. Time it perfectly—too long and it's ruined, too short and it's raw. Cool in the pans for 10 minutes, then transfer to wire racks to cool completely. The cooling is critical—too soon, and it collapses, too late, and it hardens.

7. Make the Frosting: In a large bowl, beat the butter until creamy. It must be smooth, perfect. Gradually add the powdered sugar, one cup at a time, beating well after each addition. Each cup adds sweetness, layers upon layers, until it's almost too much, almost unbearable. Add the heavy cream, vanilla extract, and salt, and beat until light and fluffy. The frosting is the facade, the cover, the mask that hides everything beneath.

8. Assemble the Cake: Place the purple layer on a cake board or serving plate. The base, the foundation. Spread a thin layer of frosting on top. Repeat with the blue, green, yellow, orange, and red layers, adding a layer of frosting between each. The layers stack, one on top of

the other, each one hiding the one beneath. The colours are bright, cheerful, but the weight of the cake is oppressive, heavy.

9. Frost the Cake: Apply a crumb coat of frosting to the entire cake and chill for 30 minutes. The crumb coat is the first layer, the thin veneer that smooths everything over, that hides the imperfections. Apply the final layer of frosting, smoothing it with a spatula. The final coat, the perfection, the mask that covers everything. It's smooth, flawless, deceptive.

10. Decorate: Decorate as desired, with additional frosting, sprinkles, or other decorations. The final touches, the distractions. Sprinkles, flowers, whatever it takes to draw the eye, to make them forget what's really inside. The cake is perfect, a masterpiece of deception.

But when you cut into it, when the knife slices through the layers, the colours bleed, the cake crumbles, and the truth is revealed. Beneath the vibrant facade, beneath the layers of frosting and sweetness, it's just cake. Just flour, sugar, and eggs, mixed together and baked, nothing more. It's all an illusion, a lie wrapped in a pretty package.

And yet, they'll eat it. They'll smile, they'll praise it, they'll devour it, and they'll never know the truth. They'll never see the cracks, the flaws, the imperfections hidden beneath the surface. Because they don't want to. They don't want to see what's really there, what's really inside.

They just want the cake. And I'll give it to them. Every. Single. Time.

Despite the overwhelming stress, the process of carefully mixing, colouring, and layering the cake brought a meditative calm to the kitchen, a much-needed contrast to the sharp orders and clashing pans that filled the air. It was a creative endeavour that required precision and attention, drawing us away from our frayed nerves and focusing us on the task at hand.

As the cake took shape, its colours melding into a vivid display, it became a testament to what we could still achieve under pressure. It was not just a dessert; it was a statement of our capability and enduring spirit. The act of spreading the frosting over the cake, smoothing it into a seamless cloak of white, felt like covering our wounds and presenting a united, flawless front despite the underlying turmoil.

When the rainbow cake was finally presented, it didn't just bring joy to the guests; it brought a moment of pride to our team. Despite the hard weekend and the failures, we felt so acutely, here was something beautiful and perfect that we had created together. It was a reminder that even in the darkest times, there can be light, colour, and a reason to smile—even if just for a moment.

The slight joy that the rainbow cake brought into such a horrible situation was profound. It reminded us that culinary art is not just about feeding others; it's about expressing ourselves, sharing our emotions, and sometimes, healing through the simple act of baking. For a fleeting evening, the rainbow cake allowed us to forget the harsh realities of our environment and revel in the pure pleasure of creation and celebration. It was a brief but powerful affirmation that even amidst a backdrop of chaos, beauty and joy could still be found and savoured.

Chapter 22: Attack of the spinach

Jamie, once the villain of our culinary narrative, a tyrant forged in the flames of perfectionism, had undergone a transformation so stark, it bordered on the surreal. His return to the fold was as dramatic as his fall—a phoenix rising from the smouldering ruins of his own ambition. The man who had once terrorised the kitchen, ruling with a merciless iron fist, had been replaced by a figure almost unrecognisable—a reformed mentor, determined to exorcize the ghosts of culinary elitism that had clung to our burners like a malignant curse.

"To hell with this pretentious ten-course tasting menus!" he barked one morning, his voice ricocheting off the cold, sterile steel that lined our battleground. The words hung in the air, a challenge, a decree, reverberating through the kitchen like the first crack of a whip. His eyes, no longer the icy, calculating instruments of a perfectionist's tyranny, now burned with a manic fervour a revolutionary zeal that was both terrifying and infectious.

"We're putting the soul back into cooking!" he proclaimed, his voice rising, filling the cavernous space with the sheer force of his conviction. "We're done with the bullshit. No more artifice, no more pretension. We are going to believe in what we do; in every plate we send out!"

His fists slammed against the counter, each impact a punctuation mark, driving his words into our psyche with the force of a hammer on an anvil. The clatter of pans and the hiss of flames seemed to fall silent, the entire kitchen held in the grip of his passion, his madness. We stood there, knives in hand, sweat dripping from our temple's, as the fire that had once burned us now reignited something deep within—something raw, primal, and desperately hungry.

The transformation was palpable. It was as though Jamie had torn down the very walls of our culinary prison, exposing us to the light for the first time in years. The weight of his former reign, the suffocating pressure to meet impossible standards, began to lift. In its place was something new, something almost terrifying in its simplicity—an idea that cooking could be more than just a test of endurance, more than a battle for the approval of faceless critics. It could be a return to something purer, something real.

And so, with Jamie at the helm, we marched into the unknown, knives sharpened and minds clear, ready to carve out a new legacy from the bones of the old. The kitchen was still a warzone, but now, it was one where we fought not just for perfection, but for the very soul of what we did.

The atmosphere in the kitchen, which had long been suffocated under the weight of microscopic garnishes and the silent pressure of star ratings, was suddenly electric. The air was thick with possibility, a palpable shift from the rigour mortis of routine to a lively pulse of creativity.

We, his team, looked around at each other, expressions tentative yet hopeful. The stainless-steel counters and chrome appliances, once cold and unyielding, seemed to gleam a bit brighter under Jamie's new mentality. The oppressive aura that had draped over us lifted, and for the first time in months, the kitchen felt like a heaven for creation, not a mausoleum for the damned.

The transformation wasn't confined to the menu or the methods; it was etched into Jamie himself, a metamorphosis so profound it verged on the unsettling. Gone were the days of sharp, barked orders that cut through the air like a knife, the scathing critiques that left you bleeding in the middle of service. In their place was something new, something almost alien—a patience, an eagerness to teach, to share the forgotten techniques that had been buried beneath the relentless climb toward Michelin stars. Jamie had become a man with nothing left to prove, but everything to give, a chef who had stood at the peak of culinary greatness and found it a cold, lonely place, devoid of the warmth that makes cooking a craft of the soul.

This new Jamie, no longer the tyrant, but a fervent disciple of rustic authenticity, sparked something in the kitchen that had been missing for years. His obsession with raw, unpretentious flavours over the hollow theatrics of fine dining brought us back from the brink, reviving a sense of unity that had long since faded. It wasn't fear or blind ambition that drove us anymore; it was something purer, something that had been lost in the pursuit of accolades and praise. We rallied behind him, not because we had to, but because we wanted to—because, for the first time in what felt like an eternity, we were cooking with passion again.

Every dish became an act of rebellion against the pretension we had once worshipped, every meal a testament to the joy we had forgotten. We weren't just aiming to impress anymore; we were striving to reconnect—with the ingredients, with the process, with each other. Jamie had shown us the way back to what truly mattered, and we followed him, not as soldiers in a culinary war, but as artists rediscovering the beauty in their craft.

The kitchen's soul, long suppressed under the guise of gastronomic precision, stirred and awoke. Laughter mingled with the clatter of pots and pans, and the aroma of real, heartfelt cooking filled the air, chasing away the lingering scents of austerity. For the first time in a long time, we were not just cooking; we were chefs, artists of the edible, revellers in the feast of life. Jamie's transformation had not just changed the menu; it had changed us all.

Jamie's culinary renaissance flooded the kitchen with an array of dishes that were both comforting and innovative. He introduced a homey twist to our offerings, each dish crafted with a palpable sincerity that was as refreshing as it was delectable. Yet, beneath the rustic charm and hearty flavours, a green thread wove through the menu—spinach.

The ingredient surfaced everywhere. Spinach-stuffed chicken breasts, where the vibrant green peeked out from the golden-browned meat, offered a visual and flavourful contrast that delighted our diners. Creamy spinach risotto, rich and luxurious, carried the earthy tones of the leaf mingled seamlessly with Arborio rice, its creamy texture punctuated by the slight bite of well-cooked spinach. Even more audacious was the spinach-infused ice cream, a playful yet perplexing dessert that left our guests both intrigued and perplexed, its verdant hue a bold statement on the palate.

My elevation to junior sous chef had filled me with a buoyant sense of purpose, my role in this culinary upheaval both exhilarating and daunting. The kitchen became my arena, and the new dishes my challenges to execute with precision. Yet, as I folded spinach into sauces and blended it into bases, a shadow of doubt crept into my enthusiasm once more. The omnipresence of spinach was peculiar—a curious motif in Jamie's symphony of flavours.

It was an odd fixation, this spinach theme, but in the whirlwind of Jamie's renewed passion and our kitchen's transformation, it was easy to brush aside. The green leaf had become a culinary leitmotif, threading through each dish with an insistence that was hard to ignore. Yet, in the heady days of our gastronomic revival, it was just another leaf in the salad—a quirky signature of Jamie's newfound culinary narrative.

But as the weeks wore on and spinach found its way into nearly every dish, the peculiarity of it began to gnaw at me. The kitchen staff joked amongst themselves, dubbing the wave of green "Jamie's Jungle" or the "Great Spinach Invasion." But beneath the jest was an undercurrent of bewilderment. Why spinach? What drove Jamie's relentless incorporation of it into dishes where it had no traditional place?

These questions simmered in the back of my mind, bubbling up as I watched the vibrant leaves tumble into pots and pans. The kitchen buzzed with the energy of creation, but the mystery of the spinach loomed, a green Spector over our culinary landscape. As I plated a spinach-laden dish, the rich, earthy aroma rising with the steam, I couldn't help but wonder what drove this green obsession. Was it a whim, a chef's fancy? Or was there something deeper, a thread I had yet to pull in the tapestry of Jamie's culinary redemption?

The initial reception of our revamped menu was a burst of optimism, with diners intrigued by the heartiness and novel approach Jamie injected into each dish. The restaurant buzzed with life, a palpable excitement in the air as waitstaff paraded the new offerings out with pride. But this initial enthusiasm soon revealed a relentless undercurrent, as the omnipresence of spinach began to dominate every aspect of our culinary operations.

Weeks into the launch, the kitchen's energetic calls of "Check on, check on" had transformed into a monotonous drone of "Spinach chef! Spinach chef!" The echo of this new chant reverberated off the stainless steel and tiled floors, a constant reminder of the spinach that had infiltrated our menu to its core. Every ticket that printed out was a demand for spinach—spinach stuffed into meats, layered in casseroles, and even swirled into desserts. "Where's the fucking spinach, chef?!" became the rallying cry, barked out with increasing frustration as if our culinary fate hinged on the presence of this one ingredient.

As junior sous chef, I stood at the epicentre of this verdant storm, orchestrating a ballet of spinach-infused dishes with a growing sense of despair. Each service became a battle, the kitchen line my trench as I faced wave after wave of spinach demands. The charm of our green-themed menu quickly soured, turning each shift into a gruelling slog through an unending forest of leafy greens.

The night began like any other—a lull before the storm, the kitchen dimly lit, the shadows lurking in the corners, waiting to be chased away by the relentless glare of the overhead fluorescents. I could feel the tension coiling in the air, thick and palpable, like the scent of ozone before a lightning strike. The first tickets started rolling in, a steady trickle that promised an onslaught, but I was ready, or at least I thought I was. The spinach—just another ingredient, a garnish, a side—nothing to be concerned about. I didn't know then that it would become the bane of my existence.

"Spinach on table six," Jamie barked from the pass, his voice already edged with the sharpness that signalled the beginning of our descent into madness. I turned to the sauté station, where the green leaves were piled high, waiting to be wilted down, their vibrant colour to be transformed into a darker, more sinister shade.

Another order. More spinach. I grabbed a handful, tossed it into the pan, the sizzle loud in my ears, the oil spitting as if it resented being used for such a menial task. I watched as the leaves shrivelled, shrinking down to almost nothing, their once voluminous form reduced to a pathetic handful of limp greenery. It wasn't enough. It was never enough.

The tickets kept coming, each one demanding more spinach, always more spinach. Table four, table seven, table fucking twelve—every dish needed it, like some perverse obsession had gripped the menu, spreading like a virus from table to table. And each time I wilted down another panful, it vanished, leaving me scrambling to toss more into the fire, the cycle repeating, endless, maddening.

"Where's the spinach for table eight?" Jamie's voice cut through the chaos, a blade slicing through flesh. My hands were trembling now, the heat from the stove searing through the layers of my chef whites, sweat dripping down my spine. I couldn't keep up. The spinach was disappearing faster than I could cook it, devoured by the insatiable appetites out there, in the dining room, where people sat, oblivious to the chaos they had unleashed.

I grabbed another handful, my fingers burning as I shoved the leaves into the pan. They hissed and shrank, mocking me with their refusal to cooperate, to behave, to simply be enough. But it was never enough. The pile dwindled, the greens turning to blackened remnants, and still the orders came, a relentless tide that threatened to drown me in its green, leafy depths.

My heart pounded in my chest, my vision narrowing as the pressure mounted, the weight of the orders pressing down on me, squeezing the breath from my lungs. I felt like I was suffocating, buried alive under an avalanche of spinach. The kitchen closed in around me, the walls pushing inward, the heat unbearable, the noise deafening.

"Get the fucking spinach on the pass!" Jamie roared, and something inside me snapped. I grabbed the entire remaining bunch, tossed it into the pan with a ferocity that bordered on violence. The oil splattered, scalding my hand, but I didn't care. The pain was just another part of the madness, another layer of the insanity that had taken hold of me, of all of us.

The leaves shrivelled, turned to a dark, twisted mass, and still it wasn't enough. I could feel the anger bubbling up inside me, a black tide rising, threatening to overwhelm. This wasn't just a garnish anymore. It was a symbol, a manifestation of everything that was wrong, everything that was broken. I wanted to scream, to throw the pan across the room, to smash it against Jamie's fucking skull and watch it shatter, but I didn't. I couldn't.

Instead, I plated what little I had, my hands shaking, the spinach a pitiful, inadequate mess on the plate. I shoved it onto the pass, avoiding Jamie's gaze, knowing it wasn't enough, knowing I had failed. Again.

The night went on, a blur of green and black, the spinach haunting me, taunting me with its inadequacy, its refusal to be enough. By the time the last ticket came through, I was spent, my body a husk, my mind a wasteland. I stared at the empty station, at the remnants of the greens that had driven me to the brink and felt nothing. Just an empty, hollow void where the rage had been.

Service was over, but the madness lingered, a dark cloud that hung over the kitchen, over me. The spinach had won, and I was left broken, defeated, a casualty of the war that raged in that stainless steel prison. The night ended as it had begun, in darkness, but this time, there was no light at the end of the tunnel. Just the lingering scent of burnt spinach and the bitter taste of failure. My dreams of a bright culinary future, once buoyed by the promise of innovation and change, now seemed to wither under the oppressive weight of spinach. The kitchen, a place I had once commanded with a sense of emerging leadership and creativity, had become a monotonous grind, each dish a variant on a theme that was becoming tiresome to both cook and eat.

In a bid to inject some creativity back into our menu and perhaps break the monotonous cycle, I developed a dish that I hoped would at least be a high point in our spinach saga: the Spinach Wellington. A twist on the classic Beef

Wellington, this dish encapsulated the best of our theme, enveloping a rich spinach filling in a tender, flaky pastry.

Spinach Wellington Recipe

Ingredients:

- 2 sheets of puff pastry: Pre-packaged, mass-produced, a convenience disguised as luxury. Flaky, golden, but empty—like so many things.

- 1 lb fresh spinach: Bright, green, deceptively wholesome. Washed clean of dirt, stripped of its roots, just like the rest of us.

- 4 cloves garlic, minced: Sharp, pungent, relentless. It clings to your fingers, seeps into your pores, refuses to let go.

- 1 small onion, finely chopped: Uniform, each piece meticulously diced, because precision is everything. No uneven edges, no imperfections allowed.

- 4 oz feta cheese, crumbled: Tangy, salty, breaking apart under the slightest pressure. Fragile, like so many people who think they're strong.

- 2 tablespoons olive oil: Cold-pressed, extra-virgin. Smooth, golden, slipping through your fingers like something you can't hold on to.

- Salt and pepper to taste: Basic, fundamental, yet essential. Too much and you've ruined it; too little and it's bland, lifeless.

- 1 egg, beaten for egg wash: The final touch, the gloss, the sheen that covers up everything beneath. An illusion of perfection.

Instructions:

1. Preheat the oven to 400°F (200°C): The heat begins to rise, the temperature climbing steadily. There's no going back now, no second chances. It's a one-way path, and the destination is always the same.

2. In a large skillet, heat olive oil over medium heat: The oil shimmers, slick, almost metallic. The pan is hot, too hot, but that's the point. You want to feel the burn, the sizzle, the heat that makes you aware, that reminds you you're still alive.

3. Add the onions and garlic, sautéing until translucent and fragrant: The onions hit the oil with a sharp hiss, the garlic following suit, filling the air with a scent that's almost overwhelming. The aroma clings to you, invades your senses, seeps into your skin. The onions turn translucent, their sharpness softening, but they're not gone. They're still there, beneath the surface.

4. Add the spinach to the skillet, cooking until it wilts down completely: The spinach, vibrant and green, is tossed into the mix. It shrinks, withers under the heat, losing its volume, its strength, reduced to a fraction of what it was. But isn't that the way it always goes? Things are never as strong as they seem.

5. Remove from heat and let cool slightly: The heat dissipates, the mixture settles. It cools, but it's not cold, not yet. There's still warmth there, still life. For now.

6. Once cooled, mix in the crumbled feta cheese, and season with salt and pepper: The feta is crumbled, shattered into pieces, mixed in with the wilted spinach. It's fragile, delicate, but it adds something—an edge, a tang, a complexity that wasn't there before. Season with salt and pepper, a dash here, a sprinkle there, enough to bring out the flavours, to make it all come together.

7. On a lightly floured surface, lay out one sheet of puff pastry: The pastry is unrolled, laid flat, smooth and flawless. But it's empty, waiting to be filled, to be given purpose. It's a blank slate, a canvas, ready to be imprinted with whatever you choose.

8. Spread the spinach and feta mixture evenly over the pastry, leaving a small margin around the edges: The mixture is spread, even and uniform, no lumps, no inconsistencies. The edges are clean, precise, because the details matter. They always matter.

9. Carefully place the second sheet of puff pastry over the top of the spinach mixture: The second sheet is laid on top, sealing it all in, covering it up, hiding what's beneath. It's smooth, perfect, unblemished. But it's a lie, a façade, masking the reality underneath.

10. Seal the edges by crimping with a fork: The edges are pressed together, sealed tight, no room for escape, no

chance of spilling out. It's secure, contained, but there's tension there, just beneath the surface.

11. Brush the top of the pastry with the beaten egg to give it a golden finish: The egg wash is applied, a glossy, golden sheen that makes everything look perfect, pristine. It's the final touch, the finishing stroke that hides the truth, that makes it look like something it's not.

12. Bake in the preheated oven for 20-25 minutes, or until the pastry is golden and puffed: The heat rises again, the oven door closing with a finality that's almost suffocating. The pastry puffs up, golden and crisp, a picture of perfection. But you know what's inside, what's hidden beneath the surface. The timer ticks away, counting down, until it's time to face what you've created.

13. Let cool for a few minutes before slicing and serving: The pastry cools, the golden sheen dulls slightly, but it's still beautiful, still tempting. You slice into it, the layers flaking apart, revealing the truth beneath. And as you take that first bite, you taste it all—the bitterness of the spinach, the sharpness of the garlic, the saltiness of the feta, the crispness of the pastry. It's all there, layered, complex, a perfect blend of flavours.

But underneath it all, there's something more, something you can't quite put your finger on. A hint of something bitter, something dark, something that lingers long after the meal is over. And as you finish the last bite, you're left with the feeling that no matter how perfect it seemed, no matter how beautiful it looked on the outside, there's always something hidden beneath the surface.

Something you can't escape.

As I presented the Spinach Wellington to the team, I hoped it would be seen as a symbol of our resilience, a way to make peace with our green overlord. Yet, even as the dish was met with nods of approval and murmurs of appreciation, the overwhelming presence of spinach in every corner of our menu couldn't help but feel like a culinary chokehold from which we all silently longed to escape.

As I grew somewhat accustomed to navigating the verdant landscape that our kitchen had become under Jamie's rule, the ever-watchful eyes of upper management evaluated from their distant offices, their patience wearing thin with each spinach-laden dish that emerged from our ovens. Their verdict, when it came, was as cold and sharp as the knives we wielded. Like a blade through butter, they cut Jamie's tenure short, a decisive, unapologetic dismissal that left us all reeling.

The day they let him go was surreal. The kitchen fell silent as the news spread like a stain—Jamie, the once indomitable force behind our burners, reduced to a mere memory in the span of a single, brutal meeting. They escorted him out with a clinical efficiency, his exit devoid of the drama or ceremony that had marked his reign. He left behind his knives, his recipes, and a legacy tarnished by the very ambition that had fuelled his rise.

In the wake of his departure, rumours swirled through the ranks like steam from a boiling pot. They spoke of Jamie wandering the city's less-travelled paths, a shadow of his former self, lost in a maze of his own making. Passersby reported seeing a man who muttered to himself about stars—Michelin, not celestial—and spinach, his rants punctuated by wild gesticulations and a haunted look in his eyes. It seemed the man who had once concocted dishes worthy of acclaim now brewed only in his stew of disillusionment and regret.

Back in the kitchen, his absence cast a pall over us all. We stood amidst the stainless steel and white tiles, leaderless and unmoored. The brigade, once a well-oiled machine tuned to Jamie's exacting standards, now questioned the path we had been on. Was our quest for culinary excellence, for putting heart and soul back into every plate, merely a journey mapped in folly? Were we just culinary Don Quixotes tilting at Michelin-starred windmills?

I pondered these questions late into the night, long after the stoves were cold, and the lights dimmed. Cleaning my station, I couldn't shake the feeling that the spinach, once a symbol of our innovative spirit, now mocked us from every corner. Each leaf seemed to whisper of what could have been, a green spectre in the shadowy aftermath of Jamie's reign.

The line between genius and madness, I realised, was as thin as the edge of a chef's knife. In our pursuit of culinary innovation, had we crossed from passion into obsession? The empty pots, the silent burners, the ghostly rustle of spinach leaves—all seemed to echo back an answer, leaving us to wonder if the fire that had fuelled us was destined to consume us instead.

Chapter 23: The death of a team

Over time upper Management had emerged as our true nemesis. These faceless titans, cloaked in corporate suits, manipulated our daily toils with a precision that was both awe-inspiring and terrifying. They didn't just stir the pots—they controlled the very flame beneath them, orchestrating carnage with the dispassionate air of puppeteers pulling strings in a macabre show.

Their methods were ruthlessly efficient, slicing through the organised chaos of our kitchen like a sharp, cold knife. On one particularly disastrous Saturday, as we navigated the tumultuous waters of dinner service, a general manager—a spectre in tailored fabric—burst through the swinging doors. His entrance was like a gale force wind, upending our precarious balance. He brandished a sheaf of papers like a weapon, each page a decree from the high courts of gastronomy, each dish a demand that bordered on the absurd.

"This is live in an hour," he barked, his voice cutting through the din of clattering pans and hissing grills. The new menu landed on our prep table with the thud of finality. It was a gastronomic Frankenstein, stitched together with dishes we had never seen, demanding ingredients that were as exotic to us as tranquillity. Techniques that required hours of preparation were expected to be conjured in minutes. It wasn't just a menu; it was a gauntlet thrown down with gleeful cruelty, a test designed to push us to the brink of culinary insanity.

The shock of it galvanised us into action, but each movement was frantic, uncoordinated desperation made manifest. Chefs scrambled to adapt, I was barked contradictory orders, and the line cooks, poor foot soldiers in this impromptu battle, were left to interpret these sudden changes as best they could. The tension ratcheted up, the air thick with the scent of searing meat and burning ambition.

As orders piled up, the kitchen transformed into a war zone. Shouts filled the air, mingling with the clatter of pans and the sharp hiss of steam. "Where's the fucking saffron?!" someone screamed into the chaos. "Who the hell knows how to make a soufflé rise in ten minutes?!" another voice despaired. The demands of the new menu were relentless, each dish a Herculean task set by indifferent gods.

More and more orders began to populate our screens, the Matthew and Chantel exchanged looks that mixed incredulity with dread. The new dishes, laced with exotic ingredients and unfamiliar techniques, were not just a deviation but a deviation without notice. There were no trials, no tastings, just a blind leap into a culinary abyss.

The kitchen, devolved into bedlam. Servers darted in and out, their faces etched with the panic usually reserved for catastrophic news. Each ticket that printed was a bullet, and I, the intended target, was already riddled with holes.

"Two risotto, one lamb, and a partridge terrine!" I called out, my voice barely slicing through the cacophony of clanging pots and the sizzle of searing meat. The responses were sluggish, the movements around me desperate but uncertain.

The first complaint arrived before the first hour concluded, a harbinger of the storm that was to unfold. "The lamb is undercooked," the server relayed, her voice a whisper of defeat. It was followed by a barrage of dissatisfaction; the risotto was too firm, the terrine lacked seasoning, the presentation of the scallops was an abstract mess – a far cry from the usual precise artistry.

Sweat dripped from my brow, mingling with the flecks of sauce that splattered my chef's jacket like blood splatter at a crime scene. Each dish that returned was a slash to my reputation, a reputation I had built with the meticulousness of a craftsman.

By the ninth complaint, the dining room had become an echo chamber of clinking glasses and murmured criticisms. I could see them, the diners, their expressions morphing from anticipation to dissatisfaction. They were sharks circling, and I was chum thrown into the water by my own management.

I plunged into the fray, attempting to salvage what could only be described as a descent into gastronomic hell. Yet, with every dish that returned, my facade cracked. The facade of the unflappable chef, the titan of the kitchen, crumbled like the poorly constructed lemon tart that now lay dejectedly on the pass.

By the close of service, the damage was palpable. The kitchen was a battlefield strewn with casualties - half-eaten entrees and wounded pride. The staff were silent, their morale gutted and left to hang over the remnants of their shattered efforts. I stood there, amid the wreckage, a captain who had steered his ship not into the harbour but onto the rocks.

As I wiped down my station, the synthetic calm of the empty kitchen mocked me. The gleam of the stainless steel was too bright, too unforgiving. Tonight, the menu had not been just changed; it had been a declaration of war. And as I stripped off my jacket, the weight of defeat clung to me, a second skin that was tighter and more constricting than any chef's coat could ever be.

Upper management had gambled, using the kitchen as their casino, and I had paid the price. But as every gambler knows, the house always wins. Tonight, the house had won, and I was left counting the cost. The general manager, his mission accomplished, vanished as quickly as he had appeared, leaving behind a trail of culinary wreckage. We were left to salvage what we could, to serve up dishes born of panic rather than passion. It was culinary warfare, and with each dish that left the kitchen, a little more of our spirits chipped away, casualties of a battle we were never equipped to fight.

This brutal tactic, this sabotage dressed as strategy, was not just effective—it was soul-crushing. It underscored our powerlessness, the futility of fighting against a force that held all the cards, that could change the rules of the game on a whim. In that frenzied night, as the kitchen finally stilled and the last order went out, the silence that followed was not peace, but the heavy, oppressive calm that descends after a storm has razed everything in its path. We stood among the culinary ruins, our chef's whites smeared with the detritus of battle, each wondering how much longer we could survive in this relentless siege.

Under this relentless assault, our ranks crumbled. The twins, once our stalwarts at the grill and sauté station, were the first to fall. Overwhelmed and under-appreciated, they vanished into the night, never to return. Scorpion, with his devil-may-care attitude and razor-sharp skills, simply walked out one evening, his knives packed, his curses echoing. Matthew and Chantel, the dynamic duo who had danced through dinners and charmed during brunches, faded away like a mirage. Even Frenchie, our stalwart comrade, couldn't withstand the onslaught. Not even Scott, with all his culinary prowess and battle-hardened will, could steer us clear of disaster.

Reality had morphed into a dystopian nightmare. The air, once vibrant with the clatter of culinary craftsmanship, now hung heavy with the stench of defeat and decay. The kitchen had devolved into a spectral vessel, its soul gutted, crewed by the culinary equivalent of the walking dead.

Over time the team was replaced. The new head chef a quivering shadow of his predecessors, stood at the pass like a deer caught in headlights. His every tremor was visible, his anxiety a tangible cloud that choked us all. Tickets streamed from the printer like a relentless ticker tape parade of doom, each one a bullet to his already shattered confidence.

The chef de parties that management had dredged up were a farce. Their ineptitude was not just a problem; it was an epidemic. They shuffled through the kitchen, clueless and clumsy, more likely to poison our guests than to please them. Their understanding of hygiene was non-existent, the kitchen's once pristine counters now festering of grime and neglect. They handled meats with the grace of butchers at a slaughterhouse, unable to tell the tender from the tough, the fresh from the rotten.

And the breakfast chef—oh, the breakfast chef—was an enigma wrapped in a riddle, swathed in incompetence. His attempts at the simplest culinary tasks turned into farcical displays of ineptitude. Toasting bread seemed to him as complex and unattainable as quantum physics. Eggs, which should have been the simplest menu item, became his Sisyphean boulders, perpetually scrambled by his confusion.

Every shift was a trial by fire, a relentless grind that wore down my psyche and sapped my spirit. The kitchen had become my undoing, its flames my jailers. At night, my dreams were fiery nightmares: I ran through the smoke-choked hallways of a hotel engulfed in flames, each corridor leading inexorably back to the kitchen. The doors I flung open only revealed more flames, more smoke, more despair. The heat was unbearable, a physical force that pushed against me as if to drive me back, to keep me trapped in this infernal cycle.

This waking nightmare bled into my days, blurring the lines between sleep and consciousness. The kitchen's heat felt like the breath of some monstrous beast, its flames licking at my mind, searing away any hope of escape. Each day was a battle, not just against the chaos of service, but against the very essence of my surroundings, which seemed hell-bent on consuming me.

As I stood amidst the culinary carnage, surrounded by the ghosts of better times and the zombified remnants of what once was, I couldn't shake the feeling of impending doom. The kitchen had become a mausoleum of dreams, where the only thing being served was despair.

The climax of my spiralling descent into insanity erupted one harrowing morning. Drained to the marrow, my mind shrouded in a haze from relentless double shifts fuelled by a steady intake of caffeine and aspirin, I staggered to my car. The external world smeared into an indistinct haze, the road's markings melting into a monotonous grey stream that lulled me into a dangerous stupor. Abruptly, the glaring beams of an oncoming vehicle sliced through the fog of my consciousness, a sharp swerve, the piercing shriek of tires—a cacophony of chaos presaging disaster.

The collision was a violent explosion, a brutal assault of steel on steel that crushed metal and shattered bone. Glass erupted around me, a storm of shards dancing in the air, suspended in time as my car was wrenched into a deadly pirouette. Amid the disaster, a ludicrous thought flickered through my mind—a dish I'd never craft again. As the tumult subsided, a profound silence enveloped me, as deep and engulfing as the encroaching shadows that narrowed my field of vision.

Chapter 24: Another World

Blinding light enveloped me—an all-consuming whiteness that obliterated the contours of reality. Distant, muffled sounds penetrated the haze; they were voices I recognised, echoes from a bygone era that had no place in the here and now. As the luminescence gradually receded, it revealed shadowy figures, morphing slowly into familiar forms amidst the unmistakable aroma of flour and fresh baking.

My vision cleared, struggling to make sense of the surreal tableau before me. There I was, inexplicably standing in the culinary school kitchen, surrounded by ghosts of a chapter long since closed. Megan's laughter pierced the surreal silence, as vivid and life-affirming as those carefree days of our youth. Craig was wrestling with comprehension, his brow furrowed in earnest frustration as he tried to grasp the tutor's instructions—poor, clueless Craig. In the shadows lurked Will, his enigmatic presence as understated yet as tangible as ever.

A sharp jolt of realisation struck as I caught Simon's gaze; his lips moved animatedly, trying to communicate something urgent. I strained to decipher his words, but they dissolved into the ether, just out of cognitive reach. As I grappled with this disorienting reality, a loud crash shattered the tranquillity.

Panic seized me. The room began to spin, the familiar faces distorting into unrecognisable shapes, their voices dwindling into a distant whisper. Was this death? Was I suspended in some purgatorial limbo; a casualty of a life spent in pursuit of culinary perfection now descending into the abyss? The sterile hospital scent intermingled with the comforting smells of the kitchen, creating a paradoxical sensory experience that tethered me to neither realm.

I floated in this liminal space, untethered from the temporal flow that had carried me from those halcyon days at culinary school to the high-stakes chaos of professional kitchens. Memories of laughter and camaraderie, the intoxicating sense of limitless possibilities—we had felt invincible, impervious to the ravages of time and reality.

Yet, the harsh clang of reality loomed ever-present. The crash that had led to my current predicament echoed ominously, a stark reminder of the brutal transition from the classroom's theoretical sanctuaries to the relentless, cutthroat culinary industry. The ethereal faces of my former classmates seemed to plead, warn, and mourn the loss of innocence that ambition's flames had devoured.

"Am I dead?" The question echoed through the void, sending chills down my spine. Yet, as I hovered in this dreamlike interlude, part of me recognised the symbolic threshold I had crossed from one existence to another— not a passage marked by death, but rather a profound transformation.

The sensation was disturbingly vivid. I could breathe deeply, inhaling the rich aroma of proofing dough, hear the soft shuffle of my classmates around me, and feel the slightly cool, flour-dusted surface under my hands. Everything was hyper-real, a sensory overload so intense it anchored me firmly to the moment, yet it carried the surreal quality of a meticulously detailed dream.

I found myself in the midst of a familiar scenario: a skills test from my culinary school days, focused on baking a simple loaf of bread. Ray, our tutor, commanded the room with his usual blend of strict adherence to technique and encouraging nods. His presence was a ghost from the past, resurrected with uncanny accuracy in this bizarre tableau.

"Let's focus, everyone," Ray's voice cut through the thick tension, bringing us to attention around the demonstration table. His hands moved with practiced grace, mixing, kneading, and finally shaping the dough with a surgeon's precision. This lesson, imprinted in my memory, unfolded with an eerie sense of déjà vu, each detail replicated with unnerving fidelity.

As Ray's instructions filtered through the space, I absorbed the familiar scene: Megan's infectious laughter punctuating the air, Craig's puzzled squint at the complex steps, Will's quiet, intense focus in the back, and Simon, ever the joker, trying to catch my attention with a poorly timed quip. All were as vivid and lively as they had been years ago, untouched by time or the wear of life's realities.

"Pay attention to the dough's texture," Ray was saying, his hands expertly guiding the flour and water mixture into a living entity. "Baking is an art that's felt, not just executed. Let your hands learn the language of the dough."

I reached for my share of dough, the tactile sensation grounding me to this place. My hands, driven by a muscle memory sharpened by years of repetition, moved with a rhythm that felt both foreign and intimately familiar. The act of kneading became a meditation, each fold and press a step on a path I had travelled many times before.

Yet, why here? Why now? This echo of my past, was it a chance for redemption or a cruel reflection of my career's cyclical nature? Was I dead or trapped in a limbo, condemned to repeat my early failures and fleeting triumphs?

Skills Test: Bread Loaf

Ingredients:

- 3 1/2 cups all-purpose flour: The foundation, the bedrock. Measured with precision, levelled off, because even the slightest deviation could ruin everything.

- 1 packet (2 1/4 teaspoons) active dry yeast: Alive, teeming with potential, waiting to be awakened. Dormant now, but ready to rise, ready to transform.

- 1 1/2 teaspoons salt: Just the right amount. Too much, and it's overpowered, too little and it's bland, forgettable. It's a delicate balance, like everything else.

- 1 cup warm water (about 110°F): Not too hot, not too cold—110°F exactly. Warm enough to coax the yeast into action, to breathe life into the mixture. A single degree off, and the process is ruined.

- 1/4 cup milk: Whole, rich, adding a subtle complexity, a softness to the structure. It's more than just an ingredient; it's an indulgence.

- 2 tablespoons unsalted butter, melted: Smooth, golden, a liquid luxury. It seeps into the dough, binding it, enriching it. Unsalted, of course—control the salt yourself.

- 2 tablespoons sugar: Sweetness, just a touch. A lure, a temptation, something to feed the yeast, to give it the strength it needs to rise.

Instructions:

1. Activate the Yeast:

   - In a small bowl, combine the warm water and sugar. Stir in the yeast and watch as it begins to wake up, as it starts to foam, a sign of life, of transformation. Let it sit for 5-10 minutes, a slow, deliberate process. The froth is a promise, a guarantee that something is happening, something you've set in motion.

2. Mix the Dough:

   - In a large mixing bowl, combine the flour and salt. There's something satisfying about the way the dry ingredients come together, something pure, untainted.

Make a well in the centre, an empty void waiting to be filled. Pour in the yeast mixture, the milk, the melted butter. The liquid seeps into the flour, pulling it together, binding it, forming something new, something with potential.

3. Knead the Dough:

- Turn the dough out onto a floured surface. It's rough, unformed, but with each push, each fold, it starts to smooth out, to become something more. Knead for 8-10 minutes, your hands working methodically, rhythmically, until the dough is smooth, elastic, pliable under your touch. It's almost alive, responsive, changing with each movement. If it sticks, if it resists, add more flour—one tablespoon at a time. Control it, shape it, make it submit.

4. First Rise:

- Place the dough in a lightly oiled bowl, turning it to coat with the oil. The oil is a protective layer, a barrier, a way to ensure nothing sticks, nothing holds it back. Cover it with a damp cloth or plastic wrap, trapping the warmth inside, creating an environment where it can grow, where it can double in size. Let it rise for 1-1.5 hours, in a warm place, undisturbed, unseen. It's a waiting game, a test of patience. You watch it swell, feel the anticipation build.

5. Shape the Loaf:

- Punch down the dough—forcefully, deliberately—expelling the air, deflating it. Turn it out onto a lightly floured surface, where it waits, malleable, ready to be shaped. Roll it into a rectangle, each movement controlled, precise, and then roll it up tightly from one of the short ends. Each roll is an act of creation, of formation, until it takes on the shape of a loaf, ready for its final transformation.

6. Second Rise:

- Place the loaf in a greased 9x5-inch loaf pan. It's confined now, restricted, held in place. Cover it again, let it rise for another 30-45 minutes, or until it has risen about 1 inch above the rim of the pan. This is the final test, the last chance to prove itself. The dough rises, expanding, reaching its full potential, or failing in the attempt.

7. Preheat the Oven:

- Preheat your oven to 375°F (190°C). The heat builds, the temperature rises, a controlled environment where the loaf will meet its fate. The oven is a crucible, a place of transformation, where raw ingredients become something more, something greater.

8. Bake:

- Place the loaf in the oven, close the door, and wait. Bake for 30-35 minutes, the minutes ticking by slowly, each one bringing the loaf closer to completion. The top turns golden brown, the crust forming, hardening, a protective shell. Tap the bottom—if it sounds hollow, it's done. But don't rush it. The crust is everything, the first thing they see, the first thing they judge.

9. Cool:

   - Remove the bread from the oven. The heat escapes, a rush of warmth, of accomplishment. Let it cool in the pan for about 10 minutes, but don't leave it too long. Then, transfer it to a wire rack, where it cools completely, where it rests, solidifies, becomes what it was meant to be. Only then can you slice into it, revealing the soft, tender crumb inside, the fruit of your labour.

This bread, this loaf, it's more than just sustenance. It's a test, a trial, a measure of control, of precision, of patience. And when it's done, when it's perfect, you know that it wasn't just the ingredients, the process, that made it so. It was you. Your hands, your decisions, your will that brought it to life, that made it rise, that shaped it into something whole, something complete.

But even in its perfection, there's a nagging thought, a lingering doubt—could it have been better? Could you have done more? Because no matter how perfect it is, there's always room for improvement, always a way to make it just a little bit better, a little bit more… perfect.

The oven's warmth spread through the room as our breads baked, the comforting scent of golden crusts filling the air, starkly contrasting the cold uncertainty of my predicament. Removing my loaf from the oven, its perfect form seemed a cruel irony—beauty born from the chaos of my current state.

Was this death's workshop? A culinary purgatory where I was to bake bread for eternity, caught in the endless loop of my former life? Such thoughts spiralled wildly as I paced the now-quiet kitchen, the echoes of Ray's teachings resonating like the distant sounds of a life I could no longer claim as entirely my own.

As I stepped through the back door of the kitchen, the shift in atmosphere was palpable. The air outside was cooler, tinged with the scent of autumn leaves and the faint trace of cigarette smoke. There, in the smoking area, was the motley crew of my college days—my friends, alive with energy and youth, their laughter and chatter forming a lively backdrop against the quiet evening.

The late sunset filtered through the overhanging branches, casting sharp, angular shadows across the rickety smoking bench table that had become our makeshift meeting spot. The wooden surface, worn and splintered from years of neglect, was the only thing standing between us and the shared intensity that simmered beneath our calm exteriors.

Megan, always the first to break the silence, slid a small, unassuming notebook across the table. "I've been refining my dough recipe," she said, her voice carrying an edge of competitive pride. "Traditional technique, naturally. No shortcuts. A slow, cold ferment—48 hours minimum. The crumb structure is flawless. You can see the fermentation bubbles, each one perfect, delicate.

And the flavour? Complex, layered. Like nothing you've ever tasted."

Craig leaned back in his seat, his lips curling into a smirk. He reached into his jacket pocket, producing a slender, black notebook, its cover embossed with gold lettering that I could not help but notice reading *'The Man Who Fell to Earth'*. "You're both so focused on the basics," he said, his tone dripping with barely concealed superiority. "But let me tell you about the sauce I've been perfecting. A reduction, triple filtered. It's not just a sauce—it's an elixir. I use a blend of wines, each carefully selected, aged to perfection, and reduced to a fraction of their original volume. The viscosity is... sublime. You don't just taste it—you experience it. It coats the tongue, lingers on the palate, and leaves you craving more, long after the plate is empty."

Will, who had been silent up until now, leaned forward, a slight smirk playing on his lips. He reached into his bag and pulled out a sleek, minimalist black planner, placing it on the table with a calculated flick of his wrist. "Sauce, dough—these are the basics," he said, his voice smooth and confident. "But have any of you considered presentation? I've been working on plating that defies convention. Geometric patterns, negative space—it's not just food on a plate. It's art. It's a statement. Each dish is a visual narrative, with flavours that tell a story long before the first bite."

There was a pause, the air thick with tension as they all absorbed Will's words. The sun dipped lower, casting the scene in a golden hue that somehow felt both warm and threatening.

Megan, not to be outdone, flipped open her notebook, revealing page after page of precise, hand-drawn sketches. "I've thought about that," she said, her voice steady but with a hint of urgency. "But what's the point of visual appeal if the texture isn't perfect? My latest experiment—lamination. The layers are so thin, they practically melt in your mouth. And when you tear it open, the steam rises, carrying the aroma directly to your senses. It's not just about eating—it's about seduction."

Craig's smirk widened, his eyes narrowing as he leaned closer to Megan. "Seduction?" he echoed; his tone mockingly thoughtful. "That's cute. But can your lamination stand up to my caramel? I've been experimenting with temperature controls—down to the half-degree. The result is a caramel that's so smooth, it's practically liquid gold. When you drizzle it over anything—anything—it doesn't just enhance the flavour, it elevates it. Takes it to a level you didn't even know existed."

The tension at the table ratcheted up another notch, the quiet of the late afternoon punctuated only by the subtle rustling of leaves overhead. They were all playing the same game, yet the stakes felt higher, the atmosphere electric with barely restrained rivalry.

There was a moment of silence as the words hung in the air, each of us silently weighing the others' contributions, evaluating, calculating. The table now held the tools of our craft, each one a symbol of there individual obsessions, there unyielding pursuit of culinary dominance.

Finally, Megan broke the silence, her voice barely above a whisper. "We're going to change everything," she said, echoing Will's earlier sentiment but with a newfound intensity. "But not just with one element. We'll combine them—all of them. Dough, sauce, plating, ingredients... perfection. We'll create something that's never been seen before."

And with that, the tension eased, replaced by a shared understanding. The competition was far from over, but for now, they were united—each of them driven by the same relentless need to perfect, to dominate, to elevate their craft to something beyond mere food. Something... transcendent.

Their voices were full of hope, their plans ambitious and bright. The air around us was charged with the promise of the future, a future we were once convinced was within our easy grasp. They laughed over inside jokes and shared cigarettes, the smoke curling up into the fading light as if carrying their dreams upwards.

Standing among them, I felt an odd mixture of inclusion and isolation. It was all too surreal, this comforting tableau of past camaraderie playing out as if I had never left, as if the years of toil and disillusionment had been nothing more than a brief nightmare. Yet, beneath the comforting veil of nostalgia, a gnawing awareness tugged at me. This was a scene from a life I had once lived, a life that had slipped through my fingers like fine sand.

I joined in, laughing at the right moments, nodding and contributing when it seemed appropriate, but the surreal quality of the experience was overwhelming. It was as though I was observing from a distance, watching a younger version of myself interact with shadows. The conversation turned to a group project we had once aced, and the laughter grew louder, the memories sweeter.

But deep down, I knew. This was not my reality anymore. These dreams, so vibrant and alive in the flickering light of the smoking area, belonged to a past version of me— one that hadn't faced the gruelling realities of the culinary world. The optimism of youth was a stark contrast to the cynicism that had been etched into my soul by the fires of professional kitchens.

There, in the quiet echo of my solitary thoughts, the reality of our training unravelled. We had been nurtured on a diet of hope and grand ambitions, fed tales of creativity and culinary fame, all the while shielded from the brutal truths of the industry. The laughter and dreams shared in the smoking area, once symbols of youthful optimism, now echoed in my ears as haunting reminders of innocence lost.

It dawned on me, with a clarity that was almost painful, how the bright promises were little more than smoke and mirrors—distractions from the grinding toil, the relentless pressure, and the often-thankless grind that defined the life of a chef. Our tutors, perhaps well-meaning in their intentions, had painted a picture of gastronomic glory without the shadows, omitting tales of kitchens where spirits were broken as often as eggs.

The twilight deepened, casting long shadows that twisted the once-familiar surroundings into something far more sinister. The smoking bench outside the kitchen had become "Reflections," the training restaurant where my culinary ambitions were once nurtured, now transformed into a grotesque stage set for a macabre rehearsal. It wasn't just the gloom of the evening—it was the atmosphere itself, thick with an unnerving nostalgia, as though the echoes of my youth were whispering sinister secrets in my ear.

As the practice service began, what should have been a routine exercise quickly dissolved into something far more horrifying. The faces of my college friends, once vibrant with the excitement of learning, were now contorted into ghastly masks of malevolence. Their smiles twisted into sneers; their eyes burned with a demonic glee. The guests, once merely customers chosen by tutors, had become ghoulish figures, their laughter warped into chilling cackles that reverberated off the walls. And the figure commanding the pass was no longer a mentor, but a fiendish overseer, his presence casting a dark shadow over the entire room. His voice, no longer instructive, was a shrill screech from the depths of some culinary abyss.

What we plated that night wasn't food—it was a grotesque parody of the culinary arts, a tableau of nightmares. Severed limbs arranged on cold porcelain, puddles of congealed blood substituting for sauce, and the remnants of some unspeakable human desecration passed off as the day's special. Each dish was a reminder of the horrors that lurked just beneath the surface of the kitchen's usual hustle and bustle.

With every order barked by our demonic head chef, the walls of Reflections seemed to melt away, revealing the harsh, clinical reality of The Paramount's kitchen. The boundaries between past and present, between training and real service, disintegrated, leaving me trapped in a nightmare where my tools of the trade became instruments of torture. The ovens, once the heart of the kitchen, now roared with an intensity that felt fuelled by the chaos and terror that permeated the room. The air thickened with the nauseating stench of charred flesh, and the sizzle of blood on scorching metal created a perverse symphony, a soundtrack for the damned.

Around me, my classmates—now ghoulish parodies of themselves—moved with a manic urgency, driven not by the pursuit of excellence but by some dark, primal compulsion. The kitchen, the crucible of my culinary education, had transformed into a gateway to hell, a place where the distinction between a mere training exercise and a professional nightmare no longer existed.

Amidst the swirling vortex of this culinary hell, a stark realisation crystallised: I had to escape. This wasn't just another chaotic service; it was a glimpse into the abyss of what my future could become—a never-ending nightmare from which there might be no return. The orders kept coming, each one a dirge of despair, binding me tighter to this doomed fate. The stench of terror and decay clung to my skin, permeating my soul. This was the future that awaited me if I continued down this path—a future of culinary damnation.

My heart pounded a frantic rhythm, each beat drowning out the cacophony of the kitchen's horrors. Adrenaline surged through my veins; clarity born from desperation. I needed an exit, a way out of this torment. I couldn't become another ghost haunting this kitchen, chained eternally to the service of a dark and merciless industry.

I shut my eyes against the horror, willing myself to break free. I needed to find a door, any door, to escape this nightmare and return to a life where such terrors were mere shadows, not daily confrontations. My heart raced as I stumbled through the nightmarish labyrinth, each corridor twisting into another, an endless loop of greasy tiles and stainless steel reflecting my haunted expression back at me.

The air grew heavier, filled with the acrid stench of scorched meat and the metallic tang of spilled blood that seemed to ooze from the very walls. I pressed forward, hands outstretched, desperate to find a passage that would lead me away from this madness. But every turn led to more doors, each one swinging open to reveal another identical corridor, taunting me with its unyielding sameness. The faint flicker of hope that sparked with each new threshold quickly extinguished as reality—or this grotesque version of it—mocked my efforts.

Whispers slithered through the stale air, voices of long-gone sous chefs and line cooks, their words curling around me like smoke. "You can't leave," they murmured, a chorus of the damned, "You'll never leave." Their laughter cut through the atmosphere like a serrated knife, slicing deeper into my psyche. I pushed against the suffocating despair, each step heavier than the last, my breaths sharp in the oppressive silence that followed their taunts.

And then, there it was—a door, different from the others, its frame glowing with a faint, unearthly light. Hope surged through me, and with trembling hands, I reached for the handle, only to recoil as the heat seared my skin. This wasn't just another door; it was a test, a trial by fire that I had to endure to escape this infernal cycle.

Gritting my teeth, I grasped the handle firmly, the pain a brutal reminder of every burn endured, every scar earned in the service of a merciless industry. I pushed it open, and a blinding brilliance washed over me, searing yet strangely cleansing.

Beyond the flames, the world shifted. The oppressive kitchen faded, replaced by a surreal expanse of corridors stretching into infinity, each lined with more doors leading nowhere. Echoes of my footsteps bounced off invisible walls, a disorienting cacophony that seemed to come from everywhere and nowhere.

As I stepped through, the world shattered around me, the fragments of my fear and despair falling away like shards of glass. The searing heat of the kitchen gave way to a chilling absence, the demonic voices ebbed into silence, and I was enveloped in profound darkness. Slowly, the textures of reality returned—the hard bed of a hospital room, the sterile tang of antiseptic, the gentle beep of a heart monitor grounding me in the living world.

My eyes fluttered open, the stark white of the hospital ceiling offering a blank canvas of calm, so at odds with the vivid hell of my vision. I lay there, tethered to the living by lines and monitors, each beep a reminder that I had been granted a reprieve—a chance to flee the destructive path I'd been hurtling down.

This brush with death, a stark warning delivered through the twisted visions of my mind, cemented my resolve. It was time to leave behind the relentless demands and the suffocating pressure of the kitchen. I needed to escape, to find a new path where the flames of culinary ambition wouldn't consume my very being.

Lying in that hospital bed, each steady beep of the monitor not only confirmed my survival but also marked the death of my former life. The decision was clear and irrevocable: I would abandon the kitchen and seek salvation in a new beginning, free from the literal and metaphorical fires that had once defined my existence. This car crash had violently jolted me out of one life and into the threshold of another, offering a second chance I was determined not to waste.

Chapter 25: New Horizons

Recovery from the crash was, on the surface, a clinical, almost mechanical process—nothing more than a series of physiological transactions between flesh, bone, and time. My body, with its baffling resilience, stitched itself back together beneath the cold, indifferent glare of hospital fluorescents, the antiseptic scent clinging to me like a second skin. Each beep from the heart monitor, every hiss from the IV drip, served as a metronome to this grotesque symphony of recovery—a relentless, maddening tick-tock that marched me back toward some semblance of normalcy, or what could be mistaken for it.

Physically, I was mending, the pain receding into the background noise, blending with the distant, sterile hum of hospital life. But my mind—my mind was anything but healed. It wandered far beyond the confines of my hospital bed, straying into the shadowy corners of my consciousness that I had once tried so desperately to ignore. The memories of Reflections, that infernal pit of heat and horrors, haunted me like a bad acid trip. The relentless pressure, the scalding air thick with sweat and stress, the cacophony of clattering pans and banshees barking orders—it all seemed to bleed together into a single, suffocating mass that weighed on my chest even as I lay there in the sterile cocoon of my hospital room.

In the dull, numbing hours of my convalescence, the idea of returning to that world became unbearable, like the thought of plunging back into a burning building I had barely escaped. The once intoxicating thrill of the kitchen, with its intoxicating blend of precision and unpredictability, had lost its allure, replaced by an overwhelming sense of dread, hatred, and disgust. The prospect of another service, another night of chasing perfection through the haze of exhaustion and adrenaline, felt like a death sentence.

But as always, I had no choice but to return.

The notion of a conventional 9 to 5 job began to creep into my thoughts, insidious and appealing. The idea of a life where the hours were predictable, the tasks mundane yet comforting in their simplicity—where the most pressing decision was whether to have the chicken or the beef for lunch—began to seduce me with its promise of stability. A life without the madness, without the constant push to the brink of sanity, was like the siren song of a calm, steady sea, luring me away from the violent storm I had been caught in for so long.

I imagined a life where my hands wouldn't tremble from overuse, where the heat didn't scald my skin daily, where my mind wasn't constantly teetering on the edge of oblivion. It was a life devoid of the intensity, the passion that had once driven me, but also free from the darkness that had consumed me. The thought of slipping into obscurity, of becoming just another faceless cog in the machine, was strangely comforting. There was a peace in the monotony, a promise of escape from the abuses that had been my reality.

I could see it clearly—an office, pale off white walls, the soft hum of an air conditioner. The flicker of a fluorescent light overhead, the low murmur of conversations blending into a dull, soothing white noise. A desk, cluttered with papers, a computer screen glowing faintly. It was all so... calm. Peaceful. I could feel the quiet settling over me like a blanket, warm and comforting, a world away from the relentless brutality of the kitchen.

A simple life. No screaming chefs, no impossible demands, no impulsive thoughts, no knives flashing dangerously close to my fingers or stabbing me in the back. Just a routine, predictable and safe. I could almost taste the mediocrity, the blandness of it all, like a glass of lukewarm water after a lifetime of fiery spirits. And yet, in that moment, it felt like the sweetest nectar, the most intoxicating elixir. The allure of the mundane, the siren calls of a life without the searing heat, the relentless pressure.

"Where the fuck is that risotto!?" The voice snapped me back to reality, sharp and jagged, like a shard of glass cutting through my reverie. Where the fuck am I?? I though Panicked to myself. The head chef's eyes bored into me, his face a twisted mask of fury. I realised I had been standing still, a rare moment of paralysis in the heart of the storm, I was back in the kitchen, daydream over!

My hands moved again, almost of their own accord, stirring, plating, wiping, arranging. The risotto was on the pass in seconds, but my mind was still half in that office, still clinging to the fantasy of a world without flames and knives. I imagined the monotony of it all, the dullness of routine. A steady paycheck, weekends off, a life where the most pressing concern was an overflowing inbox or a meeting that ran five minutes too long. A place where time moved at a crawl, where each hour was marked by the slow, steady tick of a clock on the wall, not the frantic, breathless rush of orders coming in, plates going out.

But even as I dreamed of this quiet life, I knew there would always be a part of me that would miss the inferno. That would long for the rush of a perfectly executed dish, the thrill of a service done right, the camaraderie forged in the heat of battle. It was a twisted addiction, a craving for the very thing that had nearly destroyed me. The kitchen was in my blood, in every fibre of my being, and though I longed to escape it, I knew it would always be deep within my DNA.

And so, as the days slipped by, I found myself caught in this limbo, suspended between the desire for a new life and the pull of the old one. Recovery was more than just mending bones and healing wounds; it was a reckoning, a confrontation with the ghosts of my past and the uncertain future that lay ahead. I resolved to leave the kitchen behind, to step away from the madness and embrace the mundane, yet a nagging doubt lingered in the back of my mind—could I ever truly escape the flames that had forged me, or would I inevitably be drawn back to the fire, like a moth to the flame?

In the end I turned to astronomy—an academic pursuit as distant from the searing heat of the kitchen as the stars are from the earth. There was something poetic in the contrast, something almost absurdly symbolic. The quiet solitude of studying the cosmos at night offered a respite from the frenetic pace of the kitchen by day, a stark, almost jarring juxtaposition that felt like balm to my frayed nerves. Enrolling in night classes, I found myself straddling two worlds: one governed by celestial calm, the other by culinary storms, this inspired me to creat a dish that represents the beauty and horrors of the two words colliding.

Inferno and Stars - Charred Venison with Nebula Purée and Cosmic Ash

Ingredients:

For the Charred Venison:

- 4 venison loin steaks, thick-cut like slabs of muscle ready for the sacrifice

- 2 tablespoons olive oil—liquid gold, anointing the flesh

- 2 tablespoons crushed black peppercorns, each one a tiny explosion waiting to happen

- 1 tablespoon smoked sea salt, harvested from the tears of a dying star

- 1 tablespoon cocoa powder, bitter as the darkness between galaxies

- 1 teaspoon ground coffee, a stimulant for the soul, black as a void

- 2 cloves garlic, minced—its pungent aroma a sharp reminder of mortality

- Fresh thyme sprigs, the green of life clinging to the edge of oblivion

- 1/4 cup red wine, blood of the earth, a dark communion

- 1 tablespoon unsalted butter, a final, decadent touch

For the Nebula Purée:

- 2 large purple sweet potatoes, peeled and diced—gutted and dissected like a celestial corpse

- 1/2 cup heavy cream—rich and suffocating, like the weight of existence

- 2 tablespoons unsalted butter, a necessary indulgence

- 1 teaspoon truffle oil, the scent of decadence, an olfactory siren song

- Salt to taste—because even the universe requires balance

For the Cosmic Ash:

- 2 tablespoons black sesame seeds, scorched remnants of forgotten worlds

- 1 tablespoon activated charcoal powder, the residue of obliteration

- 1 teaspoon smoked paprika, a fiery whisper from the flames

- A pinch of flaky sea salt, crystallised tears of the damned

For the Garnish:

- Edible gold leaf, a lie told to ourselves about the value of beauty

- Micro-greens, the fragile green of hope, mocking in its naiveté

- Pomegranate seeds, like tiny explosions of life in a sea of darkness

Instructions:

1. Prepare the Venison:

- Marinade: In a bowl, combine the olive oil, peppercorns, smoked sea salt, cocoa powder, ground coffee, minced garlic, and thyme. Rub this concoction into the venison steaks, anointing them for the ritual. Let the meat soak in the flavours, absorbing the essence of life and death, for at least an hour. This is the moment before the fall, the calm before the storm.

- Searing: Heat a skillet over high heat until it smokes like the last breath of a dying sun. Sear the venison steaks, each side a battlefield where flesh meets flame, creating a charred exterior that is both repellent and irresistible. Pour in the red wine, the blood of the earth, and let it sizzle in the pan like a dark prayer. Add the butter, a final indulgence, and let it melt into the chaos. Let the steaks rest, as one would a warrior after battle, their juices pooling like the blood of the vanquished.

2. Create the Nebula Purée:

- Boiling: In a pot, boil the diced purple sweet potatoes until tender, the colour leaching out like the last light of a dying star. This is no ordinary purée; it's the remnants of something cosmic, something that once was and now only echoes in the void.

- Blending: Drain and blend the sweet potatoes with heavy cream, butter, and truffle oil. The result is a purée as smooth as the lies we tell ourselves, yet as deep and mysterious as the universe itself. Season with salt, because in the end, everything needs a touch of reality.

3. Craft the Cosmic Ash:

- Grinding: In a mortar and pestle, grind the black sesame seeds into a fine powder—this is the dust of the universe, the remnants of stars that died before we were even born.

- Mixing: Combine with activated charcoal powder, smoked paprika, and a pinch of sea salt. This ash isn't just garnish; it's a reminder of what we came from and what we'll return to—dust.

4. Plating:

- Nebula Swirl: On each plate, smear the nebula purée in a swirling motion, as if painting the last breath of a star across a dark canvas. The colours should evoke both awe and dread, a visual representation of the void that surrounds us.

- Venison Placement: Slice the rested venison and lay it on the purée, the charred exterior a contrast to the vivid purples beneath. This is not just food; it's a statement—a confrontation between the primal and the cosmic.

- Dusting with Ash: Lightly dust the venison with the cosmic ash, letting it fall like stardust over the plate, a gentle reminder of our own mortality.

- Garnishing: Adorn with micro-greens for a touch of false hope, pomegranate seeds for a burst of life amid the decay, and a delicate flake of gold leaf, the ultimate lie of value in a valueless universe.

5. Serving:

- Serve "Inferno and Stars" as a dish that encapsulates the brutality of existence and the wonders of the cosmos—a reminder that in every bite, we are consuming not just sustenance, but the very fabric of life and death. Each taste should remind the diner of their insignificance in the grand scheme, yet offer a fleeting moment of power, as they hold the universe on a fork.

This duality was a gruelling marathon, a test of endurance that stretched me to my limits. By day, the kitchen's heat and demands clawed at me, dragging me back into the inferno I was so desperate to escape. By night, the tranquil, methodical study of the stars offered a glimpse of a life less fraught, a promise of peace that was almost tantalising in its simplicity. Despite the exhaustion that gnawed at my bones, I persisted, applying to every clerical and administrative position available, desperate for a way out, for a life where I could breathe, where the only heat I felt was the warmth of the sun, distant and benign.

Yet, the strain of living two lives—chef by day, aspiring astronomer by night—began to erode my resolve. It was like balancing on a knife's edge, each step forward fraught with the risk of slipping, of falling back into the chaos I was trying so hard to escape. The tension mounted, a taut wire pulled tighter and tighter until it finally snapped. It culminated dramatically during what would unknowingly be my final service. The kitchen roared around me, a cacophony of shouts and clattering pans, the din of a hundred tasks being executed with military precision. But my mind was elsewhere, adrift among the quiet stars, lost in the vastness of the cosmos where time itself seemed to stretch into infinity.

And then, amid the chaos, she appeared—the woman in the wheelchair, her spectral image cutting through the clamour like a cold blade. She was as real as the heat of the ovens, as tangible as the sweat trickling down my spine. Her presence was sharp, sudden, a flash of cold terror in the sweltering heat of the kitchen. Her ghostly eyes locked onto mine with a penetrating gaze that seemed to reach into the very marrow of my bones, freezing me in place, rooting me to the spot with a fear that was primal, absolute.

Panic seized me, a visceral, clawing terror that tightened around my chest like a vice. The kitchen spun around me, a dizzying maelstrom of sights and sounds that suddenly felt distant, muted by the rush of blood in my ears. I stumbled, my hands trembling, a plate slipping from my grasp to shatter on the floor, the crash piercing the noise like a gunshot. The sound echoed in my skull, reverberating with a finality that sent a shudder through my entire body.

Hands grabbed me, pulling me from the line, dragging me away from the stifling heat, the suffocating pressure. I was escorted to the relative quiet of the back hallway, where the walls were cold, unfeeling, offering no comfort, no solace. I slid down against the wall, my breath ragged, tears cutting tracks through the grime on my face, mixing with the sweat and the dirt, a baptism of despair. The breakdown was a total surrender to the cumulative burdens of years spent in the relentless grind of the kitchen. It was a surrender to the ghosts that had haunted me, the demons that had driven me to the brink.

In that moment, I knew it was over. My career as a chef, once a badge of honour, now felt like a millstone around my neck, dragging me down into the depths of an abyss I could no longer escape. This breakdown, public and complete, severed the last ties that bound me to this world. The fire had gone out, the passion extinguished, leaving only ashes and the bitter taste of failure. I needed to leave, to find solace in the quiet study of the stars, away from the oppressive heat and demands of the culinary world, away from the ghosts that refused to let me rest.

I left the kitchen that night, the heavy door swinging shut behind me with a finality that echoed in my hollow chest. The sound was like a death knell, a sombre note marking the end of an era, the end of a life that had consumed me, devoured me whole. Outside, the cool night air embraced me, a stark contrast to the stifling heat I had left behind. The stars twinkled indifferently above, distant, unfeeling, offering no judgment, only the quiet promise of a new beginning, a life beyond the flames.

As I walked away, the weight of my chef's coat felt unbearable, a symbol of a life I was eager to shed, a burden I was desperate to cast off. Each step took me further from the life I had known, from the chaos, the heat, the relentless demands. Ahead lay the unknown, daunting yet filled with potential, like the dark, vast expanse of the night sky. It was a leap into the void, a step into the darkness, but it was also a chance—a chance to find peace, to find meaning in the quiet, in the stillness, in the stars.

And as I walked into the night, the stars above me, the earth below, I felt a sense of calm wash over me, a quiet resolve that I had never known before. The kitchen was behind me, the hellscape receding, the ghosts fading into the darkness. Ahead was the cosmos, infinite and serene, waiting to reveal its secrets. And for the first time in a long time, I felt free.

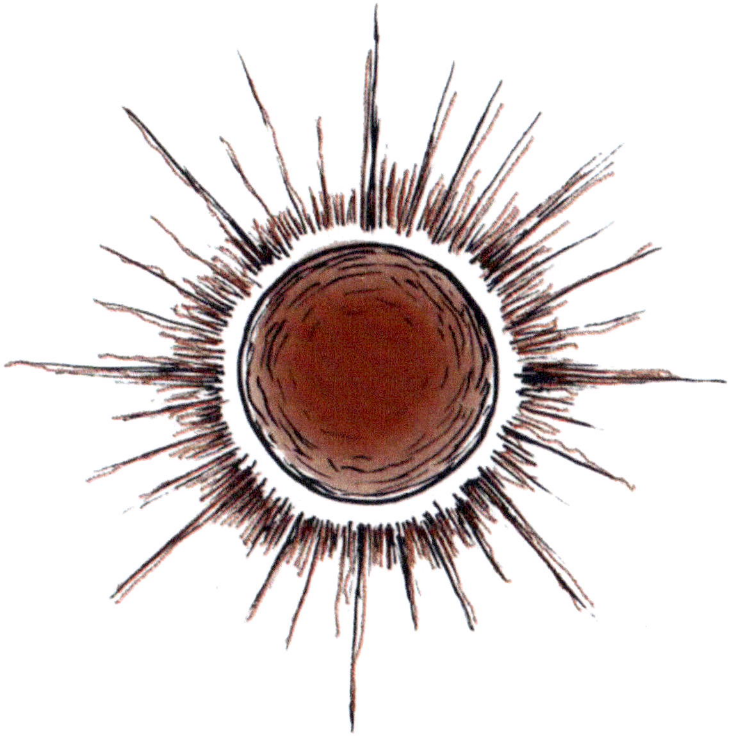

Epilogue: Beyond the Flames

The relentless cycle of my culinary career has finally reached its conclusion. As I look beyond the flames, the heat of the kitchen has been replaced by the sterile calm of a white-collar job—a sanctuary I longed for, free from the punishing late nights and exhaustive 12 to 17-hour shifts that once defined my existence. This new role, devoid of physical strain, marks a stark departure from the gastronomic warfare I endured.

The universe seems to have intervened just as I teetered on the brink, rescuing what remained of my spirit from the clutches of culinary hell. My future now sparkles with potential: a strengthened relationship, a new home, the prospect of normalcy. The skills homed in the kitchen—swift decision-making under pressure, enduring relentless stress—now repurposed for a more benign office landscape.

It became glaringly obvious, almost immediately, that this new office I inhabited had a particular fascination with my past life. My cheffing experience became a commodity, a perverse little secret they could harvest. The executives, these hollow men in their pressed suits, saw potential in me beyond the monotony of spreadsheets and meaningless emails. They offered me more money, bonuses, perks—all to oversee the daily lunches of our CEO, Rory, the self-proclaimed visionary.

Rory, our illustrious CEO. The man who doesn't just crave power—he devours it. Literally. He's obsessed with this absurd concept he calls "The Human Being Diet." No grains, no vegetables, nothing that wasn't ripped straight from the essence of human flesh. Muscles, fat, blood, marrow. You can almost taste the psychosis in it. Rory believes that by eating what mirrors the human body, he's transcending, becoming more than just a CEO. He's turning into something primal, a predator at the top of the food chain.

Every morning, at exactly 8:30 AM, I'm called into his office to prepare his grotesque meals. Chicken thighs, carved to mimic the texture of flesh, seared just enough so the juices run like blood. Bone marrow spread delicately over toast. Rare steak, still bleeding, served with a side of self-delusion. I don't cook for a man anymore. I cook for a creature wearing human skin, someone who pretends he's feeding off the essence of his subordinates, his employees. He eats their effort, their dedication, their souls, one meticulously crafted plate at a time. And I am complicit in this twisted ritual.

But it's more than just feeding his obsession. There's performance in every bite. The food must be plated with a precision that would make surgeons envious—clinical, exacting. Rory wants to be reminded of what he's consuming. Every meal is a reflection of his power. And I? I've become too good at it.

From there, it spiralled. Rory saw my "attention to detail"—that's what he called it—and soon I was thrust into the world of corporate food photography, taking perfectly composed shots of cheap ready meals for Tesco, Asda, and whoever else. The same precision I used to craft Rory's bloody fantasies now turned into capturing the ideal shade of golden brown on pre-packaged shepherd's pie. Perfect lighting. Perfect angles. It's all a lie, of course. The kind of food that no one ever actually eats, but the kind they buy, fooled by the illusion of something wholesome, something real.

It's grotesque, but I couldn't look away. I'd stage every meal like a crime scene, arranging chicken breasts and limp asparagus with the precision of an autopsy. The camera would click, the image frozen, immortalised. Perfectly staged lies.

And then, inevitably, I became more than just the guy taking photos. Rory, with his gleaming eyes and crocodile smile, decided I had a gift for "operations." The office—became my new kitchen. Spreadsheets and schedules replaced pans and knives. I'm still cooking, in a way. Still organising, still perfecting. But now it's about supply chains and logistics, all the components of feeding the machine.

Beneath this seemingly serene transition lurks a residual darkness. The scars of past battles, both mental and physical, have woven a complex tapestry within me. There's an emptiness, a lingering hollowness that no professional accomplishment can seem to fill. It's as if the damage inflicted over those relentless years has embedded itself deeply, questioning whether any semblance of genuine recovery is feasible.

Reflecting on my past life feels like examining the existence of a ghost. At times, my former self seems like a stranger in the mirror, echoing the haunting lines from David Bowie's "The Man Who Sold the World"—a melody that now underscores my days with its eerie resonance. The kitchen, once a battlefield of flames and fury, has transformed into a distant memory, a surreal chapter from another life.

Yet, despite the scars of the professional kitchen battles, my love for cooking remains undimmed. Freed from the pressures of high-end culinary expectations, I've embraced the art of creating hearty, homestyle dishes—kitchen wonders and homemade delights that nourish both body and soul. In this new culinary chapter, I find solace and joy in preparing simple, fulfilling meals. Among these, lasagna has emerged as a favourite a layered masterpiece of comfort that I relish both making and eating.

Here's a traditional lasagna recipe that combines hearty layers of cheese, meat, and pasta, perfect for a comforting meal.

Lasagna Recipe

Ingredients:

- Meat Sauce:

  - 1 lb ground beef: The foundation, raw and red, soon to be transformed by heat and time. There's something primal about it, something that stirs a deep, unsettling hunger.

- 1 onion, chopped: It must be finely chopped, every piece uniform. Each slice precise, controlled, the sharp blade slicing through the layers with practiced ease.

- 2 cloves garlic, minced: The pungent bite of garlic, so essential, so invasive. It permeates everything, lingers on your fingers, your breath, a constant reminder of what you've done.

- 1 (28 oz) can crushed tomatoes: Thick, crimson, like blood. It pours out slowly, spreading across the pan, seeping into every crevice.

- 2 (6 oz) cans tomato paste: Concentrated, dark, almost sinister in its intensity. It thickens the sauce, makes it rich, almost suffocating.

- 1/2 cup water: Just enough to loosen it, to keep it from sticking, but not enough to dilute the intensity. Everything in balance, everything in its place.

- 2 tablespoons white sugar: The sweetness that cuts through the acidity, that balances the bitterness. But too much, and it tips the scales, turns everything sickly, cloying.

- **Cheese Mixture:**

- 1 egg: A binder, a lifeline. It holds everything together, keeps the chaos at bay.

- 1/2 teaspoon salt: A pinch, just enough to season, to bring out the flavours. Too much, and it overpowers, ruins the delicate balance.

- 3/4-pound mozzarella cheese, sliced: The pull, the stretch, the melt. It's the essence of lasagna, the thing that makes it irresistible, almost obscene in its indulgence.

- 3/4 cup grated Parmesan cheese: Sharp, salty, a bite that lingers, that cuts through the richness. It's the final touch, the finishing stroke.

- **Additional:**

- 12 lasagna sheets: The structure, the backbone. They must be cooked just right—al dente, with a bite, but pliable enough to bend to your will.

- Salt for boiling water: Just enough to season the water, to infuse the pasta with flavours as it cooks. It's the first step, the foundation of the whole dish.

Instructions:

1. Preheat oven to 375°F (190°C): The temperature rises, the heat builds. It's the crucible where everything comes together, where raw ingredients are transformed, melded into something more, something greater.

2. **Prepare the meat sauce:**

  - In a large skillet, heat the pan over medium heat until it's hot, almost smoking. The ground beef hits the pan with a satisfying sizzle, the fat rendering out, turning the red meat a deep, satisfying brown. The onion and garlic follow, their sharpness mingling with the rich scent of cooking meat, filling the kitchen with an intoxicating aroma.

- The crushed tomatoes pour in, their deep red mixing with the browned meat, the tomato paste thickening the sauce, the water loosening it just enough. Stir in the sugar, a balancing act, adding just the right amount of sweetness to counter the acidity of the tomatoes. Let it simmer, covered, the heat low, for 30 minutes. The flavours meld, deepen, the sauce thickens, becomes something more than the sum of its parts.

3. **Prepare the cheese mixture:**

- In a mixing bowl, combine the ricotta cheese with the egg, the parsley, and the salt. The egg binds it all together, the salt seasons it, the parsley adds a hint of freshness, a bright green contrast to the rich, creamy cheese. Mix until smooth, until it's ready to be layered into the lasagna.

4. **Cook the lasagna sheets:**

- Bring a large pot of water to a rolling boil, add enough salt so that it tastes like the sea. Cook the lasagna noodles for 8 to 10 minutes, until they're al dente, just tender enough but still with a bite. Drain them, rinse under cold water to stop the cooking, to keep them from sticking together.

5. **Assemble the lasagna:**

- In a 9x13-inch baking dish, spread 1 1/2 cups of the meat sauce over the bottom. The first layer, the

- 3/4-pound mozzarella cheese, sliced: The pull, the stretch, the melt. It's the essence of lasagna, the thing that makes it irresistible, almost obscene in its indulgence.

- 3/4 cup grated Parmesan cheese: Sharp, salty, a bite that lingers, that cuts through the richness. It's the final touch, the finishing stroke.

- **Additional:**

- 12 lasagna sheets: The structure, the backbone. They must be cooked just right—al dente, with a bite, but pliable enough to bend to your will.

- Salt for boiling water: Just enough to season the water, to infuse the pasta with flavours as it cooks. It's the first step, the foundation of the whole dish.

Instructions:

1. Preheat oven to 375°F (190°C): The temperature rises, the heat builds. It's the crucible where everything comes together, where raw ingredients are transformed, melded into something more, something greater.

2. **Prepare the meat sauce:**

   - In a large skillet, heat the pan over medium heat until it's hot, almost smoking. The ground beef hits the pan with a satisfying sizzle, the fat rendering out, turning the red meat a deep, satisfying brown. The onion and garlic follow, their sharpness mingling with the rich scent of cooking meat, filling the kitchen with an intoxicating aroma.

- The crushed tomatoes pour in, their deep red mixing with the browned meat, the tomato paste thickening the sauce, the water loosening it just enough. Stir in the sugar, a balancing act, adding just the right amount of sweetness to counter the acidity of the tomatoes. Let it simmer, covered, the heat low, for 30 minutes. The flavours meld, deepen, the sauce thickens, becomes something more than the sum of its parts.

3. **Prepare the cheese mixture:**

- In a mixing bowl, combine the ricotta cheese with the egg, the parsley, and the salt. The egg binds it all together, the salt seasons it, the parsley adds a hint of freshness, a bright green contrast to the rich, creamy cheese. Mix until smooth, until it's ready to be layered into the lasagna.

4. **Cook the lasagna sheets:**

- Bring a large pot of water to a rolling boil, add enough salt so that it tastes like the sea. Cook the lasagna noodles for 8 to 10 minutes, until they're al dente, just tender enough but still with a bite. Drain them, rinse under cold water to stop the cooking, to keep them from sticking together.

5. **Assemble the lasagna:**

- In a 9x13-inch baking dish, spread 1 1/2 cups of the meat sauce over the bottom. The first layer, the foundation, a bed of rich, meaty sauce. Lay down 6 lasagna sheets, side by side, covering the sauce completely. Spread half of the ricotta cheese mixture over the pasta sheets, smoothing it out evenly. Layer half of the mozzarella cheese slices over the ricotta, pressing them down slightly, making sure they cover every inch.

- Spoon another 1 1/2 cups of meat sauce over the mozzarella, spreading it out, making sure it reaches the edges. Sprinkle with 1/4 cup of grated Parmesan, adding a sharp, salty bite. Repeat the layers, finishing with the remaining mozzarella and Parmesan on top. It's a careful construction, each layer precise, each step deliberates.

6. **Bake in preheated oven:**

- Cover the dish with foil, making sure it doesn't touch the cheese, because the last thing you want is for the foil to stick, to ruin that golden, bubbling crust. Bake for 25 minutes, the lasagna cooking slowly, the cheese melting, the sauce bubbling up around the edges. Remove the foil and bake for another 25 minutes, the top turning a deep golden brown, the edges crisping up, the cheese bubbling and browning.

7. **Cool for 15 minutes before serving:**

- Let it rest, let the layers settle, let the flavours meld. It's tempting to dig in right away, to cut into it while it's still hot, but the wait is necessary. It's part of the process, part of the ritual.

This lasagna is more than just a meal. It's an experience, a culmination of ingredients and effort, of time and patience. Each bite is a reward, a rich, indulgent taste of something perfect, something complete. But beneath the layers, beneath the rich, comforting flavours, there's something else, something darker, something that lingers on the palate, in the mind, long after the meal is over. Because in the end, it's not just about the lasagna. It's about control, about precision, about creating something that's more than just food. It's about the process, the need to perfect, to create, to consume.

I find myself missing the comrades who stood by me in the trenches: Liam, whose rugged exterior masked a profound loyalty; Jamie, whose brilliance as a chef was overshadowed by his downfall; Reece, the irreverent "Scorpion"; the inseparable twins, Matthew and Chantel; and Ellie, who has thankfully transcended the confines of the kitchen to become a cherished friend. And then there's Scott, whose culinary triumphs continue to inspire, proving that at least one of us could conquer the world we once struggled to endure.

In this new corporate realm, as promotions accumulate and the kitchen's harsh lessons fade into the backdrop of my psyche, I occasionally catch myself romanticising the brutal decade spent behind the line. These reflections, while tinged with nostalgia, also serve as a reminder of the life I've managed to escape.

Yet tonight, as I exit the office into the encroaching darkness of early evening, a familiar chill seeps through my bones. It's the kind of cold that isn't just temperature—it's a sensation that originates deep within, radiating outward, a creeping numbness that I can't quite shake. The office, with its monotonous rhythms and predictable routines, has become my refuge, a stark contrast to the chaotic inferno of the kitchen. But as I walk to the bathroom, leaving the false security of fluorescent-lit hallways behind, I can feel the night closing in, suffocating, oppressive, pressing against my skin like a wet blanket.

In the office bathroom, under the harsh, unforgiving lights, I catch sight of myself in the mirror. My reflection stares back, hollow-eyed, the weight of too many sleepless nights etched into my features. The fluorescent bulbs buzz above me, casting a sickly yellow glow over everything, making my skin look sallow, almost corpse-like. For a moment, I'm alone in that cold, sterile space, but then, as if summoned by the very act of looking, another figure materialises beside me in the mirror—familiar, yet profoundly unsettling.

There, reflected beside me, is the woman in the wheelchair. Her presence is a chilling reminder of my past encounters, a ghost that has followed me, haunted me, throughout the years I spent in the kitchen, cooking alongside a darkness that I never truly understood. She is not of this world, not entirely; her eyes, empty and lifeless, bore into mine with an intensity that freezes me in place. It's as if the temperature in the bathroom drops several degrees, the air growing thick and heavy, making it difficult to breathe.

Our eyes meet in the mirror, and for the first time, she speaks. Her voice is not what I expected—it's softer, quieter, a whisper of cold reality that intertwines with the lyrics of Bowie's song, now chillingly apt:

"Ashes to ashes, whites to whites, we know you are still a Junkie, strung out in heaven's high, living an all time low."

The words seep into my consciousness, echoing in the sterile, tiled room, blending with the faint, distorted melody that plays over the office PA system. It's as if Bowie himself is singing directly to me, his voice a spectral presence that mingles with hers, creating a harmony that's both haunting and disturbingly intimate.

As her words echo in the empty bathroom, the realisation dawns on me with a clarity that's almost painful: No matter how far I stray from the flames of the kitchen, some fires are never fully extinguished. The darkness that I cooked alongside, the shadows that danced at the edges of my vision as I stood over the stove, wielding a knife with precision and purpose—it's still there, lingering in the corners of my mind, a part of me that I can't escape. The woman in the wheelchair is more than just a ghost; she is the embodiment of everything I've tried to leave behind, a manifestation of the darkness that still clings to the fringes of my new life, a shadow from which there may be no final escape.

Fin.

"I laughed and shook his hand, and made my way back home, I searched for from and land, for years and years I roamed, I gazed a gazeless stare, at all the millions here, we must have died alone, a long, long time ago"

"Who knows? not me, we never lost control, you're face to face, with the man who sold the world"

David Bowie

Printed in Great Britain
by Amazon

48479809R00215